D0450631

NOEL HYND
MIDNIGHT IN MADRID

ZONDERVAN

Midnight in Madrid
Copyright © 2009 by Noel Hynd

This title is also available in a Zondervan audio edition.
Visit www.zondervan.fm.

Requests for information should be addressed to:
Zondervan, *Grand Rapids, Michigan* 49530

Library of Congress Cataloging-in-Publication Data

Hynd, Noel.
    Midnight in Madrid / Noel Hynd.
        p. cm. — (The Russian trilogy ; bk. 2)
      ISBN 978-0-310-27872-6 (pbk.)
       1. United States. Federal Bureau of Investigation--Officials and employees — Fiction.
2. Antiquities — Fiction. 3. Conspiracies — Fiction. 4. Robbery — Fiction. 5. Madrid
(Spain) — Fiction. I. Title.
    PS3558.Y54M53 2008
    813'.54 — dc22   2008049745

All rights reserved. No part of this publication may be reproduced, stored in a retrieval
system, or transmitted in any form or by any means — electronic, mechanical, photocopy,
recording, or any other — except for brief quotations in printed reviews, without the prior
permission of the publisher.

Internet addresses (websites, blogs, etc.) and telephone numbers printed in this book are
offered as a resource to you. These are not intended in any way to be or imply an endorse-
ment on the part of Zondervan, nor do we vouch for the content of these sites and numbers
for the life of this book.

Edited by Andy Meisenheimer and Alison Roth
Interior design by Christine Orejuela-Winkelman

Printed in the United States of America

10 11 12 13 14 • 24 23 22 21 20 19 18 17 16 15 14 13 12 11 10 9 8 7 6 5 4 3 2

NOEL HYND
MIDNIGHT IN MADRID

THE RUSSIAN TRILOGY — BOOK TWO

ZONDERVAN®

ZONDERVAN.com/
AUTHORTRACKER
follow your favorite authors

Also by Noel Hynd

The Russian Trilogy

1 | Conspiracy in Kiev

For Patrick and Kathleen Hildreth
and
Emily, Sarah, and Molly

"Then the bird doesn't belong to any of you?" Spade asked.

"Belong?" the fat man said jovially. "Well, sir, you might say it belonged to the King of Spain, but ... an article of that value that has passed from hand to hand ... is clearly the property of whoever can get a hold of it."

Dashiell Hammett, The Maltese Falcon

Every man is as Heaven made him, and sometimes a great deal worse.

Cervantes, Don Quixote

ONE

ST. GALLEN, SWITZERLAND, AUGUST 15

Lee Yuan had always been a bit of a mystic. Always had been and always would be. He saw things where other people didn't, believed things that other people laughed at. But his friends and peers accepted him for what he was, a product of his background, and his experience.

Right now, however, Lee Yuan was halfway around the world and completely out of luck. It was not a healthy equation for examining fading artifacts in the dungeons of an ancient stone monastery. It was not a healthy equation for anything.

Worse, Lee Yuan felt as if he were freezing to death. His hands worked as quickly as possible. His only light was that from a kerosene lantern, lit with a small acetylene torch. There was a little heat from the torch, but still, his fingers were nearly frostbitten. He had traveled far. This was where he had been told he would find it.

On a bench built in the sixteenth century, he sorted through artifacts, bits and pieces of ancient times, stuffed together in a decrepit old wooden box. The box was the size of a child's coffin. It had probably been built for that purpose, constructed by hands that had been dead for many centuries.

Monks had lived in this dwelling since the fourteen hundreds. Who knew what else, what treasures and torments from other ages, were sealed in these gloomy walls?

Well, there was only one treasure that Yuan sought.

Only one that *anyone* sought here.

He worked with bare fingertips that could no longer feel anything. Wool and leather covered his palms as well as much of the rest of his body; even his head was wrapped against the cold. He couldn't hear anything.

But he had needed dexterity in his fingertips.

First they had stung like the devil, the fingertips. But now, nothing. He had long since zoned out the pain, but frostbite was another matter. He reasoned he could only sift through these items for another two minutes before he would endanger the flesh of his fingers. Once the flesh had frozen, the feeling would never return. He had seen Sherpa guides who had come back from Tibet and Mongolia with gnarled, disfigured hands that extended only to the first knuckles.

An ivory box. A hand-carved crucifix, Italian in origin. Maybe two and a half centuries old. His brain assimilated: from the reign of one of the Clements or Innocents.

Clement the Fifth.

Innocent the Seventh.

Roman popes from the Holy See. The Bishops of Rome.

French Anti-popes from Avignon. The self-indulgent pretenders.

Gregory the Eighth.

Ignatius the Righteous.

A tremendous shiver overtook Yuan and shook him violently. His spine ached.

Yuan the Frozen.

How much colder could it get? His hands trembled. His fingers worked quickly.

Bone. The bone of a man or woman. All flesh long gone. It looked like a wrist bone.

A small gold cross, probably German, judging by the inscription that was not entirely worn away.

Yuan had been on this search for five weeks since leaving Hong Kong. Why had he ever agreed to this? Others could have come in his place to retrieve the artifact. He was forty-seven years old and probably not even the most qualified man that his employer could have sent. Sure, he was highly educated in Western culture, fluent in Mandarin, English, and French, deeply knowledgeable in the traditions of the Holy Roman Church, an expert on their strange procedures.

Send a younger man next time.

He continued to sift through the contents of the box.

A ceramic pot. A small replica of the Virgin. Splinters of wood from other objects.

The True Cross? Sure. Why not? If every splinter that Westerners had claimed to be from the True Cross were authentic, an entire mansion could be built from the splinters. What else in the box?

A small urn, probably for burning incense. Some metal chips. Tiny broken crosses. Broken into small pieces, much like Yuan's hopes.

Would this trip never end, this journey into oblivion?

From somewhere a voice spoke to him, almost an epiphany. *Careful what you wish for.*

He wished he were back home in Asia. He thought of his wife. He wondered if she was faithful to him. He wondered how long, if he didn't return, before she took up with another man. He wondered about the younger men whom he had trained and worked with. Would they laugh at him in this final quest? Or would they come after him to bring him home?

His eyes assessed the final contents of the box.

A few coins. Fragments of jewelry. Little pieces of nothing.

Nothing. Nothing at all to justify this long trek and search. And certainly nothing mystical. Now he realized that he had been scammed. He should have demanded delivery of his prize in Zurich, or Geneva, or some sane place! Not the monastery where the filthy thieves claimed it had been hidden!

What next?

His fingers could take it no more. The numbness was spreading. A bad sign. He held his fingers near his acetylene torch, almost touching the flame. He could smell the flesh thawing, or thought he could, then burning, then sudden pain. The feeling was back.

He pulled on the heavy gloves that hung at his side. No time for anything except to escape. He turned. He trudged across the small chamber to the base of the spiral stone stairs that had led him down to this claustrophobic place. If hell had frozen over, surely this was it.

He held up the lantern. He looked upward to a blackness that he hadn't anticipated. He took five labored steps upward and saw what had happened. The old wooden door — his only exit — had closed. And not on its own.

Where had his two sentries gone? His lookouts?

He put his shoulder to the door. He pushed against the aged wooden beams. But someone had bolted the door from the other side, probably the perverse old monk with the scar across the back of his hand who had led him down into this place.

He knocked furiously at the door. Then he kicked it. He called out. He cursed violently.

But he realized that he was a captive and probably no one even heard his screams. No one would come back for him for days, maybe weeks.

There was only one possible escape. He poured the remaining kerosene from his lamp against the lower section of the door and used his acetylene torch to try to burn it.

Lots of smoke. Not much fire.

He coughed violently. Then he realized that he had done exactly what his adversaries had hoped he would do. He would asphyxiate himself in an attempt to escape.

His kerosene ran out. With a final pathetic flicker, so did his torch.

Darkness descended with unwelcome speed. Then darkness embraced everything.

Not just darkness. Blackness.

Yuan was smart enough to know: light was not something he would ever see again. He settled in. So did death's messenger in a place like this: the bitter Alpine cold.

His mortal end arrived with astonishing ease.

TWO

NAPLES, ITALY, AUGUST 26

On a Saturday evening, Jean-Claude al-Masri stepped out of the passenger side of a Citroën in front of an Islamic school in Naples. He closed the car door behind him and surveyed the block. He noted a man waiting for him, a man twice his age, seated on the front steps of the school.

After establishing eye contact, Jean-Claude returned a very slight smile. They had negotiated earlier. He then glanced back to the Citroën and two others stepped out.

The man on the front steps rose to greet the arrivals. The visitors were expected.

The Islamic school was operated by a rotund, personally engaging man named Habib, an Islamic militant from the Baluchistan region of Pakistan. Habib was the gentleman who waited in greeting on this evening.

Habib was not a professional educator. While he was trained as a chemist, he had also been a merchant in Cairo several years earlier, selling everything from dried meat to television sets to small weapons, such as knives and handguns. Black market, white market, gray market. It didn't matter. These days, however, police across western Europe suspected Habib of being a liaison with radical homegrown Muslim cells in Europe. There wasn't a significant police agency from Athens to London that didn't have a dossier on him. And among those same radical Islamic groups, he wasn't just suspected of being a liaison. He was known to be one of the best.

Jean-Claude was a French citizen of Algerian origin. He had grown up in both France and Algeria, hauled around as one of seven children by an itinerant French father and illiterate Bedouin mother. Jean-Claude had bolted from his family at age sixteen and went to work as an underground laborer at the Tirek Amesmessa gold mines in southwest Algeria close to the border of Mali in north Africa. The experience toughened him and educated him to the mean unyielding ways of the world, as well as the use of demolitions and an ability to navigate through narrow underground passageways. It also incubated within him a burning hatred of the better-off people of the world; those whose fingers, wrists, ears, and other body parts glittered with the gold that came out of the earth at such an extortionate physical cost to those who worked in the mines.

After he turned twenty, Jean-Claude moved to Algiers where he fell into a life of prosperous petty crime. He worked as a burglar, a freelance hold-up man, and a break-in specialist. He drifted further under the influence of Islamic radicalism, as it was angrily preached in the mosques he attended in the afternoon and the cafes he frequented in the evenings.

Jean-Claude wasn't a theoretician and wasn't an intellectual. But what he sometimes lacked in intelligence he made up for in viciousness and anger. He learned his way around and beneath the old city of Algiers, the back alleys, the unknown side passageways through the stinking slums and the fetid subterranean routes used for centuries by traders in narcotics and human flesh. He relished these dark, unseen corridors of a barely visible world in a way that only an embittered ex-miner could. He gained some weight, some muscle, and some added meanness and social resentment.

In Algiers also, he cheerfully murdered his first two men. His victims were an English pimp, whose stable included a Tunisian girl he was sweet on, and an Israeli gem merchant, whose diamonds Jean-Claude coveted. The second murder evolved from a nighttime break-in-*avec*-stick-up gone bad. The slayings took place within ten days of each other, and in their aftermath, Jean-Claude saw fit to buy an off-the-books passage across the Mediterranean to France.

The Tunisian girl went with him but stayed only a few weeks. More importantly, he fenced a dozen beautiful diamonds with an obese Dutch middleman who knew better than to ask questions. Jean-Claude stayed in Toulouse for two years, continuing his same lifestyle and perfecting the occasional burglary or nighttime smash-and-grab. Then he moved on to Madrid, the Spanish capital, in 2006 when some plainclothes French police appeared in his neighborhood, asking nosy questions.

So now he was in his late twenties as he stood before Habib on a warm Italian summer evening. In Madrid over the last few years, he had acquired all the personal components that made him attractive to the radical Islamic movement in Spain: a raging sense of anger, a desire to do something grand for the cause, and a talent for theft and murder.

A few months earlier a Saudi man had been brought to him by acquaintances. The man had no name and was shown great deference by Jean-Claude's friends. The man outlined a small, simple, but highly ambitious plan for an operation in Spain, one for which some knowledgeable people felt Jean-Claude would be perfect.

Would Jean-Claude be interested in considering such an operation, even if it might end in martyrdom? Surprisingly to everyone, including himself, Jean-Claude said yes. He was brimming with self-confidence these days, so the idea that the operation wouldn't end in success never occurred to him.

And so here he was this evening before Habib. He had no interest in Habib's school, its students, or any aspects of formal education. The school, located in a decaying gray building that had once been a bakery, was in a section of Naples known as Little Egypt. The neighborhood was home to a growing number of Arab immigrants from the Middle East.

Jean-Claude's arrival at Habib's school was at 8:00 p.m., exactly as promised. He was a tall wiry man, Jean-Claude, an inch over six feet, mocha-complexioned, and stronger than he looked. He carried a small attaché case. As he moved toward the entrance to the school, he was accompanied closely by the two other men. The latter were both larger and heavyset.

Habib greeted his visitors in Arabic on the uneven brick steps to the school. Jean-Claude's two backups uttered little in any language. They kept their jittery eyes on the surroundings.

"It is very good of you to be here," Habib said. "My blessings upon you and Allah's blessings upon you. Come. Let us discuss things."

Habib produced a key that undid a drop bolt to the aging wooden door. Beyond this outer door there was an entrance foyer with heavy plate-glass walls. Then there was a second door. This one was made of very thick glass, steel reinforced and locked electronically, like a gate to a vault.

Habib unlocked this second door by a combination that he had memorized. As he did this, he shielded his hands from view.

Once the door opened, Habib brought his new contacts into the building. He brought his guests down a long hallway within the center of the first floor. A large gray cat seemed ready to greet Habib but then scurried out of the way at the sight of the visitors.

Habib led his guests into a small room, the principal's office. Habib drew the blinds and illuminated a small desk lamp.

"Well, welcome," he said again. "You've traveled far?"

"Far enough," said Jean-Claude.

"Of course," Habib said. "Of course."

Habib and his school had frequently been at odds with Italian educational authorities. The government saw Habib's institution as pushing its own Islamic agenda and not meeting the state standards of the Italian Ministry of Education. Arabic and Koranic schools in Italy were known as gateways of radicalization for European Muslims. Habib's school was not accredited by the Italian education authorities, and yet three hundred students, mostly the sons and daughters of Egyptian and Syrian immigrants, attended it.

But Habib was also a local hero within his community. Bearded and devout, sometimes genial, sometimes edgy, he projected, overall, a generous grandfatherly image to the families who sent their children to his school. He charged low tuition to working people, and nothing to those who couldn't afford it. He had also become the target of local fascist groups who denounced Islamic immigration in general — Habib in particular — and Italy's new secular laws, which to them seemed to give traditional Roman Catholicism a legal backseat to the faith of the unwashed and newly arrived. He was very much a contradiction. He was a gentle man, but he often drew violence. He had been a merchant for much of his life, and yet he was trained at the university level as a chemist. He was a scholar, but he also dealt with thugs. He was suspicious of everyone, yet trusting of too many individuals. Who knew where his real loyalties actually lay?

Jean-Claude sat quietly with the attaché case now across his lap.

"So?" Habib said eventually. "We are here to conduct business?"

"We are," Jean-Claude answered. "But time matters to me. So we should proceed."

Jean-Claude placed the attaché case on the table. Habib eyed it warily, its latches facing him.

"If you wouldn't mind, perhaps *you* could open it," Habib suggested.

Jean-Claude gave a little snort of amusement. "Of course," he said.

Jean-Claude unlatched it with two loud clicks. Then he turned it back toward Habib.

Habib's eyes widened. Within the case were several bricks of cash, mostly euros but a significant concentration of American dollars as well, fifties and hundreds, bound together with rubber bands. There were some smaller packets of Swiss francs.

"Count it," said Jean-Claude.

"With pleasure, I shall."

Habib flicked quickly through the money, calculating as he counted, coming out with a sum equivalent to almost sixty thousand American dollars.

Finally, Habib smiled. "Very well. Very close to the proper amount, giving consideration to the current rates of exchange. So you have made yourself a purchase," he said. "It is an honor. But ...," he said, raising his gray eyebrows in exaggerated surprise, "something perplexes me. May I inquire upon a point?"

Jean-Claude fixed him with a chilly glare, then nodded.

"A few short weeks ago," Habib posed, "when we negotiated a price, you stated that you had acquired a piece of art that you were engaged in selling. And yet the price I demanded was considerably higher than what you stood to receive upon that sale. We had quite an argument, if I recall. Yet you arrive here today on an afternoon's notice with everything that I asked for. That suggests that other funds have come from other sources, which further suggests the involvement of others beyond our immediate circle. As you might imagine, that alarms me."

Jean-Claude's tone was flat. "It shouldn't," he said.

Jean-Claude had made his living acquiring coveted property, then selling it. But it had often occurred to him that one could make even more money by selling the same item more than once. One particular purchaser from the Orient had paid in full for the artwork but then met with a terrible accident before he could take possession of the object in question. Jean-Claude, of course, mourned the man's ill fortune but was able to secure a second bid very quickly from an Italian businessman. The latter gentleman delivered a fifty percent down payment.

It's too bad, Jean-Claude mused, that he would also not be able to sell the item a third time. But sometimes a dealer had no choice except to complete a transaction.

"My first buyer met an unfortunate end. After payment was made. I have since found a second buyer. Now, where is our cargo?"

"Not far from here."

"We can retrieve it now?"

Habib opened his hands in an expansive gesture. "Of course," he said. "We will go for a short drive. As soon as I lock up the money."

"Have it your own way," Jean-Claude said. "Do you also wish to have your own bodyguards come with us now?"

Habib shrugged and laughed. "And why should I, my friend? You come here through an honest and devout contact in Madrid. You have paid in cash for the merchandise you want. You appear to be pious and a man of honor." Habib also gave a pat to his midsection to indicate that he was carrying a pistol. "And I have taken some small precautions. Aside from that, what can I do? My enemies are not you, my brothers in Islam, but rather the Americans, the Zionists, and the Christian fascists here in Italy. Some day, I know, they will come and kill me, but, *inch' Allah*, not tonight."

"Understood," said Jean-Claude with a slight nod.

"You will then excuse me for one minute?" Habib asked.

Jean-Claude's gunmen stepped aside to allow Habib to go to the door and leave the room. Habib left the door open. Jean-Claude listened to the sound of his footsteps and the direction the older man walked with the attaché case. The men in the room exchanged glances but said nothing.

Less than three minutes later, Habib returned.

"Very well," Habib announced to the room. "Your merchandise is at a farmhouse nearby. I have a van, my friends," Habib said. "We can all go together or you can follow if you wish to use your own vehicle."

"For safety's sake, we will use our own vehicle," Jean-Claude said.

"Then let us complete our business."

THREE

NAPLES, ITALY, AUGUST 26

Five minutes later, Habib was on the road that exited Naples to the south. Ten minutes later, he was outside the city limits, driving steadily through the night, one eye on the road, one eye on his rearview mirror. His van was small, old, and drafty. It rattled. From a tape player bolted to the dashboard, Arabic music whined softly, a stream of ballads by Kazeem Al-Saher, the Iraqi pop icon who now made megahits in Lebanon.

In the follow-up car, which bore French plates, one of Jean-Claude's guards drove while Jean-Claude rode shotgun. The third man was in the backseat.

Both cars moved quickly. The night was cloudy, but there were stars. The drive took another quarter of an hour on main arteries and then Habib led the way onto a side road. Next he accessed a smaller one. They went through farmland; vineyards, it looked like to Jean-Claude. Then they were on a long driveway in an area that was surprisingly rural. Finally, Habib's van rolled to a halt, and the following car came to a standstill a few meters behind it.

The travelers all stepped out in unison. There was only one building, a small barn. There was a pasture nearby. Jean-Claude surveyed it carefully as his eyes adjusted, looking for danger. But from the pasture the only movement or sound was from sheep. In the same field were several haystacks, positioned at predictable intervals and standing like tall rotund sentries in the starlight.

Habib went to the door of the barn. He fished around in a large flower pot and found a metal key, one which looked like it might have belonged to a medieval church. When he pushed it into a keyhole it turned with a loud click. He led the other three men into the barn, lit a heavy battery-powered lantern, and continued to lead the way, throwing a single bright beam before them.

The interior of the barn was half the size of a basketball court, but seemed smaller because it was cluttered. There was no livestock, only equipment and tools on a dirt floor.

"We are quite alone, my friends," Habib said quietly. "There is a farmer who owns the site, but he is a friend. And he will not be here again till Monday."

Jean-Claude nodded curtly.

Habib walked to the rear of the structure. Jean-Claude watched him carefully. There was an array of pitchforks and rakes, but Habib seemed to be trying to position himself. He put down his lantern and held his arms out at angles as if taking imaginary vectors. The other three men stood by quietly and watched. Habib shuffled his right foot along the floor as if he were looking for something in the layer of straw. Then he found it.

Kneeling, he pushed away some earth and revealed a metal ring on a trap door. Under this section of the barn, a small foundation had been dug into the earth, reinforced by wooden planks.

"I'm afraid I will need your help now," Habib said gently. "I'm an old man. Fifty-two. And your cargo is quite heavy. Would you do me the honor of some assistance?"

"Of course," said Jean-Claude.

Habib cleared away the trap door. One of Jean-Claude's assistants, a man with a nasty scar across his left brow, stepped down into a small storage area. He cleared away an array of farm equipment and then came to a piece of old canvas.

"Lift that and you will find what you want," Habib said.

The man in the crawl space lifted the canvas. Beneath the canvas was a pair of black duffel bags, new and sturdy, carefully wrapped in heavy transparent plastic. The man in the pit lifted the two bags and pushed them onto the floor of the barn.

Jean-Claude knelt down. From his pocket he drew a knife and with a click popped the blade forward. He cut open the transparent plastic and unzipped the first bag. He reached in. Within the bag were what appeared to be white bricks of some sort of plaster-style construction material. He pushed carefully through the whole bag and took an inventory. It was as expected. He opened the second bag and confirmed a similar inventory. He looked approvingly at what was before him.

"Will the owner of the barn not know this has been taken?" Jean-Claude asked.

Habib chuckled. "The owner of the barn does not know what was here. In truth, he does not know *anything* was here."

"You are very cautious," nodded Jean-Claude. "I like that."

"Cautious and reckless at the same moment," Habib said. "You could murder me and dump my body in that pit," he said, indicating the hidden foundation, "and I wouldn't be found for months. Maybe years."

"How do you know we won't?" Jean-Claude asked.

Habib shrugged. "I don't," he said.

The two gunmen were nervous. Habib smiled to the other two men, who did not return the kind gesture.

Jean-Claude zipped both bags closed and stood.

"As expected?" Habib asked. "The cargo?"

"Exactly."

"You are pleased with the transaction?"

"Completely."

For the first time that evening, Habib broke into a broad grin. "Then I am pleased too, my friend," he said.

Jean-Claude returned the smile. He opened his arms to suggest an embrace. Habib stepped forward. Jean-Claude wrapped his powerful arms around the older Arab and locked him in a tight embrace. Jean-Claude then pushed back and tried to break apart. But Habib continued to hold him and became very serious, almost like a scold.

"Let me tell you something, my young compatriot," he said. "I take one look at you, my friend, and I see a very smart but a very angry young man. About some things, I do not care. You can kill as many Western infidels as you wish. My only concern is that you do not get arrested with anything that could be traced to me."

"Why would I get arrested?"

"Informers, snitches, and traitors are *everywhere*, even in our community!" Habib said. "People loyal to the Jews, to the Americans! Are you so foolish that you do not know that?"

"I've been careful. Extremely careful."

"So far, yes. But already I hear rumors of what is afoot in Madrid.

Already I hear stories that suggest that our organizations could be counterattacked by police and saboteurs in Switzerland and Spain."

A moment passed. Habib released Jean-Claude.

"All right," Jean-Claude finally said. "We need to keep moving."

"Please help me reseal our hiding chamber," said Habib.

Jean-Claude's two assistants did much of the heavy lifting, piling farm equipment back into the storage area, then sealing it again. They covered the makeshift pit with hay. Then they left the barn, carrying the two duffels to which Habib had led them. They stashed the cargo in the trunk of their car.

Habib remained behind. Then the three travelers silently returned to their car. They drove it back to the main road and turned northward, the direction from which they had come. Jean-Claude rode in the back. Their mission now was to get as far away as quickly as possible, and this they did to perfection.

FOUR

BARCELONA, SPAIN, SEPTEMBER 4, LATE MORNING

Something told Alex LaDuca not to come out of the water. Her holiday in Spain was going so pleasantly, particularly following all the horrible events in Paris.

Some instinct told her that the vacation was about to come to a crashing end. But she finished swimming a few final strokes in the gentle surf, fifty meters from the beach and then turned leisurely to shore. The Platja de Barceloneta was a seductive place off the east coast of Spain, with smooth waves, soft sand, and the comforting warm water. The beach was a world-class one perched on the edge of Barcelona's city limits. It was almost lunchtime. The sun was intensifying. The Mediterranean was as blue as the sky above it. A perfect day to go out and swim a mile, which is what she had just done.

She reached water that was waist deep. Then she was in knee-high water and waded toward shore, enjoying the caress of the water upon her legs. She was feeling good again, fit and athletic, her mind strong and straight, her body the same. She had even purchased a new bathing suit for this trip, a red Nike two-piece. Not one of those scanty two-piece jobs that barely covered anything, "three postage stamps" her girlfriend Laura back in Washington liked to call them. But her suit was a bold one, good for some modest sun bathing but also good for a thirty-minute swim.

Red, as a guy once said to her, as in "red hot."

On this beach there were plenty of younger women who were there for the "top optional" experience, though these were mostly northern Europeans and a few North Americans. Alex wasn't about to join them, but she didn't have problems with it either. Maybe when her friend Ben teased her that she "had been in Europe too long" he had an amusing point.

Too long? she thought. Or not long enough? To Alex, Spain remained a fascinating if polarized place, a vibrant young democracy whose older generations had endured the Franco dictatorship and the strict moral authority of the Roman Catholic Church. Spain under the government of socialist Prime Minister José Luis Zapatero had become one of the most socially progressive countries in Europe. Today, the political right pulled one way in Spanish society and the left pulled in another. And then the Islamic population pulled in its own way.

The latter was a relatively new factor: More than five centuries earlier King Ferdinand and Queen Isabella had expelled Muslims unwilling to convert to Christianity. Now, as part of the worldwide migration of people from third world to first world countries, Spain was subject to an inflow of illegal immigrants not unlike that affecting the United States.

When she reached ankle-deep water, she stepped between some children at play. She smiled to them and to the bronzed, bikini-clad au pair girls who attended them. Alex was starting to feel good about life again. On paper, she was still an employee of the Federal Bureau of Investigation, on loan to the US Department of Treasury. She was still on the payroll even as she walked on the beach.

Her employers back in the United States, both the FBI and Treasury, had been generous about a few weeks of paid leave. Even the bureaucrats who oversaw her assignments agreed that she could use the R-and-R, first from a personal tragedy in February and then from nearly being gunned down in the Paris Metro in May. Before that, there had been the attack on the US president in Kiev, during which Alex had personally had a hand in protecting the president. The system, all agreed, owed her.

She kept telling herself that had been the past, her professional triumph in Kiev, linked to a personal catastrophe. It had been what God intended, she told herself. She could do nothing about the past but could do much about her own future. Yet as a little bit of a spiritual nod to the past and the future, she wore around her neck a delicate gold chain that supported a *stone* pendant, slightly smaller than an American quarter.

The pendant was of stone and had praying hands carved into it. Months earlier, she had bought it from a girl in the remote mountain village of Barranco Lajoya in Venezuela to replace a small gold cross she had lost in Kiev. In Paris, the stone had shattered, but she took the pieces to a jeweler in Montparnasse and had the pieces reset with a gold-plated steel edge around it to secure it together. So there it still hung. As a piece of beach jewelry, it nicely set off her tan and her swimsuit. Worn on a dressy occasion with a suit, it was equally handsome.

She walked toward her towel. She felt *good*. But when she reached her towel, her cell phone was ringing. It served her right for buying a phone chip that was good in Spain. She reached for the phone. From habit, she answered in the language of the country she was in. *"Diga."*

There was a moment's pause as her voice bounced off satellites. Then the response returned in English.

"Alex, I don't know where you are," said Mike Gamburian back in Washington, "but I have a pretty good hunch where you'll be in three days."

"Seriously, Mike," she said. "Nice to hear from you, but don't try to read my mind. There's this cruise ship that's sailing out of Barcelona for Fiji and the South Seas. They need multilingual hostesses who can cheat at blackjack and speak Russian. I've been hired and I'm going."

There was a pause. "Are you *serious*?" he asked.

"No, I'm not," she said. "But serves you right for calling me when I'm at a European beach and hardly wearing any clothes."

"How are you feeling?" he asked.

She pictured him in his office at the United States Department of Treasury, leaning back in his leather chair, 15th Street outside his window. Then she remembered that this was Labor Day back in America.

"Shouldn't you be in your backyard grilling botulism burgers for your family right now?" she asked.

"Should be, yes. But I'm not."

She crouched down for a moment and grabbed her towel and sunglasses. In one motion, she put the glasses on and worked the towel across her hair and shoulders. She was happy to see her newly acquired iPod, loaded with English, French, and Spanish pop and rock, and a library of jazz and classical, lay just where she had stashed it, plus the novel she was reading.

"Then you didn't call to ask me how my tan was progressing. What's going on?"

"What's your agenda for the rest of the week?" Gamburian asked.

"Are we talking on a secure line?" she asked.

"My end is fine. How about yours?"

"It's good, also," she said. "Or at least I think it is. Probably no fewer than a dozen different agencies listening, how's that?"

"Situation normal," he said.

A beat and then she added, "Well, I had it in mind to fly to London for two or three days to see some old friends and maybe see some theater. Then I figured I'd be back in Washington next week and pick up again at Treasury the Monday following and start in with whatever dull honest work you have for me. Then, if our previous arrangement holds, which it never seems to, I leave for Venezuela in a few weeks."

"How would you feel about going to Madrid, instead of London," he asked, "and staying in Europe for a little longer before coming back to Washington?"

"Why? What's in Madrid?"

"Great food, great wine, handsome macho Spanish men, the king of Spain, and bull fights. Plus relentless heat and pounding humidity that will make you cry. How does that sound?"

"It stinks, Mike. No way!"

"Good. Glad you're pumped. Can you be there in three days?"

Her hair was almost dry. She shook it out and liked the feeling. She pulled a thin voile cover-up around her upper body and remained standing. "And why do *you* want me in Madrid, Mike? I don't suppose there's a good reason."

"The Museo Arqueológico Nacional," he said, massacring all three words. "Ever been there?"

"Never."

"Here's your chance. Uncle Sam promised help with a missing item. Apparently the museum was burglarized a couple of weeks ago. There was a pietà taken."

"A *what*? Am I hearing you right?"

"A pietà," he said again.

"Like the huge one in Rome that weighs ten tons? The Michelangelo? Mary crying over the body of a slain Christ? What did they do, Mike, back a truck up to the place overnight and no one noticed? Great security."

Gamburian laughed.

"You have the reference right, Alex, but not much else. This one has a bit of a history to it. It's much older than the Michelangelo work and much smaller. A miniature. It's a carving in pink granite on a wooden base. Maybe six inches tall and eight inches wide."

"Art theft isn't my field," she said.

"But you learn quickly," he answered.

"I've heard that before and been sorry," she said. "What are you telling me? You want me to help the Spaniards with a two-bit burglary?"

"This feels like more than 'two-bit,' Alex," Gamburian said. "That's why we want to assign you to it."

"Give it to me straight, Mike," she said. "There are hundreds of major art thefts every week all over the world. What's different about this one."

"The uniqueness of the piece," he said. "And we've been picking up some rumors and theories about some small terror cells in Spain that are intent on big things. Art theft often finances major crime. So we're on guard."

"Got it," she said.

"You worked with a man named Mark McKinnon earlier this year, right? He's one of the top 'Agency' guys in Europe."

"I know him," she said without enthusiasm.

"He's on top of this, or at least says he is," Gamburian said. "He's going to be in touch with you in Madrid. Once again, you're the perfect person on the spot."

"Your flattery is going to get me killed some day."

"Better you than me."

"I'm going to hang up on you, Mike. That way you won't hear me cursing at you."

"Oh, come on. Hear me out, okay?"

Already within her, there was a feeling of disappointment. She had been doing much thinking and soul searching in the last few weeks. Following her recent activities from the brutally hot jungles of Venezuela to the snowy streets of Ukraine, she wondered if she was already burned out from this type of work. A voice within her urged her toward a job, an assignment, that would combat poverty, disease, and hate, the things she felt were the challenges of the new century, and part of how she wanted to live out her Christian faith.

"I still get to go back to Venezuela, right, Mike? Unfinished business and all."

"The Caracas assignment will happen down the road, Alex. But the US government needs to assign someone *right away*. Today. We got a request at the ambassadorial level. You're in Spain already. You're fluent in Spanish, you'll charm the socks off the *castizos* in Madrid, and you *do* have a bit of a background in art history."

"How did you remember that?"

"I didn't. I have a memory like a sieve. But I'm looking at your c.v. Christian art courses for your Master's at UCLA. Says it right here. So, listen," he continued. "If you say yes, I'll put you back on the active payroll as of yesterday morning. Instead of the money coming out of the 'Head Case' funds you'll be back on active duty. What do you say?"

A child's soccer ball with the Barcelona team logo rolled onto her blanket from nearby, pursued by a smiling five-year-old boy. Alex gave him a friendly smile and gently flicked the ball back to him with her bare foot.

She held her silence, just to let Mike twist a little in the wind.

"Still there?" Gamburian finally asked.

"Before I say yes, what *exactly* are you asking me to do?" Alex asked.

"At first, go to a meeting at the US Embassy. You'll meet some of our covert people in Spain and some people from various other European police agencies. You'll be the point person for the US government and our combined intelligence agencies while you help the Spanish government recover a piece of ancient Christian artwork. Please say yes soon: I want to go home and catch the end of the family barbeque. Spare ribs don't wait forever."

She turned and looked at the glittering Mediterranean, where tanned hard-bodied bathers romped, splashed, and laughed. She looked the other way, toward a busy promenade lined by small shops. On high white poles against a clear sky there flapped an array of flags from three dozen nations. The fresh salty air caressed her nostrils.

Europe really didn't seem so awful.

A breeze swept across the beach. Something in the back of her mind reminded her of the grittiness of Washington in September, and on top of that, the tedium of some of the desk-bound investigatory work that would be on her desk. At least here she could call her own shots.

"I suppose I could handle Europe for a few more weeks, Mike," she said.

"Excellent! We'll book you into the Ritz in Madrid as a little perk," he said, naming one of the best—and most expensive—hotels in the Spanish capital. "You'll be comfortable there."

"I suspect I will be," she said.

"Do everyone a favor and take a soft route to get there," he added. "Something that doesn't leave a trail."

In other words, she thought, don't *fly.*

"Oh, and you're going to need a new laptop. Do you want to shop for one and charge it to Treasury or should we deliver it to your hotel?"

"I'll buy one new in Madrid," she said. That way she could be sure it was never out of her sight from the time she acquired it. She could install her own software and security codes.

"Anything else?" she asked.

"Yeah," he said. "This little artifact that went missing from the museum—it's got some legend to it. There'll be a curator in Madrid who will give you the full story."

"What sort of legend?" Alex asked.

"People claim it's got supernatural powers. Spiritual stuff. Nothing you need to take seriously, but it might be an angle on why someone swiped it."

"I'll call you from Madrid, Mike. Thanks."

"Oh, and finally," he said. "You'll love this part. This missing piece?

It's called the *Pietà of Malta.* Do you like that, the Malta part? Shades of Humphrey Bogart and Mary Astor? You know the old movie, right?"

"I grew up in California and went to UCLA, Mike. How can I not? Peter Lorre and fat old Sidney Greenstreet. No tuxedo for Bogie, no Sam at the piano, and no fake fez for Greenstreet, but what the heck?" she added. "And I've read as much Dashiell Hammett as anyone under thirty."

"And no falcon, either," Gamburian said. "But still kind of cool, huh?"

"Maybe a little. Depends on who ends up shooting at me this time."

"Enjoy yourself, Alex," he said. "Travel safe. And thanks."

FIVE

SCHWARZENGEL GLACIER AND ZURICH, SWITZERLAND, SEPTEMBER 5

A late summer thaw had come to the mountains seven kilometers south of Saint Gallen. Drip by drip, trickle by trickle, the Schwarzengel Glacier had re-created itself, advancing and retreating, some of it so slowly that no one might have noticed other than the geologists who monitored the area. In this one remote spot, it was noticed only by those who took note of the changing snowscape and stared hard into the ice near Koizimfrau Ridge.

There, a heat wave had floated a glove up to the surface, one of those gloves with wool on the inside and leather on the outside, but with the fingers cut away. And then a dead Chinese national was found not far behind the glove.

Yuan was unmistakable. He was still big and strong, still wearing his parka, still bound in his tight head gear. Underneath his parka, among other layers of clothing, was a Euro Disney sweatshirt bought from a gift shop in Paris.

Donald Duck in French. The perfect absurd touch.

Yuan's dark hair was still thick too. His right eye carried a star fracture to the pupil, damage that he probably sustained in his rough trip from the basement of the monastery to this isolated location. His blue leather Hermès wallet was zipped in the pocket of his navy parka.

The wallet contained a Swiss phone card, his health card, his social-insurance card, three credit cards issued in Hong Kong, and his international driver's license, for which he'd had his picture taken two days before he left China.

His passport was there too, valid and issued in Beijing. It indicated that he was fifty-five years old and further revealed that he traveled on official Chinese government business.

Yuan wasn't alone. The heat wave had been extreme.

Also found during the melt was a twenty-year-old man who had said goodbye to his wife and newborn baby in 1995, gone snowboarding in late spring, and turned up now along with Yuan in the big thaw, his red hair still matted down on his forehead and a wedding ring still on his hand. And there was the Australian hiker, missing since 1977.

None of this by itself was unusual. The previous year, there were the two climbers who had remained roped together for more than thirty years, a man and a woman, their black leather boots still tied tight to their feet, their wooden skis still waxed and strapped to their backs. It had become part of the Alpine summer routine in this area, watching faces and corpses emerge from the big melt.

As always, the Swiss Gendarmerie Nationale was ready for the reappearance of the people who had been taken in by these mountains. They kept lists of those who were missing and waited for them to come forth.

That was the first unusual thing that the local police noticed about Yuan when his body had been found on the morning of September 5. Yuan's name was not on any of the lists. The second thing they noticed was that there was no record of him being in Switzerland or anywhere in the European Union, diplomatic passport or not. Then a third thing: under his parka was a fully loaded semiautomatic, a Glock G18.

What the Glock had to do with snowboarding or mountaineering or hiking was anyone's guess, but Lieutenant Rolf Hunsicker, who drew the investigation that would follow into Yuan's death, spent little time on that question. After all, the dead Chinaman had obviously been killed somewhere else not that long ago and then dumped in a remote area.

That conjured up three questions which would vex Lieutenant Hunsicker until they were resolved.

Dumped: How? Why? And by whom?

The cantonal police sent Yuan's remains by helicopter to a medical examiner's office in Zurich. An autopsy was performed that same evening.

Cause of death, suffocation. From smoke. And that hadn't happened out in the snow. There were also some strange bruises, and the funny configuration of the body when it had been found, as if it had been taken by helicopter to that place and then dumped from above.

Well, stranger things have happened. But if they had a chopper, that also suggested that Yuan must have had some wealthy powerful enemies. Then again, almost everyone in Switzerland had wealthy, powerful enemies as well as wealthy, powerful friends.

Sometimes they even overlapped.

BARCELONA, SPAIN, SEPTEMBER 6, MORNING

Alex stood on a platform at Estació de Sants in Barcelona, waiting for the train that would take her to Madrid. The station, built in the latter part of the twentieth century, was surprisingly modern, with none of the soaring vaults of the older Estació de França, the next depot down the line. And the subterranean waiting platforms were new, clean, and functional, having been constructed for the high-speed line that went into operation in 2008. The "AVE," La Alta Velocidad Española, the train that would take her to Madrid, was a marvel of modern rail technology. It glided smoothly into the station exactly on time at 10:16 a.m., looking like a beige spaceship.

She was playing along with Michael's paranoia. No air travel, which could be easily traced. Instead, she had paid cash for her one-way ticket to Madrid and would travel across southwestern Europe with complete anonymity.

She wore a tan skirt and a blue blouse. She scanned the platform as the train pulled in. Any followers? From long habit, she always had one eye to her back. Nearby there was a group of couples, eight people in all, that appeared to be tourists. She cocked her ear. They were speaking French. Not far from them there was a trio of American college students, a boy and two girls. Backpackers. One had an Ohio State sweatshirt and another girl had a Chicago Cubs cap with a ponytail pulled through the back.

She stepped back from the crowd and let others board first. Then she moved quickly along the platform to the next car to see if anyone would follow. She was one of the last to board.

Good. No followers. Her back was clean.

The car was crowded. She walked toward the back of the train, intentionally passed her assigned seat, then turned back. Again, no followers. She took her reserved single seat by a window. With a slight lurch, the train pulled out of the station.

Train and airline trips often lent themselves to reflection for Alex. She would carry a book but tend to ignore it after an hour. Today, however, she would dial up on her iPod music appropriate to her mood and spend the voyage in thought.

She gazed out the window and, beyond the tracks, at the farms and fields of Catalonia, followed by Aragon, then Castille. She watched an unveiling of the whitewashed walls of elegant Spanish villas wreathed in bright bougainvillea. They basked in a sunshine that was so intense that Alex put her sunglasses on. Then she watched a scattered array of medieval castles, Islamic palaces, and Gothic cathedrals pass by, interspersed with smaller towns and cities that conjured up more old than new.

Sometimes the landscape was flat and barren. She conjured up images from the literature of Spain. Don Quixote, tilting at windmills on the plains of La Mancha, even though those plains were to the south of Madrid.

She sighed to herself.

To understand modern Spain, she knew, meant to understand the past. Having studied history well and spent time in Europe at several points in her life, she was no stranger to modern Spanish history. And Spain, like so many others, was a country and a people torn by civil war.

Beginning in 1923, the government was held in place by the military dictatorship of Primo de Rivera. Following de Rivera's overthrow, the Second Republic was declared in 1931, a coalition of the left and center. over the next five years, tensions rose in all parts of Spain.

On September 17, 1936, a nationalist-traditionalist rebellion began, igniting a civil war. General Francisco Franco assumed command of the insurgent nationalists. Franco's supporters portrayed the conflict as a battle between Christian civilization on the one hand and communism and anarchy on the other. But on the other side, Republican sympathizers proclaimed the Civil War was a struggle between fascism and tyranny on Franco's side and democracy and liberty on theirs. Many non-Spanish young, committed reformers, and communist revolutionaries joined the International Brigades to fight against Franco.

Meanwhile, the troops of the International Brigades represented the largest foreign contingent of troops fighting for the Republicans. Thousands were from the United States.

Both Fascist Italy, under Benito Mussolini, and Nazi Germany, under Adolf Hitler, sent troops, aircraft, tanks, and other weapons to support Franco and his army of *nacionalistas*. The Italian government provided the Corps of Volunteer Troops, *Il Corpo Truppe Volontarie*, and Germany sent the Condor Legion, *El Legión Condor*.

The Soviet Union backed the Republicans and sent Soviet "volunteers" who often piloted aircraft or operated tanks.

In October of 1936, Franco's troops launched their first major assault on Madrid. The Republican government fled to Valencia. When Franco's forces failed to take the capital in ground fighting, however, Franco bombarded the city relentlessly from the air, then withdrew.

Franco made another attempt to capture Madrid in January and February of 1937 but failed again. The city of Málaga was taken on February 8. On March 7 the German Condor Legion arrived in Spain; on April 26 the Legion massacred hundreds of Spaniards, including numerous women and children, at Guernica in the Basque countryside. The bombing was committed forever to notoriety in a stunning mural by Picasso that he began painting just fifteen days after the event.

On March 9, Franco's army overran the city.

Less than three weeks later, with the help of pro-Franco forces inside the city, Madrid fell to the Nationalists. When the last of the Republican forces surrendered, Franco proclaimed victory in a radio speech aired on April 1.

Like most wars, this one was ugly. Tens of thousands of people had been executed, most killed by their countrymen. Atrocities were common. These included the aerial bombing of cities carried out on Franco's behalf. In the early days of the war, more than fifty thousand people who were caught on the "wrong" side of the lines were murdered. Victims were taken from their refugee camps or jails by armed people and shot outside of town. The corpses were abandoned or interred in graves dug by the victims themselves. Local police knew better than to intervene. Probably the most famous victim was the poet Federico García Lorca.

Mass graves are still being unearthed today.

The Republican authorities arranged the evacuation of children. These Spanish War children were shipped to Britain, Belgium, the Soviet Union, other European countries, and Mexico. Those in western European countries returned to their families after the war, but many of those in the Soviet Union remained in Russia after the Iron Curtain descended.

Atrocities by the Republicans were known as Spain's "red terror," and among them were hundreds of attacks on Catholics. They were unspeakable in their cruelty. Nearly seven thousand clerics were killed. Thirteen bishops and more than four thousand diocesan priests were murdered. Nearly three hundred nuns were murdered. There were accounts of Catholics being forced to swallow rosary beads or being thrown down mine shafts, as well as priests being forced to dig their own graves before being buried alive.

Other actions on the Republican side were committed by the NKVD, the Soviet secret police. The crimes committed by the NKVD were even-handed — they butchered everyone. They carried out executions not only against Nationalists, but also against all those who did not share their Stalinist ideology, even if they were fighting on the Republican side.

After the end of the war, thousands of Republicans were imprisoned and at least thirty thousand were executed. Many others were put to forced labor, building railways, drying out swamps, digging canals, or constructing monuments to Franco. Hundreds of thousands of other Republicans fled abroad, especially to France and Mexico.

In all, there were about half a million deaths during the Spanish Civil War. Ten percent of all soldiers who fought were killed, including almost one thousand Americans, most of whom were buried in Spanish soil.

In the ensuing decades, Spain remained a closed corner of Europe, a nation that had once had an empire and great artists like Goya, Velasquez, and Picasso, but which had also turned inward from the outside world. It was not until the 1950s, when the United States was seeking allies in the fight against communism, that Spain rejoined a Western alliance. Control of the Straits of Gibraltar and permission to place American air bases in Spain were no small part of the equation.

And now after seven decades, feelings in Spain have not completely healed. In late 2007, Spain finally passed a law that families wanting to unearth bodies of relatives killed during the Spanish Civil War should now receive full cooperation from the state. And the government mandated that every province in the country must remove remaining monuments to Franco.

As the train sped for Madrid, however, Alex's mind flickered from the distant past to her own personal events of a more recent coinage. Her fiancé, a member of the United State Secret Service, had been killed recently in the line of duty. She remained angry and unsettled with God at the events that had befallen her. Deep down, she had not yet learned how to forgive the people or forces that had caused Robert's death. In terms of what she now wanted from life, she remained undecided.

Like this very mission. Why accept it? Then again, why not?

Soft route, indeed.

Outside in the distance, she saw a small church and churchyard and for a fleeting half a minute, she could see a funeral in progress. She was somehow touched by the feelings of sympathy, empathy, and sorrow for the people gathered there.

It was a rural ceremony. It brought to mind a memory of her own, when she was a little girl, visiting her mother's childhood home in Mexico. Her grandmother's health had been failing for two or three years. But during this summer, when Alex was nine, her grandmother had suddenly started to run a high fever. Overnight, her breathing became difficult. The family wanted to move her to the hospital, but the nearest facility was a hundred miles away.

"*Tu abuela se está murienda,*" her mother explained. Your grandmother is dying.

"*No. Ella no puede,*" Alex answered, in denial. No! She can't!

Alex went to her grandmother's bedside. She placed her hand on the old woman's, then upon her forehead as her eyes welled with tears.

"*Por favor,*" Alex cried. "Don't leave us."

Her *abuela* managed a weak smile. Across three generations, they spoke to each other in Spanish, in the accents of Oxipalta, where the old woman had lived as a girl.

"Remember, Alex, there is a purpose to everything, a time for everything. The Creator has seen to that. Many years ago, I was young and strong. But now I am tired. I must rest. It's what God intended."

By her bedside was a small white paper bag with sand in it. The sand supported a small candle.

"Be my little angel," Alex's grandmother had said. "Light the luminaria for me. Through the light of the luminaria, my Lord Jesus will find me."

Alex sobbed and kissed her grandmother. She told her how much she loved her. She fumbled with some matches and lit the luminaria. Her grandmother smiled, closed her eyes, and never spoke again.

Alex's mother sat by the bed. A few hours later, the old woman passed away.

The next day, Alex sat by the open coffin. A young priest from the local parish said Mass in Spanish. Afterward, the family and the priest buried *abuela* in the *camposanto* by the churchyard. They laid her to rest next to her husband, who had died ten years earlier.

It was Alex's first brush with death, the first time she had tried to comprehend it. But in Alex's mind and in her heart, another luminaria had been lit, one of faith, and it still burned.

It was like that with Robert, her late fiancé, too, Alex realized. The luminaria, the simple candle, still burned. But it hadn't receded in memory as much as her grandmother's, and the flame had been lit much more recently. And yet, in the same way, Alex had moved on.

What alternative was there, really?

The final two hours of the trip passed uneventfully. Her seat companion was a gray-haired Spanish woman twice her age who was deeply engrossed in a novella. For a while, Alex gamed on her iPod, with only a casual eye on the scenery. Eventually, the train passed a glorious castle about forty minutes outside of Madrid, then through the surprisingly third world shanties of gypsies that ringed the city. Then it pulled into Madrid Atocha at quarter to three. She disembarked. Here too the station was surprisingly modern, the original nineteenth-century one serving as a kind of trainless winter garden. Gradually the familiar faces from the train disappeared into the crowds at the station and ceased to be a part of her day.

She took a taxi to the hotel, which was only about fifteen minutes away. "The Prado," the driver said as they passed the famous museum, although she had visited it many times on previous visits. As they approached a fountain with a figure of Neptune, they turned onto a crescent with a little park in the middle called the Plaza de la Lealtad and pulled up in front of the Ritz, a building that looked to be straight out of Paris.

"The stock exchange is on the other side of the square," the taxi driver said. "Maybe not a coincidence," he added with a laugh. "No poor people here."

The Ritz had been Madrid's most prestigious hotel since it opened at the beginning of the twentieth century. King Alphonso XIII, grandfather of the current King Juan Carlos II, invested his personal money into its construction. Alex had stayed there once before, about five years earlier.

The lobby was grand and immaculate. A fortuitous error had taken place in booking, and she was bumped up from a single room to a small suite. The suite not lacking for comfort, from king-sized beds to plush carpets, to reading chairs, two phones, Internet connection, and an antique desk. She opened a pair of twin windows to view the city, even though the air-conditioning was humming quietly and efficiently.

Okay. She was in Madrid. Now what?

SEVEN

The autopsy had just concluded in Zurich when a representative of the Consulate of the Republic of China arrived at the headquarters of the cantonal police. The man entered the building and approached the receptionist at the front desk very quietly. She only knew he was there when she looked up and jumped slightly, seeing a handsome but unsmiling face and dark eyes looking down at her.

"Hello," he said, with great courtesy. "I'm John Sun. I'm here to visit the body of the unfortunate Lee Yuan." He was immaculately dressed and infinitely polite. He spoke enough German to get by. He also spoke excellent English. And, with a big gracious smile, he exuded more charm in a minute than most men can muster in a lifetime. All the women in the office noticed. He was there, he said, to identify and claim the body. He had his Swiss government issued ID, standard issue for foreign diplomats in the country. No one looked at it too carefully.

The receptionist passed him along to a policeman who worked the records room. The policeman had studied in England for a year, so the language was a convenient fit. Sun got on well with his Swiss contact.

The visitor had a business card in English, Chinese, and German, as well as his consular ID. His documents confirmed his name as John Sun.

Sun joined some of the ladies for their lunch break. He hung around the police installation waiting for the release of the corpse. One of the younger women, a single blonde girl named Hana, remarked—blurted out, actually, in Sun's presence—that Sun looked very much like the sexy Chinese movie star Jet Li, who had killed about a hundred guys. Li had also, she said, bedded many beautiful ladies in dozens of films from Hong Kong to Hollywood.

The visitor expressed embarrassment over such flattery. He insisted that his own life was much more prosaic. Back home in China, before joining his nation's foreign service, he said, he had been a teacher and a gymnast.

That afternoon, Hana brought up a picture of Jet Li on her workstation computer via the Internet. She said she'd love to take him home, cook for him, and "seduce him with European culture and keep him all to myself."

The other women crowded around, admired the picture, and agreed. After that, they referred to Johnny Sun as their "movie star."

As a movie star in Zurich, however, he had a short run. He appeared only one more time, early that same evening to manage the shipping of Yuan's remains "back to his family in China." Sun was again infinitely courteous and thanked everyone at police headquarters. He wore a black suit and a funereal black tie for the pickup of the deceased. He arrived with his own vehicle and two Chinese helpers for the occasion.

Hana made an attempt to turn her school-girl fantasy into reality. Cornering him alone for a moment, she invited him to dinner at her place, he could pick the day.

He declined with grace and regret. His immediate responsibility, he said, would be to accompany the body of Yuan back to China. They—he and the corpse—would be leaving within a few hours.

So John Sun disappeared as abruptly as he had appeared. It was a strange irony: they hadn't known much more of John Sun than Lee Yuan, and they both had vanished as quickly as they had appeared.

"The mysterious East," one of the women said.

EIGHT

MADRID, SEPTEMBER 6, EVENING

At the front desk of the Ritz, Alex inquired about where to buy a new laptop. She knew there would be no shortage of expensive stores nearby, which catered to wealthy tourists and business people traveling on someone else's tab. In Madrid, being a late city even by European standards, there was an array of shops open near the hotel in the early evening. The concierge at the hotel provided her with the address of the best.

She went back to her room and threw on a pair of jeans and some comfortable walking shoes. To anyone observing her, she might have looked like a graduate student on summer holiday. In actuality, the anxiety of being back on the job was setting in, and she was already entertaining premonitions of danger, made worse by the persistent memories of the events of the previous months.

She also wished, for example, that she were carrying a weapon. She hated to use it and knew that violence leads only to more violence. Yet she had no illusions about the world and the evil of some of the people in it. Sometimes guns and physical force, lamentable as they were, were as much a part of life as food, water, and air. There wasn't much she could do about it.

She made her computer purchase within a half hour of leaving the hotel. Her clerk was a young *Madrileno* who was fascinated with her and couldn't tell her nationality until she presented her passport as identification with her credit card.

He had visited London and New York, he told her, and began speaking very good English. He wished to practice it, so she indulged him by conducting the final parts of the transaction in English.

She took her new purchase back to the hotel. She booted it and started to download the proper software. The procedure would take several hours. So she left the computer and went out again for a walk.

She was alone in a city she had loved very much in brief visits as a student many years previously. And her hotel — bless her bosses and the American taxpayers who were underwriting this back in Washington — was excellent.

After her computer was properly set up, Alex caught up with some evening sightseeing. Then, toward eleven, she had a light dinner and a half bottle of Rioja at a quiet little place two blocks from the hotel, one where she could find a quiet table in a corner, watch the endlessly interesting street scene, and not be bothered by anyone.

Might as well enjoy it, she told herself. She was already back in the government harness and as usual had no idea where that might lead. She would attend the next day's meeting, take a conscientious assessment of the museum theft, and see what she wanted to do next.

It wasn't all bad, she told herself. She was back to work and felt much better about it than she had expected she would. She was glad she had taken this assignment and noticed, as she sat in the café and tuned into several conversations around her, that she was already thinking in Spanish.

NINE

BARCELONA, SEPTEMBER 6, LATE EVENING

In the hours after picking up their cargo from Habib, Jean-Claude and his two assistants had driven northward past Naples, then the next day continued past Rome. Driving and sleeping in shifts, they eventually had driven past Pisa and Florence until they arrived at the massive shipyards of Genoa.

There they had waited until the proper ship was ready for them. The ship was a freighter named *El Fuguero*, a Portuguese merchant vessel that flew a Liberian flag. Their secret cargo remained in twenty separate packets, each weighing about five kilos, or ten pounds. For good measure, Jean-Claude had repacked them in fresh luggage purchased at an Italian department store along the route to Genoa. Jean-Claude's henchmen then left the ship, but Jean-Claude, using his French passport, bought passage in one of the steamer's inexpensive staterooms.

The next morning, *El Fuguero* hoisted anchor and sailed westward from Genoa. It was the twenty-ninth of August. It made a stop in Corsica and then another in Marseilles, where it docked for two days. There the crew enjoyed the run of the sunny old port, the bars, the cafés, the gambling parlors, and, in particular, the international brothels.

Jean-Claude had struck up friendships with a few of the crew members along the way and accompanied them on their lusty evening exploits while in port, particularly the fleshier locations. He boldly informed his new friends that he was a professional teacher with a job waiting for him to teach language in October in Brooklyn, New York. But he also cited his affection for the fresh sea breezes of the Mediterranean and wanted to enjoy a brief holiday before flying to America.

Then, after two evenings in Marseilles, the ship hoisted anchor again and sailed southward through a stretch of the western Mediterranean that was busy with cruise ships, merchant vessels, and private yachts chartered by wealthy men and the women who, for a price, loved them.

El Fuguero was never far from the coast of mainland Europe. It passed the distant mountains of the Pyrenees, the border between France and Spain, and ultimately entered Spanish territorial waters. It easily navigated the tricky currents off Cap de Creus on the Spanish coast and came within fifteen knots of Barcelona. There it stopped and dropped anchor in a peaceful but ever-changing sea, swept by sun and wind.

It was the evening of September 4. *El Fuguero* waited. So did its clandestine cargo, and so did Jean-Claude, a much appreciated passenger, who was gracious to all and raised the suspicions of none.

On the evening of September 6, a berth opened unexpectedly in the commercial shipyard in Barcelona. *El Fuguero* sailed into the harbor with the late evening high tide and docked. An hour later, Jean-Claude disembarked like any other tourist or citizen of the European Union. He had both duffel bags slung over his left shoulder and held his passport in his right hand.

As he walked past Spanish customs, he nodded amiably to inspection officers who nodded back to him.

"You care to check my bags, *Señores*?" he asked in Spanish.

"*¿Ciudadano español?*" asked one of the officers. Spanish citizen?

"*Ciudadano francés,*" he said in return. He indicated his French passport if they wished to check it.

The officers shook their heads, waving him on. Two minutes later, Jean-Claude spotted a driver who was there at the docks to meet him.

The driver was a young man named Mahoud who was a Spanish citizen, and whom Jean-Claude had recruited earlier in the year into a tiny little cell of self-styled terrorists in Madrid. Mahoud was an auto mechanic by trade. He had a sixth grade education.

Jean-Claude greeted Mahoud with an embrace. Then he shoved his two duffels into the backseat of Mahoud's car and slid in after them. He eased back and lit a cigarette as the car began to move.

TEN

GENEVA, SWITZERLAND, SEPTEMBER 7, TWO MINUTES PAST MIDNIGHT

The sunshine of the early summer afternoon that had warmed the streets of Geneva faded to dusk and then to darkness. Shortly past 8:00 p.m. the streetlights of the old city were illuminated. The many open-front cafés at lakeside were alive with the clinks of glasses and tableware, punctuating conversations in many languages.

Bankers and businessmen finally relaxed for the day, savoring what they might have accomplished or anticipating their next move for tomorrow. As best they could, they kicked back with their guests, the tourists, the idle rich, the occasional film star, and the university students. As the evening grew later, they swapped advice and attempted seductions. Some would succeed, others would fail.

The high spirits had not penetrated a secure sprawling apartment in a modern building two blocks away. There, the aging Colonel Laurent Tissot of the Swiss army sat at an ornate nineteenth-century desk before his visitor. Two in-progress packs of American cigarettes lay on the colonel's desk. A cloud of smoke gave the air within the apartment a cancerous, bluish haze.

Tissot was a short man with a slight moustache, a high forehead, and an immense bald head. Though Tissot still professed a high rank within the Swiss military, it had been years since he had worn a uniform. Tonight he wore a dark brown suit with a neat white shirt open at the collar. The suit had been elegant once, but that time had long passed. In that way, Tissot's attire matched the furnishings of the flat, as well as the business at hand.

Seated in a chair across from Colonel Tissot's desk was a second man, richly muscled beneath casual clothing. He was a Polish national known as Stanislaw, trim, very tall, and sturdy. He had wide shoulders, closely cropped blond hair, and blue eyes.

The room was quiet, aside from the rumble of traffic that rose from the narrow rue Ausnette outside. Tissot closed a file that the second man had brought to him and looked up.

They spoke in English, the shared language in which they were most fluent. "And so?" Tissot said, moving the brief meeting toward a conclusion. "The *Pietà of Malta* remains in our possession?"

"That's what my report says."

"Well done," said Colonel Tissot.

He closed the folder and rose from his desk. He walked across the room to a fireplace that bore a gas grate. Tissot knelt and gently laid the file in the fireplace. He used a cedar match to ignite the file, then turned on the gas with a key at the side of the hearth. With an abrupt whoosh, the entire file erupted in flames.

A careful, precise man, Tissot stood before the fireplace and watched the file disintegrate into a harmless gray powder.

He turned and walked back to his desk.

"So now it's the Americans," said the colonel with exasperation. "Now *they* plan to send someone?"

Stanislaw nodded and pondered the point. "The result will be the same."

"I know," Tissot said. "Fools," he muttered.

But while his lips passed a single word, volumes passed in his mind. He was midway through his eighth decade of life. He had been brought up in a world that had possessed its standards of good and evil, right and wrong. The colonel had tenaciously held those standards and still lived by them. Yet the world was a different place now. He dimly recognized a new world social order, and he did not like it. So he battled against it.

Colonel Tissot withdrew a thin file from his antique desk. He handed it to Stanislaw. The file was in English. Stanislaw scanned it.

"The American they will probably send is very young and highly inexperienced," Colonel Tissot said, reverting to English. "That is what my contacts in Spain have advised me. Foolish, foolish. But the Americans are invariably foolish."

Stanislaw raised an eyebrow. He reached to the back page of the file with his scarred left hand. He withdrew a photograph of the subject. For a moment, Tissot's gaze settled on the scar, and he remembered its origin. A decade earlier, in a drunken rage over a woman,

Stanislaw had attempted to kill a man with his bare hands. In trying to defend himself, the other man had shoved a knife through Stanislaw's right palm. Stanislaw had pulled it out by himself and used it to slit the victim's throat.

Afterward, he had bandaged the hand with a bar towel, sutured the wound by himself, and refused any subsequent medical attention.

Stanislaw glanced at a series of surveillance photographs.

"The pictures are less than ten days old," Tissot said. "Good to know who the enemy is, isn't it?"

"Yes. It is." He glanced at the pictures for a few final seconds.

Then he placed the photos back in the rear of the file and closed it. He leaned back in his chair.

"You'll take care of this?" Tissot asked.

Stanislaw gazed off for a moment. "Americans are naïve and undisciplined. The men when they travel sneak off to brothels. The women have sexual liaisons with strangers that they would dare not have back in America." The Pole's eyes twinkled. "The agent will be found dead of a gunshot with evidence suggesting that sort of immoral behavior."

Tissot raised an eyebrow in approval and nodded.

"You will have the first opportunity. Act upon it immediately, if you please. A backup team in Spain has already been engaged, but I would prefer not to use them."

Stanislaw nodded. "I expect no difficulties," he said.

Colonel Tissot leaned back in his own chair. He rubbed his tired eyes.

"Nor do I," he said. "Take the file with you. Burn it after you've memorized it. And do not make any mistakes. There is no room for mistakes."

ELEVEN

The United States Embassy in Madrid stands at the north end of Calle Serrano. It is a slab building in the style of the United Nations Secretariat, though at nine stories, considerably smaller. A metal fence runs around the compound.

At exactly 8:45 on her first morning in Madrid, Alex arrived at the public entrance to the embassy. Wearing a summer-weight navy suit and carrying her new laptop, she proceeded to the consular section. She identified herself to the Marine Security Guard at the window, who checked her official passport against information provided by Washington. He buzzed her through a door at the side, into the employees' entrance lobby, and asked her to wait.

Alex recalled from earlier visits that, given the unusual position of the building against the relentless sun of Spain, it was an incessant gripe of workers at the embassy that it was never possible to achieve a mutually acceptable air-conditioning setting for the offices on the north and south sides of the building. If the air conditioning was set to cool the south side with its greenhouse effect the offices on the north side were too cold, and if the setting left them comfortable, the offices on the south side were too hot.

She sighed. The elevators were slow and there weren't enough of them. Finally an elevator door opened, and a young man came out, smiling, hand extended.

"Hi," he said, "I'm Pete Wilkins, with the Treasury Attaché's Office. I'm your control officer. The Regional Security Office asked me to give you this. I guess you found the standard welcome in your room. But this is something different. It's your temporary embassy ID. Your data for laser eye scans has already been sent from Washington."

When another elevator arrived, Alex and her "control officer" rode up to the eighth floor. The Political Section was on the eighth floor, which is as high as the elevator rose. And yet, also from her previous assignments, she knew that there was also a ninth floor, or, as one diplomat once drunkenly put it to her, "the Felliniesque 8½ floor." This was where the black arts of espionage were practiced by the American faction in Madrid, the stuff that took place off the record and in the back alleys. An armada of microwave antennas were on the roof just above this intelligence section. Despite access from the Political Section it had nothing to do with the latter, whose business was traditional diplomacy.

On the eighth floor they turned to the left and walked down a corridor with offices on either side. They came to the room assigned to her morning briefing: Sala/Room 821.

Wilkins departed and Alex stepped in.

Small groups of conversation stopped. All heads in the room turned her way. Her eyes did a quick count. Nine players, all men, aged from their twenties to their fifties. Suits all around. Grave expressions breaking into smiles at the arrival of a woman. She didn't mind. She had long since gotten used to being the only women in a room. She had also learned how to use it to her advantage.

But at some time on some day at some point in the future, couldn't she walk into a room like this and see at least *one* other female?

She did a quick scan. Only one man did she recognize, and she didn't know if she should acknowledge him. Before she had to decide, a handsome young man with fair skin and black hair smiled and stepped toward her.

"United States Department of Treasury?" he asked. "Alejandra LaDuca?"

"That would be me," she answered.

"I'm José Diego Rivera, the chief curator of the Museo Arqueológico Nacional," he said. "Thank you for being here and my deep appreciation to your government for sending you."

"De nada," she said. "I hope I'm able to help."

"Let me introduce you around," he said. *"¿La molesta si hablamos español?"*

"No me molesta," she answered. It didn't bother her at all if they all spoke in Spanish.

The eight other participants present were each in some branch of international law enforcement. Rivera introduced Alex first to a man named Miguel Torres who stood to his immediate left. Torres was in the green uniform of La Guardia Civil, the paramilitary Civil Guard of Spain. These were the police brigades that mostly guarded rural areas, highways, country roads, and national buildings, but who were still remembered by some for an attempted coup in 1982. At that time, rogue members of La Guardia Civil burst into the parliament, firing shots in the air, then held the members at gunpoint. Even though it was las Fuerzas Armadas, the Spanish army, who had attempted the coup, not the Civil Guard, the guard was widely remembered as embracing the assault on the new democracy. In recent years, however, the Guardia Civil had also played a greater role of combating terrorism within Spain, mostly in the more remote areas and the borders.

Torres was tall and thin, dark-haired with grayish-white temple patches in a Paulie Walnuts style. His uniform hung on him as it might on a clothes hanger. His nose was out of joint, looking as if it had been broken and reset more than once.

To Rivera's right stood Carlos Pendraza, a representative of another division of the Spanish police, the Policia Nacional. Alex guessed he was the alpha-cop present, the most powerful person in terms of local authority.

The Policia Nacional were the units that dealt mostly with national security, major crime, and potential terrorism in the larger cities. Pendraza was regally featured with gray hair and a very light complexion. When he spoke, his accent carried the inflections of Madrid. He made no attempt to speak any language other than Spanish. Alex wondered if he was uncomfortable with other languages or just holding back. He also possessed a certain intelligence and dignity. He was, she guessed, in his mid-fifties and easily the oldest man in the room.

Though the two Spaniards were of competing police agencies, both were perfectly gracious when introduced. Spaniards, like most Europeans, tended to like Americans personally even if they disagreed with various aspects of American foreign policy. Both men were near the top in their divisions, but not right at the top. They were colonels, not generals.

Further to the curator's right, and to Alex's left, stood a trio of men in dark suits, all with ID tags that pegged the service they were here to represent. Like the Spaniards, they were high up in their respective organizations. Alex also knew that the representatives of the other police agencies would have been chosen with an eye to their fluency in Spanish and their familiarity with Spanish culture and law.

Closest to Rivera was a heavy-set balding man named Maurice Essen, a Swiss-German who was a representative of the International Criminal Police Organization. The latter was better known by its telegraphic address, Interpol, and was currently headquartered in a set of gray modern buildings in Saint-Cloud, France, just outside of Paris and not far from the world-class racetrack.

Next to Essen was a very youthful Englishman of Scotland Yard, Rolland Fitzgerald, and next to him was a stocky dark-haired Frenchman named Pierre LeMaitre, who had been sent by the Gendarmerie Nationale de France, the French National Police.

Fitzgerald was bright-eyed and hollow-cheeked and hawklike in the sharp quirky way he turned his head from side to side to follow conversation. He was about thirty-five. LeMaitre was small, almost chubby, his dress dowdy and his expression dour. His accent, which Alex overheard when he spoke briefly in French with Fitzgerald, had the almost rube-like inflections of Normandy. He was as unglamorous a Frenchman as she had ever seen, and she guessed that he was probably a pretty good investigator. In her experience, it always turned out that way. He hadn't gotten to where he was on looks or charm.

The introductions proceeded in Spanish, yet all the Europeans other than Colonel Pendraza were careful to say a few words to her in English. First, they wished to be courteous, but second, and more importantly, they wished to make her aware of their fluency in her native language in case it proved important later. It was the proper gesture.

Arriving last was the one other American who would be in the room, a jowly man with thick glasses, pink lips, and a clipped gray moustache. His name was Floyd Connelly. He bore an unflattering resemblance to an aging Orson Welles and moved with the speed and grace of a sea tortoise.

Connelly, however, represented the United States Customs Service. Customs people in the US, she knew from experience, tended to be plodders, more mulish and stubborn than innovative, more bureaucratic than maverick. But they also had unending access to federal records. So he was a contact she would nurture if she could.

The one man in the room whom she did know loitered outside the introductions. He was an Italian national, tall and trim with short dark hair. His name was Gian Antonio Rizzo. He was immaculately dressed in a Via Condotti suit. Rizzo was recently retired from the municipal police in Rome after having put in a quarter century on the job in that city, often with distinguished results. He also had had a less-evident employer over those years, off the books and off the record, one based in Langley, Virginia, which was how Alex happened to know him.

They had worked together in Paris. Alex had not seen Rizzo since she had checked out of the American Hospital in Neuilly two months earlier. Rizzo gave her a brief hug and spoke in English as a courtesy. They exchanged a few words, but little of substance with the other men present. There was an unspoken expectation between them that they would talk more afterward.

Rivera, the curator, glanced at the Rolex on his wrist. It was 9:00 a.m., the given time of the meeting. He moved to the head of a round conference table as an assistant closed the door to the room and departed.

Taking the cue, the assemblage of law enforcement people within the room moved to seats at the conference table. Rivera stood at the head of the table.

Rivera waited for all others to sit, then eased into his own chair. He quietly turned on an anti-bugging device that sat on the table before him.

Alex sat thoughtfully at the round table in the conference room, her new IBM laptop open in front of her. She glanced at the others and there was much she could already conclude.

First, whatever she was here for was no small matter and probably had some larger import than anything that was shared around the table today. Second, by the assemblage of people around the table, whatever the heist had been, it had already escaped the boundaries of one country — with potential repercussions to match.

And third, if Rizzo was there, it wasn't a coincidence. Her employers were hooking her up with someone she knew.

TWELVE

Colonel Tissot finished breakfast and prepared to address a day of business. As a merchant of munitions that were sold in the world's gray economy, he was a busy man on most days, particularly in a "neutral" capital like Geneva. The beauty of five hundred years of Swiss neutrality was that Switzerland was a perfect place to conduct the commerce of warfare.

Well, why not? The Swiss banks and their codes of secrecy were there for a reason, were they not?

A fastidious man, quiet and unassuming in public, Tissot dressed in a light gray suit, one of several that he had bought on a recent visit to London. He tended to be a creature of habit, leaving between nine and ten each morning to meet his clients. He was, however, wary enough to alter his movements from day to day. One never knew when some pest from the past with some grievance, real or imagined, might step forth.

Tissot locked the double bolts on his door and stepped a few paces to the private elevator that served his floor. He checked to make sure he had both of his cell phones, one in his trouser pocket, the other with a small handgun in the briefcase he carried. He knew that Stanislaw would call him during that afternoon with a progress report of his drive down the southeast coast of France.

Tissot had a rueful admiration for his employee. The man had made a lifetime occupation of killing people, first in the military and then for hire. Well, it was a mean, unforgiving world, and everyone had uses for men like Stanislaw, who were just smart enough to get a job done and just dumb enough not to try thinking on their own.

When the elevator doors opened, there was a passenger whom he had never seen before. He gave Tissot a nod and Tissot reciprocated. No words were spoken. Tissot didn't care for strangers and was leery of them. But people were always subletting in this building or entertaining promiscuous guests who stayed over. The morality of today led to a lot of strangers, Tissot mused, and he could have done without them.

Well, it would only be a few seconds, Tissot grumbled, and he did have his own weapon in his attaché case, along with his laptop.

The elevator doors closed.

Of course, Tissot pondered next, working his way through an unpleasant scenario, if this stranger in the elevator were any real threat, he would not have time to access the weapon. The man was Asian of some sort, much younger and athletic than he. Tissot had sold weapons to Asians many times. He liked them as customers but not necessarily as people. The elevator slowly descended, and Tissot put together a few other details.

The stranger in the elevator wouldn't yield the rear of the car, insisting through his positioning that he remain behind the only other passenger. Then Tissot noticed that a band of tape had been placed over the security camera in the elevator. And then, out of the corner of his eye, he saw that the man was wearing gloves.

Tissot quickly raised his gaze to the mirror in the corner of the elevator. He saw that the young man behind him was staring back at him. Tissot could read the look in an instant.

"Something troubling you, sir?" Tissot asked in English. He made a move to access the gun in his brief case.

"Yes," the stranger said.

Then the gloves were in motion. Tissot jabbed an elbow backward. He flailed and fought to open his attaché case. But the stranger ripped the case out of his hands. It thudded onto the floor.

Tissot attempted to throw another elbow and tried to stamp down on his assailant's instep. But the assailant had him by the head, one hand under the jaw, the other on the top of his skull, turning his head in a powerful twisting motion.

The grip was so tight that Tissot couldn't open his mouth to speak. Tissot resisted by clenching his neck muscles and trying to strike backward with his arms. But the stranger was an expert. He had his own body flush against Tissot's as leverage.

Then the stranger put everything he had into his mission. With a tremendous twist, he moved Tissot's head sharply to the left, then jerked it backward. Tissot felt his own muscles tighten like springs, then gradually tear with an excruciating pain. The intruder jerked Tissot's head upward, then spun it abruptly back to the left. Tissot felt as if his body was a car involved in some catastrophic wreck.

The crack of Tissot's cervical column was as loud as a gunshot. It filled Tissot's body with an immense pain that swelled and carried him into an unconscious blackness. Then Tissot's body gave one final violent contraction as death claimed it.

Tissot's body went limp. John Sun thoughtfully eased it to the floor. He let the body rest there briefly in a small moment of victory. He picked up Tissot's attaché case and guided the elevator to an emergency stop. Then he took the elevator back to the sixth floor where Tissot had boarded.

Using the keys from the dead man's pocket, he opened Tissot's door.

He dragged the corpse in. Perfect so far. No one had seen anything, and presumably no one had heard anything. No blood. Sometimes things were too easy, but he wasn't complaining.

Sun closed the door and locked it. He set aside the attaché case for a moment. He calmly dragged Tissot's body into one of the bathrooms, dumped him headfirst in the tub, and closed the door. He returned back to Tissot's front door and bolted it from within.

He then settled into the apartment of the man he had killed. He had to go through Tissot's belongings. There were certain items he wanted, and he had several hours to go through everything and look for them. But the item he wanted most, which he would take with him, was the colonel's laptop.

He found it easily.

THIRTEEN

MADRID, SEPTEMBER 7, 9:42 A.M.

Here, my distinguished guests, is the object we're looking for," José Rivera, the museum curator, continued in Spanish. "*The Pietà of Malta*. Let's take a close look at the pilfered object."

He passed around the table a series of identical files, one for each person present. Inside each, on the top page, was a color portrait of the object recently stolen. To a casual observer, it might have appeared to be a smaller and less refined version of Michelangelo's majestic sculpture, *The Pietà*, as it was known to millions of art lovers and Christians around the world. Michelangelo's masterpiece has remained at St. Peter's Basilica in Vatican City to this day.

"*The Pietà*," Rivera began, "is not just a single sculpture in Rome, but rather a singular subject in Christian art, normally depicting the Virgin Mary cradling the slain body of Jesus. As such, it is a particular *form* of the devotional theme of Our Lady of Sorrows. Any pietà depicts a scene from the Passion of Christ and is the thirteenth of the Stations of the Cross. When Christ and the Virgin are surrounded by other figures from the New Testament, the subject is strictly called a *lamentation*, although *pietà* is often used for this as well. The pietà — as an expression of faith and as an enterprise of religious art — gained popularity in Italy in the sixteenth century. Many German and Polish fifteenth-century examples in wood greatly emphasize Christ's wounds and are seen as precursors to the genre. Woodcuts from Russia in the fourteen hundreds suggest a similar fascination with the form."

Rivera paused. A trace of a smile crossed his face. "The most famous pietà, of course, is Michelangelo's in St. Peter's Basilica in Rome. Michelangelo's last work was another pietà, a different one, featuring not the Virgin Mary holding Christ, but rather Joseph of Arimathea." He paused, then added, "Michelangelo carved Joseph's face as a self-portrait. A final act of piety wherein the sculptor *humbly* placed himself in a biblical context."

There was laughter around the room. Alex always enjoyed listening to an expert on anything.

"But what we are here today to discuss, however, is what is believed to be the definite origin of this genre of work. *The Pietà of Malta*. Please look at the top photograph I've presented to you. Five centuries ago Michelangelo gained inspiration for his greatest work from gazing for many hours upon the very sculpture that was stolen from us. *The Pietà of Malta* was held by the Vatican at the time, AD 1500, and would have been accessible to him. That is the treasure that disappeared from our museum. It goes without saying that our most prized pietà must be found and returned to the government of Spain and this museum as soon as possible."

There was a rustling of documents around the room.

"I'm just curious," Rivera continued as those in the room perused the files, "as to who here might have ever seen *The Pietà of Malta* before, directly in our museum. Or how many of you are even familiar with it?"

Only one hand went up in acknowledgment, that of Rizzo, the Roman. Rivera nodded to him.

"I've also seen the big one at the Vatican," Rizzo said. "Does that count?"

"*En absoluto.* Not in the slightest," Rivera said with a sly smile.

In the photographs from the files was a small piece of artwork from antiquity. It was part sculpture in stone, part carving in wood. It was well worn from the centuries, but it was easy to distinguish what it represented.

"What you see before you," Rivera said, "is the first sculptural *lamentation* in recorded history."

The carving was that of Mary comforting the body of her slain son. The faces had eroded over the centuries, but the arms, body, robes, and legs of two figures remained clear.

"It is believed to be from the time of Constantine the Great," Rivera said. "Perhaps three centuries after the time of Christ. It was under the rule of Constantine that the eastern and western Roman Empires were united, and the new capital of Constantinople was founded on the site of Byzantium. Constantine also issued the Edict of Milan, which made Christianity legal throughout what remained of the Roman Empire. He himself converted to Christianity on his deathbed. It was thus an era when much early Christian art flourished among the artisans who were faithful to the church. So it is believed that this particular piece is from that time."

Alex and the others in the room followed along as Rivera, switching back and forth now between very precise English and his native Castilian Spanish, explained the background of the stolen object.

"This category of art is, strictly speaking, a lamentation," he said, backtracking slightly. "A *lament* or *lamentation* is, in artistic terms, often a song or poem expressing grief, regret, mourning. Many of the greatest and most timeless poems in human history have been lamentations. They can be found in the *Iliad* and the *Odyssey*, in Beowulf, in the Hindu Vedas. There are laments in the Jewish *Tanakh*, what Christians know as the Old Testament. In many oral traditions, the lamentation is or has been typically performed by women. Similarly, in the traditional music of Scotland, a lamentation is a genre of musical composition for the bagpipes. In this form, these slow pieces are a theme and variations, beginning with a slow air that is played with embellishments. The simple melody returns to finish the piece. These laments are usually named after a person; traditionally, a warrior slain in battle."

Down the table, the Frenchman LeMaitre was pouring water from a plastic container into a glass. Rolland Fitzgerald, the young man from Scotland Yard, was looking steadfastly at the hard copy of the photograph while simultaneously jiggling his laptop screen to life. Alex did a quick count and noticed that she was one of three in the room who had arrived with a laptop. The rest, older school, worked off note pads and pens. Rizzo sat resolutely with his arms folded, nothing in front of him, listening, his own personal computer in his head.

Rivera continued. "The term *pietà* originated from a custom of the Roman Empire around AD 64," he explained, "referring to the act of prostrating oneself, and putting forth an emotion of intense spiritual love, accompanied with a reverence for the Roman gods. Eventually, the term slipped from Latin into Italian, taking the meaning 'pity.' But in the context of these pieces of art, the early Christians also adopted the term and took *la pietà* to connote the great grieving sorrow over the death of Christ, as well as a reverence for the Almighty."

Rivera paused.

"Now look at the photograph."

The missing piece, he explained, was an extremely rare example of late third-century sculpture. The early pietà had been created by a craftsman in an unusual manner. The covered body of Christ was limestone. The exposed head, arms, legs, and feet were marble of a faint pink hue. On the base of the sculpture was ancient writing that looked possibly like Arabic. And the work was small by the standard of a pietà. Alex recalled Mike Gamburian mentioning that it was about six-by-eight inches.

"The original provenance of the carving has never been known for certain," Rivera explained. "But studies during the twentieth century suggested that it might have been *excavated* originally at Morgatina. Morgatina was a site in central Sicily well known for having been looted frequently and the abundance of artifacts that resulted from it. It was believed that an early civilization of Christians from Rome established a colony and a fortress there. With the fortress came a church and a monastery. And with the monastery came early artwork, much of it from the islands of Sardinia, Corsica, and Malta. Much of this was plundered or destroyed during the fifth century AD when the Roman Empire disintegrated under the press of barbarian invasions from the east, and Vandals finally sacked the city."

Alex looked up and watched Rivera. He was still speaking without notes.

"In an effort once to confirm this pietà's origin," Rivera continued, "the limestone was analyzed by computer in 1975. The samples matched a limestone found in Malta. The specific site has never been identified as it no longer exists. But there is no doubt that the limestone was from Malta. Hence the name, *The Pietà of Malta*. There is even to this day, I might add, a small town on the island of Malta that goes by the name Pietà."

He moved toward conclusion.

"Allow me one or two other historical notes. The strategic importance of Malta was recognized by the Phoenicians, who occupied it, as did in turn the Greeks, Carthaginians, and Romans. The apostle

Paul was shipwrecked there in AD 60. With the division of the Roman Empire in AD 395, Malta was assigned to the eastern portion of the empire dominated by Constantinople.

"Throughout history," he continued, "small Christian carvings and relics such as this one were collected and enshrined. It was believed that the holiness of the art would evoke a power to heal and or to intercede for the faithful owner. Similarly, if such an item had actually been in the possession of a saint, its aura and powers would have been enhanced by the contact with the saint's spirit. The fact that this faith was later exploited for money does not alter its basic character. The practice forms an interesting comment on the inherent longing for physical contact, even if once removed, with great men or spiritual leaders. Even into the present day, millions of people will place immense value on such objects."

A pause and he continued.

"Now look very carefully at the base of the carving. Much of the original engraving has been lost over the years." Rivera was indicating the area that Alex had already noticed, one that looked like ancient writing, but not European.

"What you will see," he said, "is ancient Arabic calligraphy. It combines the Arabic word for peace and a depiction of a dove. As you all know, in Judaism and Christianity, a white dove is generally a sign for peace. The Torah tells us that Noah released a dove after the flood in order to find land. The dove came back, an olive branch in its beak, telling Noah that the waters had receded and there was land once again. The same image holds through in the modern and ancient Islamic languages. The motif can also represent 'hope for peace' and even a peace offering from one man to another. The dove is represented here with wings spread, still in flight, a reminder of its role as messenger as well as the unfulfilled promise. The dove is, of course, in art also the traditional representation of the Holy Spirit, frequently seen hovering above Christ's head when He is baptized by John the Baptist."

Alex flicked her gaze around the room. All of the attendees appeared focused on Rivera's minilecture, except possibly Floyd Connelly of US Customs, the Orson Welles look-alike, who seemed to be jetlagged. His eyelids were drooping and he had obviously tuned out, even though Rivera kept glancing at him.

"Now, it has been suggested, for centuries, that *The Pietà of Malta* has had magical powers," Rivera continued. "According to legend, whoever was in possession or guardian of it, could not suffer a mortal death. Similarly, those who possessed it — nations, armies, civilizations — would never be vanquished. Hitler for example was obsessed with this object and personally snatched it in Rome in 1943 after Mussolini's overthrow. At the close of World War II, American soldiers under Patton 'rescued' it from Hitler's chalet on the Obersalzburg. The United States government owned it for a while, then generously returned it to the Austrians in 1955. It was then put on display in the museum of Vienna's Hofburg Palace yet was largely ignored. Eventually, Francisco Franco acquired it for Spain in exchange for some Austrian art that had gone to Madrid during the war. Shortly before his death, he turned it over to Prince Juan Carlos, Franco's designated successor and the future king. Juan Carlos turned it over to the Museo Arqueológico."

And there it had remained, he said, largely ignored again, until less than two weeks earlier.

"You all have further background in front of you to read. Those of you who came equipped with laptops can turn in your reports, and we will provide you with a download of the identical information. Needless to say, the overall information shared in those documents is to be privy only to those in this room and any immediate superiors who assigned you to this investigation."

He scanned the room. "I also expect you will exchange credentials and ways to access each other to work together to retrieve *The Pietà of Malta* for the people of Spain."

He paused again.

Around the table, most eyes remained trained on the files or the individual computer screens. Some nodded soberly. Floyd Connelly, US Customs, looked pleased that the meeting was over. He opened a piece of Juicy Fruit gum, chomped it, and gazed at the ceiling.

LeMaitre, the Frenchman, sitting across from him, studied Connelly with barely concealed contempt until he shifted his gaze slightly and caught Alex looking at him. He gave her a smile and turned back to Rivera.

"We know we are asking for a great achievement in a short period of time," Rivera continued. "But the recovery of this object is the only remedy we can ultimately accept. So today and tomorrow you will be briefed by me and various branches of the Spanish police as to what has happened to date. After that," he said, "I trust you will pursue this investigation with the vigor and skill of which I know you are all capable."

As Rivera spoke, from her right, Alex caught a nearly subliminal glance from Rizzo, whose gaze slid sideways for a moment to hold hers, then drifted away again and didn't return.

"Questions?" Rivera asked.

Maurice Essen of Interpol was the first to speak. "Have your local police or national police made any inroads in their own investigation?" he asked. "The use of municipal police uniforms suggest there may have been some local organization involved in this."

Colonel Torres of the national police picked up the question.

"There is nothing so far," Torres said. "We have our leads out, much as is mentioned in the report. But so far, there is nothing."

"Is there any indication that the theft was engineered with any international group?" asked Rizzo.

"No indication one way or another," Rivera answered.

Alex pondered for a moment. A few half-shaped questions and theories began to emerge in her mind. But she wanted to study the full dossier that had been given to her before she ran her thoughts in any particular direction. It was an old habit that had served her well.

Think first, then speak.

The room was quiet. There were no further questions. The meeting adjourned.

FOURTEEN

MADRID, SEPTEMBER 7, NOON

Maria Elena Gómez had turned thirty-three years old on the same day that *The Pietà of Malta* was stolen from the Museo Arqueológico in Madrid. At thirty-three, an unmarried mother of a twelve-year-old daughter, she was a woman of considerable charm and good looks, solid and wholesome in the traditional style of a working class *Madrileña*.

To see Maria at the clubs or even at a soccer match, laughing, singing, or knocking back wine with friends, one would never have guessed the stolidly mundane nature of her career and employment.

As an employee of the Madrid subway system, just a few years earlier Maria would have been limited to working in a ticket booth. But now, thanks to laws forbidding sex discrimination in employment, Maria had graduated to the Madrid Metro job that she really liked. She was a track walker.

Five days a week, after the subway shut down for the night and before service resumed the next day, armed with heavy flashlights and cell phones, she and her partner would hop down onto the tracks and walk from one station to the next. They would check the links between the individual rails and check to see if the pressure of passing trains had created cracks in rails that, if the rail was not replaced, could lead to a train jumping the tracks. Now, more recently, track walkers were on duty during the day too. They kept a special eye open for anything unusual that could be connected with terrorism. New York, London, and Madrid had all been hit savagely by al-Qaeda, as everyone knew. While the chances of a repeat were always present, no one wanted to make it easy.

It wasn't a job for everyone, but Maria liked her work.

"But, *mujer*! The darkness, the *vagabundos* in the tunnels, the filthy rats!" her female friends would say.

"No me importa nada," she would answer. And to her it *was* nothing. She didn't care a whit about dark or rats, maybe because she had been a tomboy as a girl, which hadn't sat well with the nuns when she was in school. But she had left school at the age of sixteen when her father died.

The job was steady. It paid reasonably. It supported her comfortably, if not lavishly. But she also felt as if she was doing something not just to support herself and her young daughter, but something for Spain as well. Something that protected the public. From accidents. From terror. Even from inferior Metro service.

So she took her job seriously and dutifully, which was in the family tradition. Her father had been an engine driver for RENFE, the railway company, until he died of a stroke.

From her father, she had also inherited his little apartment in Lavapiés, not far from where so many of the new immigrants from India, Morocco, and China had settled. The home was not grand and it was not in a chic or fashionable part of the ancient city, nestled onto a street with Arab tea rooms and Indian kabob restaurants. Her place was a rambling apartment in one of the old *corrales* — or tenements — of the nineteenth century. But inside, it was tidy, clean, and comfortable, a nice home all the same among friendly people from all over the world. And it was hers.

The home was her father's inheritance to her. All of it. And her father was the man she had loved unequivocally her entire life and who had loved her the same way in return. Pictures of him with Maria's mother adorned every room of her home. In his honor she still supported Atlético, the soccer team that was the perennial underdog to the much more famous Real Madrid. She had gone to the games with him when she was a small child, sitting on his knee when she was small enough, in much the same way that he had taken her to the bullfights

She still went to the bullfights at Las Ventas from time to time. She felt very much at home sitting in the pie-slice shape of the arena where her father sat along with all the real aficionados, compared to the tourists in the more expensive sections. Actually, more than the bullfights themselves, she liked walking back along the Calle de Alcalá, with its lively scene of people enjoying the bustle of the boulevard, leading up to the Puerta de Alcalá, the three-hundred-year-old neoclassical arch that remains Madrid's grandest monument.

Men in her life? From time to time. But she no longer wished to be tied down. And one of the last things in Spain that would change, she thought, would be the *machismo* aspect of the male dominated Spanish society. No, she had her daughter, a job that gave her some independence, and the little pleasures of life.

Men were a mixed lot, anyway. Except for her father, who had accepted her behavior and her pregnancy, saying *"Los tiempos cambian."* Times change.

Times *had* changed.

A lot of the change had been very visible and in her lifetime, the last few decades, the final part of her father's life and the first part of hers. Much of the change had come thanks to Felipe González and the PSOE, the Socialist Party that came into power in 1982 and completed the transformation from the stodgy, repressive Franco era to the vibrant Spain of the present day.

She remembered the latter years of the *movida*, the time when frozen morals were thawing and repressed creativity in everything from the arts to fashion to cinema was blossoming everywhere. She remembered dancing late into the night as a young girl sans chaperone, something that would have been unthinkable a few years earlier. She had even gotten pregnant by a man she barely knew, and though she hadn't married the father, she was proud of her twelve-year-old daughter, who was now an outstanding student in school.

For a woman in her thirties with minimal formal education and no husband, things were going very well.

FIFTEEN

MADRID, SEPTEMBER 7, 12:47 P.M.

As Alex was closing her laptop, Gian Antonio Rizzo moved to a position beside her. "When did you arrive in Madrid?" he asked, switching into Italian.

"Yesterday. By train from Barcelona."

"I noticed your tan," he said. "Very nice. Your legs look spectacular. Spent some time turning heads on the beach, did you?"

"Yes, thank you. Are you flirting with me already?"

"I hope so," he answered good naturedly. "I need to do something to make this otherwise-useless trip worthwhile. We're never going to find this filthy figurine, you know. Might just as well go to the flea market on Saturday and get them a piece of junk there to replace it. So let's talk about your skin hue, and the unending beauty of it, instead."

Alex smiled. "I'm not sure I'll be having much more time to work on the tan," she said, packing her PC into an equally new carrying case. "Seriously, this looks like a full plate."

"When art is gone, it's gone," he said. "Poof. Arrivederci. Hasta la vista, baby!"

"We'll see."

"But you're feeling better?" he asked. "Better than I saw you last in Paris."

"Molto meglio, grazie."

"Where are you staying?"

"The Ritz," she said. "Down the Calle Filipe IV from here."

"I didn't know America's balance of payments was so healthy they could put your investigators in a place like that," he said.

"It's not," she said, packing up her things. "The dollar is still in shambles worldwide, but the average bubba who votes doesn't know that yet. So they waste money, anyway. Like all governments. At least some of it gets thrown in my direction. If I objected, they'd probably have me investigated."

"How many dollars is that a night, the hotel?"

"Maybe six hundred," she said. "I haven't looked. But the marble bathrooms are wonderful, as is the balcony and the view. I'm on the fifth floor overlooking the Prado. What's not to like?"

"It's always helpful to understand that staying at a five-star hotel in Europe is quite a different experience than staying at one in Asia, or even in America for that matter. You'll never get the service of the Oriental in Bangkok or the amenities of the St. Regis in New York. But what you do get is a heavy dose of old-world charm. And yes, sometimes that does come in the form of a beautiful hand-loomed carpet that is a bit stained or a breakfast buffet with indifferent food. That is what I love about hotels like the Ritz. You have to take a portfolio view of the experience and not focus too hard on any one aspect. Is that your experience?"

"Yes, it is."

"Then invite me up to your room sometime."

"Not a chance," she said with a laugh. "So far I've focused on the fresh fruit that arrives each day. Today it was yellow plums. Yesterday it was Haifa oranges."

"Don't tell your taxpayers," he said.

"Sometimes being a government slave has its perks. This is one, I guess. And what the heck, I'm a prima donna, anyway, and tend to injure easily."

He laughed again. "Of that I have no doubt," he said. "Unfortunately, I come from a small backward country with an outstanding football team but a third-world economy."

"Oh, knock it off." They both moved toward the door. "You make Italy sound like Tunisia."

"Sometimes the similarity is vague," he said.

By then it had become a conversation in motion, Essen of Interpol tightly latching a computer case and talking to Fitzgerald of Scotland Yard in hushed tones, while LeMaitre, the Frenchman, picked through his pockets for a pack of cigarettes.

The two Spaniards in uniform stood at their places and waited in case anyone felt like asking them anything further. They looked disappointed when no one did.

Floyd Connelly of US Customs came over. His face was puffy up close, little red veins visible around the eyes that suggested a more than passing acquaintance with booze over several decades. He had the confused look of a man playing out the final few months before retirement, not really on top of anything any more, and torn between saying something smart and making a fool of himself.

"A lot of bull, this whole thing," he said in English. "I don't know why I was even included here."

"I don't either," Rizzo said.

"I had to fly in for this," he muttered. "I missed a golf weekend in Maryland and an Orioles-Yankees game. I thought the peet-a was a big rock in Rome, and now this guy's telling us it's a little thing that got stolen from here."

"This is one of the tinier ones," Rizzo said, switching smoothly to English. "Which is why it walked off."

"How you supposed to keep track of them if there's two things by the same name?" Connelly asked.

Rizzo blinked. "There are actually several," Rizzo added. He and Alex looked at him in the same way, wondering if he was that dumb or joking.

"Well, carry on," Connelly said, ignoring Rizzo and looking at Alex. "If you need anything, give me a holler." He handed her a business card. On it he had written the name of his hotel in Madrid and a phone number.

"I'll do that. Same going the other direction," she said.

"Yeah. Right," he answered, after taking a moment to figure out what she meant. "Right. Listen, my Spanish is a little weak, so I might give you a call just to compare notes on what was said here."

"That's fine," Alex said. "But the handouts are in English also."

"Are they?"

"But call me with any questions," she said.

"Right," he said again. "Okay."

Rizzo and Alex watched him lumber to the door and leave. Rizzo placed a hand on her shoulder, then took it away.

"Political appointee," she said.

"Capisco," he said.

"Anyway, you look like you're doing well," he said, going back to English. "I'm very glad. You were in my thoughts for the last weeks."

"Thank you."

"This work can slowly kill you sometimes," he said. "Sometimes I wake up and am surprised I'm still alive. Know what I mean?"

"Look," she said. "The Ritz is only a few blocks from here and they have an excellent café just off the lobby. I think you should buy me coffee."

"I think I should too," he said.

SIXTEEN

MADRID, SEPTEMBER 7, EARLY AFTERNOON

On the outskirts of Madrid, Mahoud's small car pulled to a halt in front of a ramshackle garage connected to a private home. The neighborhood was one of immigrants from Asia and North Africa. The home was owned by a taxi driver named Basheer. Basheer was not home at the time. He was an honest workingman in his thirties who pushed an old vehicle around Madrid for twelve hours a day, six days a week, to support his family. He had emigrated from a war-torn Lebanon to Spain in 1993. His family had found peace and prosperity in Western Europe.

Basheer was also the second member of the cell that Jean-Claude had pulled together in Madrid.

Jean-Claude stepped out and, as he always did, surveyed the street. His eyes swept quickly. He saw no danger. From a ring of keys, he found the one to Basheer's garage. He unlocked the two doors and swung them open. He glanced at his watch.

Mahoud pulled the car into the garage. They closed the garage door and waited.

In the garage, which had space for only one car, Jean-Claude flipped open a cell phone and called a certain number. A familiar voice answered in Spanish.

"Soy aqui," Jean-Claude said.

The response was rapid. *"Veinti minutes."* Twenty minutes. But, Basheer warned, he had just dropped off some lousy American businesspeople at the airport and the traffic might be bad returning. Or he might catch a fare that he didn't want to turn down.

Jean-Claude said he would wait and clicked off.

For a moment, neither Mahoud nor Jean-Claude spoke. There was taped music from Egypt on the car radio. It played softly. The garage was stuffy and hot, the sun pounding on the roof. Jean-Claude smoked. Mahoud coughed.

He switched back to Arabic. "Why don't you go stand sentry?" Jean-Claude suggested. "Outside. Stand across the street and keep watch."

"I don't want to," Mahoud said.

"I didn't ask if you wanted to," Jean-Claude answered.

Mahoud glared and hesitated. Then he opened his door, got out, and slammed it shut. He leaned forward and glared at Jean-Claude, looking as if he had something to say. He had a gun at his belt, beneath a soccer jersey. But Jean-Claude returned the glare with cold brown eyes. Mahoud exited the garage through the side door and took up his assigned position across the street.

Jean-Claude remained in the back of the old car, his duffel bags at arm's reach. There was also a rear exit to this garage, one that led to an alley that led between buildings and to safety down another street. If he felt that they had drawn a tail, this was his escape route before his cargo reached its destination. But for now everything looked fine.

His attention drifted to a side door that led from the garage into a kitchen. The door was half open. There was activity in the kitchen now. Basheer's wife, Leila, was there with her young child.

Leila was a trim Arab woman, very pretty with fair skin. She was very young, maybe eighteen or nineteen. She was dressed very immodestly because of the heat.

Jean-Claude watched her, his eyes riveted, more than a devout man should. Basheer, the taxi driver, was obviously a fortunate man in his home, not only to have such a young wife but such a sensual one too.

The child was a boy. Excellent. Basheer and his wife had been blessed with a son. If Jean-Claude ever had a family, he would want a woman who looked as good as Basheer's wife and he would want to impregnate her with many sons to continue his wars. Basheer's wife had the infant in a high chair and was fixing a meal for her offspring. She was a perfect baby machine, a nice lithe body and obviously fertile.

Jean-Claude remembered, though, that Basheer had expressed some criticism of Leila from time to time. Like many of the young Arab women in Madrid, she had some irritating pro-Western attitudes.

She didn't sufficiently hate Americans and English people, or even Spaniards. Worse, she seemed to like them and even like their culture. She and a friend, for example, had snuck off to a Batman movie and apparently liked it. The unfortunate Basheer had to raise his hand to his wife over that and punish her so that similar transgressions would not mar their future.

Leila glanced in Jean-Claude's direction but obviously didn't see him in the car. She continued to go about her business, fixing the meal, feeding the child, entertaining an unseen watcher with her half nudity.

Then, perhaps from feeling unseen eyes on her, she glanced again at the garage. This time, she did see him. She was startled.

Jean-Claude's instincts told him to look away quickly, but he didn't follow them. His eyes were riveted. He was seeing something that he hadn't often seen in his life. So he stared awkwardly, and then smiled.

He smiled in spite of himself. Basheer was a primitive pious man. If he knew his wife had been seen in this state, Basheer would be prone to violence against both of them. He was a simple man and that was how he normally reacted.

All sorts of scenarios ran through Jean-Claude's head, none of them good. At the very least, he hoped Basheer's wife would simply close the door and never mention the incident.

Instead, she did the unpredictable. She did nothing. She didn't close the door, and she didn't cover up. Instead, she suppressed a delicate little smile and went about her business with her child.

Jean-Claude would later remember thinking, "People are right." Leila is "too Western." But he didn't look away, either. And in this case he didn't seem to mind.

SEVENTEEN

MADRID, SEPTEMBER 7, MIDAFTERNOON

Alex and Rizzo arrived at the Ritz and soon found their way to a café located on the back patio of an inner courtyard. As they found seats in a comfortable shaded area, it occurred to Alex why Rizzo had been assigned to the case.

Italy had the most art crime of any country in the world, with approximately twenty thousand art thefts reported each year. Russia had the second most, with approximately a tenth as many. Italy was also the only country whose government took art crime as seriously as it should. Italy's *Carabinieri* were the most successful art squad worldwide, employing over three hundred full-time agents, so if Rizzo had contacts within their ranks, as assuredly he did, he would be invaluable.

"So," Rizzo finally said, "it's been about two months since I saw you last. You've managed to enjoy yourself a little bit, I hope."

The café was shaded and fans blew cold air outdoors from within the air-conditioned hotel. Despite the bad associations with the events in Paris that had nearly cost Alex her life, she was glad to see someone here she recognized, and, for that matter, someone she trusted.

"I think I'm managing reasonably well," she said. "The government gave me some time off. They don't want me to turn into a nut case a few years down the road and sue them for abusive employment practices."

"Ah, America," Rizzo said with a laugh. "I wish I were American. I wish my ancestors had gotten their tails onto a freighter out of Calabria and done me the favor of a lifetime."

It was her turn to laugh. "Anyway," she concluded, "I've been vacationing in Switzerland, Portugal, and Spain. Just collecting my thoughts, hanging out on beaches, doing a lot of reading, getting back into shape, listening to my iPod in six different languages, seven if you count English and American separately."

"I do. And my congratulations on a wise use of your time," Rizzo said. "So you didn't return to America at all?"

"I did actually, yes," she said, "for two weeks in June. Too many memories there for now. So I picked up some different clothes and came back over here."

"I understand," he said. "Are you carrying a gun these days?" he asked.

"Not in Spain. Are you?"

"If I reached to my right ankle I might find something," he said.

Via the waitress, a pitch-black espresso arrived for Rizzo, a double poured over ice, and a small pitcher of iced tea with mint for her.

"So you've been hanging out by yourself mostly?" he asked. "Not missing the warmth of human contact?"

She smiled. "If you're snooping around to see if I'm romantically linked again, already," she answered, "shame on you."

"My apologies. I'm only curious after your welfare," he said.

"It's too soon for me to be involved with anyone new," she said.

"There was an American gentleman whom I met briefly in Paris," he said. "I believe he was a wounded veteran from Iraq."

"Ben," she said.

Rizzo answered yes with a nod.

"Ben's been a wonderful friend. Like a brother to me at this time," she said. "He's planning to get his law degree now. We keep in contact by phone and he worries about me."

"As do I," Rizzo said.

"What's new in your world? Last time I checked, for example, you had two employers."

"I've retired from the Metropolitan police in Rome," he said, almost proudly. "As long as the government stays out of bankruptcy I have an ample pension."

"And the 'other' job?" she asked.

"That's why I'm here," he said. He cleared his throat. "As a special advisor to the Holy See, which would hope that a religious relic would find its way back to its rightful owner."

"Of course," she said.

"Or, stated more directly," Rizzo said, "this has drawn the attention of the pope because it's the earliest known pietà, and the Old German Man hopes that it gets returned soon." Alex smiled. "Which leads me to a few questions," Rizzo said.

"Go ahead," Alex answered.

"Why *are* we in Madrid, aside from the fact that some underworld *pozzo* made off with a paperweight that the museum should have locked up better?"

"I was going to ask you the same question," Alex said.

"Art treasures often disappear into thin air once they leave the museum," he mused. "Why the big commotion over this one?"

"I was hoping *you'd* tell *me*."

"I don't have answers today," Rizzo said, "aside from what I just said about the Vatican and its interest." As he spoke, he was eyeing the young waitress, who managed a smile as she was pouring tea at the next table.

Rizzo looked back to Alex.

"They asked me to come to that meeting and told me you'd be there," Rizzo said to Alex. "That was enough of an enticement."

They paused for a moment and the waitress departed. "But you do have some experience in art theft," Alex said.

He rolled his eyes. *"Troppa esperienza,"* he said. "Too much. Before I moved to homicide in Rome I did *furto del arte*. Sounds like *commedia del arte*, but much more serious. Here's something to remember, though. Art crime represents the third highest-grossing criminal enterprise worldwide, behind only drugs and arms trafficking. Billions of dollars and euros per year, most of them stolen to fund international organized crime syndicates or terrorists or guerilla movements in Asia, South America, or Africa. Should I go on?"

"Feel free."

"Most art crime is perpetrated by international organized crime," he said. "They either use stolen art for resale, or to barter on a closed black market for an equivalent value of goods or services."

"What about individually instigated art theft?" she asked. "Crimes perpetrated for private collectors?"

"More unusual than you'd think," Rizzo said. "People like that are so wealthy they don't care about the money. Plus they want the prestige of being able to show a valuable piece."

"So whoever the gang was who robbed the *Museo* . . . ?" she asked, shifting gears in the middle of her own sentence. "They were — "

"An organized gang of some sort. But look, as soon as you get into this field, you're getting into a very dirty business with very dangerous people." He paused. "You want to look at something pretty, you go look at the sunset or the mountains. You show me a Van Gogh or a Picasso and sooner or later I'll show you some sleazy ownership, a thief, and eventually a murderer, a tax cheat, or a swindler. How's that? Art is like that: always something beneath the surface. Art theft is like that too. Only more so."

"What about the big galleries?" she asked. "The people who do the big auctions in New York, London, Paris? Rome? Here, Madrid?"

Rizzo scoffed. "Some of the most disreputable people I've met in my life have lived in mansions with ten cars in their garage and a Rodin sculpture in their backyard. Some of the most honorable lived under the bridges of Rome or Paris. The art dealers have no monopoly on duplicity and amorality," Rizzo said, "but they practice both better than anyone else. All over the art world, they turn a blind eye to cash transactions. Things move around from country to country; people change their ownership more often than their owners change their underwear. Smuggling is a dirty word, but 'import-export' isn't, even though it means the same thing. There's no market for a painting or a sculpture that can't fit in a suitcase. That pietà that was stolen here? That would fit into a suitcase."

She laughed. "Tell me how you really feel."

"They're worse than politicians," he said.

Rizzo glanced around the café and sipped his espresso.

"Look," he continued, musing further, "art crime is easy and it pays. There are many valuable pieces that are worth millions and weigh only a few kilograms. Transportation is easy and many high-profile museums hosting multimillion dollar works have disproportionately poor security measures. That makes them susceptible to thefts that are slightly more complicated than a typical smash-and-grab, but with huge payoff."

"Such as this one?"

"The curious thing is that what was stolen was an antiquity," he mused further. "It dates almost from the time of Christ, give or take a couple of centuries. That's a strange thing to target. The robbers were in that museum and had access to anything. So what do they do? They take a remote piece with a comparatively low market value. That's the part I don't get."

"So someone wanted that piece specifically," she theorized.

"Sure. You could go with that thesis. But why? And then again, the market in antiquities is perhaps the most corrupt and problematic aspect of the international art trade," Rizzo said. "Antiquities are often regarded by the country of origin as national treasures. There are numerous cases where artworks displayed in the acquiring country for decades have become the subject of controversy. One example, the Elgin Marbles, moved from Greece to the British Museum in 1816 by Thomas Bruce, Seventh Earl of Elgin. Yale University's Peabody Museum of Natural History is engaged in talks with the government of Peru about possible repatriation of artifacts taken during the excavation of Machu Picchu by Yale's Hiram Bingham."

He paused long enough to wink at the waitress and indicate that he could use more espresso.

"The question arises frequently," he continued. "What's theft? What's excavation? If a piece of art was stolen from one country two hundred years ago, how is it any different to steal it back from a museum today?"

"But we're not talking about a country stealing something back," she said. "Are we?"

"Not yet," Rizzo said. "But who knows where this leads? Maybe the Maltese want their pietà back. I understand," added with a wink, "they never got their falcon."

He shrugged. More espresso arrived.

In thought, Alex fell very quiet. Rizzo picked up on it quickly.

"What?" he asked. "What are you thinking?"

"I was the least experienced person in that room today in the field of art theft. But I do know a few things about criminal motivation. A theft on such a grand scale with a high but secret cash purchase price is exactly the type of transaction that funds various organized crime enterprises around the world. Would that be the case here?"

"No reason why it couldn't be."

"And that could include terrorism," she said.

"That is a *considerable* fear here. No one wants to jump there without evidence. But what's the expression in English? The 'elephant in the room'?"

Rizzo put out cash for the waitress and waved away any change. The young woman gave him a low bow and scurried off.

"Are you going to work on this case actively?" Alex asked.

"I'm going back to Rome tomorrow," Rizzo said. "Or maybe the day after. I'll give it some attention. It will be on the top of my list but so will a few other things. What about you?"

"This one fascinates me, just a bit, at least. I think I'm hooked."

"Then I will leave you with three thoughts," he said.

She waited.

"One: perhaps the most famous art theft of all time occurred in 1911," Rizzo said, "when the *Mona Lisa* was stolen from the Louvre. The French poet Guillaume Apollinaire, who had once called for the Louvre to be 'burnt down,' came under suspicion. He was arrested and put in jail. Apollinaire pointed to his friend Pablo Picasso, who was also brought in for questioning."

"Are you kidding?"

"Why would I joke about world-class crimes?" he said with a grin. "That's point number two. Picasso as a youth had been an art thief. He stole some sculptures from the Louvre. They were returned eventually, but it's another reason why he was a suspect in the theft of *La Giaconda.*"

Alex shook her head, half in amusement, half in disbelief.

As they made their way to the door, Rizzo continued.

"Both Picasso and Apollinaire were later exonerated, and at the time the painting was believed to be lost forever. Two years later, the real thief was discovered, a Louvre employee named Vincenzo Peruggia. He stole it by putting it under his coat and walking out the door with it. Peruggia was an Italian who believed da Vinci's painting should be in an Italian museum. He kept the painting in his apartment for two years, then grew impatient, and was finally caught when he attempted to sell it to the directors of the Uffizi Gallery in Florence. It was exhibited all over Italy and returned to the Louvre in 1913. Know how much time Peruggia served for the theft of the most famous piece of art in the world?"

"Tell me," she said.

"Four months. In Italy he was hailed as a patriot. And set free. Who says things never work out for the better?" said Rizzo. "Maybe next time I'm in that museum I should steal something for myself."

Alex would have laughed, but she wasn't certain it was a joke.

"What's the third thing?" she asked.

"Just this," he said.

He put his hands on her, drew her close, and kissed her on the cheek.

"I was really worried about you," he said. "I'm glad to see you back to yourself, as much as can be hoped for right now. You're a good person. I admire you. You know where to contact me, and you know I will help you in any way I can," he said.

"Grazie mille," she said. "You're more than kind."

"Actually," he said, "I'm the most disreputable person you know. It's just that I'm on your side."

EIGHTEEN

Finally, after a half hour's wait, Jean-Claude thought he heard something outside. Then he knew he did. The sound of a car engine. Diesel, rattling to a stop.

Friend or enemy, he didn't know.

Under his shirt, he gripped his gun.

Then, almost on cue, Jean-Claude could tell from Ceila's reaction who was present. She quickly pulled on a robe and her headwear. To be caught this way by her husband might result in a thrashing and she knew it. She also picked up the child and carried him to another room. Within a few more seconds the garage doors swung wide open.

It was Basheer. His taxi was parked outside. It was an old blue Mercedes Benz, an elderly 300D workhorse of a vehicle.

Jean-Claude stepped from the back of Mahoud's car. He walked to the street and embraced Basheer. Both men looked around. They saw nothing that didn't fit within the neighborhood. Old men sitting at the café a few doors down, mothers keeping watch on children. Many parked cars, but only ones they recognized.

Mahoud made a hand gesture from across the street. All clear. He had seen nothing amiss.

Jean-Claude gave a head gesture to Basheer. Basheer helped him retrieve one duffel bag, Jean-Claude carried the other. They loaded them quickly into the trunk of Basheer's Benz and took off. Mahoud remained behind, moved his own car back to the street, closed and locked the garage, and departed.

They drove across the city to another destination, a pastry shop operated by a Muslim couple named Samy and Tamar.

Samy and Tamar were a likeable young couple in their twenties who operated a pastry shop in El Rastro, a neighborhood named after the Sunday market held within its bounds. The quarter lay within the triangle formed by the La Latina Metro stop, Puerta de Toledo, and Glorieta de Embajadores and was in the larger neighborhood of Lavapiés, an artsy, bohemian section of Madrid. In medieval times, Lavapiés had been the Moorish and Jewish quarter located outside the city walls. The neighborhood has retained an outsider character with visible immigrant communities from Morocco, sub-Saharan Africa, and India. Samy and Tamar enjoyed living there. They had many friends and liked to sit in the cafés until late at night, laughing, drinking tea, telling jokes, and watching sports on television.

Lavapiés was undergoing a process of gentrification as more and more cafés, bars, and galleries opened every day. Samy and Tamar had many friends who worked for the government and even several friends who were British or American. Sometimes this created odd situations as both Samy and Tamar would rail against American and English "colonialism" throughout the world. Yet never, even in their bitterest diatribes, did their friends ever feel the two young Muslims were railing against *them*. The hatred wasn't personal, it was *political*.

Samy and Tamar had been recruited into Jean-Claude's cell two months earlier. They too hated America deeply for what they felt Americans had done to Muslim people worldwide. This, despite the fact that Tamar loved to dress Western in public, with skirts above her knees, and liked American movies and music. Fortunately, her husband permitted it, within reason. So they lived happily together.

And they too were happy to be conduits for Jean-Claude's cargo.

So when Jean-Claude dropped the cargo at the bakery, Samy personally stashed both bags in a locked area of a deep walk-in pantry in his bakery.

He was thrilled with what he had and happy to be part of Jean-Claude's team and mission.

NINETEEN

MADRID, SEPTEMBER 7, 4:23 P.M.

As a warm afternoon faded in the Spanish capital, Alex opened her laptop on a table on her small balcony at the Ritz. She had a soft drink on ice and had changed out of her "meeting" clothes into more comfortable duds: shorts and a T-shirt, an outfit that made perfect sense in terms of relaxation, but too casual to wander around the starchy old Ritz or even this very dressy neighborhood.

She settled into a comfortable cushioned chair. Five floors below traffic rumbled along the Paseo del Prado, though the crescent in front of the Ritz was quiet.

As the computer booted, Alex's gaze drifted out across the city. Madrid had been the capital of the Iberian Peninsula since the middle of the sixteenth century. She gazed over the ancient city and felt a surge of excitement and fascination. It would be nice, she told herself, to come back here someday with time to burn, time to enjoy at her own pace the museums, nightclubs, and sporting events. She would love to watch Real Madrid, the city's world-class soccer team play a game at Estadio Santiago Bernabeu or catch a bullfight at Las Ventas, the world's most famous bullring. She would like to come back here someday with someone she loved.

And then her thoughts tripped a mental landmine, one of sadness and longing, one of still painfully missing her fiancé, Robert, who had died early that year. The memories set off a wave of bittersweet loneliness within her, one she fought almost every day for at least a few moments. She knew what had happened in Kiev, but she hadn't fully accepted it.

Alex looked at her watch. She sighed.

She clicked into her secure email and looked for anything that might have come in during the last few hours. Predictably, several of the men who had been at the meeting at the embassy had already checked in with her. Pierre LeMaitre of the French National Police had been the first, followed by Rolland Fitzgerald of Scotland Yard and Maurice Essen of Interpol. None of them had anything new for her.

Floyd Connelly of US Customs, the pudgy old Orson Welles look-alike, had sent an empty email. Alex wondered what to make of it, other than the notion that the man was quickly emerging as a blustery old fool. Somewhere he had a secretary who did his job for him.

She was about to exit the email when another note popped up from Fitzgerald at Scotland Yard. He had a brief file touching on anti-US terrorist activities in Spain and attached it for Alex's consideration.

It was filled with rumors and conjectures, as well as a shopping list of predictably Islamic names and addresses of mosques. Nothing substantial. Nothing specific. Just a maze of nasty implications floating around, waiting to make sense or waiting to have some sense made of them. Stuff like that could be a gold mine. Or it could send her a hundred eighty degrees in the wrong direction. She finished but then scanned again to see if she had missed anything.

She had. Almost.

She found an email from her occasional employer in New York, Joseph Collins, who financed mission work in Latin America. It had been Collins who had bankrolled her visit earlier in the year.

Alex wrote back, telling him she was in Madrid on a new assignment. And she would, she promised, keep him informed.

She moved on. Time passed.

Her fingers went to work on the keyboard, and she fired back a response to the Englishman Rolland Fitzgerald, thanking him. At least the man was thinking. Then again, so was Alex.

As recently as 2004, she recalled, the deadliest terrorist attack in Europe had occurred in Madrid: ten synchronized blasts on trains, nearly two hundred killed, fourteen hundred wounded. Al-Qaeda had been responsible.

The victims on that infamous day had not necessarily been Americans, but the Spanish government and any members of humanity who happened to be in the wrong place at the wrong time. But it further occurred to her, just from the perspective of her own employer, the multitude of targets within Spain linked to the United States: embassies, consulates, USO clubs that had been targeted in the past, and naval bases at Gibraltar and Barcelona. Then there was the massive US naval installation for the Sixth Fleet at Rota on the other side of the bay from Cádiz, west of Gibraltar. The facility was a Spanish base, but with a massive US presence.

Her thoughts teemed. And then suddenly, she was mentally maxed out, very much on overload.

She glanced at her watch: 7:16 in the evening.

If it was a quarter past seven in Madrid, it was the same number of minutes after 1:00 p.m. in the eastern United States. She still had some telephone credit cards, so what good were they if she didn't use them?

She needed someone to talk to, so she dialed a number in northern Virginia and got her friend Ben on the line.

They talked. A lot. Alex put her feet up onto the railing of the balcony and pushed, leaning back in her chair, then rocking slowly. Time flew.

Almost an hour later, she hung up the line, her spirits lifted temporarily. But during the call, the sky had darkened a little with some clouds that had rolled in from the Pyrenees to the far north. The late afternoon had long since made its transition to evening now and she could see the computer screen better. In the distance, across a rooftop, a neon Tio Pepe sign, an ad for the largest selling sherry in the country, glowed bright red across the rooftop of a commercial building.

A second surge of homesickness was upon her, as were thoughts about Robert. She knew it was best to get out of the hotel room.

She packed up her laptop and took it with her. She went to the same café as she had frequented the previous evening, sat at the same table, and felt better for being out, even when she flipped open the laptop and reviewed museum documents until 10:30. Then she surfed the web for relaxation a bit, had a final Carlos Primero, a distinguished Spanish brandy, and shut down her computer in favor of her iPod.

Eventually, it was midnight. She walked back to the hotel, alone on busy sidewalks in a very safe neighborhood. When she reached her room, she was exhausted.

She made no pass at any further work. She showered and went to bed. In her dreams, she was an innocent young girl again, laughing in the company of her beloved parents, playing in the warm surf of Southern California. The strong hands that picked her up and tossed her around in the water belonged to her late father.

She slept beautifully. Not everyone that night was as fortunate.

TWENTY

The evening after meeting Colonel Tissot, Stanislaw had gone to his home and packed. He had a car at his disposal with a fraudulent registration. He would get into the car the next morning and begin to drive. The *autoroute* would take him down through France, and he would make Barcelona within a day. Driving was more arduous than flying, but driving gave him the temporary anonymity he wanted.

He had done enough research on his prey to know that in reality, Alexandra LaDuca was not about to cavort with a man she hardly knew. But the local police in Spain wouldn't know that. A death is a death is a death in the police ledgers, and he would be long out of the country under another false identity before the dead woman's body was even cold.

He planned an early getaway from Geneva the next morning. Thus, he was soundly asleep by midnight and resting very comfortably when his eyes inexplicably came open in the middle of the night.

Some sixth sense told him that he was not alone. He felt his heart start to pound, and he felt a sweat start to pour off him as he lay in his bedroom under the covers. He knew from his days as a mercenary soldier, sleeping in the field, that rolling over would accomplish nothing.

Instead, he slowly moved his arm. He moved it cautiously so his sheet would not rustle. And he moved in a way that brought his hand to the holster that held the pistol that he hung by his bedside every night. He hung it there for two reasons. Women found it an aphrodisiac when he was lucky enough to lure one back to his apartment. But the better reason was that of self-protection.

In terms of a home break-in during the dark of night, every second counted.

His hand found the holster. And the holster was empty.

He hadn't failed to put the gun there. Its absence proved that he wasn't alone. And its absence also told him that the enemy was waiting patiently for him to realize that the gun was gone, so that there would be a hideous panic in the moment of death.

In the dark, the full force of a lithe, powerful body came down on him, pinning him to the bed. Hands in latex gloves — hands that were like vices — pinned the upper part of his body. The hands were like steel. They clamped tightly.

Stanislaw let loose with a horrendous howl of profanity. He flailed and tried to fight his way forward, to escape the grip of the intruder.

Then there was a final sensation, that of a cool steel point pressing to the side of his neck, the point of something very sharp and very cold, like an ice pick.

A final kick, scream, and thrust and then Stanislaw felt the point of the pick penetrate his flesh, much like one feels a hypodermic needle. But this needle was several inches long. Pushed by a powerful hand, the blade shot upward into his jugular vein and slid onward through his head like a bolt of lightning.

When it went into his brain, a piercing blackness accompanied it. He shuddered a final time and was dead before the intruder withdrew the blade.

John Sun relaxed and withdrew from the sleeping area. Methodically, he placed the murder weapon in a zip-lock bag, the kind currently favored by airport security pests. He would later throw the pick into the Lake of Geneva. He went to the washroom and rinsed off his gloves but did not remove them. These days, in the era of DNA and micro-forensics, one could never be too careful. Get arrested in Switzerland, and he'd never see the light of day again. Even his government wouldn't be able to get him out. Not that he was worried.

He returned to the dead man to make sure the dead man was a dead man. No movement, no pulse. Good. He breathed a little easier. He went to all the windows — there were only five in the apartment — and drew the blinds. Once again, one could never be too careful. Out of a sense of decency, he drew a cover over the dead man's body. Like Colonel Tissot, the body would start to stink in about seven days and would draw investigators to the apartment. But by then,

Sun would be long gone from the country and possibly even from Europe.

The apartment had a good audio setup in the living room, so he went to it and turned on some music. Most of the dead man's music collection was not to John Sun's tastes. But he did find some classical stuff, some Mahler and some Brahms, and he hooked up some restful, mournful stuff. He had killed two men today, partly out of retribution, partly because it had been his job. But it did set him in a mournful mood. No Verdi *Requiem*, so Mahler would have to do.

Then, for two hours, Sun prowled his second victim's apartment. He found many items of interest, but the preeminent one was the file that the dead man had acquired less than twenty-four hours earlier.

Thoughtfully, he settled into a chair and read it, putting two and two together quickly.

Sun had a keen eye for attractive women, and his gaze settled almost immediately on the surveillance photographs of Alexandra LaDuca. This was the first time he had ever seen her, either in a photo or live, and it was the first time he had ever encountered her name. The file was clear as to what she was: an American agent who would be assigned to a case tangential to the late Pole, the late Colonel Tissot, and that star-crossed little statue that some busybodies had swiped from a Spanish museum, putting this whole skein of events in progress.

An American agent and a female one at that, as the pictures made clear. Interesting.

Alex LaDuca. Well, he had computer access and some very good backup people. He'd be able to find out more about this woman within a few hours, not the least of details being where and how to find her, if necessary.

He read the snippets about her background and then went back to the pictures.

The clearest photograph of Alexandra LaDuca was one week old. Color, shot from a surveillance camera in Barcelona. A trim woman in her late twenties, short dark hair, at ease on the streets of Barcelona, walking in a T-shirt, a short denim skirt, and sneakers, hardly the vision of a tough investigative agent. But appearances were frequently deceiving.

Another photo, taken from a greater distance, showed her on the beach in a red Nike swimsuit, and a third photo showed her at a café, sitting alone, reading a novel.

It was very strange, he pondered, where these back-channel paths sometimes led. He set the file aside near the door. He would take it with him. He then spent another hour prowling the apartment.

Around 4:00 a.m., he emerged from the lobby of Stanislaw's building onto a quiet Geneva street. He walked two blocks, an American baseball cap down across his eyes just in case, and he found his car exactly where he had left it.

In another minute, he was gone, leaving the streets behind him quiet and lifeless.

TWENTY-ONE

MADRID, SEPTEMBER 8, 7:15 A.M.

The next morning, Alex left her hotel and went for an early walk to get into the pace of the city. She had breakfast at a nearby café, opened her laptop there, and went to work as the city started to awaken around her.

In the background material that the curator, Rivera, had spoken of when he gave his introduction, someone had written an overview of art theft in the world of 2009.

"I say a prayer every time we hang a new show," said one woman, the curator of a private gallery in London, setting the anxious tone of the material that followed.

"Historically, the most significant catalyst for art theft is war," began the first section. It continued:

Conquering armies have claimed and redistributed artifacts of value since war began. World War II brought violence and destruction on a scale previously unseen. The confiscation by the Nazis of tens of thousands of artworks created by Jewish artists or belonging to prewar Jewish collectors prompted the drafting of the "Convention for the Protection of Cultural Property in the Event of Armed Conflict" in 1954. This was created to protect art, just as the Geneva Convention was created to protect civilians. Yet in 2003, professional thieves, working under the camouflage created by the invasion of Baghdad by US forces, looted the Iraq National Museum and other museums, libraries, and archaeological sites, making off with over 12,000 artifacts.

Scholars worldwide have demanded that the authorities in Baghdad hold the thieves responsible according to the rules laid out in the aforementioned convention. Authorities caught an American scholar trying to smuggle pilfered statues into the States in June of 2007.

From 1933 through the end of World War II, the Nazi regime maintained a policy of looting art for sale or for removal to museums in the Third Reich. Hermann Goering, head of the Luftwaffe, personally took charge of hundreds of valuable pieces, generally stolen from Jews and other victims of genocide. In 2006, title to the gilt painting *Portrait of Adele Bloch-Bauer I*, by Austrian artist Gustav Klimt, was restored to Maria Altmann, an heir of the prewar owner. Provenance in this case was easy to establish; Bloch-Bauer, the subject of the painting, was Altmann's aunt. Altmann almost immediately sold the painting at auction, and it was resold to Ronald Lauder for $135 million. At the time of the latter sale this was the highest known price ever paid for a painting.

War could not only redistribute art but also destroy it, the report reminded Alex. Original paintings by Joan Miró and Roy Lichtenstein were destroyed during the attacks on the World Trade Center in New York in 2001. And two generations earlier, ceremonial bells confiscated from Zen temples in Japan by the Japanese army were melted down for submarine propellers.

Clue: The Great Museum Caper — the popular board game came to mind; and she recalled the *Pink Panther* movies and eighties-era television, with images of sleek black-clad thieves slipping through skylights, dangling in comic splendor from grappling hooks, and avoiding alarm-triggering laser beams to snatch valuables. The images that she recalled glamorized theft and the cleverness of the crooks.

Could one hate a thief who looked like Cary Grant or George

Clooney? Could a female *really* hate an art pilferer who had a six-pack like Brad Pitt or the sultry good looks of an Andy Garcia? But the real world of art crime, she knew, wasn't quite that way.

She kept reading.

The thieves who had swiped Edmund Munch's *The Scream* in Oslo a few years earlier were as subtle, sophisticated, and charming as a kick in the kneecap. They had held terrified museum guards at gunpoint and ripped the painting from the wall. These days, armed smash-and-grab was the *technique du jour*—because it worked.

Her pal Rizzo's words echoed in her mind.

High-value small items, easily portable.

Lousy security systems.

Even if resell value were five percent, the rewards were well into six figures and the risk of apprehension low.

Looking at other notable instances of art theft worldwide, the report continued:

> We see some of the same tactics used on television. In April 2003, a piece of artwork by Salvador Dalí was stolen from the Riker's Island Correctional Facility in New York City during a fire drill and replaced with a forgery. In 2002, thieves dug an eighty-foot tunnel into the National Fine Arts Museum in Asuncion, Paraguay, escaping with a million dollars worth of paintings. . . .

Yes, Interpol could be handy. But Alex knew this from playing *Where in the World Is Carmen Sandiego* as a kid. The report continued:

> Some objects will be stolen, protected, and stolen again. The value of an art object has a dual identity, one is a dollar figure, and one is a value that exists in the mind. Art thefts occur with motivations that range from high-minded to ludicrous. Some art thieves believe that they will appreciate the piece more than their victim, as in an unsolved case involving

a Pablo Picasso drawing stolen from a yacht in Miami in August 2007, possibly related to a feud between rival collectors ...

High values stimulate greed, which stimulates theft. A seventeenth century cello built by Antonio Stradivari and estimated to be worth $3.5 million was stolen from the home of a member of the Los Angeles Philharmonic Orchestra in April of this year. The thief was unable to sell the cello as police closed in and the cello was discovered leaning against a dumpster near a Korean restaurant in the same city.

In 1973, Richard Nixon gave "goodwill" gifts of moon rocks encased in clear acrylic to 135 nations. Most of these rocks have been stolen, including the rock given to Malta, which was swiped in June 2007. The moon is a highly prized collectable. In 2002, some NASA student interns stole a six-hundred-pound safe containing 3.5 ounces of moon rocks worth millions of dollars and tried to sell them on eBay. Greed and possessiveness could lead to the dismantling of the moon into saleable parts.

Art theft also comes in the form of fanatical obsessions and impulsiveness. A New Hampshire man was arrested last year after stealing a painting of a cat drinking out of a toilet from the bathroom of a veterinary clinic. There are framed artworks hanging unguarded in almost every restaurant bathroom in the country. An anonymous artist in Portland boasts that he has stolen dozens of rubber filters from the urinals of public bathrooms with the intent of making art from them. A Thomas Paquette painting stolen from a show at Colby College in 2001 was taken because the thief liked the painting. Paquette, quoted in the *Morning Sentinel* in 2001, said

"It's somewhat of a compliment for someone to risk going to jail for one of my paintings."

Alex leaned back and sighed. Facts. She hungered for facts.

There was a harsh note in the file at the conclusion, a fact of sorts:

The "grandest" museum caper in the United States remained unsolved almost twenty years later. In 1990, thieves had stolen a dozen paintings from the Gardner Museum in Boston. The thieves were dressed as Boston police officers and swiped five works by Degas, four Vermeers, and two Rembrandts. The paintings were valued at over $100 million at the time of the theft.

Not a bad night's work. Who said crime didn't pay?

A reward of fifteen million dollars was posted and accomplished nothing. Almost two decades later, all the works were still missing. Not a trace of any of them had ever surfaced.

Poof! Bye, bye, baby! Into the thinnest of air they had all gone.

Here was perhaps the highest profile art theft in history. There was a massive reward and legions of investigators public and private had explored the case. Arguably, if that theft had eluded resolution, how was anyone to make any headway in the disappearance of a small stone carving from an outstanding but secondary museum in a secondary world capital?

She tried to draw conclusions and was left with only one. If one wanted to recover a piece of stolen art, the best way to recover it was not to allow it to be stolen in the first place. So many of these museums and galleys, she noted with a sigh, seemed particularly adept at locking the barn door after the horses had been stolen.

Recovering a piece?

Debatable at best.

Almost a fool's assignment.

TWENTY-TWO

MADRID, SEPTEMBER 8, EARLY AFTERNOON

Today, Maria Gómez worked in the Metro with her usual partner, Pedro Felipe Santiago. They were working a fashionable section of the city known as Bourbon Madrid, east of the old city, observing the stations together. Tighter security now meant dayshifts.

As they strolled through the Metro stop called Antocha Renfe — after the mainline train station of Atocha, which the Metro stop served — the residents, tourists, and business people swarmed around them, briskly on and off the shiny new silver trains. Maria and Pedro stood together on the busy train platform and surveyed the crowd. Not too far away, above them at street level, less crowded at this hour, were the tree-lined blocks of the Paseo del Prado, once an idyllic meadow where the Habsburgs had built a monastery in the sixteenth century. Pedro, her partner, was more than just a peer. He was a good friend and a solid supporter at work. Thus she was surprised when he dropped a small bit of news on her when they walked the tracks that Friday from Antocha Rente to Anton Martin.

Pedro would be taking the next week off. The official reason was to visit his ailing mother in Malaga. But the real reason, he confessed to Maria, was that he was going to be spending a week with a woman he had just met and whom he was falling for in a big way.

The complication was that she, the woman he wanted to spend time with, was married to a man in Madrid, a man from a good family and who worked in the financial industry. The woman and her husband had agreed to separate, and Pedro was free to go off with her. But public appearances had to be maintained for all parties.

Hence, the charade about the ailing mother.

Maria smiled when Pedro brought her up to date on the newest developments in his life. They were, as they discussed it, in the stinky darkness beneath the Calle de Antocha, with heavy traffic rumbling overhead. The sunshine of Malaga to the extreme south was a world and a half away. But Maria wished him well, even though she suffered a small pang of envy. Then she posed the inevitable next question.

"If you're away," she said, "who will I be assigned to work with?"

Pedro already knew.

"José Luis," he said, referring to another track walker: José Luis Martínez Márques.

Maria suffered a little cringe. She knew Márques. She didn't like him or his approach to the job. He liked to let things slide. His observation techniques were careless, his reports shoddy. But the union protected him.

"Well," she said. "It's only a week?"

"*Sí.*"

"I can put up with anyone for a week," she said. "Even Martínez Márques."

They laughed, Pedro and Maria, and turned their attention to a safety hazard. There were a pair of emergency lights that were flickering deep in the tunnel under Calle de Atocha. These would have to be replaced. They began making a report on a handheld computer.

At the same time, they both became aware of a tapping sound, like someone hammering or chiseling, somewhere on the other side of the walls. Both were aware of it but neither said anything. They carried keys that could unlock doors that led to some of the old passageways that wound their way under the city. But no one ever went in there. A train rumbled into the station and glided to a halt. When it had left, the tapping sound had stopped. So they gave it no further notice.

TWENTY-THREE

MADRID, SEPTEMBER 8, AFTERNOON

On a cluttered backstreet next to the Rastro, Jean-Claude watched the block for a quarter hour before crossing the street and trying the door to a small shuttered shop across the way.

The door was locked. But from within, a meaty hand pushed aside a curtain. Two dark eyes peered into Jean-Claude's, then past him, and then a bolt dropped from within. The door opened quick, Jean-Claude entered, and the door closed and locked again.

Jean-Claude found himself standing in a compact, cluttered establishment that seemed to sell both everything and nothing.

The two men exchanged cautious greetings in Arabic.

"You're aware of the nature of my visit?" Jean-Claude asked.

"I am," Farooq answered, "but only in general terms." Farooq retreated to a position behind a high counter. Jean-Claude assumed, given the nature of his business, he kept at least one weapon there. He held aloft a plump finger, indicating that Jean-Claude should wait for a moment. He walked to a table behind his counter and turned on an old television set. He adjusted the volume up high, then turned back to his customer.

"Now," Farooq said. "Perhaps you could explain your needs in greater detail? But do keep in mind that for reasons of security, I keep very little in stock here."

"I understand," Jean-Claude said.

"Good. Then I would like to understand too. What is it you desire?"

"Detonators," Jean-Claude said, continuing in Arabic, "for explosives. A series of very good ones with a zero failure rate."

Farooq nodded amiably and his eyes twinkled with mischief. "I suppose you're going to tell me that you're in the construction business," he said.

"I wouldn't be foolish enough to tell a lie like that," Jean-Claude answered, "and you wouldn't be foolish enough to believe it."

"Perhaps you could share with me a bit about your project," Farooq said. "I sense that you have given yourself a challenge, perhaps an ideological one."

Jean-Claude kept quiet.

"What sort of explosives will you be working with? What exactly do you require?"

Jean-Claude said nothing.

"I could supply you with a very basic device that should work for you," Farooq said. "It would be similar to a standard blasting cap with a primary consisting of a compound formed from lead azide, lead styphnate, and aluminum. It would be pressed into place above the base charge, which is usually TNT."

"I have explosives more sophisticated and more powerful than TNT," Jean-Claude said.

Farooq's attitude changed slightly. His expression darkened and his tone of voice became more grave.

"What might your target be?" he asked. "An individual? Several individuals. A vehicle? Moving or stationery? Large? Small?"

"A building," said Jean-Claude.

"A building or the people in it?" Farooq asked.

"Both," Jean-Claude said.

"Very good," Farooq continued after a moment. "For your purposes then, might I suggest a relatively new item known as a 'slapper' detonator? This variety uses thin plates accelerated by an electrically exploded wire or foil to deliver the initial shock . . ."

"No," Jean-Claude said. "I consider that type of detonator unreliable. I'm seeking a British item known as a Number Ten Delay switch, which is unavailable in Spain except through merchants such as yourself."

The Number Ten Delay was a sort of "timing pencil." It consisted of a brass tube, with a copper section at one end, which contains a glass vial of cupric chloride. A spring-loaded striker was held under tension and kept in place by a thin metal wire. The timer would be primed by crushing the copper section of the tube to break the phial of cupric chloride, which then would slowly eat through the wire holding back the striker. The striker would shoot down the hollow center of the detonator and hit a percussion cap at the other end of the detonator and the combustion would follow. A delay switch ranged from ten minutes to twenty-four hours, accurate within plus or minus three minutes in an hour's delay and plus or minus an hour in a twelve-hour delay.

Farooq nodded thoughtfully. "I see," he said. "Then for the first time I understand the high quality of explosives that you have. In what form are the explosives now?"

"Twenty individual bricks," Jean-Claude said.

"They would be military quality then, I would suspect."

Jean-Claude said nothing, which was an implied yes.

Farooq thought for a moment then washed his hands at a sink behind his counter. "And you have them in your possession, these explosives?"

"Spare me the stupid inquiries. Would I be here if I didn't? Again, I know the product that I need. Can you get them for me with no chance that they can ever be traced."

Farooq was toweling his hands dry by now. "I believe I can," he said softly.

"Perfect," Jean-Claude said after a few minutes of examination. "I need two packs with the twelve-hour delay. Can you get them for me?"

"Yes, I can. It will take a few days, but I have my own resources."

"How much will this cost me?"

The owner wrote an outrageous money figure down on a piece of paper.

"I will also require the entire payment in advance," Farooq added.

"You're a robber!" Jean-Claude snapped.

"I am a businessman," the dealer said. "And, my friend," the old Arab said. "You are not just buying detonators and the ability to strike at Western infidels. You are also buying my silence and good will. I have been in business for a long time. There must be a reason, and the reason is that my first dissatisfied customer will return and kill me. So I don't expect you to become one. My price is high, but I deliver with discretion and safety for the buyer. So do we do business or do I ask you to leave?"

Jean-Claude glared at him. Then he nodded, peeled off a wad of money, and paid.

TWENTY-FOUR

MADRID, SEPTEMBER 8, AFTERNOON AND EVENING

From the National Police Headquarters, Alex walked back to the Ritz, relaxed for an hour, and then fired up her laptop again. She was trying to get an overall feel of art theft, a grip on it and the people who commit it. There was no way to approach a case without having a feel for it.

Hours passed. She had a light dinner delivered to her room. She felt stale, almost unproductive. She had learned a lot this day but wasn't sure she had made any real progress or yet had an angle on the case. After her dinner, she prowled through more odds and ends about art theft and art thieves.

Item: The original of a Norman Rockwell reproduction titled *Russian Schoolroom* was found in the collection of the American movie mogul Steven Spielberg in 2007. Spielberg had paid about $200,000 for the 16 x 37 canvas in a legitimate purchase and then had alerted the FBI immediately when he learned of its questionable provenance.

Item: Art thieves—as professional criminals—do a simple risk-versus-reward evaluation. They know that even if they receive only a fraction of the work's market value, the cash gained was at low risk of death or injury. And museums and private collectors are an easy touch.

Item: Nor had anyone seen any trace of the biggest art theft in European history. In February of 2008, a gang swiped four paintings worth an estimated $163 million from the E.G.

Buehrle Collection in Zurich, Switzerland. They took works by Paul Cezanne, Edgar Degas, Claude Monet, and Vincent van Gogh.

"These paintings were extremely valuable on the open market, but they never went onto the open market," said a Swiss detective at the time. "So they're priceless but they're also worthless."

Item: Some thieves often try to ransom the art back to the museum or the insurance company. Usually, an insurance company would rather get art back at a fraction of its original price than pay the owner its insured value. Ransoming art to an insurance company through an intermediary adds ten to twenty percent to the market value, which often turns into quite a lot of money.

Item: Art thieves rarely face justice. A work of art does not require a title document in order to be transferred from one owner to another, so a stolen object easily enters the legitimate stream of commerce. Even if the original thief can be identified, there is also a statute of limitations on prosecution for theft.

And a final item, having its numbing effect on Alex:

Even if a stolen work is recovered, the original owners may not get it back. Art stolen from a Los Angeles mansion in 2003 and sold in Sweden remained with its Swedish purchasers. Even though the thief was caught, the Swedish government refused to return the paintings, claiming that according to Swedish law, the auction buyers had purchased the paintings in good faith. Laws governing art theft were a maze of contradictions from one country to the next, often offering the trained investigator little more than frustration.

Alex leaned back and took stock. Whoever had pilfered *The Pietà of Malta* from the museum in Madrid was not to be mistaken for a high-society, tuxedo-wearing, *Thomas Crown Affair* style thief.

She stared at her computer screen, a picture of confusion and doubt. Maybe it was time to return to America. She could opt out of this *Pietà of Malta* case very easily.

Maybe she should, she told herself.

She closed out of her laptop, drew a breath, and watched evening settle in across the city.

TWENTY-FIVE

MADRID, SEPTEMBER 8, EVENING

The Iberia flight from Geneva to Madrid glided into its landing trajectory at 10:15 that evening. In a business-class seat by a window, John Sun gazed out the window and watched the lights of the city stretch out below him. Then the plane descended from its path in the purple sky, and as the 727 banked, the traveler picked up the lead-in lights that beckoned the aircraft into Aeropuerto Barajas, one of Europe's busiest and most modern facilities.

There was much on his mind. In one capacity or another, he had presided over three deaths in Switzerland. Now he was just as happy to be out of the country. The farther and faster he got away from the place, the better he would feel. The business of death, the back-alley enforcement of his nation's interests, was never an attractive business. He was experienced in it and efficient at it, but that didn't mean he was wedded to it or even liked it. In fact, in ways that he couldn't even explain to himself, it always unsettled him. Then again, the world was a cruel, nasty place, and all other rules of life followed from that one.

So what else could he do?

His mind was flooded with thoughts like these as the soil of Spain rose to meet his arriving flight. He glanced downward through his window and saw that the flight was above the grassy terrain leading to the runway.

Then the grass was replaced by a stream of runway lights and then a blur of numbered panels, white on gray-black asphalt. Then came the welcome thump and bump of the tires. There followed the roar of the brakes and the lifting of the wing flaps, and then the deceleration on the runway.

Sun had actually been hoping to go home to his special lady, but at least he had had a few hours in Switzerland to pick up a piece of jewelry for her, a beautiful diamond and gold bracelet. This he carried with him, though it was the least of his concerns right now. There were others to deal with first and an assignment that started to appear open-ended. So be it. Life had its strange twists and turns. Even the cultural icon of his grandfather's generation, Confucius, would not have disagreed with that.

The plane rolled smoothly to a halt. It taxied to a gate.

John Sun was traveling light as always. He passed easily through immigration. He spoke fluent Spanish with the agents while also keeping an eye on the uniformed Spanish police who patrolled the airport with automatic weapons. He also easily spotted the plainclothes people. In his peripheral view, he also checked the surveillance cameras, both the obvious ones and the hidden ones. It was almost a game to him to find them without looking directly at them.

Then he passed through customs with equal ease. A trio of uniformed customs officers, two men and a woman, waved him through to the concourse.

Now he was officially in Spain.

TWENTY-SIX

MADRID, SEPTEMBER 9, MORNING

The Museo de Arqueológico is perhaps Madrid's finest museum, after the immense Prado. The museum stands like a mid-nineteenth-century fortress on the Calle Serrano, not far from the Ritz and not far from the American Embassy. Founded by Queen Isabel II in 1867, the building houses archeological treasures excavated from Spanish soil from prehistoric times to the present. Key attractions have for years included religious art from countless centuries, including seventh-century votive crowns from Toledo, ceramics from the ancient civilization at El Argar, a carved ivory crucifix that had been carved for King Fernando I and Queen Sancha in 1063, which included within it a space for a sliver of wood from the True Cross and an extensive collection of Roman mosaics and Islamic pottery. It was by no coincidence that *The Pietà of Malta* had been on display here.

Alex met Rizzo at the front of the museum the next morning, an hour before the institution would open to the public. They were joined by Rolland Fitzpatrick, the young Englishman, and LeMaitre, from the French SNDCE. A private guard took them to the office of José Rivera, the curator.

Floyd Connelly, the unpredictable representative of US Customs, had also expressed interest in joining them, Rivera announced, so they waited for him for several minutes. After a quarter hour, however, Connelly was officially labeled a no-show.

Thereafter, the brief tour started.

Two weeks earlier, Rivera explained in Spanish as they walked the first floor together, three nimble thieves armed with automatic weapons had tunneled under the three-story Museo Arqueológico late at night, penetrated the museum through a basement wall, and then emerged in the uniforms of the Policía Municipal. They had bound the four guards on duty and sabotaged the alarm system that would have alerted Madrid municipal police of a robbery in progress.

The thieves had ignored the vast collection of seventh-century gold crowns from Toledo province, the priceless Islamic pottery, and the Roman mosaics to find *The Pietà of Malta*.

They knew exactly what they wanted and exactly where it was located. Conveniently, since the museum was arranged chronologically, their target had been on the first floor, easily visible and accessible. The leader smashed its glass case, grabbed it, and the gang of them were out the door with it within five minutes.

As Rivera guided his visitors from the site of the penetration to the actual site of the theft, he engaged in a back-and-forth of questions from the four detectives. LeMaitre and Fitzpatrick had an old-school style about them, despite their comparative youth, and made handwritten notes in their notebooks. Rizzo followed with arms folded much of the time, but held a small recorder that took in every word for later review. Alex trusted her memory and frequently found note taking a distraction, so she listened, tried to sort out the most salient details, and wrote down nothing. She knew she could always consult back with Rivera or any of the others present.

The tour concluded in front of the broken display case, which had been emptied of other antiquities by the museum staff and put on display elsewhere. The case had been taped up and cordoned off, though there was still an air of ignominy about it. It stood in shame on the main floor like a cat with a broken tail.

"Fingerprints, there were none," Rivera said in conclusion. "DNA tests haven't helped. Our security cameras have no good pictures of the thieves, as I'm sure the local police explained to you in your meetings yesterday. These thieves were very good and very careful."

"Something I've been wondering," Alex pressed, continuing in Spanish, "many of these other pieces would have an infinitely higher value on the black market. So I'm trying to understand their mindset. What is it about this piece that is completely different from any other object here or, say, in the Louvre or in one of the great museums in London or New York?"

Rivera thought for a moment, then smiled slightly. "Very perceptive question," he said. "You've read all the material I gave you?"

"Yes, I have," she said.

"Nothing stands out?" he asked.

"Many things stand out. But nothing is *sobresaliente*. There is no single feature that dominates all others. So again, I'm trying to put my mind inside an expert's."

Rivera smiled. "All right, since you asked, there *is* perhaps one aspect to this piece that *I* find particularly engaging," Rivera said. "It's something I note as a good Christian and as a Roman Catholic. It's in the material I gave you, but to some degree it's buried. Do you know where I might be going with this?"

"No tengo la menor idea," she answered. Not in the slightest.

"There was a young Italian of the twelfth century named Giovanni di Bernadone," Rivera said. "I'm sure my distinguished guest from Rome, Gian Antonio Rizzo, can tell us the name under which Bernadone is better remembered."

Rizzo nodded slightly.

"As anyone who survived fourteen years of Catholic education could tell you," Rizzo said, "Giovanni di Bernadone later became known as Saint Francis of Assisi. He was the founder of the Franciscan order, patron saint of animals, birds, anything that creeps or crawls, and more recently the blasted Green Party and our soon-to-be-completely-ruined environment."

"And for what is St. Francis best remembered?" Rivera pressed.

"Aside from the crows and the jackasses?"

"Aside from *los cuervos* and *los asnos*, yes."

"St. Francis was an early evangelist," Rizzo said. "When St. Francis lived, Christianity had been established in Europe for many centuries, but Francis sought to spread it into Islamic territories. At great personal risks, I might add."

"That is correct."

"Not too much different from today," Fitzgerald added.

Rivera smiled. "St. Francis of Assisi went to Egypt on a mission of peace about eight hundred years ago," Rivera said. "This was at the time of the Fifth Crusade, launched by Pope Innocent III. In 1219, Francis left, together with a few companions, on a pilgrimage of nonviolence to Egypt. Crossing the lines between the Sultan Malek-el-Kemel and the Crusaders in Damietta, he was received by the caliph, whose Islamic army was defending the Holy Land from the Christian armies. Francis challenged the Muslim scholars to a trial of true religion by fire. But they refused. So Francis proposed that he would enter a blazing fire first and, if Francis left the fire unharmed, the sultan would have to recognize Christ as the Savior of mankind. The sultan didn't take Francis up on his offer. But he was so impressed that he allowed Francis to preach to his Islamic subjects. He didn't succeed in converting the sultan or very many of his subjects. But the last words of the sultan to Francis of Assisi were, 'Pray for me that God may deign to reveal to me that law and faith that is most pleasing to him.'"

The journey of Francis of Assisi, as a poet, as a minister, and as a lay evangelist, Rivera stressed, was one of attempted reconciliation between Islam and Christianity. For that reason, St. Francis was revered in the Islamic world for many centuries up until and including modern times. "By scholars of both religions," Rivera concluded, "he is often seen as an architect for interfaith dialogues."

"St. Francis was also an accomplished poet in his own right," Alex said, recalling. "When I studied Italian in Rome many years ago we read 'The Canticle of the Sun' and 'The Canticle of the Creatures.' The poetry was dense since it was Italian from the late Middle Ages and early Renaissance."

"Thank you," Rivera said good naturedly. "What a wonderfully overeducated bunch of detectives I have here. It's refreshing."

"Well, I did my Renaissance studies too," Rizzo said. "*My* only further comment is that Saint Tom had a more benevolent view of the ragheads than that scoundrel Dante Alighieri, whose *The Divine Comedy* placed Muhammad in hell with his entrails hanging out. Justifiably to modern readers, I might add."

There was laughter around the small circle of five.

"That may be *more* than what we need to know, Senor Rizzo," Rivera answered with a sly smile. "But I mention all this because in contemporary accounts of the burial of St. Francis in 1226, there is an account that a friend placed a 'lamentation' in St. Francis's tomb with him. No one knows exactly why, but perhaps it was because Francis was the first known person to manifest the 'stigmata,' the wounds borne by Christ from the crucifixion. So a 'lamentation' would be a logical item to accompany Francis to the grave. And, as *The Pietà of Malta* has an Arabic inscription, and as St. Francis's tomb has been disturbed at least three times over the centuries, there is further conjecture — no *proof*, mind you, but further *conjecture* — that it was *this piece* that actually went into the ground with St. Francis. Hence, perhaps, its mystique. Hence, the notion that a certain supernatural aura is attached to it, one that transcends an earthly grave. After all," Rivera concluded, "it is very possible that this particular piece went into the earth with a saint and then returned to the living world."

The laughter by now had dissolved. Alex felt a little chill.

Into the grave and out of it. What *had* she gotten into? Yet she also noted the link to the Islamic world.

"Resurrection. Eternal life. The property of a noteworthy and revered saint, and a link to the Islamic world of the Middle Ages. All part of the equation here, my friends," Rivera said. "All part of the unique aspects of *The Pietà of Malta*. So when you ask about qualities that set it apart from any other object in the museum, and perhaps even the world ... to *my* mind? I have just told you."

His voice trailed off.

"Well?" the curator finally added in conclusion. "Need I say more?"

TWENTY-SEVEN

MADRID, SEPTEMBER 9, AFTERNOON

Jean-Claude stood at the intersection of the Calle de Maldonado and the Calle de Claudio Coello. He studied the street. In front of him was an upscale residential neighborhood, behind him more of the same. There was also a public square, trees, and traffic.

It was almost 3:00 p.m. There were more pedestrians than he could count, a steady bustle. Well, he reasoned, within crowds there was always anonymity as well as danger.

His eyes settled on the green-and-white face of a Starbuck's coffee shop that had recently opened. For a moment, he was filled with rage. Was all of Europe going to be Americanized? Was the entire world? He stifled his rage, knowing he would have his day of reckoning within the next week or two. Out of force of habit, he adjusted the long sweatshirt that he wore. Under it was a small pistol, low caliber, Italian-made.

He walked south twenty meters until he came to the doorway of a small three-story building. There was an art gallery on the first floor and apartments above.

He pressed the door code. A buzzer sounded and a big door creaked open.

Jean-Claude stepped into the building. There were two men in the corridor, his accomplices, Samy and Mahoud. They waited on the main floor, a corridor that led up to expensive apartments but also to a small portal that led to the utility closest where the trash was assembled.

The two men stared at him. Then Samy nodded. Jean-Claude moved forward and Mahoud led him to the stairs that went to the basement. On the way down, they both picked up powerful battery-powered flashlights.

The basement was damp and dark, with spider webs, scattered

pieces of garbage, and broken bottles. It stank of mildew and smelled of rats. They crossed the old floor. There were things left over from an exterminator's kit.

"Aquí!" said Mahoud. Here!

Mahoud led Jean-Claude across the floor to an old stone wall.

"How old is the wall?" Jean-Claude asked.

The friend shrugged. How old was the foundation of European cities? From the time of James II? From the time of Torquemada? Mahoud shrugged. What difference did it make?

Mahoud had worked construction for much of his teen years back in the Middle East. He was powerfully built, which was one reason he had been recruited. He put his strong hands upon some stones and the stones started to move. The rocks were old and clammy and heavy, but they fit together in the wall like a Rubik's cube of masonry.

Jean-Claude watched intently, then lent a hand himself. They removed a dozen rocks from the wall, then another dozen. Gradually a hole emerged at waist level, a hole big enough for a man to pull himself through.

Jean-Claude and Mahoud kept moving stones. After a few minutes, both men had broken a sweat. But the hole was four-by-four.

"Enough," Mahoud said. "Come with me."

Mahoud lifted himself up and pulled himself through. With a short jump, he landed on dirt on the other side. He turned and extended a hand as Jean-Claude came through the hole in the wall after him. They were now on a winding path that would lead them under the city.

With their torches casting long yellow beams in front of them, they hunched their shoulders low and followed a bizarre underground passageway that wove around and between the basements and sub-basements of the buildings on the street above them. Mahoud knew the route because he had discovered it himself, tipped off by another Spaniard born in the Middle East who bore no liking for the American presence in Spain.

The pathway was dirt, at times very narrow, at other times heavily strewn with the debris of many years. Rumors had it that some of these passageways dated all the way back to the Inquisition of the 1400s. Other rumors maintained that the passages had been active in the Civil War of the thirties, controlled largely by anti-Franco Republican forces who would emerge to the streets, take potshots at Franco's soldiers, and disappear again during the final treacherous endgame at the fall of Madrid. But there were an equal number of stories about brutal subterranean ambushes by *Franquistas*.

Jean-Claude and Mahoud moved quickly. Above them, they could hear the distant rumblings of the city. They could smell the sewer. At times, they passed directly under thick floorboards of houses and shops and could even hear muffled voices.

Then eventually, they reached a dead end, or appeared to.

"This," said Mahoud, "is the difficult part. My friend, if you're claustrophobic . . ."

"I'm not . . ."

"Then we continue," he said. "It's about thirty meters. It's filthy and it's a crawl."

Mahoud went to his knees and loosened about twenty bricks from the base of the wall. Mahoud pulled them out and built them into a neat pile.

"I'll go first. Keep your arms extended at all times. Pull yourself along. There's no glass or concrete. It will take us about ten minutes. Maybe more. In some areas the clearance is very low. In these areas you must push yourself along. I suggest going on your stomach but you could do it on your back."

Mahoud went first, ahead of Jean-Claude by about ten meters. The crawl space was a nightmare of tightness and loose bricks. But Mahoud had been through here already and knew the parameters. They crawled under one house, had a little breathing room, and then crawled under a second. They pushed and prodded their flashlights along in front of them. Only someone driven by fanaticism would have attempted such a crawl. Only a fanatic would have made it.

When they came to an open space twelve minutes later, their limbs were creaky. But Mahoud had led his commander to a large passage, one that led to yet another chamber. They were now faced with another aging underground wall. Mahoud had already excavated a small hole in that, and he led Jean-Claude through that hole too. Then they came upon a stash of tools: hammers, crow bars, and various instruments of excavation.

"This is as far as I've progressed," Mahoud said. "But if I have help, I can be under the United States Embassy within another week. You have all the explosives?"

"I have them," Jean-Claude said. "But I need detonators. Then we're in business," Jean-Claude said. Despite the fact that he was dreading the reverse crawl back to the outlet to the street, he was pleased. He was, in fact, ecstatic.

There were only five members of their cell, and they had all the equipment and knowledge they needed. Nothing could possibly go wrong.

An hour later, Jean-Claude was back up on the Calle Maldonado, two and a half blocks north of the embassy. His clothes were filthy, but no one seemed to notice or care.

He walked across the street and looked in the direction of the American coffee shop. It was filled with wealthy foreigners, to his mind, packed with the cultural imperialists that he so hated.

If he had his way, he'd blow up the coffee shop too.

But first things first. This morning, Jean-Claude had received a message from a man named Lazzari, an Italian of Turkish descent. Lazzari had had something to do with the shipping of the explosives from Italy to Spain. And now Lazzari wanted some money to keep quiet.

So today, instead of blowing up the American coffee shop, Jean-Claude just glared at it, cursed everyone in it, and spat. It was unending, this war against the infidels. No wonder it had been going on for centuries.

TWENTY-EIGHT

MADRID, SEPTEMBER 9, EVENING

Wrapped in a plush white Ritz towel, Alex stood in front of the mirror at the sink in her hotel room. She was working on her hair with the hotel hairdryer when her cell phone rang in her bedroom. She clicked off the hairdryer. She looked up and the ringing stopped.

Then, seconds later, it rang again, as if the same caller was trying again.

Or as if the caller knows I'm here.

She managed a quick jog to the phone and picked it up while the call was still live. *"Diga,"* she said.

"Alejandra?"

It was a male caller. The voice had an accent and was not a voice she recognized.

"Si," she said. *"Quien es?"*

Remaining in Spanish, the caller answered. "This is Colonel Torres of the Guardia Civil. We met the day before yesterday. At the embassy."

"Yes. Of course." Now she had a face to go with the name. "What can I do for you, Colonel?"

It was not unusual for a call to come in so late. She glanced at a clock at her bedside. It was after 9:00 p.m. That was still early for a Madrid evening.

"Would you be available this evening?" he asked.

"Is the invitation social or professional?" she asked.

"Professional, I assure you."

"Keep talking."

"We've located *The Pietà of Malta*," he said.

"You've what?"

He repeated.

"We've located *The Pietà of Malta*," he said. "We have it in our possession."

"Why that's wonderful!" Alex said.

A beat and he added. "Well, yes. And, no. It is and it isn't."

"Why are you calling me?" she asked.

"We would like *you* to take possession of it. And return it to the museum tomorrow."

"If you have it or know where it is, why don't you?" she asked. "It belongs to Spain, not the United States. I would think the home team would want to make the big play."

There was a silence. "I don't understand," the voice said.

"We're in Spain, Colonel," she said. "Apparently, you've found the item. Might it not look better if a division of Spanish police returned it?"

There was something about this that didn't smell quite right. She fumbled with a pen and a pad of paper on the desk in her hotel room. She took the phone from her ear quickly and replaced it. Good. The incoming phone number was displayed. "There is a problem," he said.

"Then you need to explain the problem if you want my assistance," she said.

The incoming number started with *91*. The call was generated by a Madrid exchange. So far so good. She wrote down the whole number. Then she fumbled through her wallet, and the card section where she collected business cards.

She heard him sigh. "Is this line secure?"

"It's secure," she said.

She found the card of Colonel Torres. The numbers matched. She relaxed slightly.

"The return has to be done through an intermediary," the caller said.

"Why?"

"We are speaking off the record? In confidence?"

"If we need to."

"The pietà cannot be seen to have been in the hands of the Civil Guard at all," the caller said. "Internal politics. There's guilt and culpability, some of which would land upon this department. There would be repercussions, questions asked about the methods taken to effect the return of the 'lamentation.' It would be best if none of that happened."

"So I can't admit how I found the pietà so quickly?"

"No."

"Then where do I say I received it from?" she asked.

"Make something up."

"Suppose I don't find it a good idea to lie," she said. "Or maybe I just don't want to lie."

"Make something up anyway," he said. "I know a bit about you. You know how to make situations work. There is no truth that can't be bent. Everyone knows you have contacts. You don't always have to explain them."

He hesitated, then spoke again.

"And I assure you, there are many people in Spain who will be grateful for your intercession. You would have friends here in important places for years to come."

"I don't doubt your word, Colonel," she said.

"It's important that a non-Spaniard take it," the voice said. "And it needs to be done tonight."

"Why?"

He started growing angry. "All right, don't bother!" he snapped. "I thought it would be best to try a woman, but maybe a woman isn't up to danger outside of a bedroom late in the evening. Forgive me for—!"

"Excuse me!" she snapped.

"Buenas noches!" There was a silence. She tossed away her towel and moved around the room with the phone to her ear. She started to pull together her clothes in case she needed to go out after all.

He changed his tone. "It's important that a non-Spaniard bring the pietà back," he said. "Please, Signorita. Will we do business or not? We know you and we respect you. So we know that placing the lamentation in your hands would be proper."

Some nasty little voice inside her told her this was a trick. A trap. Something was wrong. But the number on the phone didn't lie.

"So this is Colonel Torres I'm speaking to?" she said.

"It *is*, Señorita."

"Do you mind if I verify that?"

"In whatever way you wish."

"How many people were in our meeting yesterday?"

He thought for a moment. "Nine."

"Where was I sitting?" Alex asked.

"Across the round table from me. On my left were Scotland Yard, Interpol, and the Frenchman. On the other side were the Italian, Rizzo, and the American, who looked bored."

"What was I wearing? You're a career detective. I'm sure you'd notice such things."

"A most attractive navy blue suit and an off-white blouse. No jewelry other than a watch, which was gold with a leather band."

"Very good," she said. "So what do you want from me tonight?" Alex asked.

"I want you to be at La Floridita bar at midnight," he said. "Stay by the bar and watch the door. At midnight you will see a policeman come in. Our uniform. Civil Guard. He is a sergeant. Three stripes on his right arm. He will stand near the door and look around as if he is looking for someone. Then a second man will enter. He will be a member of the guard too. You will notice that both men will be armed. That is to reassure you. But do not acknowledge them. They will stay for a moment and look around. Then they will leave, as if they have not seen whom they are looking for. Wait for two minutes, then leave and follow them. Go out the door to your left. Walk for two blocks. You will arrive at where the Calle de la Bolsa intersects with the Calle de la Paz. You'll see a police car there. They will have a box in the trunk of the car. It will contain the pietà."

"And I'm just to take it?"

"They will open the trunk. The lamentation will be in a brown wrapper in a leather satchel. Inspect it if you like. I would suggest returning it to the museum tomorrow shortly after it opens."

Alex liked to think she had good antennae. Something seemed too easy about this, too pat.

"And if I don't show up tonight?" she asked.

There was an ominous pause. "When you show up, do so alone. Good evening, Señorita."

There was a click. Suddenly her room was very quiet. She looked at the print out on the phone. Three minutes, fifty seconds. A gut punch of a call.

Her eyes rose. She looked at herself in the mirror, clad in undergarments. She felt like a schoolgirl, in well over her head, inadequate, not knowing how to navigate the internecine warfare of a foreign nation's power establishment and politics.

She drew a breath and steadied herself

She quickly went to her notes from the previous day.

Sure enough. Same number. Torres. Civil Guard.

Okay, that much made sense. But not much else did. She looked at her watch. It was 9:30 now.

She wished she had obtained a gun.

Conventional wisdom: Going out like this was potential suicide without being armed.

Updated conventional wisdom: Sometimes the height of paranoia was a healthy exercise.

She tried to reassure herself. There was always room for some simple corruption to factor into any case. It might even have been the main factor. The thieves had worn Guardia Civil uniforms and now the head of that unit was trying to steer the pietà back where it belonged.

Obliquely, that made sense. Didn't it?

Her mind was in overdrive. To her own embarrassment, she even thought of the reward money. She knew she couldn't accept it, but she could direct it to a charity.

Okay, that tipped her a little in favor making the transfer.

She processed information rapidly. She had more dangerous things in her life than this. Serving as a target on the streets of Paris. Going undercover many years ago against some Cuban-American hoodlums. Standing in the central square in Kiev while RPGs rolled it.

One side of her said she had survived the past so she would survive the present. The other side of her said that she was playing Russian roulette. Spin the dial too many times and you wind up dead.

She thought for another moment.

Show up alone. Well, that was one thing that wasn't going to happen.

TWENTY-NINE

MADRID, SEPTEMBER 9, 11:49 P.M.

Stepping through the doorway of the dimly lit cocktail bar, Alex's first impression of La Floridita was that of being transported to another decade. The bar gleamed with chrome and wood, Deco-style lamps, and elliptical tangerine-colored chairs. The bar was reminiscent of the bar of an ocean liner in the 1930s.

She looked for Rizzo, whom she had called before she left, and didn't see him. Normally he was dependable. Surely he would be there shortly. Bad feelings started to quickly creep up on her.

The place was crowded. Not noisy, just crowded. She scanned the chrome and leather bar stools. Then she glanced across the dark nooks and crannies of the room, linked by staircases and galleries. The lighting was so dim that she could barely make out who was there. Much easier to get the drop on someone entering than someone already nestled in. Whoever had set this up had done it for a reason.

Where's Rizzo? She didn't like this. Not at all.

Just retrieve the artwork without getting killed.

She liked the music. It settled her. Latino pop. Mexican stuff. She recognized the raspy, sexy voice of Paulina Rubio. *"Yo te Seguo Aqui."* Appropriate. The familiar tune calmed her. But her insides suddenly felt like there were a dozen butterflies on a mating dance within her chest. She had an instinct about things going the wrong way, and the instincts were on red alert right now.

Where's Rizzo?

Then came a familiar male voice from close by. "Alex . . . ?"

The voice floated out of thin air and above the techno beat that accompanied Paulina Rubio. Alex looked in every direction, mildly disoriented.

"Soy tu apoyo," said the voice. "Behind you." A hand tapped her shoulder. She jumped and turned.

Thank Heaven. It was Rizzo.

"Hello, Gian Antonio."

He had been seated near the door, so he could cover the back of anyone he saw enter. Now he sheltered her from the crowd, a drink in his hand.

"You're jittery," he said, switching to English.

She exhaled. "Am I?"

"Like a dozen scared cats," he said. "Follow me. I'd suggest a drink. Don't tell me you don't need one, because you do, and don't tell me you don't want one, because I'm getting you one, anyway."

"All right," she said.

He had a wineglass in his hand. He placed a hand across her shoulders, and she didn't object. He guided her to the bar. "They have a nice fruity *cava tinto* here," he said.

"If you're having one," she said.

"I'm having three," he said and gave the bartender a nod. "Maybe four if things go in the wrong direction. This is my third and I don't like the mood of the evening."

"Me neither," she said.

The barman caught Rizzo's gesture. He poured red wine quickly into a Burgundy-style glass. The wine was six euros, Rizzo gave the man a twenty and didn't look for change. Alex thought she caught a piece of an explanation. The man also gave Rizzo something else from the bar, wrapped in a paper napkin, a plastic knife and fork or something. She couldn't see and knew better than to ask.

"Let's move down the bar a bit. Gives us a better vantage point," Rizzo said, speaking English in lowered tones. "Never know what you're going to spot."

She followed. Rizzo found a place toward the end of the bar where they could see the door and the floor around them.

She leaned in close to him, speaking directly into his ear, and quickly brought him up to speed on the phone call she had received and why they were there. He listened carefully, asking only the most occasional quick question.

"I'm not sold on any of this, either," he said. "Something's wrong somewhere. Too easy."

"Civil Guard. Can I trust them?"

"You shouldn't trust anyone," he answered. "It's bad for your health. Didn't your mother teach you that?"

"I trust *you*."

"I'm an exception," he said. "I'm a Roman but I have Sicilian blood."

"I thought your family was from the north of Italy. That's what you said in Paris."

"They *are* from the north. Everyone from the north is from the south. FIAT plant at Torino. An entire generation migrated north to build cars that don't work very well. Look, it'll probably be okay tonight. I'll cover you closely."

"Thanks."

"Whatever you do, when you get close to their police car, be careful. If there's a door or trunk to open, insist that someone else do it. The only thing you want to touch is the clammy old artwork, and you want to touch that as little as possible. You have gloves?"

"No."

"I do. Here. I brought them for you." He fished into his pocket and came out with a pair of latex gloves, the kind used for kitchen work

"Do you think of everything?" she asked.

"Of course not. But I stopped by the restaurant of my hotel and stole these. Actually, they gave them to me but what does it matter? Can never be too careful," he said, his brown eyes sliding sideways, working the room. "I bought you another present too," he said. "Don't say no, and relax, it's not a peignoir."

He made a surreptitious movement with his free hand, as if to pass something to her out of everyone's sight. She took the cue and reached. It was the package in the paper napkin.

Their eyes met. She looked down. He had acquired an ice pick from the bar. She took it and the hint that went with it.

"If you have trouble on the street," he said gently, "go for the eyes or the jugular. If you're down low, an upstroke toward the groin would do the trick. I would have brought you a gun if I'd had time," he said. "But short notice, you know?"

"I know. But thank you," she said again. She lifted her glass and offered it toward his. "Cheers," she said as she tucked the pick into her pocket. It was stubby and sharp. It had a wooden handle and four inch spike.

A slight smile. "Cheers," he answered. "An ice pick's a handy thing to carry. There's not a bus or a truck you can't bring to a halt with the proper use of one of those, not to mention the driver. And so much classier than a gun, right?"

"Right," she said. She drank.

"Salud," he said.

"Salud."

Alex sipped. Rizzo quaffed. He was right. The wine was outstanding. Then something clicked in from earlier in the evening, on the phone, when Rizzo had said that he knew the place. Obviously, he knew it well and the barman probably knew him.

"So how are you enjoying retirement?" she asked finally.

"Never been busier," he said.

"Your American 'interests'?" she asked.

"You could say that," he said. "Bless your government. They'll keep me working till I'm a hundred years old because they can't go a week without having some small political, diplomatic, or security crisis here in Europe. So may the incompetence and mismanagement of your government continue forever. If I live long enough I'll be a rich old man."

"Hey," she said. "Look."

She indicated the doorway where an armed man in a green uniform had strolled in. Not that unusual, except he was armed, which the Civil Guard people hadn't done till recently and still didn't do all the time.

"Your mark?" he asked.

She glanced at her watch. Midnight. The timing worked. "Maybe," she said.

Alex and Rizzo watched as a noisy pair of men came to the bar near them. Two men with one woman. They seemed to be having some sort of good-natured argument, but Alex couldn't understand. It was Greek to her as well as to everyone else.

"Let me get a better look," she said to Rizzo. She stepped away.

The uniformed policeman stood and looked around, as if he were searching for someone. Then the other cop entered. Two Civil Guards in uniform, both armed. Burly, thick-waisted men with pistols on their hips.

Alex looked back to Rizzo, where he stood among the Greeks. She gave him a nod. This was them, she was convinced. He gave a nod in return and made a quick motion of touching his heart, which she took to mean, be careful.

The woman who was with the Greeks was tall, slim, and leggy, in a short blue dress. She looked like a dream or trouble or both. Rizzo tried to not let her distract him aside from the first appreciative glance.

The two policemen left.

"Corrupt cops?" Alex asked.

"Something smells wrong. Be very careful. I'm going to be ten seconds behind you."

"Only ten?"

"Maybe five," he said. "I'm coming through the doorway as soon as you're outside," he said. "Just get the artwork and get away from them," he said. "Do everything quickly, don't stand in any one place too long. Keep an eye on windows for snipers. I wish I'd brought my own backup."

He gave her hand a squeeze. Not lust this time. Real concern.

"Go," he said.

Alex gave him a hug and set her half-full glass down on the bar. She turned and moved toward the door.

Rizzo reached to her glass as he watched her. He raised her glass to his own lips and finished her drink.

One of the Greeks grinned, turned to him.

"Thirsty?" the Greek asked in Spanish with a sneering smile.

"None of your lousy business," Rizzo snarled in English, "so get out of my face."

The man turned, still smiling, but confrontational.

"You're not very friendly, are you, old man?" the man answered in English. "What happened? Your woman just walked out on you?"

The woman who was with them peeled away. Rizzo worked on the man's accent. It wasn't quite Greek. Once again, something was wrong. His hand moved for his weapon.

"You going to get away from me or do I have to break you in half?" Rizzo asked.

"An old guy like you?" the man asked. He laughed and so did his pal.

"Go to hell," Rizzo responded. He followed that with a sharp colorful obscenity and a little push. He took a step away from the bar. Alex was out of his sight by now, and he needed to move.

The man took exception to Rizzo's language and stepped in front of him. Rizzo pushed him again, pushed him hard, and the man budged and shoved back. An instant later, Rizzo also realized that he had been skunked.

An arm grabbed him from behind and locked hard around his neck. A yoke job and a perfectly professional one. Rizzo knew the drill. With his heel, he smashed down onto the instep of the man behind him and uppercut with his elbow. But then he felt a jab in one of his buttocks. It was a sharp jab that was hot with pain, then suddenly very cold.

Meanwhile the man in front of him brought up a knee to Rizzo's groin, a knee that felt like an express train when it made contact. And Rizzo continued to feel an iciness radiating far down in his backside, from the middle of the left buttock on outward, where he had been stabbed with a needle.

With a speed faster than light, Rizzo realized that the Greek wasn't a Greek. The lousy Eurotrash accent was something more ominous than Greek, maybe.

Tunisian or Algerian or Moroccan.

An accent from a hot, oppressive country with a lot of hot sand, stinking camels, and obnoxious people stuck in the seventeenth century, in his humble opinion. Rizzo realized that a trap had just sprung shut and the pain in his buttock was turning to a cold numbness because someone had jabbed a hypodermic needle into him and he was a goner, for this evening at least, if not for good, depending on what they had loaded into the syringe . . .

His vision blurred and he eyed the door. Then his eyes widened. His assailants released him and he stood with a wobble.

What a small perverse world this was!

He then spotted another strange face. An Asian guy who was looking at him from the midpoint of the bar and seemed to understand what had happened. Rizzo swooned, wishing the Asian would help him or do *something*.

The Asian had the movements of a big cat. He turned and quick-stepped out the door in Rizzo's place, following Alex and, in Rizzo's opinion, closing a trap on her.

Now she had a stranger on her back, not the noble old Roman bodyguard.

Rizzo cursed violently. Darkness was descending on him, but he still had lots of fight, more than his opponents expected from a geezer. With a chopping motion, he brought his hand up toward the Greek-speaking guy in front of him, a guy who was dumb enough to stand there with his hands down, just watching.

Rizzo caught the man in the Adam's apple and felt a solid crunch on impact, a crunch that was loud enough to draw the attention of people at the bar.

The man recoiled and coughed violently.

Rizzo grabbed the man's throat and tried to squeeze. He tried to claw.

Rizzo felt the flesh tear against the clawing of his fingernails. But Rizzo was losing strength fast. He threw an elbow backward, hitting the man behind him — the one who had jabbed him — in the ribs. But then something that must have been a fist came out of nowhere and walloped him across the back of the head.

The blow stunned him.

The ceiling spun away.

Rizzo knew he was losing consciousness. The foreign hands upon him were firm, and they threw him against the wall. He continued to fight and cursed in slow motion. He was furious. He hadn't lost a bar fight in thirty years, but he was sure on the short end of one tonight.

There was laughter, and Rizzo heard them explaining to the bartender in Spanish, "... our friend has had too much to drink," followed by more laughter.

"I saw you hit him," the bartender said. "Get out of here before I throw you out."

"We're leaving. We're leaving."

Rizzo knew expletives in at least a dozen major languages and launched as many as he could. Then he settled slowly to the floor as his assailants moved away and toward the door.

Darkness overwhelmed Rizzo. As he lost consciousness, he wondered if he would ever gain it back or whether this was lights-out for good.

THIRTY

MADRID, SEPTEMBER 10, 12:01 A.M.

Alex emerged from the bar alone and stopped on the sidewalk outside. The neighborhood was busy.

She looked both ways. She checked the street for vans or suspicious cars. The area was a minefield of things she didn't like. Groups hanging around talking, single men, couples smooching in doorways, people sitting at outdoor tables that overflowed from other bars. Any single one of these groups, or any single person within them, could be transformed into a lethal adversary at any moment.

Her insides were so tightly coiled that she saw the whole architecture of the neighborhood in terms of menace. The traffic flowed the wrong way, approaching her from behind, meaning anyone could follow. She guessed that might have been by design.

"Okay," she said to herself in a whisper. "Move!"

Far to her left, almost half a block away now, she saw her two cops, a duet of green uniforms moving at a quick pace.

Well, no turning back now. She walked briskly. Get this over fast. Make this your own type of smash and grab. No nonsense permitted. God bless Rizzo and his ice pick.

She felt in her jacket pocket and found the pick. She clutched it and felt her sweaty palm on it. She crossed one street corner. So far so good.

Now, once again: Where is Rizzo? She threw a sideways glance over her shoulder and didn't see him. Where was he? She looked again.

Come on Gian Antonio. Don't be slow about this. Timing is everything.

She continued walking. A second street corner crossing.

Okay, two thirds of the way there. So far so good. She was still alive. She tried to steady her pace. She knew Rizzo had to be back there somewhere. He *had* to be.

Far up ahead she could see the end of the block. She knew she needed to turn the corner to follow … She quickstepped her pace, got there, and did a quick evasive maneuver. She went out into the street, so as not to be too close to the building. She wished Rizzo would close ranks with her.

Where was he? How could she have lost him? Unlike the busier main street, the side street was quiet. Up ahead a parked car with Guardia Civil markings waited, as per the plan.

On the side street, windows were barred and grates were down against the night and the people who populated it.

In her gut she had the same feeling she had had in Kiev before all hell had broken loose. Was it an animal sense by now, an instinct telling her that danger lurked somewhere? Or was it just a survival skill, telling her to play the game carefully?

Then she could see the cruiser clearly. One of the men in uniform stood leaning against the front hood, near the tire, his arms folded, watching her approach. The other stood by the rear trunk. He was several years younger than the man in front. No nametags. No ranks. Like the rest of the evening, these guys didn't look right. It wasn't just that her radar was beeping now, the alarm sirens were raging.

She stopped short, about twenty feet in front of them.

"*Buenas noches,*" she said. She would handle this in Spanish.

"*Buenas noches,*" one of them answered. They almost laughed.

"*La pietà,*" she asked. "*¿Dónde está?*"

They both smiled. Something was off with their smiles too.

"In the trunk," they said. The man in uniform at the rear of the car stepped away, several paces, very carefully. By now she knew, this was no ordinary transaction.

Where is Rizzo!

She didn't want to turn. She knew better than to take her eyes off two players in a quasi-criminal transaction.

"Be a gentleman. Open the trunk for me and bring it here," she said.

"Come get it," one of them said.

"No. I've come this far. The final few paces are up to you."

Her hand remained on the pick. But she felt naked. They had guns!

Where is Rizzo!

Then she heard footsteps behind her. Comforting ones. That had to be him, didn't it? She felt eyes on her back. She felt a presence, maybe twenty feet behind her.

There was a moment of standoff.

"I brought a friend," she said, still in Spanish.

"You shouldn't have done that," the man to her left said.

"Just give me the pietà if you have it," she said.

There was another moment of hot sweaty standoff. Five seconds that played out like a month. She cocked her head slightly and glanced behind her to see where Rizzo was, angling so that her eyes were only away from these two creeps for a millisecond.

No Rizzo. Actually, she saw where he wasn't. But she could see a man she had never seen in her life before. An Asian, sharply dressed in a dark suit. Midthirties. Handsome. Killer-good-looks handsome.

Now it all made sense. She had been trapped and set up. She turned back toward the car. There was movement behind her, as if the Asian were jockeying for a better angle. She watched the men in front of her and saw something strange in their eyes too.

She was certain: the three of them were together and she had waltzed into their trap.

Then she read the look of the men in front of her. Their hands were moving slowly toward their weapons. She would have fled, but quick movements are suicidal during a crossfire.

In front of her, both of the uniformed men reached for their side-arms. And a voice came from behind her. The Asian screamed out in English.

"Alex! Get down! Get down! Get down!"

She saw the guns come up in the hands of the men in front of her. Big, mean, automatic pistols. Urban warfare stuff.

The two men spread out quickly to their sides to get a better angle on her pursuer. She was right in the middle. Her mind was so filled with pounding blood, fear, and danger that her instincts took over. She knew that if she moved to the left or the right, she would be in the line of fire from the Guardia Civil and if she stayed upright she could be shot in the back.

So she went down, hitting the pavement hard as the gunfire broke out all around her. She ducked and threw her arms and hands over her upper torso and her head. She waited to feel the impact of a slug and the searing pain that would hit her.

The gunshots resonated with a terrifying sound. The ammunition sailed all around her. In a vision that would play out in her mind forever, just like the dark bloody visions of earlier this year in Kiev, she saw the younger Guardia Civil man take a shot in the center of the chest.

The shot propelled him backward against the car, where the force of his recoiling body kept him stationary for several seconds even though his own weapon had flown from his hand and into the air. A second shot from behind her hit him and threw him sprawling onto the hood of the car, where he remained.

In the same instant, the second Guardia Civil man, the older one, fired at the man behind Alex. He got off a barrage of shots from his automatic pistol. Some of them flew directly over her prone body at the Asian. But he must have missed with every one of them because the shots from behind her kept coming in return.

Four, five, six of them. Several of the bullets impacted across the Guardia Civil man's chest. He reeled and spun. But the final shot from behind Alex was the coup de grace. It hit the man square in the center of the face.

Alex, cringing, unable to pull her gaze away, had an excellent view. The final bullet blew away the left side of the man's skull. The hat flew away, as did a bloody mass of brain and pulp. The body spun wildly, spasmed, tumbled over the rear trunk of the car, and rolled wildly into the Calle de la Paz.

Two dozen shots must have been fired, all in the space of a few seconds. Everything was quiet for a moment. Then Alex heard the footsteps from behind approaching her.

Alex turned her head, gasping for breath, a hot sweat soaking her, convinced that the death that she had evaded in Kiev would now find her on a Madrid sidewalk several minutes past midnight on a warm summer night.

She slowly rose with her hands against the sidewalk. Her eyes widened at the vision behind her. Bathed by the light from a streetlamp, the gunman behind her stepped forward. There was a pistol at the end of each arm.

The vision was surreal. He had carried the weapons much as he had fired them, with a precision and carriage that was almost inhuman. No wonder he had been able to fire off so many rounds at once. He had been firing with two weapons at once. But the accuracy had been as astonishing as the speed. He stood no more than twenty feet from her. And now a revised realization. He wasn't with the fake cops at all.

Yet before him now, she was helpless. Sweat poured off her.

"Go ahead," she said, reverting to English.

He gave a nod. "I will," he said. He spoke perfect English.

Run, she thought. But to where? She didn't stand a chance.

She saw him raise both weapons and take several paces forward. He stood now no more than five feet away from her. The guns came up. She looked him in the eye.

"What's in your pocket?" he asked.

"An ice pick."

He looked bemused. "Why? Is it snowing?"

She said nothing.

"Don't make a move," he advised. "Stay there."

Both guns came up. First the left. He fired once. Then the right. He fired a second time.

She felt no impact. Why was she still alive? She turned to the fallen men in Civil Guard uniforms. He had fired a final shot into the heart of each of the prostrate bodies. Hardly necessary, but a gory punctuation point to the killings.

"They were sent to kill you," he said in English that was almost too perfect.

"What?"

"They were sent to kill you."

"The pietà?" she asked. "In the trunk of the car?"

"Don't be silly," he said. "They don't have it. The trunk was open to stuff you into it."

He used his left hand to train one pistol on the trunk of the car and he fired several shots. Alex heard the bullets smash into the car. Then there was an explosion that propelled her several feet along the sidewalk and into a sprawling tumble. She looked back and the police car was in flames. Whatever had been in the trunk had exploded and had ignited the gasoline as well. The cruiser was an inferno.

She stared at it in disbelief, then jerked her head back to the gunman before her.

"Next time, be more careful," he said. "I only want to rescue you once. You'd do best to get out of here fast."

With movements that were quick and proficient, almost catlike, he tucked his pistols under his jacket. He turned and walked briskly away, not looking back. She heard sirens in the distance, drawing closer. She gathered herself and climbed to her feet. She felt some tearing to her jeans where her knee had hit the ground hard. One of her elbows was bleeding also.

The gunman was already gone. She couldn't believe how quickly he had disappeared. She turned toward the darker end of the block and fled. Halfway back to the hotel, she found a taxi and took it the rest of the way.

THIRTY-ONE

Colonel Carlos Pendraza of the Spanish Policia Nacional stood with his arms at his side on the Calle de Balsa and methodically looked at the carnage before him. A dignified man, ill-at-ease to overt manifestations of temper, he surveyed the scene and quietly seethed.

Another horrendous high profile crime on the streets of Madrid. He could tell in an instant that the two men dead in Guardia Civil uniforms were not Spaniards. Not true Spaniards anyway. It was just another example of the international *gentuza* — the riffraff — bringing their discontent to Spain.

When would it end? he wondered. With what would it end? Certainly the leftists in the government weren't going to do anything to suppress this stuff. He felt a deep disgust, a deep rage, and a deep helplessness.

And he also felt a sharp echo from the past.

As a young police officer in 1973, Pendraza had been part of the police detail that had protected a man named Carrero Blanco, Franco's hard-line prime minister and the man seen as Franco's most likely successor.

But within six months of being named prime minister, Carrero Blanco was assassinated in Madrid by four members of ETA, a Basque separatist organization that was still dangerous in this new century.

To murder Blanco, the ETA had placed close to two hundred pounds of explosives in a tunnel they had excavated under the street. Then they had set off a blast by remote control while Blanco rode from his home to a Roman Catholic Mass. Blanco had traveled in a specially built armored Dodge Dart. Pendraza had been in the second car following the Dart and had been badly injured by broken glass and hugely traumatized by the events of the day.

The blast catapulted Blanco's vehicle over the church it was approaching. It landed on a second-floor balcony on the other side of the street. In a macabre touch, its twisted remains remained to this day on display, part of a grim memorial at the Spanish army museum. The explosion only took place about a half block from the United States Embassy.

Henry Kissinger, then the US Secretary of State during the Nixon administration, had been visiting Spain at the time. Had Kissinger been Catholic, not Jewish, Kissinger might easily have been in the car with Carrero Blanco at the time, and the ETA would have taken out a US cabinet member as well as their own prime minister.

This incident was the origin of the modern widespread practice of sealing manholes when a high profile procession is to take place.

This assassination, dubbed *Operación Ogro* by those who carried it out, was in retaliation for the execution of five political opponents by the regime and was applauded by many opponents of Franco's regime.

In his first speech to the Spanish parliament in February 1974, Carrero Blanco's successor promised many reforms including the right to form political associations. Though he was denounced by hardliners within the regime, the transition had begun, and it never ceased to gnaw at Pendraza that Blanco's murder rewarded the purposes of those who had killed him.

But the incident hadn't ended there either. One of the ETA members who had assassinated Carrero Blanco, a man known only by his nom de guerre, *Argala*, was himself assassinated by a car bomb in the south of France five years later. The killers this time were a Spanish far-right group organized from inside the navy, assisted by neo-fascists from France and Italy.

Argala, was the only one who could identify the mysterious man who handed to ETA Carrero Blanco's schedule and itinerary. According to a former member of the Spanish army who participated in the bombing against Argala, the explosives that killed Argala came from an American military base, either stolen or "donated to a good cause."

This morning, Pendraza had been sleeping soundly with his wife of twenty-six years beside him when his phone had rung to report the shootings on the Calla de la Bolsa. Ripped from a peaceful sleep only half an hour earlier, he now stared forward. Pendraza had had more than enough of the scenes that lay before him. He wondered again where it would all end. Why couldn't Spain remain the sweet isolated place he had known as a young man? At age fifty-seven, he felt as if he were a hundred.

Behind him, on the other side of the police lines, a crowd gathered. Police had strung crime-scene tape everywhere. Technicians doing their jobs. A couple of ambulances were present to take away the dead, and there were more police cars than Pendraza cared to count, not even including the unmarked ones.

Pendraza's brown eyes slid uneasily over the death scene. He felt his blood pressure rising.

These days in Spain, he raged to himself, he heard and read a lot of foolish things. A lot of revisions of history. But more than ever, Pendraza felt that the late, great *Caudillo*, General Franco, had saved this great country, and for that matter *la civilización español*, from the unwashed Bolshevik hordes. Spain would have turned into Poland or Cuba if the reds and the pinkos had had their way. And today it was no different.

He looked at what had happened on the street, then turned in anger, and went back to his car. Now he was officially involved in this. So officially or unofficially, whoever had been a part of this was going to pay. That was a promise he made to himself, and to the spirit of Franco.

THIRTY-TWO

MADRID, SEPTEMBER 10, MORNING

At a few minutes before 11:00 a.m., Alex stood in the front lobby of the Ritz. She positioned herself near the large front entrance but stood back from it. She could see vehicles in the arrival area without being seen from the street.

She had been up for three hours already after a nearly sleepless night. She had located Rizzo in a Madrid hospital and had been burning out the secure phone channels to Washington. Now she stood patiently waiting for a ride, as promised on one of those calls.

She did not know how hot a target she might still be. She edged toward the door, giving the doormen a polite nod every time they looked her way. On her left knee, a few inches below the hem of a stylish blue skirt, she wore a fresh bandage from where she had hit the sidewalk the night before. Beneath a blouse and suit jacket, there was a similar bandage on her elbow.

She stepped to the doorway and looked at the city of Madrid beyond the old hotel. Past the stand of chestnut trees that insulated the hotel from the street, traffic churned around the plaza in the middle of the Paseo del Prado, with its fountain featuring Neptune on a chariot pulled by mythological sea beasts. Normal for a weekday morning.

At one point during the Civil War, the front lines had been only a few dozen streets to the west, on the street of Paseo del Pintor Rosales, which overlooked the park called the Casa del Campo. Republican defenders had ridden into action on streetcars that ran up the boulevard known as the Gran Vía. The hotel itself had at one point closed its doors to guests and become a hospital.

A black unmarked Mercedes eased to a stop in front of the Ritz. It was one of those special-orders favored by police and antiterror officials around the world. Within its gleaming steel chassis, it had the most bomb and bullet-resistant armor plating that the trolls of Stuttgart could weld. The tinted windows had the world's best bulletproof glass, and the occupants could roll through traffic on the most shred-proof tires known to humanity.

A driver stepped out, a hulking armed police officer in a suit. He had a shaved head and a cadaverous face. He stood about six-feet-five and looked as if he broke people in half for breakfast. He came around and opened a rear door. As he opened it, a black Cadillac Esplanade pulled to an abrupt halt behind the black Mercedes.

Friends? Enemies? They could have been either. But from Alex's phone calls this same morning, she knew exactly who was arriving.

The Mercedes carried the VIP. The second vehicle was the body-guards' car. It was filled with four more officers from the National Police. Three were armed with automatic pistols beneath their summer-weight jackets, and one sat with an Uzi across his lap.

The two in the front surveyed their commander's car. The two in the back watched the front portico of the Ritz. Alex left the lobby of the Ritz and moved quickly toward the Benz. The first bodyguard spotted her immediately and walked to her.

"Alejandra?" he asked in Spanish.

"*Soy yo,*" she said. It's me.

"I'm Miguel. Come with me," he said.

Miguel stood close to her in a protective pose, his body acting as a shield, almost pressed against her, his arm around her shoulders but not touching. Miguel was so close that, from brushing against him, she knew he was wearing a bulletproof vest.

He guided her to the car door. The normally attentive Ritz door-men knew enough to stay away. Alex slid into the backseat. The driver closed the door, moved quickly around to the driver's side, and jumped in.

In the backseat of the vehicle sat a very unhappy Colonel Carlos Pendraza of the Spanish Policia Nacional. Pendraza nodded to her. They spoke in Spanish.

"*Buenos dias,*" he said.

"*Buenos dias,*" Alex answered.

"My sincere apologies for the events of last night," Colonel Pendraza said.

"Apologies are unnecessary," she said. "Last night wasn't your fault, I assume."

"Of course not!" he said angrily. "And I've spent more than an hour on the phone to Washington," he said. "I assume you have too."

"I've been asked to definitely stay with this investigation," Alex said. "I spoke to my superior at the Treasury Department. Originally, I was asked to come here as an observer in the theft of *The Pietà of Malta.* Now my bosses have asked me to take more of an investigatory role. With the permission of the host government," she said.

"You have our permission, of course," he said. "And you'll have any measures of support that you need from the government of Spain. Aside from that, please try not to get killed in our country."

"I'll try not to," she said.

"I've tried for thirty years myself," he said. "I've been successful. So far."

The Mercedes moved quickly out into the morning traffic on the plaza, joining the rumble of cars and trucks and the whine of motor scooters already on the plaza. The sun broke above the neighboring rooftops and blasted the streets.

Madrid in September. Already the day promised to be a scorcher. Colonel Pendraza allowed a moment to pass. Then he switched into fluent English.

"We need to talk," Colonel Pendraza said to Alex as the car moved through the streets of Madrid. "We're honored to have you here working with us. And my deep condolences for your personal loss in Kiev."

"Thank you," Alex said.

Pendraza remained in English, recalling for a few moments the time he had spent as a naval attaché with NATO, where he had used his English every day and, as Alex noted, refined it to a high level of proficiency.

"This third gunman," Pendraza finally said, "this Asian man you described when you phoned Washington and when you phoned me. You have no idea who this could be, whom he might be working for, whom he might represent?"

"No idea," she said.

"He fits the general profile of someone in whom Interpol has a current interest," the colonel said. "And of course, with a public shooting, every police agency in Spain now has an interest too."

"Of course," she said.

The Mercedes jostled a bit in traffic. From the corner of her eye she saw Miguel give a slashed-throat gesture to another driver.

"I assume also that you may have watched the morning news," Pendraza continued. "Or seen the local newspapers. The events of last night at Calle de la Bolsa and Calle de la Paz are all over the media."

"I've seen it," she said.

"Which of course will mean there will be journalists pestering us," he said. "It was much easier in the old days when one could discourage such things."

Pendraza raised his eyes and voice to the driver. "Miguel?" he asked.

Without taking his eyes off the traffic, Miguel reached his thick hand to the seat next to him. He picked up a package wrapped in brown paper and handed it from the front seat back to Alex. Meanwhile, the armored sedan navigated the roundabout at the Plaza de Cibeles, then shot onto the westbound Calle de Acalá, traveling past, then away from, the massive Greco-Roman fountain that featured Cybele, the goddess of nature.

"If you're going to work with us in Spain, we suggest you carry something in case you need to protect yourself," Colonel Pendraza said. "We arranged everything with your embassy and with the proper departments here in Madrid."

She accepted the package. By its weight and feel, she knew what was in it.

"*Muchas gracias,*" she said.

Alex unwrapped the package and pulled out a small nine-millimeter Browning automatic. It came with a belt holster and a permit to carry in Spain, issued two hours earlier at the Oficina Central of the National Police. There was also a box of ammunition, fifty rounds.

She hefted the pistol in her hand. It was a good fit.

"Acceptable?" Colonel Pendraza asked.

"Very acceptable," she answered. "Thank you."

"We received your photo and your personal information from

Washington. Please note that your permit runs for one year only. Should your case conclude before that, as we hope it does, and you wish to leave Spain, we will ask for the permit to be returned."

"I understand," she said.

"If you wish to use one of our ranges to get the feel of the weapon please call my office," he said. "Arrangements will be made upon your request."

She turned the weapon over in her hand, examining it. The metal was cold, the design sleek. As Colonel Pendraza continued to speak, she loaded a magazine and fixed the holster to the right side of her skirt. Then she put away her new sidearm and looked back to the colonel.

"How is Señor Rizzo?" she asked. "My friend Gian Antonio? He sounded okay, but it was hard for me to tell."

Pendraza shook his head. "Much the same way I am this morning. More angry than anything. You'll see him in a few minutes."

"And do you know anything more about what happened last night?" she pressed.

"The uniforms and the car were stolen from the Civil Guard," Pendraza said. "Or sold illegally. Who knows with those people? Traitors are everywhere in the Civil Guard."

In the corner of her eye, she thought she saw Miguel, the driver, react with a snort of agreement.

"And the original phone message that sent me to La Floridita?" Alex asked. "My own phone showed that it came from Colonel Torres' phone."

"Someone used a signal scrambler," Pendraza said. "It mimicked the signal from the Guardia Civil phone network. Whoever was out to lure you knew you'd look at the numbers as a rudimentary precaution."

"So whoever was after me would have had access to Colonel Torres' number," she said. "Not only that, but the caller knew what I had been wearing as well as what transpired in the room."

"As I said, traitors are everywhere in the Civil Guard. But that's not to be repeated outside this car."

"I understand," she said. "But whoever the opposition is, they have a degree of technical sophistication," she said. "To intercept and mimic a cell phone signal is not that common. Equally, if whoever the opposition is right now is the same group that stole the pietà from the museum, that further suggests that this was more than a simple grab of an art object for money. Obviously, there is something further afoot."

"Precisely," said Pendraza. "But what?"

There was no answer. Not yet.

Up ahead lay a large white building, modern, sixteen stories in its central tower, with slightly lower wings. Alex knew it was a medical facility, one of the best in Spain. It reminded her of Los Angeles's iconic old City Hall, as made famous on the old *Dragnet* re-runs.

"I've been in my job for many years and have seen many things," Pendraza said. "So I think I am entitled to some conclusions. You'll forgive me, Señorita, if I offend you."

"Please speak freely," she said.

"I am not so much a Spaniard as a European," the colonel began. "My mother was German, my father Castilian. My father was an army officer on the side of Franco, which, in my opinion was on the side of Spain against the advance of communism. But I'm not proposing to tell you about my father; I am going to speak about my mother."

Alex watched the cityscape go by. Smart shops and chic restaurants. Then they came to another building. "See that?" Pendraza asked.

She looked. He was indicating a mosque.

"I see it," she said.

"We are told that Islam is a religion of peace, and that the vast majority of Muslims want to live in peace. But fanatics rule Islam at this moment in history. These fanatics wage several dozen shooting wars worldwide. They slaughter Christian or tribal groups throughout Africa and are gradually taking over the *el continente nero* in an Islamic wave. The fanatics mutilate their women. They bomb, behead, murder, or 'honor kill' women in their families who wish for a few personal modern liberties. *Los fanaticos* take over mosque after mosque. *Los fanaticos* zealously spread the stoning and hanging of rape victims and homosexuals. The so-called 'peaceful majority' is silent and intimidated before these ... these butchers and barbarians!"

Alex listened in silence. The colonel glanced at his watch and continued.

"It was the fanatics who bombed our trains and transportation system a few years ago," he continued bitterly. "My niece, a beautiful university-educated girl of twenty-two whom I had known since she was an hour old, died in that cowardly attack. She was an art student, Alex, and if you do not mind my saying so, she looked a bit like you. Her husband had his arm blown off. And for what?" he asked angrily. "So that the Muslim people in Spain could feel better about themselves?"

"I'm sorry," she said.

"Why do they come here if they do not want to adhere to the conventions of Western society?" he asked. "Why do they abuse our Christian sense of decency and citizenship? But to ask these questions in public is to invite a firestorm of protests. So we speak here in the car, you and I, and Miguel who understands English perfectly and understands my heart and conscience just as well. And I share this with you so that you know how I think, so that there will be no surprises."

His look went faraway for a moment and then returned as Alex kept silent.

"The Soviet Union was comprised of millions of Russians who just wanted to live in peace, yet the Russian Communists were responsible for the murder of twenty million people. China's huge population was peaceful, but Chinese Communists killed seventy to eighty million people. The average Japanese individual prior to World War II was not a sadistic warmonger who wished to fight China and America. Yet Japan slaughtered its way across Southeast Asia with the systematic murder of ten million Chinese civilians. Most were killed by swords, shovels, and bayonets. And in our recent lifetime, Alejandra, Rwanda. Could it not be said that the majority of Rwandans were 'peace loving'?"

"The case could be made," she said.

"We miss the obvious lessons of history," the colonel said. "The sane majority rarely speaks until it is too late. For us who are entrusted with the safety of the public, we must pay attention to the fanatics."

"So you think the museum robbery and the events of last night tie into terrorist activity in Spain," she said. "Is that what you're saying?"

Pendraza laughed softly. "I have a gut feeling, Señorita. I also have files on more than one hundred current investigations of terrorist activity in Spain."

"May I see them?" she asked. "Those files?"

He turned on her, with surprise. "*All* of them?"

"If you don't mind."

He looked away. "No. I don't mind at all," he said. "I'll have them sent to you later today by secure *correo electrónico*. You also might be interested in some information at the medical examiner's office. That's one of the places we're going today. All right?"

"Excellent," she said.

"You'll hear a lot of things in Spain today," Pendraza said. "A lot of revisions of history. But mark me well on this. General Franco saved this country from the Bolshevik hordes. We would have turned into Poland or Cuba if the opposition had had their way. And today, it's no different. There are alien hordes. Enemies among us. I will fight them until they die. Or till *I* die."

The vehicle eased to a halt in front of the hospital. Colonel Pendraza held a hand aloft to indicate that everyone should remain until their car doors were opened for them. Miguel was out in a flash and so were the Spanish police officers from the following car. They were beside their commander's vehicle so quickly that Alex guessed they had jumped out before it stopped moving.

Alex watched silently as a protective barrier of armed police surrounded the colonel and his passenger, including from within the building. Two policemen brandished Uzi-style automatics in full view.

There was a strange silence, and Alex could see some tension on the colonel's face. Obviously, Pendraza was on guard, perhaps even more than usual because of the events of the previous night. The doors to the Mercedes opened.

"Come along, Señorita," he said, switching back to Spanish. *"Vamos al trabajo.* Now that you know how I feel and who I suspect, let's go to work."

THIRTY-THREE

MADRID, SEPTEMBER 10, NOON

I don't know how I let them get the bloody drop on me," Gian Antonio Rizzo grumbled. He was in an understandably sour mood as he sat on the edge of his hospital bed.

Two women attended him. Normally Rizzo might have been pleased with such a development, but not today and not these women. According to their hospital name tags, which they wore on their lab coats, one was a female nurse named Eliza and the other was a doctor named Jenny Morin.

They stood before him, carefully examining the repair work that had been done on him from the night before. But at the moment, Rizzo was talking past them in English, to Colonel Pendraza and Alex, who stood respectfully to the side and allowed the medical people to work.

"I'm getting careless in my old age," he said, obviously giving no credence to what he was saying. "Well, there'll be repercussions for those two mutts who mugged me in that bar. I'll promise you that much!"

"I only found out what happened to you this morning," Alex said.

"I got my fingernails into one of them, you know," Rizzo said with satisfaction. "Fingernails!" The Rizzo of the hospital room — seething, aggrieved, injured — was not a happy man.

As the doctor and nurse examined Rizzo's scalp, he flexed his right hand for the colonel and for Alex. "Took a little of the skin off one of their faces," he said. "I wonder how he's enjoying shaving this morning."

On the right side of Rizzo's skull, above the ear and visible as Dr. Morin removed a bandage, was a red lump that had the size, shape, and texture of a purple plum. It was still red and angry, wet from a combination of antibiotic cream and blood that continued to seep, and it looked to Alex as if Rizzo had taken a few stitches to close the gash.

Rizzo continued his vent with a torrent of profanity until Dr. Morin, in English, told him in so many words to clean up his vocabulary.

"Sorry," Rizzo muttered. "Hey. But tell my visitors what happened, how they knocked me out."

Dr. Morin was a dark-haired lady of around forty with a formidable, intelligent face.

"They put a needle in his left buttock to knock him out," Dr. Morin said. "If his mouth was as foul last night as it has been since they brought him in, it's no wonder," she said. "I would have wanted to knock him out too."

"Very funny," Rizzo said.

"You're lucky it wasn't worse," she said.

"You don't know half of what was going on," Rizzo said.

"I'm not sure I want to," the doctor said good-naturedly.

Rizzo winced as the doctor examined the head wound with latexed fingers. "Am I going to be able to recite Greek poetry from memory after a shot to the head like that?" he said, his tone becoming mildly flirtatious.

"Could you recite it before?" she asked, sniffing out the old joke.

"No."

"Then you won't be able to now," she said, withdrawing her hands. "But the injury is clean and the X-rays didn't reveal a fracture. Your AIDS test from the needle came back negative too. You're lucky. Again."

"X-rays of my head revealed nothing," Rizzo said, glancing to Alex. "How do you like that?" Colonel Pendraza snorted slightly.

"Do you still have the headache?" the doctor asked.

"No."

"Be honest."

"Okay, I still have it," he said.

"You probably will for a few days," Dr. Morin said. She looked back to Alex and the colonel. "Senor Rizzo has a mild concussion also. There's going to be some discomfort to that."

Rizzo looked back to the doctor. "Tell them what they gave me in the needle," he said. "These are my work associates."

"An injectable form of flunitrazepam," the doctor said. "Powerful sedative. In America it's often used as a veterinary medicine for horses."

"A Mickey Finn with a needle," Rizzo said. "It's also one of those 'date rape' drugs." He cursed his assailants and again swore speedy vengeance upon them. The colonel gave a shrug that conveyed the notion that if Rizzo unofficially took out a couple of street felons, it would be a civic improvement.

Rizzo paused, then looked at Alex. "What happened on the street?" he asked. "Did you get that bloody pietà?"

"No."

"No?"

A glance to Colonel Pendraza from Alex. Pendraza lowered his gaze.

"It was an attempted ambush," Alex said. "Fortunately there was an extra gun in play and it covered my back. So I'm here to tell about it."

"Extra gun?" Rizzo asked, squinting. "What extra gun? Who?"

"We don't even know. When you're discharged, we'll give you access to what we know."

"I'm ready to go now," Rizzo said. "What do you think, doc? Can I be on my way?"

"I can't keep you here," she said, placing a fresh bandage on the wound and then stepping back from the patient. "But I'd like to. At least for a day or two for observation."

"Two days? Forget it." Rizzo said.

"It's your choice if you want to check yourself out. I can't stop you, but I'd advise against it. If a blood vessel broke suddenly in your brain, you'd be dead before an ambulance could get you here."

"And if one breaks while I'm here, I'll be dead before the nurse can get in from the coffee machine," he said. "I can sign myself out?"

"If you wish to," she said. "And again, I emphatically advise against it."

"Thank you. Show me where to sign," Rizzo said.

He got to his feet but was unsteady. Alex reached forward and extended a hand.

"You *really* want to check yourself out?" Dr. Morin asked.

"Bloody right, I do," Rizzo snapped. "The coffee here this morning was unbearable. I think they were trying to poison me."

Half an hour later, Colonel Pendraza, Alex, Rizzo, and their armed escorts were back on the street in front of the hospital. They climbed into the colonel's car, Rizzo sitting up front riding shotgun, Colonel Pendraza again in the rear with Alex.

Rizzo continued his diatribe. It was difficult to tell for whom he had the greater anger, the men in the bar who had assaulted him or the hospital staff that had treated him.

Nonetheless, another twenty minutes of weaving through morning traffic in Madrid and they pulled up at the side entrance to a nondescript brick building on the outskirts of the city, about two blocks from the Plaza de Toros de las Ventas, where the great bullfights were held.

The building was set between a dental office and a Chinese restaurant, on a busy narrow street that was cluttered with traffic. With no external marking other than a small sign, this was the office of the medical examiner for the Policia Nacional.

The car doors opened. Pendraza jumped out and walked at a quick pace, a phalanx of bodyguards around him, Alex, and the unsteady Rizzo.

A few minutes later, the three of them stood over two steel slabs where a pair of male bodies in red canvas bags were set forth for their examination.

Alex winced. Pendraza and Rizzo stood stony faced.

The wounds had been stitched shut and the dried blood had been cleansed away. But the gunshots had smashed into the heads, necks, and upper chests, ripping away flesh and pounding the bones of the recipients. Each corpse was missing part of the skull. Each man had been shot through the heart and neck. Alex had seen many corpses in her life. Too many, in fact, and the events of Kiev came rushing back to her as she looked at these. And yet these, in their own way, were particularly horrifying.

Never mind the fact that they might have killed her. The gunman who had covered her back had dispatched these two men with an unholy precision.

One half of one man's head had been hammered away by bullets and the remaining eye socket was hollow. The other man's face had been completely smashed in by gunfire so horribly that Alex wondered whether it had been done intentionally to make identification difficult, or pathologically out of some unknown vengeance.

"These were the two men in police uniform?" Pendraza said. "To the extent that you can recognize them."

Rizzo looked at the corpse that had half a head remaining. His eyes slid back to Alex. He gave her a nod.

"I agree," she said. "That's one. Not much question really if you picked up the bodies at the scene of the shooting. Any identification yet?" she asked.

"No," Colonel Pendraza said. "They weren't police; you know that. Exactly who they were and why you were targeted, we don't know. I can only assume it has something to do with the pietà, but you've been in this line of work. It could have been left over business from something else."

"Possibly," she said.

"We'll do DNA and fingerprints to the extent possible," the colonel said. "Dental isn't possible because the oral cavities have been destroyed. We have some bullet fragments. Those might tell us something. Anything else here?" he asked. "Either of you? Any thoughts at all?"

"Just the machinelike precision of the shooter," Alex said. "I've never seen anything like it before. And I'm not sure I will again."

"Unless it saves your life again," Rizzo added. "Good Lord."

"Unless it saves my life," she said, "yes. Point well taken."

"And then there's the picture that begins to emerge," Alex said. "Two men posing as police officers, another two in the bar, along with a woman. Whoever we're dealing with begins to look like part of a fairly extensive organization. And then there's the actual museum thieves who probably were none of these people."

"I like the way you think," Pendraza said. "I agree with you."

Colonel Pendraza motioned to a lab technician, a young woman in blue scrubs. She rezipped the bags, then summoned more help from the next office. The team at the morgue would return the bodies back to the deep freeze.

THIRTY-FOUR

MADRID, SEPTEMBER 10, EARLY AFTERNOON

Alex moved quietly through the lobby of the Ritz and took the elevator up. The hallway on the fifth floor was quiet. A maid was working with a vacuum cleaner in a room two away from hers. The maid gave Alex a polite nod as Alex passed.

Alex came to her own door, paused out of caution, listened, heard nothing from within, and swiped her room card in the slot. She pushed the door forward. The door was still moving when Alex saw two legs lazily folded, belonging to a man in a suit sitting on her sofa.

"LaDuca!" roared out a booming male voice. "Finally! About time you got here!"

American, with slightly mid-Atlantic Coast inflections. It was a voice that she recognized instantly. She pushed the door the rest of the way open, reaching by instinct for her new weapon at the same time. The legs unfolded and shifted toward her. She stepped forward without closing the door, her pistol aloft and pointed.

The man looked at her. The man's hands were in plain sight, holding no weapon.

"Oh, honestly, Alex. Don't be overly dramatic." Mark McKinnon, the CIA's chief honcho assigned to western Europe, whom she had most recently worked with in the ragged aftermath of Kiev.

McKinnon gave her a smile. There was a bottle of Bushmill's Irish whiskey on the table in front of him, with a bucket of ice and a bottle of water. There was a glass in his hand. He seemed more relaxed than he should have been, but it was Bushmill's Eighteen Year Old. The good stuff relaxes a man real fast.

But someone else was in the room too, and that someone was behind the door.

She stepped away but was not quick enough. From the other side of the door came a lithe, agile man of about six feet. He had his hand on her pistol like a velvet hammer, quickly turning her hand upward against the thumb, removing the pistol quickly, and taking it from her. He did all this with such a deft touch that he managed to not hurt her at all, much like a parent removing a dangerous toy from a child's possession.

Then with a leg, before she could say anything, he pushed the door shut and they stood eye to eye.

"Hello again," he said. No smile. No emotion.

"Come on in, LaDuca! Have a drink with us!" boomed McKinnon, finally standing. "And relax, would you? It's about time you formally met Peter Chang. Peter's come all the way from Peking. I know you've seen him before, and I think you're going to like working with him. Know what? My guess is that you already do!"

Peter Chang smiled very slightly. Then it was gone again.

Up close, he had movie star good looks. An Asian Adonis in a fine suit with a classic Western tie and a light blue shirt. His eyes were dark and sharp, his stature strong but nimble. His hair was perfect. Werewolf of London, she found herself thinking.

Peter gave his head a slight nod. He checked her pistol for ammunition and safety catch, and, with a little showboating Jackie Chan–style move, flipped it around in his hand so that the barrel was pointing away from her.

"Nice piece," he said. "New acquisition? You didn't have it last night."

"If I had," she said, "I might have used it."

"That would not have been good," he said. "If you had tried, one of us wouldn't be here right now."

Then he returned the weapon to her, still loaded.

"My apologies if I scared you last night," he said.

His English was impeccable, just like his marksmanship had been. He could have worked on Saville Row as a tailor or at Claridge's as a hotel manager.

Her nerves settled slightly. She took back her Browning, then took McKinnon up on his invitation and sat down. It was, after all, her room, even if the taxpayers were footing the bill.

"So, LaDuca," said McKinnon, as Alex found a place in a comfortable chair. "How are you enjoying your visit to Spain . . . so far?"

"I've been here in Spain before," she said. "More than once. There was a tax case back in 2004. The FBI sent me because they needed someone who spoke Spanish and French."

"So you know your way around?" he asked.

"As I said, business a few times. And that's aside from the trip I made when I was a college student."

Chang sat quietly, his eyes set upon her like a pair of compass needles pointing north.

"Yeah, I guess those were the days," McKinnon said. "College years. I remember them myself."

"Prewar Berlin and the rest, huh?" she said. "Marlene Dietrich in the clubs, right?"

"Ouch! That was nasty."

"So is finding you here. The lobby wouldn't work for you to wait?"

Chang followed the repartee back and forth.

"No, it wouldn't," McKinnon said. "Not with Peter at my side, not with the security cameras all over the bloody place, and not with a couple of Madrid cops — who weren't Madrid cops — shot dead last night. What a bloody mess. And anyway, what's the point of our agency having master keys to every hotel in Madrid if we don't use them from time to time?"

"I have no idea," she said.

"Oh, I'm sure you do," he said. "And by the way, your file did say you were here on the 2004 tax case and that you did visit Malaga with a boyfriend named Damien in 1997. Damien later went into the military, did you know that?"

"No, I didn't. I haven't seen him for more than a decade. So why don't you tell me something else I don't know, like what you're doing here and what's going on, at least from your jaded end of things. Who were the people in the cop uniforms and who jabbed a needle into my partner last night?"

"Bullfight fans. Tourists. The opposition. Liberal Democrats. How should I know? That's partly what we're gathered here so happily to discover."

There was also some bottled water on the coffee table in front of her. She made sure the cap was still factory-sealed, then opened it and poured some into a glass.

"Can I interest you in a whiskey?" he asked. "It's already on your room-service bill, so I might as well offer you a drink."

"Maybe later," she said. "Maybe I'll need a drink after I hear what you have to say."

McKinnon laughed. "Spain is a funny place," he mused. "The present is all caught up with the past, and the past is something most people don't want to talk about. Yet it keeps repeating itself, doesn't it? When I was a young case officer in Madrid back in the 1980s, Reagan visited. Are you old enough to remember him?"

She was, of course. "No, Mark," she said, "but I studied him in history class. Same as Washington, Lincoln, and Elvis Presley."

But McKinnon was on verbal cruise control. All accelerator and no brakes.

"Reagan visited," he continued, "and after a bourbon or two, got away from his script. The president made an uncalled for remark about how it was too bad that the Americans who fought in the International Brigades had fought for the '*wrong* side.' They fought *against* Franco, in other words, instead of being on the side of Franco, Hitler, Mussolini, and the long and wonderful tradition of fascism and anti-Semitism in this hot, unwashed country. Well, you can imagine how that went over. The Spanish Left organized a ceremony of *desagravio*. Do you know what that is, LaDuca?"

"It means 'atonement' in English," she said. "Except I also know from my time here before that there's a strange Spanish ceremony called a *desagravio* that can be made on behalf of someone else who may not feel apologetic at all."

"Exactly," McKinnon said, punctuating the air with a finger. "You got it. In this case, the unrepentant one was President Reagan. The so-called atonement ceremony took place in the Plaza Colón. You know, that square where they got a statue of Columbus?"

"Hence the name of the square," she said. But if McKinnon got the dig, he wasn't letting it show.

"Remember, this was 1986," he said. "There were still a number of broken-down old *brigadistas* alive, people who had fought against Franco in the 1930s. I was sent to keep an eye on the event. The Plaza Colón was hung with the old flag of the Spanish Republicans, a genuinely ugly, meaningless old rag with vertical purple, white, and red stripes. It looked like a cheap beach towel from a gas station giveaway. Anyway, the old anthem was played, one of those surprisingly bouncy 'workers' paradise jingles' from the early days of Bolshevism, before the whole cause of Communism was thoroughly discredited. The main speaker was a man named Enríque Líster. Fifty years earlier as a young Communist, Líster had been one of the more effective self-taught generals of the Republican Army that fought against Franco. If I remember correctly, and there's a chance I don't because my brain has begun its voyage into the sunset, the ceremony took place in an auditorium *under* the plaza. I was in this highly uncomfortable seat, admiring the beauty of all the Spanish wives. Anyway, it wasn't an important event, really. Nothing happened except a bunch of decrepit old lefties blew off some steam about Reagan and America. But I had a real sense of history, you know what I mean? A feeling that I was watching a final curtain call from a long-passed age. And yet, know what? All those old polarized elements from Spanish society? There're still around today."

"Quite correct. I've seen a bit of that recently," Alex said, thinking of Colonel Pendraza.

McKinnon poured himself another whiskey. "You'll see a lot more before you're safely out of here," he said. "Count on that!"

The bottle was down about four fingers. Chang didn't have a glass going. McKinnon sipped some water also. Alex was about to interrupt, but McKinnon appeared as if he were about to add something. She rarely interrupted men when they were drinking because they frequently said too much, later to their displeasure.

"I had the same feeling around the same era here in Spain when I attended a lecture at a Catholic school by a man named Serrano Súñer," McKinnon continued. "Ever heard of Súñer?"

Alex shook her head. "No," she said. "Don't know the name."

"That's because you're too young. What are you now, Alex? Mid thirties?"

"Same as last time you saw me which was two months ago," she said. "Plus you know I'm twenty-nine if you just read my c.v."

"Peter?" he asked, looking to the other guest, almost surprising him. "*Súñer?* Name set off any alarms for you?"

For the first time, Chang spoke. "Súñer was Franco's brother-in-law, wasn't he?" Chang answered.

"Exactly," McKinnon answered. "Bright fellow, you are. And you're the same age as Alex, I'd guess."

"I'm forty-one," Chang said.

"That proves my point," McKinnon said. "Anyway, in the 1930s, during the Civil War, Súñer represented Spain in talks with Hitler. Hitler wanted Spain to get into the big war in Europe. Súñer suggested the creation of a national 'movement' out of the Falange and the Carlists to match the fascists in Italy and Nazis in Germany. Then they'd all go to war together and keep the Americans and Brits busy on the western front while Hitler could go at it with the Ruskies in the east. Well, Franco wasn't buying into that one. He was determined to keep Spain *out* of World War II to make sure he had some soldiers left in case Uncle Joe Stalin marched his Red Bastard soldiers right up to the Pyrenees. And he *did* stay out of it. But the dispute ended in a falling out between the two men. Not really important anymore," McKinnon said.

"Then why mention it?" Alex asked.

"What?" It was obvious he wasn't quite in the bag, but well on his way.

"Why mention it?"

"Well, it was a curious feeling," McKinnon said. "To speak with a man who had personally conversed with Hitler."

A moment passed. McKinnon rubbed his eyes and looked at his watch. "God!" he said. "We've been here since 10:00 a.m. Let me hit the boy's room, then we'll talk more, okay?"

"Okay," Alex said.

Chang gave her a shrug. McKinnon rose with effort and wandered off to the washroom, leaving Alex and Peter Chang to stare at each other.

"Thanks," Alex finally said, "for saving my life."

"No big deal," Chang said.

"Actually, to me it was."

THIRTY-FIVE

MADRID, SEPTEMBER 10, EARLY AFTERNOON

For Maria Elena Gómez, the new week was not going well.

José Luis, her new partner this week in Pedro's absence, was an even bigger pain to work with than she had imagined. On their first day together, he had been as aggravating as any man she had ever had to work with. He was slow and inattentive to detail. His attention would wander, he would want to sneak off for cigarettes, and he had a *machísmo* attitude that she found unbearable, an attitude best exemplified by her doing all the work and him supervising. Or so it seemed.

She had had more than enough of him as they inspected the electrical junctions at the Sevilla station in the old city. While Maria was busy noting a frayed cable that could short circuit if any rain swept down into the station, she looked up to find him not taking the notes as she suggested, but rather watching a gaggle of American girls in shorts and minis, as they waited for a train.

"Are you here to look or are you here to work?" she asked him.

"I'm here to look," he said.

"Then why don't you find another partner?" she snapped.

"Because you're prettier than most of the cows who work for the Metro."

"I should report you for a remark like that," she said. "Maybe I will."

"I'll deny I ever said it," he smirked. "You know how women imagine things. If you come on to them, they complain. If you don't, they're insulted."

She handed him a clipboard, almost throwing it at him. The American girls turned and watched the argument and grinned. One of them whipped out a disposable camera and snapped a flash picture. Maria felt humiliated.

"Just shut up and work," she said tersely as a train rumbled into the station. "Or I will report you. I swear."

He growled but finally got the message, taking the proper notes as she gave them to him, filling out the proper maintenance request that would be turned in at the end of the day.

They track-walked to the next station, Banco de España, in near silence, moving slowly. They twice stepped to the side en route when the red warning lines cautioned them about an advancing train. They found nothing worthy of note in the tunnel. Then when they emerged at the Banco de España station, José Luis was at it again. When they came up into the station, they were confronted by a huge Real Madrid billboard featuring the goalkeeper, Iker Casillas making a brilliant diving one-handed save.

José Luis took the occasion to sing the praises of Real Madrid.

"I support Atlético," she said sharply.

He laughed. *"Sabes, no comprendo que una bonita mujer sensata como tú seas hincha de ese equipo de perdedores."* I don't understand how a pretty girl like you could be a fan of a bunch of losers like that.

"Por que no te callas!" Why don't you just shut up? "For the rest of the week."

José Luis smirked in response. She knew that lurking beneath the surface, he was one of those men who didn't feel women should even have these jobs walking the tracks. She was in a genuinely foul mood by now. The attack on Atlético she even felt as a shot at her late father. She felt sadness mixing with her anger and wished the week was already over.

But it wasn't. Not by a long shot.

THIRTY-SIX

MADRID, SEPTEMBER 10, MID-AFTERNOON

McKinnon lurched back into the living room of the suite. He sat down hard, a crash landing of sorts, into the big chair.

Alex turned to him.

"Let's talk about *The Pietà of Malta*," Alex finally said. "And maybe you can also bring me up to speed on why we're here and why two people have already been shot dead right in front of me."

"Of course," McKinnon said. "But everyone in this room needs to get to know everyone else in this room. Peter, you've been here in Spain before, also, haven't you?"

"Several times," he said. "This is one of my favorite places in Europe."

Turning to him, Alex asked, "And you speak Spanish, I assume?"

"*Claro que sí, Señorita*," he said. "Spanish, French, English, Cantonese, and Mandarin," he said. "Interchangeably."

"Peter works for the Chinese government," McKinnon said.

"Which branch? You don't exactly look like a trade delegate, looking to dump a lot of cheap toasters on the *Marcado Común*."

"The Guojia Anquan Bu," he said without a smile.

"The Ministry of State Security?" she asked. "Peking's version of the CIA."

"Exactly," McKinnon said. "Our counterparts, and, as is often the case with counterparts, sometimes our interests coincide. As in this case. Let me backtrack. Mr. Chang has worked with the Agency in Europe before."

"So the Chinese government has an interest in *The Pietà of Malta* also?" Alex asked.

"Very much so," McKinnon said. "*The Pietà of Malta*. It's like a 'black bird' — a Maltese Falcon — for our new century."

Alex waited for a moment. McKinnon's eyes jumped to Peter's

then back again. "When you were at the embassy earlier this week, Alex, you attended a briefing by a Señor Rivera, the curator of the Museo Arqueológico."

"That's correct."

"And the curator mentioned that this missing artifact had a tie to St. Francis, the highly revered saint, at least according to legend."

"That's right. That was mentioned," Alex answered. "And if the case is so important to the two of you, why weren't the two of you at the briefing?"

"I wasn't invited. And I wasn't even aware of the case till Peter contacted me."

"That doesn't make sense, Mark. You had someone in that meeting on your agency's behalf," she said, thinking of Rizzo.

"Very true. And as you yourself know, sometimes the Indian chiefs don't know what the braves and warriors are up to. May I go on?"

"Please do."

"I've done a bit of study on this myself in the last week," McKinnon said. "First eight years of my own schooling, I went to Catholic schools in Chicago. Nuns. Franciscan order. A bunch of tough-assed old Irish biddies with red faces, black-and-white habits, and the usual fondness for hitting you with a ruler. So I know a bit about St. Francis and how he is known in the modern world."

"In what sense?" she asked.

"His evangelism. Do you know where I'm heading with this?" McKinnon continued.

"I discussed the point with Señor Rivera yesterday," Alex said. "So what's the point? How does this impact the theft of the pietà?"

"On our black bird? Follow along. The US government was asked to help the Spaniards recover *The Pietà of Malta*," McKinnon said. "Were any tangible leads offered to you in your meeting yesterday morning?"

"No," she said. "None. A lot of information, but no leads."

"So you were in a roomful of people poised to accomplish nothing, in other words," McKinnon said.

"Keep a lid on that wise-guy stuff, okay, Mark? You know how these things work as well as I do," she said.

"Sure. But that's where counterpart agencies would appear to have common goals. Peter's government wishes to see that the pietà is returned also."

"What interests do the Chinese have?"

"Peter will get into that with you later today in a one-on-one," McKinnon said. "Right now, suffice it to say that Peter represented a wealthy buyer in Peking. The buyer had his interests, and his interests were betrayed."

"A wealthy individual buyer or the Beijing government?" she asked immediately, turning toward Peter.

"For now, let's say both," Mark said. "In China today, these things usually overlap."

"Understood. Betrayed how?" she pressed.

"They paid," Peter said, "and the bird, the pietà, was not delivered."

"Hence, Peter's presence in Europe," McKinnon said. "He works much the way you do, Alex. Assessing problems, inventing solutions to them. Sometimes painfully difficult solutions."

"I'm flattered by the comparison," Alex said.

"As am I," said Peter, interjecting politely.

"But here's where we get into the hardball," Mark McKinnon said. "We feel the larger part of the operation, if there is one, might be against the United States in some way. America has a huge number of targets in Spain, as you know. One can only protect so much for so long. And a high-profile US inquiry into the *motives* behind the theft might accelerate whatever plans are out there against us."

"But," she said, picking up his line of thought, "if we were able to work through another agency, with Chinese help for example ..."

"Exactly. There would be no tip-off to the opposition. It would look as if we're just trying to get a chunk of granite back for the dumb Spaniards who were careless enough to let it get stolen in the first place. So let's look at the big picture here," McKinnon said, turning back and focusing on Alex. "You're now involved here in the black-bird investigation. What attributes do you bring to the table? Well, there are all the obvious ones: brains, looks, ability to penetrate certain circles and blend in, a knowledge of several languages, some of which might not seem to apply to this case but might in a broader sense. But often it's not *what* you know, it's *who* you know."

She shook her head. "Still not with you," she said.

McKinnon and Peter exchanged a glance.

"I understand you speak Russian," McKinnon said. "And Ukrainian."

"So do several million other people."

"Forgive my subtlety," McKinnon said. Then he ambushed her. "You had a previous relationship with a Ukrainian mobster named Yuri Federov, didn't you?"

The question jolted her. It took her a second to answer, to sense where he was leading.

"I wouldn't call it 'a relationship,'" she finally answered, putting aside any possible innuendo. "I worked a case earlier this year in which he was a principal. Again, you know that because you worked the same case."

"Of course. Your last report suggested that Federov had withdrawn to Switzerland, possibly into a semi- or complete retirement. He has also dropped off the Agency radar screen, which would indicate that he has withdrawn from the business. That, or he's dead. Have you seen him recently?"

"No. Not since I saw him in a hospital room in Paris," she said.

He held her gaze.

"You're sure?" he asked, seeming more sober than he had all day. The question was a direct challenge. "Good will is flowing through my veins by the quart today, LaDuca, so if you *have* seen him —"

"Right!" she said, cutting him off. "I'd forgotten! We had a late dinner together a week ago at Taillevant in Paris. Then we crossed the channel and spent a wonderful weekend in Brighton, knocking back lager and fish and chips. Just a good Episcopalian girl recovering from the death of a fiancé by bedding her six-cylinder Russian hood." For good measure, she followed all this with an uncharacteristic but colorful reflection on Mark's ancestry.

Unwavering, McKinnon didn't miss a beat. "Come, come, LaDuca. But you *do* know how to find him. Your final report on that Kiev case suggested that you might."

"I *might*. It depends on whether the information he gave me is good or not. So I don't know if I do or don't have a way to contact him, because I've never tried."

"So then you have an address filed somewhere?" McKinnon pressed.

"Not so much an address, but a procedure."

"Would you mind sharing it with us?"

"Seriously, I would. I have the procedure memorized, but right now, I can't quite recall it."

McKinnon sighed and took a long sip of whiskey. Peter Chang's eyes were like a terrier's, fascinated, sharp as tacks, working McKinnon and Alex back and forth.

"Should I remind you that you're talking to a superior?" McKinnon said.

"Should I remind you that you're not acting like one," she said. "Should I also remind you that as a member of the CIA you also have no hierarchical superiority over someone working for Treasury or the FBI? You're in your world, I'm in mine, and I don't have to do squat for you."

"True, true. However, somewhere in this mess about the new black bird, we need some interagency cooperation and some access to Comrade Federov. We need access if for no other reason than to pick his disgusting mind. And the best girl to pimp that access for us would be a girl named Alex LaDuca. So consider this a cross-agency request already cleared by your 'jefe' Mike Gamburian in Washington."

"You think Federov had something to do with the disappearance?" ignoring McKinnon's metaphors.

"Not necessarily do I think that," McKinnon said, "but look at the big picture. Federov has dealt in stolen munitions and war material in the past, and he has been involved in art thefts. He once brokered a deal for a submarine to Colombia drug runners. Whether he's retired from crime or not, and assuming he's alive, we could bet that he has the phone number of someone who has the phone number of someone in whom we may have an interest."

"Sure," she said. "But you haven't told me how this connects with *The Pietà of Malta*."

McKinnon raised an eyebrow and looked at Chang. "Peter?" he said.

"Alex," Chang said, "if you don't mind, Yuri Federov's name came up when I did some business in Switzerland. The business was with a gentleman who most likely brokered the sale of the bird. A Colonel Tissot. And I use the term 'gentleman' very loosely."

"And what was said?" she asked. "Between you and Tissot?"

"There was nothing specific," Chang said. "Nothing damning, no particular bit of business," Peter answered. "But from what I learned from Monsieur Tissot, it was as if Federov was someone that needed to be worked around. Maybe he was not involved in the case itself, but the case was in his orbit, his underworld hegemony."

"Can you show me the reference?" Alex asked.

McKinnon picked it up from there. "Who needs a reference? Whether Federov is alive or not, his corporations out of Odessa still have financial interests in shipping all over the Black Sea and the Mediterranean. That's enough right there to question a hood like that. You know what shipping is like in those stretches of water: you show me a boat, I'll show you smugglers."

"Not to mention the fact that ships of that nature would be excellent conduits for any sort of contraband," Chang added. "From weapons to stolen art objects."

"So," McKinnon continued, "Federov, your Ukrainian bottom pincher, might be able to tell us something." McKinnon held a long pause. "If only we had someone who can find him."

"He's Russian, by the way," she said.

"Okay, your *Russian* bottom pincher."

"*Now* you want me to find Federov," she said, turning back to McKinnon. "And then grill him?"

"Not exactly," McKinnon answered. "We want him to find you. *Then* you grill him. Did you ever see *Jurassic Park*, where they put the little nanny goat out as bait to lure the dinosaur? In this case, you're the nanny goat."

Peter was shaking his head.

"And why should Yuri Federov talk to me?" Alex asked. "Where's my leverage to get any information out of him?"

"He still has a tax situation in front of the IRS," McKinnon said. "It limits his business dealings around the world, exposes some of his personal assets in the United States and its territories, and restricts his entry into the United States."

"So I could offer some flexibility on his tax problems?" she asked.

"That's what I'm saying," McKinnon said. "As long as his information proves useful. Check with your bossman Mike about that. The fix is in with Treasury if you can finagle a deal. Does this have a logic to it?"

She pondered it and let go with some information from her side.

"My instructions, if I ever wanted to get in touch," she finally explained, "were to go to Geneva and register at a certain hotel under my real name. The next day I was to have lunch alone at a certain restaurant. I'm supposed to go there and ask for a captain named Koller and tell him that his aunt from New York sends her regards. I'm to sit by the Lake of Geneva reading a book at eleven the next morning. I will be met by someone, possibly even Federov, himself. I'm to repeat the procedure until he contacts me. Or until I get tired of not being contacted."

"So he lives in the Geneva area?"

"That's my guess, but I don't know that as a fact."

McKinnon smiled. "There," he said. "After all that, wasn't that easy? Peter will go with you to Switzerland, keep a discreet distance, and try not to kill everyone who makes a pass at you." McKinnon said. "Think of Peter as your bodyguard, your backup. He seems to have shown a certain talent on that front. Would that work for you? If I were you, I'd be very pleased to have a gun like Peter watching my backside. Did you ever see *The Bodyguard* with Whitney Houston and Kevin Costner? Think of Peter as Kevin Costner, but with some Jackie Chan factored in."

"All right," she said after a moment's thought. "That might work."

"The only other question now," McKinnon said, "is when can you leave for Geneva? It's about a two-hour flight from here, but that won't make any difference because you don't want to fly. No flight records. And you should carry a gun, which I see you already have, so you can't exactly do a Texas two-step through the airports."

"Tomorrow?" she asked. "The day after tomorrow?"

"The day after tomorrow would be perfect," he said, "if you could get your butt on the move that fast. Can that be done, considering this is an urgent request from those who sign the checks that allow you to cavort at a hotel like the Ritz in Madrid?"

"Okay," she answered. "That can be done."

"Perfect," McKinnon said.

Then Peter turned to her. "I thought you and I might have dinner tonight," Chang said. "Get to know each other a little better. How does that sound?"

She looked him squarely in his sharp, dark eyes.

"Dangerous," she answered. "But the answer is yes. I owe you something, don't I?"

Peter leaned back in his chair. For the first time, he smiled broadly.

THIRTY-SEVEN

MARSEILLES, SEPTEMBER 10, LATE EVENING

Hassan Lazzari, a Turk by way of Sicily, sat nervously in a nearly deserted café on the grand port in Marseilles. He was nursing a coffee and was positioned carefully at a small table away from everyone else. He sat there like a large stone, his posture erect, his features fagged, his face unshaven for the last few days.

It was late in the evening, night to most people. Lazzari was looking over the lights of the harbor and the tourists walking by the piers. Far up on the hills, overlooking the harbor, stood the Chateau d'If where the Count of Monte Cristo had been imprisoned, at least in the famous novel, and long before a popular sandwich was named for him.

Well, Hassan Lazzari didn't feel like having a sandwich and didn't much feel like any more coffee either. But he did feel imprisoned, imprisoned by his nerves and a sense of impending disaster.

The coffee was lukewarm and he had lost interest in it. He was there to become rich, to accept a bag full of money, but so far nothing had happened. He started to slouch. Then he straightened up in his chair when he saw a Frenchman approach him and figured it was the man he was waiting for. He figured that, because the approaching stranger — with hands visible — was carrying a small tote bag and looking right at Lazzari.

The Frenchman approached the table. "Mind if I join you?" he asked. They spoke French.

"Not if you brought the money," the Turk said.

The Frenchman indicated a small duffel bag next to him. "Would I be here without the money?" he asked.

"You might be," the Turk said. "No way of knowing."

The Frenchman smiled indulgently.

Lazzari leaned back and allowed his outer shirt to fall open. Under

171

his left armpit there was a powerhouse of an automatic pistol. The Frenchman's eyes fell onto it, then lifted back into the Turk's eyes.

The message was clear. No nonsense. Nonsense would be dealt with quickly, efficiently, and brutally. That's the message that Lazzari was sending.

The Frenchman put the bag on an empty seat. The Turk looked at it nervously, reached to open it, but flicked his eyes back and forth between the bag and the delivery person.

"You're Jean-Claude?" the Turk asked.

"I'm Jean-Claude," the Frenchman said.

"How do I know that?"

"You don't. And why do you care, anyway? Your money is there. Count it if you like."

"I'm not going to pile up twenty-thousand euros on a café table, you fool," Lazzari said.

"Then we'll go to a back room if you like. I know the management here. The evening man Fajit is a friend of mine."

"No back rooms," the Turk said. "No friends."

As if to reassure his client, Jean-Claude cautiously pushed up his shirt sleeves and laid his hands on the table.

"What might I do to put you at ease?" Jean-Claude asked.

"You can keep quiet, to start with."

Then, impulsively, the Turk sighed and leaned forward. He leaned so far forward that he lifted up slightly from his seat. Reaching out, he roughly shoved his hands all over Jean-Claude's shoulders, ribs, and waist, frisking him thoroughly. He groped at Jean-Claude's crotch, under it and around it, searching for any trace of a weapon.

The Frenchman kept still and did nothing to protest.

The Turk eased back down in his seat.

"Why would I come here to deceive you?" Jean-Claude said. "You give me too much credit. You're the one who has outsmarted us and the one who will profit tonight. Count the money," he said, nodding toward the bag. "Everything you asked for is there."

The Turk pulled the canvas duffel back to him. Without pulling any money out, he kept Jean-Claude and the rest of the café in view as he quickly inventoried the money.

It looked as if it was all there. He pulled out a few banknotes at random and scrutinized them. He liked what he saw, which had a calming effect.

"It looks good," he said. "All right. It looks good." He closed the duffel and prepared to stand. He still didn't like this setup. He didn't like it at all and wanted to be out of there as quickly as possible.

He looked back at Jean-Claude.

"I will give you a few words of warning," the Turk said. "I'll tell you one time. I should be back in Italy by noon tomorrow. If I am not, keep in mind that I am Sicilian in addition to being Turkish. I have relatives and friends. If anything happens to me while I'm transporting this money, you personally will be hunted down within twenty-four hours by some of the most savage killers in Europe. Then you will be tortured with knifes. You will be left to die slowly in an unspeakable way that will make you wish that you had never been born. Is that clear?"

Jean-Claude again smiled tolerantly.

"You've made your point and you've made it very clearly," Jean-Claude said. "I think of this as part of the cost of doing business. A tax, so to speak. I don't wish any aggravation past this evening any more than you do."

"You will not hear from us," said the Turk who for the second time attempted to leave. But Jean-Claude held his hand, keeping him at the table.

The Turk's other hand inched toward his weapon.

"There is no need for a firearm," Jean-Claude said disdainfully. "But now I just need assurance from you. I need your word to me that this is the only 'tax' the people in my organization are going to need to pay to you. I've already removed the little 'bugs' that you were so conniving as to place in our shipment of merchandise. And I have had the entire shipment searched millimeter by millimeter to make sure there are no other little hidden presents for us. So actually, you would have difficulty locating us after our mission is complete. So let's just be clear that neither will ever see the other again under any circumstances."

"You have our word," said the Turk.

"Then you have ours as well."

Jean-Claude extended a hand. It was firm, strong, and dry. Their hands clasped.

"Travel wisely with the money," Jean-Claude said.

The Turk gave a little snort in return.

"I have an accomplice with a rifle in a window across the street," Lazzari said. "You will give me ten minutes to leave. If you move from this table, you'll be gunned down like a rabbit. If you reach under your clothing to find a weapon I may have missed, you'll be gunned down also. If you make any effort to come looking for me or my brother, you will also be killed. Understand?"

"I understand perfectly," Jean-Claude answered. "I'm in fear of my life here. There is no way I would dare to do anything."

He sat back down and smiled.

"That's good. That's good." Lazzari said. Yet somehow, Jean-Claude was too calm. He hadn't sounded convincing to his business associate.

Fretfully, Lazzari turned on his heels. He moved swiftly along the narrow passageway between café tables. He hit the sidewalk, his pace accelerating. Jean-Claude watched him go, doing a slow count of seconds as the Turk disappeared with a bag of money.

THIRTY-EIGHT

MADRID, SEPTEMBER 10, LATE EVENING

They sat at a table that evening, Alex and Peter Chang, at a small restaurant in the Bailén amidst remnants of Moorish Madrid and in the shadow of the grand Basilica de San Francisco. They were in a small room with burnt-ochre walls and oak paneling, a quiet chamber behind a noisy brass tapas bar. They sat in a booth in the back that afforded both of them cover, as well as a view of both the entrance and the exit.

In Spanish, with an affable young waiter, they ordered a dinner of tuna steaks in soy and ginger with a bottle of Rioja. When the waiter departed, Alex switched the conversation back to English.

"You speak Spanish with a very slight accent," she said, "but your English is perfect. Better than most native speakers, I'd say," she said. "And what there is of an accent almost sounds British, but with a few American inflections thrown in. How did that happen?"

"I was born in Hong Kong and grew up there," he said. "I went to British schools on the island and then later in England when I was older. My mother was a teacher, my father owned a shipping company. Only five ships, but papa kept them busy."

"Only five, huh?" she said. "That's five more than most people."

"Then, when I was in my early twenties, I spent a few years in New York."

"Doing what? Working?"

"Political studies. Columbia University. New York City," Peter Chang said. "I was a teaching fellow and earned my master's degree. I lived in New York for five years. I loved the place. Broadway theater. The smut of Times Square. Two ballparks and the dirty pretzels from the vendor who was always outside the School of International Relations on 110th Street. What a city!"

He finally grinned. There was a chilliness to Peter, she noted. She had to push hard to get past a cautious exterior. She wondered what lurked beneath, passion or poison.

"As you know, Hong Kong was a crown colony of the United Kingdom when I was growing up," he continued. "My family remained even after the transfer of the island's sovereignty to the People's Republic of China in 1997. I went back, horrified that Peking now controlled the island. But it wasn't as bad as I'd guessed. One thing led to another, and the new government offered me a very comfortable career."

"Impressive résumé," she said.

"You flatter me," he said.

"But hardly as impressive as your abilities with a pistol," she said. "Or should I say, *pair* of pistols? Where did you learn *those* skills?"

"I was taken aside, given special treatment, special training. Same as yourself."

The waiter arrived with the bottle of Rioja and the conversation jumped back to Spanish. Peter did the tasting, gave his approval, then asked for the wine to be decanted so it could air. The dialogue between Alex and Peter stayed on small matters until the food arrived and, not by surprise, turned out to be spectacular.

Peter lowered his tones and switched back to English when the conversation turned serious again. "Let me bring you up to date on *The Pietà of Malta*," he said. "Our own intelligence knew the trail of a transaction involving the bird. Black market sale: $1,250,000 from the sale of a stolen piece of art. The physical transaction of the artwork was made in Switzerland with the money returning to Spain by electronic transfer."

"So someone paid to have it stolen?"

"Someone paid *a lot* to have it stolen," Peter said. "Which brings us to motivations."

"Arguably it could have been a private collector," she said. "One of those immensely wealthy people who get their charge merely out of possessing the item. Or it could have been stolen by people who wanted to raise money. But if the money returned to Spain, what was the purpose of it?"

"Here we get into the notion of artwork financing criminal activity or terror activity. And the latter would most likely be aimed at America or Americans," he said. "Listen, another agent from my agency went to Switzerland to intercept the transaction. The agent carried five checks on the Bank of Hong Kong to complete the transaction."

"And?"

"He was murdered when he was supposed to retrieve the carving from an old monastery," he explained. "Then his body was dumped in the mountains. Concurrent with his disappearance, the checks were cashed through an Arab bank in Ri'yad. And as I mentioned, much of the money eventually came back to Spain by electronic transfer. It was laundered first through Zurich, then through a bank in the Cayman Islands."

Alex picked up on the explanation.

"So whoever was brokering the deal had your agent killed, took his money, then sent the pietà in another direction. Perhaps to the Middle East. Or at least, that's what we speculate."

"You could put forth that theory," Peter said.

"Do *you* put forth that thesis?" she asked.

"Most of it. Or variations on it. It's the foundation of what I'm working with."

"Bad way to do business," she said, harkening back to those who had brokered the sale of the stolen art.

"Yes. It's a *very* shortsighted way to do business," said Chang with a certain iciness. "Selling the same stolen art work twice. Or at least twice. It leaves everyone unhappy and puts in motion some very unfortunate repercussions."

"I can imagine," Alex said.

"It was enough reason for me to fly to Switzerland to arrange for the agent's body to be sent home to China," he said. He paused very slightly. "While I was there, I picked up where the other agent left off and embarked myself on the trail of the bird and the transactions involving it. How's your tuna?"

"It's fine."

"How's the wine?"

"You're consuming the same meal as I am. Both are excellent. Why are you changing the subject?"

"I'm not."

"When were you in Switzerland?"

"You *are* a lady tiger, aren't you? Persistent and not easy to distract from a line of inquiry."

"I can be. When were you in Switzerland?"

"I was in Switzerland four days ago. I knew you were to be assigned to the case," Chang said. "But I had no authorization to make contact with you until I consulted with both my people and the Americans. But I also knew you were potentially a target."

"How could you have known *that*?" she asked. "You would have had to have left Switzerland before I knew I was assigned to the case."

"You're smart," he said. "I'll give you five seconds to think about it. I doubt if you'll need all five."

She used three of them. Then, "Ah. Federov!" she said.

"Correct. I knew you were going to be assigned, because when I passed information about the brokerage of stolen artwork along to the CIA in Rome, Federov's name came up. Mark McKinnon saw the name and knew you had previous dealings with the Russian. So Mark contacted me before he contacted you. That's also obviously why the opposition, whoever they are, knew you were to be assigned. And that's why they drew a target on your beautiful head."

"But backtrack for a second. How did you find the Federov connection?"

"I hacked the computer of a certain Swiss businessman."

"You what?"

"I hacked into his computer and downloaded all the contents into mine."

"His computer wasn't coded?" she asked.

"Not very efficiently." Chang answered. He laughed. "I'm Asian so I'm good at those things. The Switzer was a dumb old white guy as far as security software went. It wasn't much of a challenge. And his laptop was like a little box of gold," Chang said. "That's one of the things I wanted to talk to you about tonight."

"So talk," she said, only slightly distracted by the best tuna filet she had ever encountered.

"I also recovered the banking records that showed exactly into what account the checks from China had been deposited. Normally, the trace on a route of a check deposited in Switzerland will hit security roadblocks and we'd need the help of the Swiss authorities to follow the money all the way back to the deposit."

"Usually that cooperation is forthcoming," she noted.

"Yes. But one is always at risk of certain bankers alerting the opposition by letting the depositor know that questions were being asked. So I hacked into the system for the complete records of that account," Chang said. "I followed the money."

Her fork stopped in mid-motion. "You hacked into the entire Swiss banking system?" she asked.

"Well, just one of the big banks. That was enough this time. Okay, I needed some help from one of our Hong Kong–trained techies. So she flew over from London for a day and got the job done. It's like a Trojan Horse virus via microwaves on the bank's main computer. If we know what account to connect with, we can drop our virus in and monitor transactions, past and current. From there we can monitor any other account that receives or disperses a transaction from the first account. Then the Trojan Horse self-destructs leaving no trace."

"Do the Swiss know you have this capability?"

"Some of the banks do," he said. "Sometimes they ask *us* for some help figuring out what their depositors are up to. One dirty hand washes the other."

She shook her head in amazement. Tens of thousands of depositors with numbered accounts wouldn't have found Peter's tale anywhere nearly as amusing.

"Anyway," Chang continued, "the money was dispersed to other accounts within minutes after it had cleared. One of the accounts was in Spain, two were in Saudi Arabia. We followed the international routing numbers and sent our Trojan Horse after it."

"So that would link the people who were fencing *The Pietà of Malta* to people in the Middle East as well as Spain," she said.

"It would appear that way," Peter Chang said. "But the first deposit was closely followed by another deposit and a similar transfer," he said. "For the same amount of money. And then the second transfer dispersed the money almost in the same manner, except there was fifty thousand dollars siphoned off, which went to a bank in Athens that specializes in trade with the Mideast."

"Did you get names off the accounts?"

"Not real ones. No surprise there. The trail dead-ends into fake passports and IDs. Very professional stuff, by the way."

Thinking it backward, she said, "Athens, huh?"

"Athens. Yes. Why is that significant?"

"When my Italian buddy had a needle stuck in his butt the other night," she said, "he said the people who did it were speaking Greek. Maybe that's nothing. Maybe it suggests we're on the right track."

"Maybe. And maybe not," Peter Chang said. "Look, my brief only addresses the sale to China, my government's displeasure on how the transaction was handled, and the fate of the gentleman who was murdered in Switzerland. But as long as I'm in this, I don't mind assisting you with your own investigation. Don't get me wrong — I'm being paid to do this. Paid very well. And I, on behalf of my government, don't personally like our opponents here either. So now you know pretty much everything that I know. If you'd like me to stay with you on this, I'm here. If not, I'll walk."

"I'd be honored if you stayed with me on this," she said.

"So I'll cover your back, and, if necessary, you cover mine," he said.

"It's a deal."

She reached across the table. They shook hands. His hand was intense and strong. It almost gave her a shudder. She finished her plate, and the last few sips of wine with it. She was feeling slightly buzzed, a safe but pleasant level.

A busboy arrived and cleared the table. The waiter arrived with a dessert menu. Alex maintained her will power for almost a quarter minute until the waiter talked them into taking some coffee accompanied by a plate to share of *buñelos de viento*, puffs of choux pastry stuffed with sweet vanilla or chocolate cream.

"Death from gunfire is one thing," she said with a shrug. "Death from triglycerides and cholesterol is something else. What's on your agenda for tomorrow?"

"I need to do some banking," he answered. "Accompany me when I do it. There are some things you should see."

"Can we do it in the morning?" she asked. "First thing?"

"That would be best," he said. "Did you have a conflict?"

"I was going to go out to the Escorial," she said, "and perhaps the

Valley of the Fallen where the big monument stands to the Civil War dead. It's about an hour outside the city. Ever been out there?"

"No."

"Interested?"

"I am," he said. "I have a car. I can drive."

She considered it. "Okay," she said. "On a professional level, right?"

"Completely," he said.

"It's a deal."

THIRTY-NINE

MARSEILLES, SEPTEMBER 10, LATE EVENING

As soon as Lazzari was out of Jean-Claude's view, the Frenchman was on his feet, moving down the same pathway between the tables. No shot rang out from across the street, no backup leaped forward with a pistol.

Jean-Claude arrived on the sidewalk. Perfect timing. Split second, but perfect. He looked in Lazzari's direction, about ten meters down the sidewalk.

"Monsieur!" he yelled. "Monsieur Lazzari!" He shouted as if it was an afterthought, as if he had forgotten something.

The Turk turned quickly, one hand clutching the tote bag, the other on his weapon within his outer shirt.

"You forgot something!" Jean-Claude yelled.

What the Turk had forgotten was to keep his guard up until he was out of the country. The distraction was just enough.

From an alley beyond the curb stepped a masked figure—Jean-Claude's accomplice—with something in his hands. Quickly, professionally, as efficiently as someone flipping a ribbon around a gift-wrapped box, the masked man looped a piano-wire garrote around Lazzari's neck. And then with the force of two powerful arms yanking at full strength, he pulled the wire in on itself closed. It zipped like a razor through the flesh, veins, and cartilage of the neck until it closed onto the spinal column.

Lazzari, a strong man himself, fought for no more than the final few seconds of his life. The gun flew from his left hand and the tote bag dropped from his right. His neck spurted like a broken water pipe, blood squirting and flowing from the deep sharp incisions left by the wire.

His assassin boldly dropped him, wire still in place, turned, and disappeared into the alley. Closely behind him followed Jean-Claude, who stopped only to retrieve the bag of money. Then he too disappeared into the alleys and darkness of Marseilles along a carefully planned route of escape, as minutes later, horrified residents surrounded the dead body and local police began to converge on the scene.

FORTY

MADRID, SEPTEMBER 11, LA MADRUGADA, 12:34 A.M.

Alex was back in the Ritz in another hour, in her suite by herself, the door bolted.

She opened her laptop and went to email messages.

On the top of the list, Joseph Collins, her Venezuelan mentor, wrote back to wish her well. He said he had some new developments, but they could wait. She fielded the email, answered it, and went on.

Colonel Pendraza of the National Police had made good on his pledge. He had transferred one hundred thirty-eight files to her by attachment, each of them having to do with some antiterror operation in Spain, large or small, but mostly large.

Alex dug into them for an hour.

Item: Three people in Malaga had been arrested in connection with a plot to plant car bombs around that Spanish city. The conspirators had been trained at a camp in Pakistan linked to the Islamic Jihad Union. Eight others were under investigation and had fled Spain. Spanish authorities said those arrested shared a "profound hatred of Americans."

Item: In early June, eight men of Somali citizenship had been arrested in Portugal while seeking to make connecting flights into Barcelona. Portuguese police maintained that one of the men was a senior al-Qaeda leader. All had been turned over to "covert American operations" for "further inquiry."

Item: Noted in passing: al-Qaeda leaders have frequently threatened to strike again in Europe in audio and video warnings. Antiterror experts within the Policia Nacional said recently that the pace of the warnings has picked up in recent weeks.

Associated item: Intercepted al-Qaeda documents have indicated activities of small sleeper cells within Spain, intent on acting independently but with major force.

Item: Analysts in Madrid were alarmed over the publication of cartoons of the Prophet Muhammad deemed offensive by many Muslims, as well as a lack of opportunities and sense of marginalization in Muslim communities. These social currents have put Europe squarely in the crosshairs of radicals. Porous borders and years of open immigration policies have added to the problem, they say.

Item: Police in northwest Spain had arrested seven people in connection with a terrorist plot to blow up aircraft flying from Spain to the United Kingdom. The plot involved hiding liquid explosives in carry-on luggage, and six to ten flights would have been targeted. A senior Spanish counterterror source said she believed the plotters were to carry a "Spanish version of Gatorade" onto the planes and then mix it with a gel-like substance. The explosives were to be triggered by an iPod or a cell phone, the source said . . . *[NB: Cross/ref: US.doj.gvt. 4543b-0-09]* The intelligence that uncovered the plot "makes very strong links to al-Qaeda," a senior US administration official remarked in telephone message with Policia Nacional. The official said it was believed the plot had been close to being operational.

Lord, what a world, she thought to herself. More examples of man's inhumanity to man, the violence and moral vacuity of the modern world. And how, on top of her personal feelings, was she ever going to make sense of all these reports, much less spot any link to the disappearance of *The Pietà of Malta*?

Good question. She didn't have an answer. Not tonight, anyway.

Her eyelids flagged. She was confused, afraid, paranoid, and tired. She scanned the list of messages.

Anything of interest?

No. Nothing.

She shut down the laptop and crashed into bed.

She worked Peter Chang over in her mind. She wondered if he was somehow playing both sides of the street, having sold his credibility to the CIA in Rome. Was he now serving up peanuts in return for a chubby annual stipend on the tab of the American taxpayers? Had he successfully hustled Mark McKinnon, who was looking increasingly burned out and unprofessional?

And was Peter now hustling her? For business reasons? Personal reasons? Something about him set off alarms.

After a few unsettled minutes, Alex drifted off to sleep. She slept surprisingly soundly, more out of fatigue than peace of mind.

FORTY-ONE

MADRID, SEPTEMBER 11, 7:45 A.M.

Alex rose the next morning at 7:00 a.m.

There was a health club nearby affiliated with the hotel. She pulled on a sweatshirt, shorts, and sneakers and was out of her room by 7:15, walking quickly though the streets of the waking Spanish capital. She was in the pool by 7:35. Without stopping, she did thirty laps before returning to the Ritz.

She felt good.

She ordered breakfast from room service and opened her computer. She threw off her gym clothes and donned a hotel robe. When breakfast arrived, she took both her breakfast and her laptop on the balcony. She loved the view of the city in the morning, even with its dull smoggy haze filtering sunlight onto the old buildings, modern apartment houses, trees, and busy streets.

She opened her laptop and set to work.

Email. Messages. A bunch from home. One from Ben that made her laugh. His first term at law school was about to begin. He was anxious to get started.

She thought of phoning him but remembered it was the middle of the night. He might not have minded, but she didn't anyway.

Another email from Joseph Collins. He said one of his employees would be in Spain during the week of September 18. Could the employee come by for a conversation, he asked. Things in Venezuela were heating up.

Alex wrote back and said that was fine, but she didn't know when the current assignment would end. She would most likely be at the Ritz in Madrid, and Collin's rep should look for her there.

Then business. She switched into her secure email account, the one she used for work. There was some stuff from Treasury pertaining to her current assignment. Synopses of other ongoing investigations in the United States that might have links to her own. She scanned them and found nothing that fixed her attention. There was one from her boss, Mike Gamburian, in DC asking for a few sentences of an update on the case. A small progress report.

Well, she could give him a small progress report because the progress was small. How's that, Mike? She sent him an update, but made it politer than she might have wished.

Then there were a few emails from the others who had been at the meeting at the embassy, the one in which she had been introduced to *The Pietà of Malta*. The black bird, as everyone now had taken to calling it.

LeMaitre, the Frenchman, had sent her a few links having to do with terror cases in France. Then there was something from Essen at Interpol, which she read. His stuff seemed to be consistently closest to the mark, but still there was nothing that she pegged as important.

Then she sighed.

There was another email from Floyd Connelly at US Customs.

Mr. Empty message, she now thought of him as. How the heck did the man keep his job in this day of mandatory computer literacy? She wondered what political hack had given him his job and was still protecting him.

She opened the message and looked at it.

Subject: Pietà of Malta
Date: Fri, 10 September 2009 12:47:01 - 0400
From: "Connelly_F" <Floyd_Connelly@USA
          Customs.org> Add Mobile Alert
To: "A_LaDuca" <A_Laduca@usdt.prv.org>

Once again, the text was jaybird naked. What was he trying to communicate?

Anything?

This was the third blank she had drawn from him. She sighed again. She clicked on Reply and wrote as diplomatically as possible.

```
Subject:  Pietà of Malta
Date:     Fri, 10 September 2009 12:47:01-0400
From:     "A_LaDuca" <A_Laduca@usdt.prv.org ·
To:       "Connelly_F"  <Floyd_Connelly@USA
          Customs.org>  Add Mobile Alert
```

Hey, Floyd ... I don't mind communication, but empty messages are not my thing. ;-) Nothing's coming though, my friend. Do you have anything interesting? If so, please be sure to attach properly or if it's easier, call me on my cell phone. Okay? I'm always happy to hear from you if you have something. Alex LaDuca

Then she hit Send and off into cyberspace went her message.

This Connelly guy was a piece of work, no?

Floyd, Floyd, a message in a void.

She needed a nickname for him, she mused, as she sipped her morning coffee and spread some delicious Spanish marmalade on toast. What would it be, the nickname?

"Pretty Boy" or "Pink"?

Well, not to be mean, but certainly not the former.

The latter? Pink?

Then she had it. The perfect nickname for him in her mind: *Gutman*. As in the Sidney Greenstreet character in *The Maltese Falcon*.

Connelly was Gutman. She laughed. Who was *she*? Samanatha Spade? Well, she'd been called worse. In fact, she liked the notion. She laughed again. Might as well have some small measure of fun with this nerve-racking pressure. She realized she was getting a little punch drunk with all this terror stuff, with the mounting demands to connect with *The Pietà of Malta*.

She went to Colonel Pendraza's attachments. More vile stuff. More attempted terror in Spain. She speed-read six files. Again, nothing.

She clicked out of email. She glanced at her watch. It was almost 9:00 a.m. She finished breakfast. Enough nonsense, she told herself. Keep moving.

She went to various websites and studied her options for getting from Madrid to Geneva without using airplanes. Yes, she could rent a car, but she didn't feel like driving. She went to a site for the European rail system and figured her next move. She would take an overnight train from Madrid. She could book a sleeping compartment and at least have a comfortable night. Well, that might be perfect. Or as close to perfect as she could hope for.

The train offered her anonymity plus a little bit of adventure. *Strangers on a Train, Murder on the Orient Express.* Why not? She thought of a couple of old European gems. *Closely Watched Trains. The Sleeping Car Murders.* She laughed.

She looked at the schedule. The train she wanted would depart from Madrid the next night and get her just north of Barcelona to the Spanish city Figueras by the following morning.

Then she could transfer to Montpellier in the south of France near Marseilles and follow that with another transfer to one of the zippy French TGV's, *trains de grande vitesse.* She would be in Geneva by the next afternoon and, she reasoned, would be able to check into the hotel by four.

She knew Geneva reasonably well from previous visits.

Okay, perfect. Traveling with a firearm was a pain, but this way she could make the best of it. She used a credit card to secure a reservation. She had a prepaid card in pseudonym for just such purposes. She would buy the hard copy of the ticket from a machine. No passport or ID checks. Perfect, again.

This was what traveling soft was all about. It frightened her that she had become so good at it. She went back to email.

Nothing new.

She finished with the laptop and closed it. She dressed in comfortable clothes for the day. Snug blue jeans of a very light cotton. A yellow T-shirt and a navy blue windbreaker. Just enough upper body coverage to conceal her weapon if she chose to carry it, which she did.

By 10:00 she was downstairs at the front entrance to the Ritz, bringing her laptop with her.

Peter Chang was already there, standing beside a maroon Jaguar. He was in a sharp Hugo Boss suit and open-collared shirt with wraparound shades. A Cantonese James Bond. Peter was chatting amiably in Spanish with the doormen. The doormen had allowed him to park in a *Prohibido Estacionar* zone to wait for her. Alex wondered what the maroon Jag had to do with Chinese socialism but lodged no questions or complaints. It was a beauty of a car.

Peter spotted her immediately but didn't even break a smile. He opened the car door for her, politely waving the doormen away from the assignment. Moments later they were out into traffic and on their way to the bank.

FORTY-TWO

You really want me to see all this?" Alex asked.

Alex stood with Peter Chang in the subterranean vault of El Banco de Santander. The branch was one of the largest in the city, as well as the most secure. They stood in a private room where Peter opened a safety deposit box from the vault.

"I don't mind that you see what's in the box," Chang said. "Look, we're working together. I have to trust you and vice versa. Do you have your passport with you?"

"Of course."

"I want to add your signature to this account," he said. "That way, if you need to, you can get in and out of this box without me."

He lifted an attaché case onto the desktop. He had carried it from the car. Using his thumbs, he clicked the locks and the latches popped up with sharp metallic snaps. Then Chang opened the case. There were papers neatly arranged in a file, a weapon in a special case, a breathtaking load of cash bundled together, and a small gift box with slick white wrapping paper and a red ribbon.

He hefted the money in his hands. "Money," he said. "I love money." He was all business.

"In its place," she answered.

"There's ten thousand euros here," he said. He flicked his fingers over the neatly bound stacks of bank notes. "Half in fifties, half in twenties. There are a few tens. If you're in Spain and get stranded, or I'm not here, or I've disappeared or had to go back to China, help yourself to a reasonable amount. I mean, if you need a good lunch or dinner, just come in and grab a hundred euros. That's about what it costs, doesn't it, these days?"

"Just about," she said, going along with it.

She watched in mounting wonder. He moved the money, tied up

in fat tactile packs, into the safety deposit box. He then opened the metal case. Within it was a small black handgun, a Chinese-made nine millimeter automatic.

"Nice, yes?" he asked.

"Very," she said.

He handed it to her for her examination. She used a tissue to hold it so she wouldn't leave fingerprints on it, a move that amused him. She recognized the gun as a Norinco M-77B, a variant of the Type 77 pistol issued to the Chinese military and police.

"I'm surprised that thing didn't set off the metal detector at the door," she said.

He smiled and tapped gently on the case.

"This is the newest thing," he said, referring to the metal composition of the weapon's case. "Cool, huh? It's like a Stealth bomber. It stymies the metal detectors so anything in one of these boxes flies under the radar."

"Incredible," she said.

"I'm Chinese, hey. We're technologically advanced. Haven't you read all that stuff in the journals these days? *The Economist*? *The Atlantic* in your country? Nostradamus said the Chinese would rule the world, remember that? Well, you might live to see it. Why are you looking at me strangely?" he asked.

"I can't decide whether you're brilliant, just full of yourself, or both," she said.

"Both," he answered. "You're not the first to notice. And anyway, the bank knows who I am, and they look the other way. You know how banks do that when they want to. So bringing the gun wouldn't have been a problem, anyway."

"They know who you work for?"

"Who do you think opened the account?" he said.

The gun, packed neatly away, followed the money into the box.

Chang reached for the gift-wrapped box and seemed slightly ill at ease. "This part's personal," he said.

"Christmas shopping?" she asked, looking at the gift box. "Do they have Christmas in China?"

"In the cities, among the ruling class," he said. "I can't speak for what goes on in the countryside. Like it?" he asked.

He handed the box to her. It weighed less than a pound and it turned over easily in her hand. She examined the box. The wrapping was from one of Zurich's finest jewelers.

"Well, it's nicely wrapped," Alex said. "What's in it?"

"I picked it up for a lady friend," he said.

"Special occasion?" she asked.

"You might say so."

"Mother? Wife? Sister?"

"No, no, and no," he answered. Suddenly into personal relationships, the steely reserve faded for a moment. He had a gorgeous smile and even laughed.

"But a special lady friend?" Alex pressed.

"Definitely."

"I didn't know you had a special lady friend."

"How would you?" he asked. "You hardly know anything about me, and all you know is what I want you to know, anyway. And the truth is I have several."

"Several what?"

"Lady friends," he said.

"Ah. You get around the world. So you have a 'stable'?"

"Don't be vulgar," he insisted.

She looked at the box, hefting it in her hand again.

"Engagement? Wedding?" she asked. "Too heavy to be a ring or a bracelet. Too light for crystal. Wrong size box for a necklace."

She smiled and reexamined the package. Intrigued, she said, "I don't suppose it would do me any good to *ask* what it is? To ask what's in the box?"

"Ask me," he said.

"What's in the box?"

"It's a secret," he said. "I refuse to tell. But thanks for falling for my offer."

He grinned and took it back from her.

She stared at the box, then looked at him. "Peter, how stupid do you think I am?" she asked.

He glanced up. "What do you mean?"

"That's the pietà. You recovered it in Switzerland."

He said nothing.

"I don't care if we stash it here, but my job is to get it returned to the museum, so if that's it, I want it."

"That's not the pietà," he said.

"Let me open it," she said.

"No," he said. He stepped back and for one horrifying moment, she thought his right hand was going for his weapon. It was like that with Peter. Little movements, little innocent quirks, she was starting to interpret as keys to much larger things.

"Then I'll draw my own conclusions, Peter," she said. "And this is going to impact our working together because you're holding back something important from me."

He looked angry. "If I walked in here soaking wet and shaking out an umbrella and told you it was raining, you'd still go look out the window."

"Can you blame me?"

"All right," he finally said. "Go ahead. Just open it carefully," he said, "because I need to reseal it, and I don't want it arriving looking like I found it under a bench in Hong Kong."

He put the package in her hands. She hefted it again, convinced that he had outfoxed her. She undid the ribbon with care. There was no tape on the wrapping paper. As she unfolded the paper, she saw his hands move slowly. One hand again was near his gun. He was looking her in the eye, hands on his hips.

The paper fell away. She paused. The box was sturdy cardboard, about five inches by five inches, bearing the mark of one of Zurich's finest jewelers. Under his intense gaze, she opened it.

There was a blue velvet bag within. His hand drifted a little closer to his weapon. She stopped, then persisted. She opened the bag and slid the contents out into her hand.

The bag had contained a sturdy étoile bangle in eighteen-karat gold, sprinkled with modest diamonds. The piece was modern and streamlined, yet timeless. The diamonds were round and set in platinum. There was nothing else in the box. She had guessed one hundred percent wrong. It probably had a price tag of five grand but it wasn't any lamentation.

"It's really quite beautiful. Some girl is lucky."

"Try it on," he said. "Let me see how it looks on a woman's wrist."

"Really?"

"Why not, at this point?"

She slipped it on her wrist. It had a fabulous look, a magnificent feel. She had never owned a piece like this. Her first car had cost less. Her parent's home where she grew up probably had a lower tag in dollars. Before she got too used to it, she took it off and handed it back.

"Okay," she said. "Thanks. And sorry."

"Aaaaah, in a way I can't blame you," he said. "At least we cleared the air."

"Right," she said.

Carefully she rewrapped it, taking great effort to get the paper and ribbon back perfectly in place. She handed it back to him and he put it into the box.

"Now let's get out of here," he said. "And will you sign the forms that give you permission to access the box? It would be a good idea."

"I have nothing to lose by doing that," she said.

They left the bank and went to his car, where they had both stashed their weapons under the front seat. Within a half hour they were at the city limits to the northwest of Madrid, and shortly after that they were driving on a new autoroute leading from the city into wealthy estates and farmlands to the northwest of the capital.

"You wouldn't mind some American jazz, would you?"

"Not at all. I rather like it."

"Louis Armstrong. Duke Ellington. Miles Davis. Absolutely the best."

"If you say so," she teased.

"You have better candidates?"

"In jazz?"

"Yes."

"John Coltrane and Dave Brubeck. They were at least equals."

"Anyone currently you like?" he asked.

"I like a jazz singer named Sarah Montes," she said, after a moment's thought. "Am I allowed to name a woman? You only named men."

"Sure. I don't know Sarah Montes."

"Then you should buy a CD next chance you get. Picture a sexy blond woman in a sexy slinky red gown standing in front of a black grand piano wailing her heart out for you."

"Very good answer. Do you know sports too?"

"Pretty well."

"I used to go see the Yankees when I lived in New York," he said. "I liked the Yankees. Still follow them when I can. I like Wang, their pitcher from Taiwan."

"The Los Angeles Angels are my baseball club," she said, "and I've always liked the Giants in football."

"English football?" he quizzed. "I follow that. Manchester United."

"Arsenal rules," she said. "I loved Thierry Henri. And that Pirès. He's hot."

He laughed heartily this time. "What *don't* you know about?" he asked.

"Chinese," she said. "Of the six languages I speak, that's not one of them."

He nodded thoughtfully. "Thanks," he said. "You just reminded me. I need to make a call."

He pulled out his cell phone, snapped it open with a deft flick of the wrist, and made a call. He spoke in Mandarin, or at least she assumed it was Mandarin. And for a moment a strange feeling came over her.

He could have been talking about her, plotting her death, saying anything, and she wouldn't have known. She tried to read his expression but couldn't. The dark side to him wouldn't go away.

He clicked the phone shut and returned it to his inside jacket pocket. She gazed at the Spanish highway that unfurled ahead. They rode for the next several dozen kilometers in silence, except for the cool jazz.

She took the occasion to glance through his collection. Ellington, Coltrane, Davis, Johnny Hartman. Everyone in his collection was dead. It set just the wrong tone.

FORTY-THREE

Digging, digging, digging.

Over the last few days, Jean-Claude and his associates had made enormous progress. From the basement of the old building on the Calle de Maldonado, they had tunneled and edged their way southward a full city block. Working during the day, when street noise would cover the sounds of their activities, they had taken down small sections of old walls that had been under the city for centuries.

Mahoud and Samy had done the heavy work. Samy's wife, Tamar, had brought drinks, sandwiches, and pastries during the day. Basheer had watched the entranceway on the Calle Maldonado and had also done some digging.

When they removed rocks and passed through the new passages, they were careful to then reassemble the walls as they continued on their path. No point to arouse the suspicion of anyone else who might be prowling. They could assemble or re-assemble from either direction as they went in and out.

They traveled in pairs, each with a small shovel, a few hammers, and picks. Each carried a small handgun in case of an extreme emergency. Tamar kept a kitchen knife on her, just in case. The cell of self-styled *jihadistas* was small and tight. Jean-Claude, the leader and organizer, was the only one who would travel by himself. All five were Moroccans by birth except for Jean-Claude, who was French by birth and Moroccan by origin.

They were like rats. They scurried along, perilously close to contact with the overall workaday population of the city, yet they were subterranean and unobserved.

After months of planning, their underground passageway had pressed alongside and underneath the Calle Claudio Coello. Then it crossed underneath the intersection with the Calle Juan Bravo.

JeanClaude himself was with the group and doing some excavation himself the day they got that far.

Jean-Claude had everything he needed up until this point. Electricity, a ventilation system, and small pumps to remove groundwater. In some areas he had wood roofing to bolster the makeshift walls and ceilings. In most areas they had clearances nearly six feet high and about five feet wide. Yet there were those spots along the path where they were forced to crawl through low, cramped, wet spaces that hardly allowed any air.

They followed a series of old cellars. They came mostly to crumbling walls where weak spots could be found and exploited. In these spots they pushed their way through to the next chamber and continued.

A few meters south of the Calle Juan Bravo, they hit a hard impasse. A construction gang from many years in the past had used one of the sub-basements as a repository for every bit of discarded construction refuse known to man: rotting old planks to hard chunks of concrete the size of boulders, to bags of garbage and wine and beer bottles from lunches consumed decades ago.

It was a roadblock. But Jean-Claude had anticipated something like this.

When his workers reported the impasse, he went with them. He carried with him a remote-controlled detonator, a PVC pipe, potassium nitrate, kitty litter, corn syrup, and a safety fuse.

This was risky. Jean-Claude needed to set off a small explosion via a modest pipe bomb about twenty feet under the middle of Madrid. He ordered his underlings to remain behind. Then, working with his own hands, he cleared as much rubble from the chamber of blockage as he could. His explosives were not the powerful sophisticated ones that had come all the way from Iraq. Rather it was routine stuff, about the amount that loggers might use to break apart a tree stump.

Of course, there was always the chance that the charge was too big and by setting off a modest underground blast, he might inadvertently create a sinkhole that would bring down everything from the street above: cars, buses, people, parts of buildings.

There was also the chance that the blast would ignite a fire. A fire like that would prohibit him and his cell from carrying out the rest of their plans. But he didn't have much choice. He had to get past this underground chamber of rubble, and there was no room to excavate it. Best to turn part of it to dust.

The area was stinking and wet where he planted his bomb. Nothing should burn very easily. And in terms of lives and property, none of the potential losses came back on him. Those who suffered would all be Spaniards and foreigners who were tied up in the pro-Judeo-Christian Western economic system that exploited Islam.

So why should he care?

He used an old Casio watch as the timer and set the moment of ignition for one hour hence. He planted the small pipe bomb where he hoped it would blow a hole in each direction, creating a further passageway to his destination at an address under a building on the Calle Serrano. His detonator today was simple, an old-style low-tech blasting cap. He double-checked everything as the seconds began to tick away. A full minute was gone when he finally turned and hurried away.

The rest of his team had already dispersed for the day, though they left a few bricks and stones out of the established route so that Jean-Claude could travel faster. Within a quarter hour, his small knapsack over his back, his pistol tucked into a roomy pants pocket, he was all the way back to the building on the Calle Maldonado. Moments after that, he was back up to the street, anxious but breathing easier.

He walked out of the building and joined the crowds for a pleasant summer mid-afternoon in Madrid. He looked at his watch and pondered his next move.

He walked to a café that he reckoned was about a hundred feet from where the flash point of the blast would take place. He took a seat at a table, ordered a drink, and waited, checking out the Western women in the café as he did so.

He counted the minutes. And the seconds.

In his mind, he went through a secret countdown. The time eventually drew very near. His agitation increased.

He looked in the geographic direction of the impending blast.

A voice from nearby made him jump. *"¿Señor?"*

He whirled around and his heart nearly stopped. Two uniformed police officers from the city of Madrid peered down at him, eyes behind reflective sunglasses, weapons hanging crisply at their sides.

Jean-Claude was speechless.

"*¡Señor! Su documento nacional de identidad, por favor!*" repeated the ranking cop, asking for his identity card.

"Why?" Jean-Claude asked.

"Don't ask us why, sir," the ranking cop pressed. "Do you have your card or not?"

Jean-Claude went to his rear pocket where there was a small billfold. He thought of the gun in his other pocket and processed quickly the scenario of shooting his way out of this. The only ID he had was his real one, the French one. But to not produce an ID would be to invite further questions, further searches.

He produced the ID and handed it to the lead cop.

Without asking, the second cop picked up Jean-Claude's backpack and looked into it. Luckily, it was empty, other than tools. But the cop wasn't satisfied. He picked up a chisel and turned it over and over, examining it with growing suspicion.

The lead cop continued to eye the small ID card issued by the French government. He raised his glasses for a good look. His gaze jumped back and forth between Jean-Claude and the card.

"*¿Frances?*" the lead cop asked.

"*Si. Oui.*" Jean-Claude answered. He knew if he were asked to stand up, things would get worse.

"What are you doing with these things?" the second cop asked of the tools. "Breaking into cars? Homes?"

"I'm a workman. A carpenter," Jean-Claude said. Then he added, with a smile, "Like Jesus."

The two cops didn't think that was funny. Not at all and particularly not coming from a French Arab. They only glared. Jean-Claude knew he had miscalculated with that remark.

"*Se levanta, por favor,*" the lead cop said. Stand up!

Jean-Claude's insides nearly exploded. He would have bolted, but the second cop had blocked his exit, not by coincidence. The second cop's meaty hand was on his sidearm also. Not by coincidence either.

The first cop pulled out a handheld tracking computer and ran

Jean-Claude's ID through it like a credit card. He waited. Cop number two engaged the suspect in small talk.

"Where is your job? As a 'carpenter,'" the policeman asked with obvious cynicism. "What *exactly* do you do?"

Jean-Claude talked his way through a pack of lies and half truths. The cop did not take notes.

"Why are you in Spain? Where do you live?" the cop asked next. Cop number one was eyeing his computer. The gun in Jean-Claude's pocket felt as if it weighed a hundred pounds.

There was silence. Everyone else in the café was now staring. Even the proprietor had moved into a position to watch but knew better than to interfere with the police.

Jean-Claude told more lies but told the truth about his home address, which he now knew might not be safe to go back to. He was registered with the local authorities, as required by law. A lie here would have raised even more suspicion. The sweat continued to roll off him. Then the first cop stepped back a pace and did something that Jean-Claude liked even less. He pulled out a small digital camera and took Jean-Claude's picture, so fast that Jean-Claude couldn't object, not that it would have mattered.

The cop checked the image he had taken, then put the camera away.

Jean-Claude glanced at his watch. There was a quiet moment.

"Late for something?" the second cop asked.

"Just wondering about the time," Jean-Claude explained.

"Why would it matter?" the cop asked.

"It doesn't," said Jean-Claude.

"Then why did you look?"

"I just looked. That's all."

"*Maldito moro,*" muttered the cop. Damned Arab. "Why do you people come here?"

Jean-Claude held his tongue. Then he felt the detonation. He was certain! He had felt a small shock wave, a small rumble, from the point of impact about a hundred feet away. It was much like the feeling of a truck rumbling by on a city street, or the sensation New Yorkers feel when a subway train rumbles under a building. Then it was gone, the rumbling, vanishing as abruptly as it had arrived.

He had heard it. Or thought he had. He glanced around in every direction, the second cop still fixing him in his gaze. Much as Jean-Claude was thrilled by the explosion, he felt as if he had guilt written all over him. He half expected to see some kind of commotion on the street, people asking questions, people wondering. Like New York after September 11, like London after the horrible attacks on the transportation system in September of 2005, Madrid had remained a city on edge, a city jittery at the sound of any strange, loud noise.

But there was absolutely no notice being taken here on the streets.

None. The pipe bomb had contained itself, at least for now.

Then the lead cop put the computer away. *"Esta bien,"* he said.

He returned the ID card. The second cop tossed the knapsack back to the ground, still open, the tools rattling, the cop still glaring.

The first cop looked him up and down. "You don't belong here. People here wash. This isn't a bar for workmen or riffraff."

"Árabes," the second cop muttered.

Jean-Claude held them in his gaze and suppressed everything he might have wanted to say. "I can drink here like anyone else," he said.

"Then drink," said the cop.

It was only then that Jean-Claude realized he had never touched his coffee.

"I will," he said softly. And he did, as the cops departed and the café settled down again.

Jean-Claude drew a long breath and exhaled. Not far away, just up the block, loomed the United States Embassy and all the security that surrounded it. Jean-Claude glared at all the Americans around him, glanced away, then fully understood why he had been questioned and why he would have to be much more careful in the coming days.

And that photo! Where was *that* going to show up?

He knew the whole equation for him in Spain had now changed. He knew the explosion he had set off that day would have kicked up massive amounts of dust and smoke. And there still could be a collapse on the streets or a fire. But there could be no question of moving forward, as rapidly as possible.

That photograph. Time was limited!

FORTY-FOUR

OUTSIDE MADRID, SEPTEMBER 11, 1:47 P.M.

By noon they had come to their first destination, the austere gray palace of Escorial, built more than four centuries earlier by King Felipe II. Unlike many of the great palaces of Europe, this one had its macabre touch. The inner courtyard had been conceived as a contemplative retreat and as a mausoleum. It had served as a final resting place for the revered Carlos I of Spain, Felipe's father, who had also been the Holy Roman Emperor Charles V.

They took the official tour, which lasted less than an hour, and then spent another hour exploring the architecture by themselves. The gigantic building, with its almost three thousand windows, was situated on the slopes of the Guardarrama mountains. From its top floors, it offered a view in every direction of what had once been the Spanish Empire, from Italy to the south, to the Netherlands to the north, and to the Americas in the west.

Walking these grounds put Alex in touch with centuries of Spanish civilization. Peter, always wishing to add to his knowledge of Western culture, observed critically and with great interest, asking questions of the guides when necessary.

They paused for a late lunch at a café in the nearby town of Santa Cruz, after which Alex glanced at her watch. "We still have time for the Valley of the Fallen," she said. "It's more modern. I have a feeling I'll relate to it better. Still game?"

"Still game," he said. "What is it, this place where we're going?"

Moments later, they stood by the roadside outside the restaurant. Alex scanned the horizon and found what she was looking for. A white stone cross stood many stories high on a peak ten miles in the distance. "See that?" she asked. "That's where we're going."

They slid back into the car and she took out a map. They drove southward for another half hour on a winding highway that passed by bulls, those reared for bullfights, grazing in green fields. Then the road abruptly rose into a hot, foggy mountain. The road led into Santa Cruz del Valle de los Caídos, the Valley of the Fallen, where Franco's most megalomaniacal monument had been built.

During the 1950s in this place, thousands of prison laborers, many of them who had been prisoners of war from the Civil War, tunneled hundreds of yards into a granite mountain ridge to build one of the world's biggest and most sinister basilicas. The church was now part of a Spanish Civil War memorial. It stood beneath a cross nearly fifty stories high, a cross that on a clear day can be seen from scores of miles in every direction.

The site had expressed Franco's desire for national atonement in the 1950s when Spain made her first shaky steps of returning to the world community. Franco's rule, as Franco himself liked to see it, was not a victory of the Falange, the Spanish version of fascism, but of a traditional Catholic conservative Spain. Franco, on his crusade to save Christian civilization in his homeland, had modeled himself after monarchs like Philip II. To Alex, the site brought to mind the architecture of the Third Reich.

Alex and Peter Chang solemnly walked the grounds of the basilica and the giant cross. The day was brutally hot. In this place, the remains of murdered Republicans were unearthed from mass graves and trucked to the valley to be mixed with dead Nationalists, so it could be designated a place for all Civil War victims.

Here also was the tomb of Franco and the founder of the Falange Party, Franco's onetime rival, José Antonio Primo de Rivera, son of the dictator of the 1920s. The site culminated at the high altar with the graves of those two men. As Alex and Peter stood before it in silence, they noticed several fresh bouquets of flowers laid on each tombstone. A young Spanish family meandered glumly through silence, gazing up at the glowering statues of soldiers and saints. On the plaza outside, there was a view toward Madrid. Above their heads, a series of dark rain clouds moved in and the top of the giant cross disappeared within the sky.

"Okay," Alex finally said around five in the afternoon. "I've had enough for one day."

"Me too," Peter said.

A few minutes later, they were back on the road. Several kilometers into the return trip, Alex spoke again.

"Something occurred to me late this afternoon, Peter," Alex said. She spoke over the efficient hum of the air-conditioning in the Jaguar.

"What's that?" he asked.

"We're looking for this *Pietà of Malta*, or looking for the reasons someone stole it. I was thinking about how we started referring to it as the 'black bird.' Like in the movie."

"Yes," he said. "So?"

"Well," Alex continued, "it occurs to me that, in the movie, everyone's chasing the bird all over the place. But in the end, the bird they're looking for is a fake. It doesn't exist. Or at least the real one never appears."

Chang frowned. "What are you suggesting?" he asked.

"Maybe *The Pietà of Malta* isn't really out there," she said.

"Oh, it's out there," he said.

"How do you know?"

"Three people dead in Switzerland. Another two in Madrid. And that's just what we know about."

"You've actually seen it?" she pressed.

"I know that it exists," he said.

"But have you actually *seen* it?" she asked.

"I'm certain that it exists," he said. "It's out there somewhere. The black bird. *The Pietà of Malta*. Whatever you want to call it. More than likely right under our noses. That's what happens with stolen art."

"What happens with stolen art is that it never gets recovered," she said.

"This case is going to be different." For a moment he drove silently, obviously thinking. "Well, okay, there's another theory too," he said. "No one will ever find *The Pietà of Malta*. Or at least not in our lifetimes. You know as well as I do that sometimes stolen art disappears forever. And you know what else? Sometimes the thieves get scared. They fail to move it, and they don't want to get caught with it. So they destroy it."

Alex folded her arms and gave the impression, accurately, of being ill at ease with his explanations and the direction of their dialogue.

"We have no choice but to move forward," he continued. "Even if we don't find the pietà, it's our task to follow the trail of money. What conspiracies were put in motion by this? *That's* our mission, not a little chunk of plaster from eighteen centuries ago. My job is to roll up the network of people who harmed one of my peers. Your job is to protect your country in case the theft is somehow financing an operation against America. Am I correct?"

"True enough," she said.

"And now I'll offer you something that you *will* like," he said. "It's an offer, not an obligation. So you're free to decline it."

"I'm listening."

"Two of my peers have arrived in Madrid from China," he said. "I'm joining them for dinner. Will you come along and meet them?"

"Where would we be meeting?" Alex asked.

"I know a little tavern," he said. "It's very Spanish. A little touristy maybe, but not far from your hotel. There's nice food and good drinks. Late in the evening they have live music."

"Who are your peers?" she asked.

"They work with me. They're friends as well as coworkers."

"From China?"

"Yes. From Shanghai. I think you'll like them."

"What line of work exactly?" she asked.

He smiled. "Same as you and me. Dirty stuff for our respective governments."

"Ah," she answered. She thought about it. "All right," she said. "I'm interested."

"What time do you have to leave tomorrow for Geneva?" he asked.

"Evening," she said. "Late. I'm taking an overnight train. What about you? Are you flying or driving?" she asked.

"I'm going to fly."

"I envy you. How do you move your gun from country to country?"

"I don't," he said. "I stash it here and get another one in Switzerland."

"Of course," she said. "I might have known."

She watched the roadside sail by. There was a light rain falling now, and Peter was doing about eighty. She might have objected but didn't. He seemed completely in control.

"Here's the drill in Geneva," she finally explained. "I check in at the Grand Hotel de Roubaix. I don't know where it is, but I'll find it on the map. The next day I'll go to a café on the rue Sevé. It's called Chez Ascender. It's run by a Hungarian who's a friend of Federov's. That's where I'll ask for Koller. You know the rest of the drill because I told you."

"Yes. I understand it," he said.

"My guess is that you should try to meet me in the hotel bar. Let's say six p.m. the second day I'm there. Keep an eye open over your shoulder and I'll do the same. We don't want to advertise that we're together."

"Okay," he said steadily. "That makes sense."

"This dinner tonight with your friends. What time?"

"Ten p.m. The place is called Tavern de Carmencita. The staff of your hotel will know it. Or should I pick you up?"

"I'll walk," she said. "And I'll be intrigued to meet your peers."

"They're more than peers. They're friends."

"I'll meet them anyway."

"They will have women with them," Peter warned.

"So?"

"Hired women."

She laughed. So did he. "*Expensively* hired?" she asked.

"Without a doubt. My government pays very well."

"Then I wouldn't want to miss it."

FORTY-FIVE

MADRID, SEPTEMBER 11, 10:00 P.M.

By 10:00, Alex was sitting down to dinner at Carmencita's on the Calle de Liberdad. The menu was more Basque than Spanish, but old bullfighting posters, photographs, and memorabilia adorned the walls, presumably to keep the tourists happy.

Peter had offered her an arm as they went through the door. She hesitated at first, then took it and liked the feel of it. His arm was like iron under his suit jacket.

Peter's two peers were there already when Alex arrived. The first was introduced as David Wong. The given name of the other, a slightly taller and stockier man, was Charles Ming. They were both in their early thirties, handsome, endlessly masculine, and very fit. They stood, shook Alex's hand when introduced, and gave her a polite bow. Each was accompanied by a drop-dead gorgeous girl. David had a sultry blonde with an easy smile. Her name was Sabrina, and she looked as if she were Russian or Polish.

Ming had with him a leggy brunette in a minidress. She was French, even though she gave her name as Holly. Everyone smoked except Alex. In Madrid, smokers had not yet been exiled to the streets. Ming and Wong and their companions were already into a second round of drinks when Peter and Alex settled into their table.

Alex did a quick scan. She couldn't tell if either of the men were carrying weapons, but she assumed they were. Both of the girls gave Alex a welcoming smile. Then it came out that Charles and David worked *for* Peter. He was their boss, even though he was only a few years older.

From that, Alex made a deduction: they were all there on the same assignment, having to do with *The Pietà of Malta*. And from there she deduced that this must have been a case of some significance to the Chinese to have assigned so many people to it from such a distance.

The group spoke English, occasionally lapsing into Spanish. The two girls mostly kept quiet, sipped drinks, and smoked. Sabrina, the blonde, was seated right next to Alex. At one point she turned and spoke in a low voice.

"Are you working?" Sabrina asked.

"What?"

"You're working tonight?" she asked again, giving a nod toward Peter who was telling the rest of the table about the trip that afternoon.

"Yes, I am," Alex answered, going along with it. After all, she was being paid to be there.

Sabrina smiled, nodded, and gave Alex a wink. At first Alex was uncomfortable with the insinuation, then, after a glass of wine, almost found it amusing. By coincidence, Peter's arm found its way around Alex's shoulders at about the same instant.

All right, she decided, no harm, no foul. She would play along, keep her ears open, and listen. The less any outsiders knew about her real job, the better.

A waiter appeared, took another round of drink orders in Spanish from Peter and Alex, who ordered red wine, and left dinner menus at the table. The talk around the table progressed. And quickly, Alex realized that she was looking at the face of the new China.

Peter, at forty-one, was maybe five years older than the other two men. But right before her eyes, China's first generation of only-children were waving good-bye to the old line Communist Party and saying hello to Moët, Prada, and Rolex. To listen to Peter and his two friends, laughing more heartily as the evening went on, was to believe that Shanghai was becoming the biggest boom town in history since Las Vegas. Around the table, they began swapping one-upsmanship stories of the prosperity of their new nation.

"Hey, my sister was in Chinese *Vogue* last month," Peter said. Quickly and proudly, he reached in his wallet and pulled out a clipping, cut neatly from a magazine. He produced a picture of an Asian gazelle who had his face and his features. Everyone leaned forward to check out the picture of Peter's sister.

Her name was Jennifer, Peter said, and she worked for IBM in Shanghai. Like all young Chinese on the cutting edge of fashion and trends, she had adopted an English-language first name, as American-like as possible.

The picture, in color, showed a world-class babe in her early twenties, done up in a white cashmere sweater, a raspberry leather miniskirt, and designer leather boots.

"Jennifer *loves* Chanel," Peter said with brotherly pride. "Ten years ago in China no one knew what Chanel was. Now my sister is addicted. She shops forever."

"She's *very* pretty," Alex said.

"Look at her," Peter said. "Immaculate hair. Perfect teeth. Manicured nails. Fluent in English, Japanese, and Cantonese, and she is feminine as feminine can be. She is the new Chinese woman in miniature," he laughed. "The economic miracle made flesh."

"Very nice looking flesh," Ming chipped in.

"Is she married?" one of the other girls asked.

Peter laughed. "Married? No, no! She's having too much fun. She has five boyfriends at the same time, and they all spoil her mercilessly!"

"Five?" Alex said. "*Five!* I don't think I've had five in my life!"

Alex's remark set off laughter around the table.

"Peter is just showing off because he *has* a sister," Wong said. "Peter was privileged. Hong Kong born. The rest of us are from one-child families."

"Because he's from Hong Kong he thinks he's better than the rest of us," Ming added.

"I *know* I am," Peter said, halfway through his second drink, an oversized gin and tonic.

"Peter already owns seven cars," Ming volunteered to Alex, as more drinks went around. "Did he tell you that?"

"No, he didn't," Alex said. "Are you kidding me? Is that true? Seven?"

"It's true," Peter acknowledged with a grin.

"What do you own?" she asked.

"Not much," he answered. "A few old wreckers."

Around the table, the lie didn't fly.

"Ha!" Ming said.

"Peter owns a Porsche 911, a Mercedes, a BMW X5, a Mitsubishi

Evolution, and a Toyota Yaris," said Wong, lighting a cigarette. "And that doesn't include the company Jaguar that's at his disposal in Europe."

Peter shook his head with a grin and tried to dismiss the subject. But he confirmed it was true about all the cars.

"That's only five that you named," Alex said to Charles Ming. She turned to Peter. "What else do you have back in the 'worker's paradise'?"

"Okay, okay," Peter said. "I also have a Peugeot, which I bought a year ago when I was in France, and I have an American 'collectible.' My favorite."

"What's that? Some hot Corvette or Mustang?"

"No, it's a 1970 Ford Colony Park station wagon."

"You drive around Shanghai in a Colony Park station wagon?" she asked.

"When I can," Peter said.

"He's never home to drive them, but he owns them," Ming taunted. "So his six-dozen girlfriends borrow them."

Wong added that Peter had inherited wealth. "His father owned five merchant ships, five hotels, and two hundred apartments. Some Communist!"

Again Peter brushed things off. "You know what they say about communism," Peter said. "It's the longest and most difficult route between capitalism and capitalism."

"You're going to get into trouble for giving away state secrets," Wong warned.

Again, the table laughed although Holly and Sabrina seemed a little left out. "Peter needs to be 'reeducated'," Ming taunted in good humor.

Peter, meanwhile, was making a hand signal to the waiter, who gave a quick nod of understanding.

"China today is crazy," Peter said, turning back to Alex, and explaining. "The money. The poverty. The urbanization. The exhaustion of our natural resources. The opportunities in China are beyond anything that anybody in Europe or America has ever seen. It's insane, but everyone goes along with it."

"My family was happy if we had food," Ming added, but less jokingly. "You in Hong Kong were already wealthy. Many of us in China were still struggling."

Ming continued. "My cousin is nine years older than me. She grew up during the Cultural Revolution. I grew up after it. She works in a factory that builds coffeemakers and sells them to the West. I cannot even imagine how hard her life has been. And she is *my* cousin. Peter's sister is what's known as a 'Shanghai princess,' a girl who has been raised in wealth and privilege."

Ming, it turned out through further conversation, was moving up in the world. He had just moved in Shanghai from a scrappy little neighborhood to a place named New California Estates. It was a private Western-style compound with huge villas made of fake adobe and a whole miniarmy of private guards. He showed Alex a picture of his home. Ming's minivilla had a manicured lawn, a deck overlooking a man-made lake, a barbecue pit, an ornamental well, and a perfectly groomed Labrador retriever.

"My dog's name is Clinton," Ming said.

"Named after the American president," Wong chided.

"The dog is a female. It's named after the ex-president's wife," Ming said. Ten years earlier, Ming said, his family had nothing; now not only did he have this house but he also bought an apartment for his parents. The economic thaw had started during the Clinton years in America, and so many young Chinese felt gratitude. Naming a pedigreed dog after the ex-first lady, to Ming's way of thinking, was the very least he could do. Alex thought of several smart remarks but didn't make any of them.

The waiter, responding to Peter's hand signal, appeared suddenly with a bottle of champagne and six glasses. He opened the bottle and poured drinks all around. Alex watched as Peter slipped the waiter an American hundred dollar bill and declined change. A tip. The waiter, his evening an instant success, gave Peter a low bow.

Wong's background was closer to Ming's than to Peter's. He had been brought up in Xinjiang, in the far northwest near the old Soviet border. His parents had been forcibly relocated there in the seventies. The Cultural Revolution had been the greatest disaster of their lives. Before the Civil War, he explained in a side conversation to Alex, his grandparents had been landlords, so they were considered capitalists. The Red Guard had come around one day with a vengeance and ordered them to the remote countryside.

"They didn't want to go work in the fields," he said, "but they were taken there and then left in the middle of the countryside. They had to build their own house. We were miles from anywhere. The government wanted to keep us apart from the local people. The nearest village was a two-hour cycle ride away, and it had nothing, only a little market."

Alex's curiosity was piqued. "That must have been terrible beyond belief," she said.

Her comment allowed Wong to open up even more.

"My parents were at the Shuanghe Labor Reeducation Camp," Wong said. "It was a prison farm near the Russian border. The other inmates were mainly young pickpockets, burglars, and brawlers. In the camp, guards and prisoners used the word 'reeducation' to mean you'd be locked up in a small cell and struck with electric prods or beaten. Afterward, you'd have to write a self-criticism. Then there was another form of daily torture. During the hours between breakfast and the second and final meal in the late afternoon, no one was allowed to use the toilet. My parents told me little more than that about the camp. I never wanted to know more. How could I?"

"I'm sorry," Alex said. She was.

"The same government apparatus that tortured my parents today makes me rich," he said. "Some days I find it confusing. Most days, I don't think about it."

He shrugged. Then he buried the thought with a long gulp of Moët and Chandon.

A wave of culture shock flowed through Alex. In almost everything she had read on China, sooner or later the phrase *human rights* turned up, coupled with the terms *policeman*, linked with words such as *torture* or *brutality*. And yet here was David Wong in Versace with a Polish babe in a slashed-to-the-thigh Liz Hurley. Next to him, Ming was a David Beckham look-alike-wannabe with pouffy hair, hanging all over his knockout French bimbo. These days, the iconic image of a lone figure standing up to a tank in Tiananmen Square was a relic of the past.

More champagne went around the table.

"So," Alex said, "does anyone ever criticize the government?"

"Of course," Peter answered. "It's common knowledge that the government is corrupt and is hiding scandals. And that they don't tell the truth. Everyone knows."

"What about democracy?" Alex asked.

"We can vote for representatives," Wong said quickly. "But in China there are too many people. True democracy is not possible."

"Why would anyone want nine hundred million unwashed, uneducated peasants from the countryside telling the government what it should do?" Peter added with dismay. "That would be absurd! The decisions of state are best left to the educated elite."

"Fine for you since you're part of it," Alex said.

"Of course. But look at the economic miracle of the last two decades. We are obviously doing a lot that is right. Our system might not be like yours, but for China it has worked."

"What about human rights?" Alex said. "Like detaining prisoners without trial? Like torture."

"Like Guantanamo?" laughed Ming. "One cannot always control the excesses of our government."

"So," Alex finally said, "is this really what Deng Xiaoping meant when he talked about 'socialism with Chinese characteristics' almost thirty years ago?"

"It might not be what Chairman Deng meant," Peter answered quickly, "but it's what it has become, for better or worse. A lot of business success is through the traditional virtue of *guanxi*, through elaborate social relationships." Well educated, male, and born in Hong Kong, he had been in a perfect position to profit.

"Okay then," Alex finally said. "You have all these luxuries and material successes," she said. "What about spiritual stuff?"

"Of what sort?" Wong asked.

"Maybe inner beliefs," she said. "A personal creed or a set of morals or a code?"

"Like a religion?"

"Call it that if you like," she said.

"You mean like Lee Yuan?" one of the younger two men said.

Alex wasn't sure who had mentioned the name, but conversation at the table stopped cold. It was as if someone had fired a shot. Peter's eyes widened slightly, as if to admonish whoever had crossed a line. And a line definitely had been crossed because both Wong and Ming, well lubricated as they were, had a regretful look to them.

"I've never heard that name before," Alex said. "Who's Lee Yuan?"

More of a pause. "Lee Yuan is why we're here," Peter said.

"Why's that?" she asked. "I'm not following."

Peter began to explain, obviously taking great care with his words.

"Lee Yuan was a wonderful man," he said. "He was a mentor to the three of us. A mystic perhaps. A great teacher and friend. He recruited all three of us into the current positions we now hold."

"I see."

"We would not be where we are today," Wong said, "if he had not handpicked and groomed us."

"He is no longer with us," Peter said. "He died recently. To honor him, his memory, his spirit, we are attempting to complete his final mission. There is a tradition. If a person perishes from this earth and an important part of his life's work is left unfinished, those who held that person in high regard are honor bound to pick up the fallen standard and finish that task. Sometimes such things are very small. Other times the task is great and may take a lifetime. The three thousand mile march begins with a single step, after all."

"That's a noble tradition," she said. "I can't argue with it."

"Thank you," he said. "But that's why I'm here, it's why my associates are here. Lee Yuan was a spiritual man. So we wish to accompany his spirit down his chosen path."

"So his soul can rest?" she asked.

"Think of it that way if you wish," Peter said.

Peter's eyes flicked away from Alex and onto the two other women at the table. The gesture was so quick that she would have missed it if she hadn't been looking directly at him. But she caught it.

"That's really all I can tell you for right now," he said. "I won't hide anything important from you. Maybe I'll think of more later. Or on another day. But that's all you need know for now."

"Thank you," she said.

He nodded. Then his serious expression gave way to a smile. The waiter returned and the conversation went back into Spanish. Orders for food were taken and another bottle of Moët replaced the dead one on the table.

Dinner was excellent. A live band started playing toward midnight, and the two younger Chinese agents pulled their partners out onto a small dance floor. Chang watched them go, turned back to Alex, smiled, and extended a hand to her. He motioned to where people were dancing.

"You have to be kidding. I haven't danced for quite some time," she said.

"Let's change that now," he said. "Please? I'd be honored."

She drew a breath. The images of her personal tragedy flashed in front of her. She thought of Robert and thought of the discussions they'd had before he died. If anything happened to either of them, the other could go on and create a new life.

"Okay," she finally said.

Out onto the floor they went.

The name of Lee Yuan did not come up again that evening.

Alex did not weave back into her hotel suite until well past 2:00 a.m.

FORTY-SIX

MADRID, SEPTEMBER 12, MORNING

On fewer hours of sleep than she might have preferred, Alex rose the next morning later than the previous day. It was almost nine when she opened her eyes. She checked her email, the personal account first.

There was something from Ben back in the States, which she opened first. Then she quickly switched into her secure account for Treasury. She wished to read everything in her Inbox before sending anything.

There was nothing from Floyd Connelly, who this morning was neither Pink nor Pretty Boy. She prowled through the latest links from her associates at Scotland Yard, Interpol, the Spanish and French police agencies, as well as Rizzo in Rome. Rizzo was in a newly explosive and churlish mood. He'd had DNA tests run on the tissue sample beneath his fingernails and was fuming that there had been no matches yet.

She scanned some new attachments from her contacts. Nothing good.

Hunched over the laptop in a T-shirt and navy track shorts, her dark hair hanging carelessly to the side of her face as she inclined over her work, she again looked more like a graduate student than a skilled investigator from the United States Department of Treasury. And a funny bit of doggerel rebounded from her own youth years ago. A phrase her mother used to say: A fool can ask more questions than a wise woman can answer.

So what was she this morning, Alex wondered in a little pang of self-criticism. A fool or a wise woman, dancing into the early morning hours at a Spanish tavern with an agent of Chinese state security whom she had just met a few days ago? Did a fast and loose social life fit her current mood and lifestyle?

Well, it *had* been most enjoyable. And Peter hadn't made any move toward her at the end of the evening. Was she disappointed by that? The mood had loosened between them . . .

Hey! She said to herself. *Reality check: you're on duty! Behave!*

The previous evening, Peter had revealed something of interest, something perhaps that he might have otherwise not wished to mention. Lee Yuan. Maybe it was something she could parlay.

She went back to the attachments from Colonel Pendraza. She had become adept at skimming them quickly. She worked her way through them.

Two Germans who belonged to neo-Nazi skinhead groups in Munich had been arrested in Luxembourg, charged with illegally selling to police informants twenty pounds of dynamite to be used against synagogues across Europe. Policia Nacional agents in Tunisia had arrested another neo-Nazi after he allegedly tried to purchase ingredients for deadly sarin nerve gas and C–4 plastic explosives from an Interpol undercover agent. A key tip had come from an Israeli born prostitute. Then a biggie: members of the Irish National Police had raided the Antrim county home of a former Provo and discovered an arsenal of more than 250,000 rounds of ammunition, fifty pipe bombs, and ten remote-control briefcase bombs. No longer useful for the conflict in Ireland, the old IRA gent was trying to move the stuff to the Middle East. Then there was something about the movement of HDX explosives from Iraq through Cyprus. Interpol had been on the case and had lost track of the HDX shipment there. The explosives may have moved east, they might still be in some mountain hideaway. Who knew until someone set them off? This dead-end tale gave way to two stories about the same "honor killing" of an Iraqi girl in Naples who had gotten pregnant by an Italian boy. The girl's uncle had killed her before killing himself.

Alex blew out a long breath. But her fingers busied themselves at the keyboard again. Something had occurred to her while she was asleep, and she had now formulated her approach to it.

She went back to her secure email account and went to Mail. In the address box, she typed in a message in English to be sent to every person who had been at the embassy meeting five days previously.

Maybe, maybe, maybe . . .

Maybe by keeping her ears open and not getting too soused on the champagne, she had heard something of note.

In the course of my investigations concerning *The Pietà of Malta*, the name of "Lee Yuan" surfaced last evening. Has that name been in any way involved in any investigation in any of your records? I have reason to believe that "Yuan" (possibly a pseudonym) may also have been on the trail of our so-called black bird. Would you please run this name across your files and get back to me with a response as soon as possible? My information indicates that Yuan was a Chinese national and was very possibly traveling in Europe on a Chinese passport, perhaps diplomatic.

Please note also, that, as the name is transliterated from the Chinese, there may be other variations to the spelling. I have obtained this name from a source I consider highly reliable, so I would appreciate your feedback as quickly as possible.

Alex LaDuca
Ritz, Madrid

She hit Send and leaned back from her laptop.

She sat quietly for several minutes and waited to see if there was any immediate response from anyone. There was none. She closed down the laptop. She felt her attention flag. She needed a break. She threw her swimsuit into a tote bag and hit the local gym again.

Weights and a swim.

Ninety minutes later, refreshed, she was back on the balcony, hammering at the keyboard of the laptop, and the wireless connection was trying to scan through more of the documents from the National Police. She continued to come up empty, however. And she knew there was nothing she could do now. She passed the afternoon in Madrid, walking, visiting some small stores, but preoccupied. She checked in on email several times during the day and while her associates gradually, one by one, acknowledged her inquiry, none had anything new to direct back to her.

Yuan's name rang no immediate bells anywhere. She felt disappointment.

There was no reply at all from Floyd Connelly, whom she increasingly considered worse than useless, or from Essen at Interpol. Rizzo in Rome said he was shaking as many trees as possible and would see what he might have by the following morning. The French National Police had nothing on Yuan and neither did the two Spanish agencies.

Fair enough. Lee Yuan may have had no bearing on recent events after all. Or maybe, she wondered when her darkest notions took over, the whole story was a bit of concocted fiction. Maybe she was being played for a sucker by Peter and his sharp little gang of Sino-warriors.

She had the uncomfortable feeling of being a fool but didn't know whose. In a final email dispatch of the evening, she sent to her museum contacts her tentative itinerary to Switzerland, CC-ing Mike in Washington. It was a debatable step, but she decided long ago that it would be better to have your peers recover your body than to just disappear forever.

When evening came, Alex grabbed a light dinner toward eight o'clock in a tapas bar. She had the inclination to phone Peter but knew that there was always the chance that one of their cell phones or even both were no longer secure. Since it was part of the overall plan to not reveal their association to any enemy, calls needed to be kept at a minimum

She arranged with the hotel for an evening check-out, finished the final details of packing, and went to the train station by 10:00 p.m. She boarded the train and found her private compartment. She was tired from the previous late night, so she eased into her bed with a couple of books. A final check of email came up empty.

The train, while fully boarded, stayed in the station for two hours before pulling out and hitting the open tracks. At this time she tried to settle in for sleep, carefully placing her loaded gun at her bedside.

Alex had not taken an overnight train for many years and had forgotten how tactile the cozy charm of the train was. The feel of the steel wheels on the rails had a comforting rhythm to it. It lulled her to sleep almost immediately.

FORTY-SEVEN

MADRID, SEPTEMBER 12, AFTERNOON

That same afternoon, Jean-Claude was down in his tunnel again. And he could barely conceal his delight at what he saw. The blast had blown a perfectly sized hole in the debris. It had cleared a route to the other side of the Calle Juan Bravo.

The pathway was dirty. It was musty and dusty and ankle deep in water. But he managed to crawl through it. Then, scanning ahead, pointing his flashlight, he could see that the pathway continued for maybe another thirty meters before encountering another wall. He examined his new location and realized that he was still working in a closely parallel path to those taken by Metro workers, electrical workers, or telephone technicians. There were several old power grids and telephone junctions along this route.

Well, the chamber had been cleared. His people were ready to work again.

Jean-Claude retraced his steps, went back, and reassembled his small underground army.

Within another two hours he had his team of subversives reassembled and went back to work. This time they were punching through some old bricks to enter a corridor that would run parallel to the Metro tracks.

Jean-Claude felt wonderful. Everything was falling into place perfectly. Now for the next step. He needed that set of detonators for the big blast. He had already placed his order. He would go back to see the man in his neighborhood named Farooq who could acquire such things.

Farooq's name was promising. It meant "one who distinguishes truth from falsehood." Maybe it was why everyone trusted him.

Allah be praised.

FORTY-EIGHT

MADRID TO GENEVA, SEPTEMBER 12 - 13 , EN ROUTE/OVERNIGHT

In the middle of the night, as the train wheels rumbled beneath Alex, the sharp sound of someone trying the doorknob to her compartment jolted her awake. She sat upright, her weapon pointed toward the door.

She kept still and said nothing, feeling her heart pounding. The doorknob continued to rattle from a strong, insistent hand on the other side.

Then she heard sounds from the other side of the door. A man's voice. Very angry. The man spoke French. The door thumped. It sounded like he had put his shoulder to it.

Alex scurried to her feet and peered through the peephole. The hallway was dimly lit, but she could see a man and a woman, lurching.

The attempt at entry stopped, followed by a brief but noisy hallway discussion in heavily accented Midi French.

It was an obscene accusatory argument. They were drunk and obviously at the wrong door.

From what she could catch of the dialogue, it sounded like the drunken husband was finally wandering back to his own compartment after falling asleep elsewhere on the train. His wife had waited up for him.

Or something.

Alex smirked slightly. But for good measure, she kept her gun trained at the door in case this was some sort of cover for a sudden break-in. And she moved away from the door in case anyone suddenly fired a bullet through it.

When it was quiet again, she went to the door, pistol aloft in her right hand, and opened it slowly. The corridor was empty.

She returned to bed and slept.

The next morning she arrived in Figueras, the final stop in Spain.

The day was warm and sunny, a pleasant late summer day in Europe. She was dressed casually, light jeans and a T-shirt, dark glasses, her gun in her purse this time, right next to her US passport.

She connected in the Figueras station with the train that would take her to Montpellier in France. There was no longer a stop for customs. After a ninety-minute trip, she then changed trains again in Montpellier for the Train de Grande Vitesse, which would speed her to Geneva.

She sat in a coach car next to a Frenchman who was a banker out of Dijon. He initiated the conversation and presented her with a business card. They spoke French. He was intrigued when she said that she was American and intrigued a second time when she said that she worked for the United States Department of Treasury.

Instinct again. She had a funny sense about him, maybe that he had been waiting for her. But the conversation went nowhere.

He nodded and went back to his reading. A few minutes later, his cell phone rang. The conversation was brief. Then he closed the phone and turned to her.

"I'm going to be changing seats," he said.

She nodded and rose, stepping to the aisle.

"Would you like the window?" he asked.

"It doesn't matter," she said.

"Take it," he said. "You might prefer it. And my associate likes the aisle."

He stepped past her with infinite courtesy. He turned and disappeared toward the rear of the train. Alex slid back in and sat down. She slid to the window, waited, and made sure her weapon was accessible under her jacket. She kept her hand near it. With her other hand, she flipped open a mirror from a makeup case. She positioned it and herself so that she could see anyone approaching from the train cars ahead of her, while watching the rear via the mirror.

She knew something was up. A minute passed and she spotted a heavy-set balding man approaching her row from behind. He was in his mid-forties and built like a brick outhouse. She had seen him once before in her life, at the meeting at the embassy.

Maurice Essen of Interpol, the Swiss-German who was a

representative of the International Criminal Police Organization. He stopped at her row and glanced to her, indicating the open seat.

"Is this seat free?" he asked in very good English.

"I believe it's yours, Maurice," she said.

He smiled graciously. He sat down.

"If you've gone to this effort to follow me so you could speak in person," she said in low tones barely audible above the sound of the train, "you must have something pretty good."

"That or I believe *you* do," he said. "I flew to Montpellier this morning so I could take this train so we could talk in person," he said.

"About what?" Alex asked.

"An open case before Interpol and the Swiss federal police," he said. "Lee Yuan."

"I might have known."

He continued in English. "The Swiss police retrieved Yuan's body from a glacier a few weeks ago," Essen began. "The government of China took an immediate interest in it. The Chinese had apparently sent one of their top young agents to retrieve the body, a charming fortyish man who traveled under the passport of John Sun. Sending someone to retrieve a corpse is *not* normal procedure for the Chinese. They normally ask for corpses of their nationals to be disposed of efficiently at the local level. A nice, cozy crematorium usually. So the request to ice the body and hold it was highly unusual."

"So this Yuan fellow had to have been important," Alex said.

"And there was nothing normal about this John Sun, either, the fellow who came and got the body out of the country as fast as possible. Sun had a diplomatic passport to cut through some red tape. Not everyone travels on one of those, not even Chinese body-snatchers."

Alex listened in silence, assimilating as many details as quickly as she could, trying to picture the scene that had unfurled in Zurich.

"Now, the behavior of the Chinese was *so* unusual," Essen continued, "that it drew the attention of both the Swiss Gendarmerie Nationale as well as the local cantonal police in Zurich. So they shadowed this John Sun. They had two-man teams on him twenty-four seven while he was in the Zurich area. They even went to the trouble to shoot some surveillance photos on the street."

Essen reached to an inside jacket pocket. He pulled out a trio of surveillance pictures and showed them to Alex.

The pictures told her what she had already surmised. John Sun was Peter Chang. Or maybe Peter Chang was John Sun. Or maybe it was an equation that she hadn't quite mastered yet. But the surveillance photos confirmed to her that she and Maurice Essen were discussing the same man. She was certain.

"Ever seen him?" Essen asked.

"I'm not sure," she lied.

For several seconds she stared blankly and coldly at the image of the man she had danced with until 2:00 a.m. two nights earlier, whose arms had held her, and who had given her a friendly platonic kiss on each cheek in the lobby of the Ritz when he had escorted her back to the hotel.

"I really can't say," she said.

"Of course not," Essen said. "Well, to use an expression I once learned in America, he's a slippery SOB, this John Sun, so I hope you're not helping him if you want our help. In Switzerland he apparently 'made' his watchers, an experienced counterterror team, and slipped them. He went in and out of a department store on the Hildenstrasse in Zurich. Or at least he went in because no one saw him come out. It was there that he vanished."

"Why are you interested in him?" she asked. "From what you've said, he didn't break any laws. Not yet by your accounts, anyway."

"Our initial focus had been more upon Yuan than his custodian," Essen said. "What exactly had Yuan been up to in Switzerland that would land him in a glacier with lungs filled with smoke? So the Swiss tried to determine who Yuan had been and what his mission had entailed. An informer told them that Yuan had been in Europe to effect a transfer of cash for some bill of goods. The Swiss police hadn't known whether it was drugs, weapons, or maybe jewelry. The informer hadn't known. There was plenty of speculation to go around, and it went in several unsubstantiated directions."

Conspicuously absent so far, Alex noted, was any mention of the high-ticket *Pietà of Malta*. But her own theories were starting to emerge. And on the subject of theories, the Swiss police had some fairly sinister ones about John Sun.

"Two atypical murders in Geneva took place within twenty-four hours of Sun's disappearance from Zurich," Essen said. "One victim was an old crook named Laurent Tissot, a Swiss. The other was a man known as Stanislaw Jurjeznicz, a Pole. Sun somehow had moved about the country like a phantom. Just as his surveillance team had not known anyone who could disappear so quickly, they had never seen a diplomat who could have slipped in and out so fast. So when they ran a check on his passport, they discovered it was one of those mysterious 'Made in China' specials. It dead-ended into the Beijing computers. The passport was real but the owner wasn't. Not quite, anyway. And the two dead men in Geneva—the Swiss national and the Polish national, both with ties to the underworld—had links to a shady deal gone sour. The Swiss then went through all their street surveillance cameras in the significant parts of Geneva, including bank ATMs, and connected 'Sun' with the time and place. That, in turn, connected Sun to Yuan and possibly to two murders."

"With respect," Alex said, "what you're presenting is a highly circumstantial case."

"That's right," Essen said politely. "So, I'll ask you again, maybe as a hypothetical, do you think you might have seen or encountered the individual we know as John Sun?"

"I see a lot of people every day," she said. "Nothing stands out."

"This man would stand out. Of course," Essen said with a slight sigh, a tiny decent into anger as he answered, "keep something in mind. We have established that the Switzer and the Pole knew each other, did business with each other, based on the accounts of respected informants. So any information you can give us in return, particularly on the whereabouts of 'Sun' would be of infinite interest, particularly if he can be located on Swiss soil where he can be brought in for questioning. We consider Sun highly dangerous. This is evident, in consideration of the deaths of the Pole and the Switzer."

"I understand," she said. "If there's a time at which I can help you with this, I'll be pleased to do so."

"Of course," Essen said. "Good day, Ms. Alex. We'll appreciate your cooperation in the future."

"Of course," she said.

Essen rose, gave her a curt old-world bow, and returned in the direction he had come. The seat next to her remained empty.

She stared for several minutes out the window as the landscape of southeastern France flew by. There were moments in life — messages, acquisitions of knowledge — that were made up of too much stuff to be digested whole.

This was one. Or maybe this was several of them, all jammed together. Eventually, she steepled her fingers before her and thought deeply. Just in terms of Peter, which way should she proceed? What if Peter had murdered two men in Switzerland to cover his own crimes or something even more devious?

Alert him that Interpol was on his trail?

Alert Interpol that Peter would be joining her in Geneva?

Run the whole thing past Mark McKinnon, hope he was sober enough to make a correct decision, and proceed on his instructions?

Every potential step had something right with it and something wrong with it.

To alert Interpol was to betray Peter, who had saved her life.

To ignore Interpol was to betray the working relationship she sought to develop for this and future cases. Did professional loyalties trump personal gratitude? Or was it the other way around?

Alex pondered.

Do nothing? Always an option for the fainthearted or the unduly cautious. But doing nothing was sometimes the wisest route. She brooded.

Reality check. Back to Square One: her assignment was *The Pietà of Malta*, its recovery, and any issues attendant to its theft. Who could help her more? Peter? Or Interpol?

A question like that should have been a slam dunk. But instead, she had no answer. She had the funny sense of not knowing Peter Chang at all, or maybe knowing him all too well. She wasn't sure which.

The train arrived exactly on time in Geneva in mid-afternoon. As planned, she checked into the Grand Hotel de Roubaix in Geneva as late afternoon was fading into evening. She had dinner at the hotel, went out for a walk, returned, bolted her door, and did a final check for email.

Finally she made a decision.

No bolt of lightning would illuminate the whereabouts of *The Pietà of Malta*, no magical key would put everything in perspective. But now there was a crucial new piece to the puzzle.

She went back to her computer. She typed an email to both Mark McKinnon in Europe and her boss Mike Gamburian back in Washington, inquiring by name about Laurent Tissot and Stanislaw Jurjeznicz. She wrote:

```
I don't know. It might be nothing, but I'd appre-
ciate anything you have on either of these two.
Their names have surfaced.
Alex.
Geneva
```

She felt clever and compromised at the same time. Like Peter on the subject of Yuan and perhaps on the subject of *The Pietà of Malta*, she had not exactly told a lie. She had instead declined to tell the complete truth.

She waited for a few minutes. She found a cognac in the hotel's overpriced minibar, and poured herself a double.

Then the email account flashed again with an incoming message. Something back fast from Gamburian, who must have been at the tail end of a long business day. No hits on the Pole, but there was some preliminary stuff on Tissot. After a stint in the Swiss Army, he was a career shady character, but mostly an arms merchant. Tissot was not an outright crook, but usually in the gray area of the law and the dark gray area of ethics and morality. Gamburian finished,

```
More details to follow,
I'll try to boot up an entire file tomorrow a.m.
in DC. Cheers, stay safe.
```

She wrote back and thanked him. But now she was exhausted. Absolutely and positively. She shut down her laptop, made sure the door to her room was bolted, set up her weapon again, and settled into bed, her mind still teeming, trying to factor a dead arms dealer into the mix but not quite able. Not yet, anyway.

After several minutes, she realized not only that she was still awake, but she hadn't even managed to close her eyes. She was staring at the dark ceiling, watching the play of shadows and light from the curtained window, and conscious of some distant movement in the adjoining hotel room, on the other side of her closet.

She opened up her iPod. She channeled into some light classical music, which did help her relax. Then, as sleep crept up on her, and as she was on the verge of dropping off into its soft embrace, more events and theories interconnected.

And another startling realization was upon her; as she worked scenarios in reverse and tried to distill inner truths from what she had been told, she had another answer.

Somehow, Peter had connected either Tissot, Stanislaw, Lee Yuan, or the pietà itself to Yuri Federov, the man she was in Geneva to find. Possibly he had done this through the computers of the man he had killed. She remembered Peter boasting about how he had broken into their database. Or possibly he had done this through other means. But from there, Peter — the name she continued to think of him as — went to Mark McKinnon, her CIA guy, with whom he had worked before.

Peter needed a way of accessing Federov. But why?

McKinnon, she theorized, had gone to the State Department and Alex's c.v. had spun off a link to Federov. So McKinnon had contacted her boss, Mike Gamburian, and her phone had rung on a Barcelona beach. Conveniently, she was still in Europe. Hence, very late at night in a Geneva hotel room, she had the answer to a question: How had Peter known that she was assigned to the case before she did?

Well, it was a thesis, at least. It made sense. And then she realized, so did something else. Yuri Federov must have been in a position to know something about the pietà's disappearance. Otherwise, finding him wouldn't have been so critical.

It all made a tidy little bundle. And the tidy little bundle was part of a massive mess. Several people were already dead, the perps were still out there, and who knew what the motivation of the theft had been, where the money had gone, and—almost least important now—who knew where the lamentation was?

Well, she would put all this to Peter when she saw him and see what he had to say about it. She even had a bargaining chip: Interpol was on his tail, and he might not even know.

Then she found something new to worry about. Maybe Interpol had nailed him already when he had crossed the border into Switzerland, even though he had probably changed passports. Maybe she was on her own again. And maybe she was now under Interpol surveillance. She might have to work the department-store routine herself.

She blew out a long sigh. A third cognac helped. Her eyelids came together. It was past two thirty in the morning. The bed was finally comfortable. So, for a short while, she slept.

FORTY-NINE

In the hour before dawn, Alex's eyes flashed open. She lay very still in bed. Somewhere close to her there had been movement in her hotel suite. But where?

The room was very dark. Her eyes tried to adjust. She made no movement in bed but slid her gaze to the night table. The LED on the clock radio told part of the story, but only a small part.

It was half past five in the morning. Very few good things happen at half past five in the morning. She counted her heartbeats. They accelerated. She knew she was not alone in her bedroom.

But how? She knew she had thrown the chain on the door. How could anyone have entered? Whoever was there was still in the room with her. She let her eyes adjust more and she looked for the pistol that she had left near the clock radio.

That told her for sure that she was not alone. The weapon that she had carefully placed there was gone.

Oh Lord, Oh Lord, Oh Lord!

She felt herself start to sweat. Feigning restlessness, feigning sleep, she kept her eyes open just as slits and rolled over. She forcibly had to control her fear because in the darkness two figures loomed right at her bedside. They were both men. They were big. Their arms were at their sides and neither appeared to hold a weapon.

These men were professionals, otherwise they couldn't have entered so furtively. They were between her and the door. That wasn't an accident, either. *Oh Lord, Oh Lord, Oh Lord!* Her heart raced. Her sweat glands were in overdrive, her entire body was overheating. Her heart thundered. The only defense she had left now was to make the first move.

She bolted up in bed and swung her right hand at the closest man. But the two intruders made their moves at the same time. The nearest man threw out a powerful arm to stop her blow. She tried to force her way up from the bed, but even as she kicked, the second man grabbed her legs above the knees, forcing her back down.

His grip was powerful and overwhelming. She realized that both these men had stocking masks over their faces, and she knew that neither was Peter. Where was Peter now when she needed him again?

Then all of the weight of one of the men came onto the bed and onto her legs, pinning her.

She cursed violently in English. She fought back with elbows and two flailing hands, but the first assailant was adept at what he was there to do. He held down her right arm and forced her upper body down onto the mattress. Amidst grunts and curses, she felt something rip. It was her nightgown.

Then she smelled something that reminded her of ether or some medical sedative. Instantly, she knew what would follow.

She kicked and struggled, but her legs remained pinned. She fought with her left hand, striking incessantly at the head of the closest man. But she couldn't manage an effective angle on him.

She couldn't do any damage. Within seconds, he pushed a cloth to her face.

The cloth was warm and wet. It had the noxious medicinal scent that she already smelled. Her assailant forced her head back down. She felt as violated as she had ever felt in her life.

The chemical was powerful. It overwhelmed her immediately. The strength went out of her body, and the fight went out of her arms and legs.

Suddenly, the struggle didn't matter, because it was over. Alex was drifting, losing consciousness, losing the ability to fight. *Losing my life too?* she wondered. *Who are these people?*

What are they going to do to me? Rape me? Kill me? Both?

She tried to move her head, to breathe fresher air, but the powerful hand of her assailant kept the cloth and the vapors against her face. She felt as if her whole body were spiraling down a tunnel. They were speaking a foreign language, but she was so far gone she couldn't unravel it. She didn't even know whether she knew it or not.

Then the whiteness faded. Her body eased its struggle and consciousness gave way to an abyss of blackness.

FIFTY

Alex's eyes flickered, wavered, and came open.

She had no idea where she was. Her first realization was that she was alive. Then she realized that she was lying in a strange room under a single sheet and blanket. There was a pillow under her head. The bed was comfortable and clean, the sheets fresh.

She blinked again. She felt groggy. She let several minutes drift by, feeling as if she were floating. Finally, she tried to sit up, supporting herself on one elbow, but lost balance and slid back down again.

What had happened the night before? She had been abducted, right? Now it seemed as if she had imagined it. Then, as her mind focused back to reality, she knew. It *had* happened.

Her brain buzzed. She felt as if there were butterflies in her head. Her body ached where the two assailants had grabbed her.

She sat up again and this time was able to remain steady on her elbow. Across the room a double window that looked out onto sunlight and trees. There was a blue sky beyond. There was a door across the room on the other side. It was shut. There was a dresser and a mirror. The room had the feel of a private residence, the guest room of a comfortable home. For the first time in her life, she was waking up not even knowing what country she was in.

She looked across the room. Her attention fell upon the dresser near the window. It was low and wide, three rows of drawers, two drawers to a row. On top of the dresser was a fresh bouquet of flowers. Behind the flowers was a mirror.

Her weapon was gone. No surprise there. She looked at her wrist. Her watch was gone also.

She pushed the bedcover and sheet aside. She swung her legs off the bed to stand up. Realizations came upon her one by one as her brain began to function again.

The next realization was how she was dressed.

Holy — —! She was wearing something that she had never seen before, much less worn. It was a deep ruby-red cheongsam, a traditional Asian silk gown with intricate gold embroidery. It felt cool against her body, and at that moment she realized that all her other garments had been removed, with the exception of the stone pendant that hung around her neck. Not only had she been abducted, but, yes, she *had* been undressed then re-dressed.

The gown flowed to her ankles but was slit at the side. She blinked and felt lightheaded. The moment passed.

On the floor by the bed was a pair of slippers. She slid her feet into them. They fit perfectly. Cautiously, she tried to stand, but wobbled, then sat back down hard on the bed.

Another second and she was up again, successfully this time. She took a few tentative steps that carried her to the window. She looked out. She had been correct. She was in a private home of some sort and was looking down into a garden. Beyond was a comfortable array of outdoor furniture. An expensive sitting area. The garden must have been an acre or more. She carefully studied what appeared to be the perimeter between this house and those that were contiguous. She noted quickly that there were high walls, maybe twelve feet, and on the top of the walls were wires, both barbed and those that formed a security link. She noted the position of the sun and the shadows it cast and reasoned that it was late morning.

She turned quickly and found exactly what she was looking for. In the corner of the room, where the wall met the ceiling, was a small security camera. She moved to the closet and opened the door. Neatly assembled on hangers were her clothes from the hotel. How nice. They had probably checked her out too. Maybe they had settled her bill for her as well.

But the next thing that occurred to her was much more ominous. If she had been abducted quietly overnight, she was here without backup. She would have no way to rendezvous with Peter or even contact him. And chances were, he would be unable to find her. Alex didn't even know where she was, so how would Peter find out?

She turned toward the door, placed a hand on the knob, and turned it. It opened easily. She stepped out into a hallway onto the second floor landing of a modern house. There were other rooms in each direction, but she overlooked an entrance hall on what appeared to be the first floor below. There were stairs that led downward.

She saw no one. But she heard a distant man's voice. A one-way conversation. She couldn't discern what language and figured that the man was on the telephone.

She moved to the stairs. She began to walk down. The stairs had a slight creak to them, so whoever had abducted her now definitely knew she was up and awake, even if they hadn't been watching via the camera.

At the bottom of the stairs, she was in a wide entrance hall that dominated the first floor of the house. To her left she saw a formal dining room with rich green walls. In its center was a long mahogany table that seated twelve. To the other side of the hall was a living room with plush sofas and several sitting areas.

There were various paintings on the wall — originals. She spotted a Picasso etching and a Miró. The living room, on second glance, was dominated by a Lautrec poster, again obviously an original, in exquisite condition. Minor works by major artists. Seven-figure price tags.

In the back of her mind, she was processing the conversation that she was tuned into, a man's voice coming out of a study. It was in English, heavily accented, and seemed to be a consultation with a lawyer or financial advisor of some sort. There was some sort of legal flap in Canada.

It stood to reason. The owner of this place was rich, rich, rich. Art treasures and homes like this weren't left by the tooth fairy.

She turned from the living room and walked softly to the open door of the study.

A handsome, rugged-faced man was seated at a wide desk with an enormous aquarium behind him.

He looked up at her and offered a broad smile, as if, on a very personal level, he was nothing short of thrilled to see her. He held aloft an index finger, indicating he would be another minute on his phone call.

She gave him a slow nod of assent. She more than recognized him.

Next to her in his office was half a wall of CDs. There must have been two thousand of them. She scanned the titles as he continued on the telephone.

Rachmaninoff. Peggy Lee. The Dixie Chicks.

What was it about high-testosterone Russian big shots that made their musical tastes so quirky? Was it the vastness of eastern European geography, or the bloody absolutism of the region's history, or just something kinky in the DNA? She knew that John Gotti had liked Sinatra, Jerry Vale, and Bobby Darin, but who would have guessed that Yuri Federov was a fan of seventies Schlock Rock and had a complete set of Deep Purple? *Spend a first night in a strange man's home*, her friend Laura had once said to her with a wry smile, *and there's no end to the things you discover about him.*

How true it was! At her feet was a short stack of books and magazines that had slithered over onto its side. There was something about yoga, recent copies of *Paris Match* and *Der Spiegel*, a hardcover book with bookmark — *Paris: The Secret History* by Andrew Hussey — an oversized volume about Chelsea Football, and a couple of collections of comparative religious philosophies.

She turned back toward him as he concluded his phone call. Federov clicked the phone shut and placed it on his desk. He leaned back in his chair, almost to the fish tank, and smiled even more broadly.

"Good morning," she said in English. Her tone was cold.

"Good morning," Yuri Federov answered.

FIFTY-ONE

Sleep well?" Federov asked. He leaned forward again and folded his hands.

"Not particularly, thanks to you."

"The bed was uncomfortable?" he asked.

"What do you think? I ought to have you arrested for abducting me," Alex said.

"You ought to, yes, but we both know that as much as you'd like to, you won't," he said. "So why are we even talking about it?" His eyes ran her up and down. "You look beautiful in that gown, by the way. You wear red so nicely. It's yours to keep."

"I can't wait to get rid of it."

He laughed. "Take it off right now and drop it on the floor if you wish. I would have no objection!"

She unloaded on him with a creative run of profanity.

"Wrong color?" he asked, raising an eyebrow.

"Wrong way to present a woman with a gift," she said.

"I apologize sincerely. But I'd be deeply honored if you would keep it."

"I'll think about it, all right?" she said, an edge remaining to her voice. "Am I your prisoner?"

"Of course not! You're my guest."

"There's a difference?"

"Absolutely."

"Then I'm free to go?"

"Whenever you'd like," Federov answered, "but again, we both know you won't, not without what you came to Geneva to accomplish. I understand you very well, Alexandra. Educated, strong, articulate in several languages; there are very few women like you. But you have an 'Achilles heel,' if that's the phrase. *You* don't understand *me*."

He reached for a humidor on the side of his desk and pulled out a small cigar.

"You don't get the impression that I might be a bit indignant about the way I was brought here and the way your staff seems to have undressed me completely and then dressed me up in a garment that pleases you?"

"You really don't like the gown? I think it's rather beautiful, more so with you in it, of course."

He lit the cigar with a flourish.

Then she said, "The gown is very nice. And you know that's not the point."

"Then what *is* the point?"

"How I got here! Being undressed and re-dressed by strangers, your staff, presumably."

"I had you brought here," he began, "in an unorthodox way because I could not take the chance that you might be followed if I summoned you here on your own. I didn't wish to meet with you in a public place, for the safety of both of us. But I do wish to help you with whatever request you're here to ask of me. As for being undressed and re-dressed by strangers, my staff, as you say — that didn't happen. The men I sent to bring you to me knew that the utmost care was to be taken and you were not to be harmed in any way."

"Just terrified!" she said, interrupting.

"It had to be done like that," he insisted. "Then you were brought here. You were handed over to me with the gentleness and care that one would use in placing a raw egg in a mother's hand. I carried you upstairs myself, and I changed you myself. So the eyes of no strangers were upon you. I am an old friend."

She felt a cringe within her. "Seriously. Don't flatter yourself."

"Acquaintance? If I'm neither friend nor acquaintance, why do you come to Switzerland to ask favors of me?"

"You're a business associate."

"Well, I hope to eventually be more."

"Like what?"

"Your lover, perhaps. Soon."

"When hell freezes over," she shot back. "Where are the rest of my things?" she asked above his laughter.

"Your clothes are in the closet of your room," he said.

"I know that. What about my gun?"

He leaned forward and reached to the side drawer on his desk. He opened the drawer and pulled it out. The Browning was in its holster, the magazine removed. He laid the weapon and the magazine on the desk in front of him, complete with bullets. With the gesture of an open hand, he offered them to her. She walked to the desk and picked up both. She held them and folded her arms.

"Why don't you sit down and we'll talk about why you're here. I might be able to help. Coffee? Tea? I have a staff here. You must be hungry."

"Food and some answers," she finally said. "Those are offers I can accept."

Federov rose from his desk and led the way, offering an arm that Alex declined by ignoring. There was an awkward moment as Federov slowed, but then he continued. They passed through the expansive front entry hall and into the dining room, passing a set of double doors that Alex had not noticed the first time. She also now saw that there was a single place set, as if to await a late-rising guest, which, of course, she was.

Federov motioned graciously to her seat. She took it and he held the chair. Somewhere along the way since she had seen him last, he seemed to have taken up the study of manners, though he wasn't always an "A" student.

She sat. He moved to a place at the head of the table, allowing an empty chair as an interval, obviously so as not to crowd her. Now that her fear had subsided, as had her shock at being abducted, she realized she was quite hungry.

Federov leaned forward and reached to a small bell on the table. He rang like an English aristocrat of the nineteenth century. A small woman named Lucy emerged from the kitchen and gave Federov a nod and fixed Alex with a smile that suggested that she thought that Alex was a girlfriend of the boss since she had spent the night.

"What would you like?" Federov asked. "For breakfast, I mean."

"What are you offering?"

After a moment of discussion and negotiation, it was settled on scrambled eggs, toast, milk, and tea. Lucy gave a polite nod, vanished, and was soon making noise in the kitchen.

Alex turned back to Federov. She fingered the stone pendant that hung on the gold chain around her neck. Federov noticed the touch. She moved her hand away.

"Before you have questions for me," he said, "I have many for you."

"Go ahead," Alex said. "You ask me one, then I'll ask you one, How's that?"

That, nodded Federov, was just fine.

"You're an intelligent woman," he said. "When I was changing you into your robe," he said, "at one point all you had left was that stone pendant. Why do you continue to wear it?"

"It saved my life once," she said. "Who knows? It could again."

"Saved physically or saved spiritually?"

"Both."

"So it's a religious symbol?"

"Yes, it is. Praying hands." She paused. "I used to wear a gold cross, one that my father gave me when I was a girl. I lost it on that bloody day in Kiev."

"Ah," he said. He seemed ill at ease in recalling the event. "I'm sorry. You lost a lot that day."

"Yes, I did."

"And yet you still believe in a benign God and these Christian superstitions," he said, returning the conversation to the pendant.

"I choose to, yes," she said.

"Because you always have?" he asked. "Because that's what you were brought up with?"

"I believe because I sense a presence out there that's bigger than this world or any person in it," she said. "I believe because sometimes my prayers are answered and because my faith offers meaning to my life. And why are you asking me this?"

"Because I'm interested. If there's something to this religion thing, why would I want to miss it?"

"You seem to have missed it so far," she said.

"Never too late. Isn't that what they say? I was brought up in an atheistic society, so that's what I was trained to believe. Well, perhaps I'm midway through my life. Or perhaps someone will shoot me tomorrow. Arguably, I could become 'born again,' no? Like your Jimmy Carter."

"I suppose, over the course of human history, stranger things have happened. Look," she said, "in my society we have a choice of whether we want to believe or not. This is what I believe."

He made a dismissive gesture with his hand. "But I could also say it's all nonsense," he said. "And it enhances your life in no meaningful way. Religion is irrational. Not just yours, but Islam, Judaism, Buddhism. All of them."

"Is that what you think or are you engaging me in a debate?"

"Maybe both."

"Then I can easily prove belief in God as rational," she answered.

"Let me hear you do it. In any language you wish."

She stayed in English. "Have you ever heard of 'Pascal's Wager'?" she asked.

"No."

"Pascal's Wager is one of the most famous arguments in the philosophy of religion," she said. "It was first devised by Blaise Pascal, the seventeenth-century French philosopher, in his book *Pensées*. He suggested that rational people should believe in God even if it is impossible to prove whether he exists, simply because it is a better bet."

"A better bet?" Federov laughed. "A fixed horserace is a good bet."

"Suppose you believe in God, but God doesn't exist. Then there's nothing to lose. But assume He does exist. The prize for a believer could be as high as eternal life in paradise. Nonbelievers, on the other hand, might roast in hell."

"Like I probably will?" Federov said.

"Weigh the gain or loss in wagering that God exists," Alex said. "Pascal theorized that if you gain, you gain all. If you lose, you lose nothing that you already had. Wager then, without hesitation that God exists and live your life accordingly. You would be irrational *not* to."

Federov blinked. In the kitchen, Lucy had turned on a television. Distantly, Alex heard some sort of inane quiz show, this time in French. At the same time, not that Alex was ready for surprises, two more surprises sauntered by — a pair of majestic Abyssinian cats whom Federov introduced as Lara and Tonya.

"Zhivago?"

"Thank you," he said. "Most people miss that." He laughed. "When I lived in Odessa I had a dog named Zhivago. A wolfhound."

"I'm not surprised," she said.

"And Pascal," he said, moving the discussion backward, "I'll bet this Pascal was a Jew."

"For the record, Pascal was a French Christian. He offered his wager to persuade nonbelievers to believe."

"Apparently it didn't work," he said with a laugh. "The French are endlessly godless people."

"And you're not?"

"I am too. You are right. Tell me something else," he said.

"Like what?"

"I'm a retired man. I am not an educated man, but I have begun to do a lot of reading. And thinking. I believe I have a soul, so I'm looking for salvation for my soul perhaps. None of us lives forever, and I've done terrible things in my life, just as terrible things have been done to me. Tell me about forgiveness."

"I'm not a theologian," she said. "I'm merely a churchgoer, and honestly I don't go as often as I should or might like. If you're really interested, maybe you should go to a church or two and see what suits you. They'll be glad to have you once they get over the shock of seeing you there."

"I like the way you insult me," he said. "I don't let very many people get away with it."

"And I don't allow very many people to abduct me."

"Do you practice forgiveness yourself?"

"I try to. That's what Jesus taught."

"Then you should forgive me for abducting you and for changing your clothes."

She had never underestimated the retired gangster's intelligence, if in fact he was retired, which she wondered about. But in doing so much reading, his articulation had improved. In a way, she wondered how he could be the same thug who had murdered people in Ukraine and New York and had beaten prostitutes that had worked for him. Then again, her own faith said much on the subject of spiritual redemption. All sinners were invited into heaven's open door through faith. With such peace with God also came the inner peace of the certainty of salvation.

This was not the first time that Federov had expressed a fascination with her faith. Was it a sham or some sort of test?

"All right," she said. "How's this? You're forgiven by me for yesterday."

"Thank you."

"Don't do it again."

"Perhaps I won't."

She began a counterattack in her argument.

"But of course I can only forgive you on a personal level. Only God can forgive sins completely, and you don't believe in God, so there's no way you can pray for forgiveness."

"Perhaps I will change. Perhaps if you stay with me, if we spend time together, you will sway me with your example."

"I'll tell you this much," Alex said. "Man receives forgiveness through a sincere expression of repentance to God, and Jesus taught that He completes this in the act of forgiving others. Forgiveness is about healing, and through forgiveness, Christians embody their mission to live as a people who are reconciled to God."

"All because Jesus forgave those who executed Him?" Federov asked.

"Think of that act as a rock dropped into the middle of a pond. An example by which all other acts can be judged. The means for humans to forgive other humans is the same means as God's forgiveness of mankind, the death and resurrection of Jesus. When Jesus said, 'Forgive us our sins as we forgive those who sin against us,' He was giving clear instructions on that relationship."

"Curious," he said. "How do you know all this?"

"Bible study. Whether you want to believe in it or not, it's literature, it's history, it's the culture of much of the world. So it's worthy of study and discussion."

"Then keep talking."

"Why are you leading me through all this?" she demanded, almost angry.

"Because I am intrigued. And I've never met anyone who was so well-versed in your Christian philosophy. Please. Do me these favors, and I will owe you several."

"The disciple Peter came to Jesus and asked, 'Lord, how many times shall I forgive my brother when he sins against me? Up to seven times?' Jesus answered, 'I tell you, not seven times, but seventy-seven times — or seventy times seven,' I forget which."

"So tell me. Those people who attacked your president in Kiev and had your future husband killed. In your heart, have you forgiven them?"

"That's a nasty, difficult question."

"We agreed to exchange questions and answers. So that is my question, and I want my answer."

She barely needed to think about it. "No," she said. "I haven't forgiven them. Not yet."

"So you who wear the stone of praying hands around your neck, you are not Christian, either. You're no better than I."

"There are differences."

"Such as?"

"I'm trying."

He nodded. "Point," he said, leaning back from the table. "Nor do I think I'll ever be there."

Lucy appeared with a breakfast tray. She set the eggs and toast before Alex as Federov fell silent. Tea was in an antique teapot. She opened two fresh jars of preserves and set them within arm's reach. Then Lucy quietly vanished back into the kitchen.

"It's time for me to ask you a question," Alex said.

"Please."

"How did your people get into my room and how did you know I was in Geneva?"

He smiled.

"I knew you were in Geneva because you did what I told you to do," Federov said, addressing the second half of the question first. "You checked into the Hotel de Roubaix. I own the hotel. I have a list of names of people. I'm to be alerted immediately if any check in."

"And how did your people get into my suite? The door was bolted."

"When you checked in, your name triggered giving out one of my special suites. There's a passage into the room from a passage within the walls between rooms. They came through your closet."

"And you probably have the suite bugged and somewhere there are surveillance cameras too, I'd now guess," she said.

"You catch on quickly."

He paused and looked as if he were about to add something. "I watched you shower after you arrived. You are a genuinely beautiful woman."

"I ought to slap the daylights out of you."

"You already forgave me for yesterday."

She began her breakfast. She felt his eyes upon her.

"We could make a wonderful team, you and me," he said in a more subdued tone. "I need a smart wife."

"Continue with your courses at charm school and keep searching."

"I have more than twenty million dollars in the banks in Geneva, Lausanne, and Zurich. My wife would never have to work. You would be a very wealthy woman. You could assist me with my American taxes and help run my companies. We — "

"We should talk about *The Pietà of Malta*," she said. "*That's* what we should do."

"What is that?" he asked. "*The Pietà of Malta*?"

"A piece of third-century Christian art, possibly the inspiration for Michelangelo's great work. It was stolen from a museum in Madrid a few weeks ago."

"You think *I* have it?" he laughed.

They both knew it was a serious question.

"I don't even know what it is," he said. He held up two empty hands, as if to suggest that sometimes he told the truth but this time he *really* was telling the truth.

"One of my associates turned up your name in association with a Colonel Tissot in Switzerland," she said. "My associate seemed to suspect a link."

Federov's eyes narrowed.

"I do business with many people," he said. "Or at least my remaining companies do."

"My source suggested a closer contact than just general business," she pressed.

"That might be the case," he said. "Would this be a Laurent Tissot? Geneva?"

"I believe so," she said.

"He's a weapons dealer," Federov said. "But you knew that."

"Yes, I did," she said. "But now I'll offer you a tidbit, in case you were unaware. Tissot *was* a weapon's dealer, not *is*. He's out of the business now. Permanently."

For a moment, Federov looked surprised. "Oh. I see," he said. "I did not know. That's very helpful. Thank you."

"Let me present a theory to you, Yuri," she said. "A suggestion of what might be going on. You don't mind listening, do you?"

He didn't bat an eyelash. "I don't mind," he said.

"There was an attempt on my life in Madrid. Someone thought I needed to be killed because I was a contact between American intelligence and you. That suggests you know something of value to us, even if you don't know exactly what it is. The only common link in all this is the late Monsieur Tissot, who brokered the deal for the missing art. Or so we think."

"All right," said Federov, who was following.

Alex, who was warming up to this, kept her gaze on Federov's eyes. Squarely.

"And of course the late Monsieur Tissot isn't in much of a position to speak to us now, is he? Little too late for him to cut himself a deal, if you know what I mean."

Federov pursed his lips and smiled a little. "Right you are," he said.

"So I guess that brings us to the paramount question that I have for you," Alex said. "What business might you have done with Tissot? When, where, and why? No use to go into ancient history, either. We're looking for activity within the last six months."

"Well," he said, with a very Ukrainian and very arrogant shake of his head. "I don't know these things off the top of my head. I'd have to check with the people who run my companies."

"Which companies?" she asked.

He was silent.

"Which companies, Yuri?" Alex repeated. "Come on now. This is important."

"And this all figures into some stolen artwork?"

"We suspect much more." She added as a hint, "This is a major opportunity for you to get Washington off your case, Yuri. A chance that might never come again."

"Ah, yes, I see," Federov said. "Yes, I'm still having difficulties with your Internal Revenue Service. Several million dollars' worth."

"I was advised of that," she said.

"If I enter the United States again or a US territory, I'm subject to arrest. Perhaps you could help me there."

"It's negotiable," she said.

"You are here to deal?" he asked

"Assume I am," she said. "I work for Treasury. I know people in the tax division."

His attention went far away and came back again. His eyes narrowed.

"I knew Colonel Tissot through my shipping interests in the Mediterranean and the Black Sea," he said. "I have companies in Odessa and Istanbul. There are smaller offices in Cagliari in Sardinia and at Nicosia in Cyprus," Federov said. "I am no longer an active partner in these companies, so whatever Tissot has been involved in recently, I do not know firsthand. This is the truth. People keep their eyes on my shipping interests for me. I pay them well, and they know I will have them killed if they steal from me. So the businesses run smoothly. I own warehouses there too. I can make inquiries. For me, people will have answers."

Alex drew a breath and eased back in her chair.

"That would be perfect," she said. She paused and played her best card. "In terms of the IRS," she said, "if I were to present Washington with a speedy wrap-up to this affair in Madrid, I would think your tax bill might vanish completely."

"Completely?"

She nodded. "But I need a speedy and complete wrap-up to my art theft and its details, including who did it and why," she said. "If I get everything I want, in terms of business, then you do too. Fair?"

"Fair," he said. He nodded. "I can have preliminary answers for you within a day," he said. "Would you care to wait here at my home where you are completely safe? Or should we move you back to the hotel?"

"I'd prefer the hotel," she said. "And a room without a fake back wall to the closet."

He laughed. "We can arrange that."

FIFTY-TWO

For Maria, Friday hadn't been quite as bad as the previous four days of the week. Still working with the irritating José Luis, they did a morning inspection of the sprawling Metro stop at Ruben Darío. The inspection was coordinated with another team, which included agents of the Guardia Civil, to secure the ventilation system beneath the chaotic traffic roundabout over their heads.

They broke for lunch. Maria went her way, José Luis went his. Maria avoided all the American fast-food places but found a little sandwich shop not too far from the square and purchased a bocadillo, a sandwich on French-type bread. She took her sandwich to the park, sat, and relaxed. During lunch, Maria flipped open her cell phone and called her daughter who was also on her lunch hour.

The normal mother-daughter conversation the world over.

"¿Qué tal el cole hoy?"

"Regular," her daughter answered.

So much for details.

Maria Elena rang off. Amanda could be exasperating from time to time. Most times, actually, but no more than any other teenager. And in the same way that Maria had loved her father, she loved her daughter.

Punctually at 1:00, Maria returned to the northern entrance of the Ruben Darío stop. There was no sign of her coworker, José Luis. Not surprising, she simmered. He had been late returning from lunch every day this week, so why should this day be any different? It was obvious why he had no regular partner. He was a lousy, careless worker.

He turned up again at twelve minutes past the hour, garlic and wine on his breath. She could barely conceal her contempt. Hardly speaking, they went back down into the Metro station and, following one train, jumped down onto the tracks. They set off eastward toward the stop at Nuñez de Balboa. It was a seven-block inspection, one of the trickiest on her route, and she wished anew that her regular partner was there. The seven blocks would take the entire afternoon under the best of circumstances. José Luis was slow as frozen molasses sometimes. She already knew it was going to be a crappy afternoon.

They proceeded slowly, stepping out of the way of several trains as they rumbled through the dim tunnels. There was a work crew at Paseo de la Castellana, installing new junction boxes. The men were hot and dripping with sweat but getting their assignment done. She didn't envy their work. Her own work, while she liked it, took her away from daylight and God's open sky more than she might have cared for.

They continued to the section of tracks beneath the intersection of Calle de Serrano and Calle de Juan Bravo. She had walked this stretch many times over the last several years. She knew it had a certain feel, same as every other section of the city had a certain feel both above and below the streets.

She slowed down.

"¿Qué pasa?" José Luis asked.

"I don't know," she said. "Something's off here."

In the dim light, she could see the look of dismay on his face. As usual, he wanted to shortcut everything. "Stop," she said.

He stopped. They stood on the tracks. She cocked her head. There were all the usual noises in the distance. Her hearing was so acute that she could tell that the nearest train was in the tunnel behind them, about five blocks away on the other side of Rubén Dario.

"Something's wrong," she said.

"Nothing's wrong," he said. "Let's keep moving."

"I hear something I shouldn't. Like a hammering or a digging. Or both."

"Hammering and digging don't sound anything alike," he said.

"Keep quiet!" she said again.

José Luis stopped and folded his arms. He too began to look around but not to locate the source of the noise.

She cocked her head again.

"The American Embassy is only one block from here," she said.

"Well, that explains what you hear," he said. "The Americans are probably torturing prisoners in the basement."

"Not funny!" she snapped again. "Would you rather be speaking Russian today?"

"Anyone can do anything they want to the Americans as far as I'm concerned," he said. "Why should we care? They don't care about us. And in any case I don't hear anything."

He paused. She walked to the northern wall of the tunnel, not far from a locked door that led to some of the old wartime passageways. She listened and could hear the offending tap-tap-tap-scrape-scrape-scrape noises better.

He launched into a tirade. *"Vosotras las mujeres siempre estan imaginando las cosas! Es como con mi mujer no sé quantas veces me ha despertado porque ha oído un supuesto sonido raro!"* You women are always imagining things. It's like it is with my wife: I don't know how many times she's woken me up because she's heard a 'strange noise'!

"No soy ninguna mujer histérica. Yo—si quieres creerme o no—he de veras oído algo raro que no son los ratones que suelen espantar a tu esposa y hacerla interromper tu descanso!" I'm not a hysterical woman and—whether you want to believe me or not—I've really heard something other than those mice that wake up your wife and make her interrupt your sleep.

He gave her a mocking laugh.

"Oh, the devil take you!" he said. "I've got a weak bladder from lunch. I'm going to disappear for a minute, okay?"

He gestured to the direction in which they had come. Plenty of dark dirty walls back there. Now she understood what he was getting antsy about.

"Fine. Take your time," she said.

She waited a moment and watched him disappear.

Then she explored along the wall until she came to the decrepit service door that led to the old tunnels and passages. She shined a light on the lock. It was a simple padlock but it was one of the newer locks that had been installed along this stretch within the last year.

She rattled it. The noises she heard stopped.

She reached to her belt and found the master key.

She unlocked the padlock, pushed the door open, and stepped through.

Maria Elena found herself in a dark, stinky place. There was little light, uneven space to walk, and the stench of rats and fetid water. She ran her light around the chamber and then nearly jumped out of her skin.

There was a man kneeling there, staring at her. He had been working on something, and she had interrupted him. He had been making the noises she had heard.

He was a slight dark man with closely cropped black hair. His skin was mocha colored, and his eyes were dark. There was a scar across his forehead, and there was little doubt in her mind that this was the man she had heard.

There was a pile of dirt near him and he had a collection of tools. Chisels. Shovels. Hammers.

For a moment, he seemed frozen in the beam of her light.

"¿Quien es usted?" she demanded. *"¿Qué hace?"* Who are you? What are you doing?

The man in front of her said nothing. Nor did he give her any time to react or save herself. Rising from a crouch, he pulled a pistol from under his black sweatshirt. He swung it in a smooth motion at her, and he fired. There was a flash but no noise, followed instantly by a feeling of tearing and ripping at the midpoint of her gut.

The pain radiated, and the man fired a second shot. The second bullet hit her in the chest, also, not too far from the first.

She dropped everything she was carrying.

The pain was intense, then it was gone. The next thing she knew was that the filthy ground had come up and smacked her in the face. She was on the ground, her chest torn open, her whole being in shock.

Then a blackness descended quickly, one unlike anything she had ever experienced.

Maria Elena thought of her father and her daughter again for the final time. She imagined herself safe at home again, in the warm embrace of people she loved, both living and dead.

And then she died.

FIFTY-THREE

GENEVA, SEPTEMBER 16, 9:00 A.M.

Sunday morning in Geneva. Quiet streets. Quiet city.

Alex rose well before 9:00 a.m., re-ensconced at the Hotel de Roubaix. After coffee, she found her way to the Holy Trinity Anglican Church, known locally in Geneva as the *Église Anglaise*, for a morning service in English. She had been there twice before on visits to Europe. The church, a gray stone edifice that would have fit in easily in England or in the United States, was situated near the center of Geneva on the Rue du Mont Blanc, between the bridge and the railway station. It was a short, pleasant walk from the hotel on clean streets past closed shops.

Attending a service in English reminded her of home. It felt right. The congregation came from many different nationalities and backgrounds, which she liked. The pastor was an Englishman who had just returned from Africa. He discussed poverty around the world. His words made her think again of Barranco Lajoya in Venezuela, and the pendant that still hung around her neck.

She took communion. In the final moments of prayer, she prayed for the souls of her parents and for her late fiancé, Robert. She hoped God was listening. When she departed, she felt refreshed. She told herself she should attend services more often when people aren't shooting at her in various places around the world. Or, she continued wryly, maybe she should attend more when they *were* shooting at her.

She found a café open a block from the hotel and bought a Swiss weekend newspaper. She read an amusing account in French on the new American president's current battles with Congress. She had a light brunch. An hour later she was back at the hotel. She sat in a corner of the lobby, waiting, this time working on her laptop in a wi-fi zone. The two people whom she needed to have find her in Geneva were Peter and Federov. They both knew where to look for her. So she kept herself visible.

She accessed more of Pendraza's files and continued her long march through them. An hour passed. She cross-referenced names and places from his files against what Interpol had sent her and what she had received in small batches from the French and Italian police and from Washington.

But her mind increasingly evoked unfavorable scenarios involving Peter. What if Interpol had picked him up? What if he had been detained when reentering Switzerland? There was a good chance that Interpol knew exactly who they were looking for, and, just as she had not completely shared information with Interpol, they probably had not shared everything with her.

Back to the laptop screen she went, one eye on the lobby, the other on the screen, glancing up and down, not completely locked in on anything. Cross-referencing, looking for links, there were overlapping references that triggered each other, but nothing definite — nothing that made sense. When, she wondered, would it?

Black bird, black fog, or black hole? Toward 2:15 p.m. she looked up from where she worked, Out of the corner of her eye she spotted a man entering the lobby, walking slowly, looking around.

The vision jolted her. Peter!

She held her position and kept her eyes on him. For several seconds she tried to weigh everything that had happened between him and her, and everything she had learned about "John Sun" and the events in Switzerland. What was he hanging around with her for? To guide her safely through to the recovery of the pietà or to cut her throat when it served his purposes. In Kiev, reluctantly, she had killed someone as well, and she prayed that God would someday have mercy on her. But was Peter any worse than she was, or vice versa.

Something told her that she would have to continue her present path, to keep giving Peter the benefit of her doubts. But was it an angel telling her or a demon? God or the Devil?

Peter turned. She caught a huge expression of relief on his face when he saw her. He made no acknowledgement but walked to her.

"Thank heaven!" she said.

"Yeah," he said with a long sigh. "Me too!"

Then, impulsively, she stood. They embraced, then broke apart quickly. "Let's go to the bar," she finally said, gathering her laptop and other things. "It's more private, but we can still keep an eye on the door."

"That would be good," he said.

"Follow me."

"I've been looking all over for you," he said. "I came to the hotel yesterday and you had checked out. I went to all our fall-back places. I sat for hours in that obnoxious Russian café. Nothing. You okay?" he asked.

"I'm okay. You?"

"Yes. I didn't know whether to leave town or just ditch completely. I figured I'd give it a couple more days, at least till Tuesday. Tried to get McKinnon on the phone but it's a weekend."

"He should have picked up the phone anyway," she said as they entered the bar.

Peter shook his head. "He's got some girlfriends," he said. "When he goes to visit them, he carries a different cell so his location can't be traced. I don't have that number."

"You've got more problems than that," she said. "You've got some you don't even know about."

He seemed to tense. "Uh oh," he said.

They settled in at a table.

"Anyway, I was with Yuri Federov," she said. "Spent the night at his place, but not the way that sounds."

"You talk. I'll listen," he said.

"Fine bodyguard you are," she said, relaxing slightly. "His people walked through the hotel walls and abducted me."

"What?"

A waiter appeared. They ordered soft drinks and finger food. There were other Americans in the bar, so as a mild precaution, Alex switched to Spanish and spoke in low tones. She brought him up to date on the events of the last several hours. Then Peter, continuing in Spanish, ran though his own set. He had experienced no problems with the Swiss police, he said, but had been completely flummoxed when he had come to this hotel and there had been no record of her arrival or departure, or at least none they were willing to share.

She sensed Federov's hand in the mix on that detail too but didn't explain.

When they were caught up, she shifted the topic of the conversation. "Do you know what we're going to do now?" she asked.

He hunched his shoulders. "You tell me," he said.

"We're going to trade information," she said.

"About what? Are we on the black bird again?"

"I think so. I'm going to tell you something for free," she said. "And then I'm going to ask you a few questions. And since what I have to say is going to have considerable value to you, I expect you to give me straightforward answers in return. Shall we try that?"

"Nothing to lose," he said.

"I have information that a certain 'John Sun' was in Zurich very recently, an emissary of your government. Except there is no John Sun. John Sun is a pseudonym for another agent of the government of China, one that will remain nameless right now."

His eyes settled in on her. "Keep going," he said.

She told him what she learned about John Sun without revealing her sources. "So I take it that it would come as a double surprise to you to learn first that John Sun's fictitious identity has been blown. And second, that Interpol is looking for a Chinese agent traveling on a different passport who might match Sun's description."

A long pause, and, "It would, yes. And this would be a very good thing for me to know. Thank you."

"You're welcome."

"I should plan accordingly," he said.

"Yes, you should." She paused. "I get the idea that somewhere, stashed away in various dead drops, car panels, and safety deposit boxes, you probably have a whole library of passports, diplomatic or otherwise. You could also pass for American, Canadian, or English if you worked at it, Peter. So why limit yourself to your native country?"

"I don't. Very insightful, Alex."

"You don't mind if I call you 'Peter,' do you? It's possibly your name."

For the first time, a laugh. "It's my name." He thought for a moment. "You could even check my Columbia University records."

"I already did," she said. "Or at least I had my boss in Washington do it for me. Roar, Lion. Wasn't Barack Obama there around the same time?"

"He was there several years earlier. Fortunately for both of us, we didn't know each other."

"That *is* a good break," she said. "For both of you."

"But what I don't immediately understand," he said slowly, "is how the Swiss police might have positively linked 'Sun' in Zurich to 'Sun' in Geneva."

"I can only guess," she said. "And my guess would be this: within their bureaus, this case has attained some importance. And similarly, if they had been more aggressive in retrieving the ATM surveillance photos in Geneva from Tissot's neighborhood and shown them around the gendarmerie in Zurich where Sun retrieved that body, they might have gotten a match much faster. It's a hypothesis, but it's a sound one."

"But all Asians look alike, right?" he asked facetiously.

"Maybe, but in your case that would work against you, not *for* you, wouldn't it? You wouldn't even want to be picked up to have to explain things, would you?"

"No. Of course not."

"Are you, as Peter Chang, traveling on a diplomatic passport?"

A pause as he sensed the direction of this. "No," he said.

"Then you could be detained, couldn't you? Arrested, actually. And there's even the fair chance that your arrangement with your government is such that they couldn't admit who you are. Not for several years."

"It could happen," he said, after another pause, "if I were unlucky. Or careless."

"Then if I were you, I would be very careful," she said.

"Who else knows about this?" he asked.

"No one."

"So," he said, "not to put bad thoughts in the air, if anything happened suddenly to you ..."

She laughed. "That would work out poorly for you too."

"Why's that?"

"Suppose you were picked up and questioned about the two

murders in Geneva. Were your two peers, David and Charles, in Europe yet?"

"No."

"The date of the murders was September seventh and eighth. I was alone that night, myself. In Barcelona. In my hotel room."

He smiled.

"So who's to say I wasn't there, also?" he said.

She nodded. "And thank you for saving my life in Madrid the other night. What goes around comes around. Karma," she said.

"Karma," he agreed. "Now, what did you want to ask me?"

She unloaded. "Why did Lee Yuan want *The Pietà of Malta*?" she asked. "Why did he *personally* want it?"

"What makes you think he did?" Peter asked.

"I hate it when I ask a question and get another one in return," she said. "But the other night you mentioned your personal connection to Lee Yuan. And you mentioned finishing his business for him. Well, if it were just a wealthy collector in China who got swindled, I don't think you'd be here. So my guess is that Lee Yuan wanted the carving himself. It wasn't delivered to him, his money was taken by criminals who were out to finance some activity somewhere else. But they didn't bargain on who he was or the fury they would unleash by harming him."

"You need to consider who Lee Yuan was," he said. "Let me explain. Lee Yuan was a man each of us respected greatly in his later years. But he had a very difficult life. The great events of the time, the turbulence of recent history, surrounded him. In one sense, the events gave rise to his greatness as an individual. In another sense, they compromised his time on earth."

"In what way?" she asked.

"Yuan was a boy during the Great Leap Forward," Peter said. "He was five years old and his family was sent to camps in the countryside for reeducation, same as millions of others. Same as the parents of David Wong, whom you met the other night. Yuan's parents were practicing Christians during the Cultural Revolution. Practicing religion was considered social turmoil. But they were devout people who continued to practice. They had come of age in the era of Sun Yat Sen and Chiang Kai Shek. They were products of their time, some say heroic, some say foolish."

"What do *you* say?"

"I am too smart to say," Peter said with a smile. "They were what they were, and the past is the past. It can be rewritten, but the truth cannot be erased. They were arrested for owning Bibles. And Yuan's father was a Christian scholar. He was particularly fascinated by the works of St. Francis of Assisi. He owned books on Saint Francis too."

"Ah," she said.

Peter paused, then continued.

"After their books were burned, Lee Yuan's parents were held in a Beijing detention center for nearly a year as the Red Guard considered what to charge them with. And still they prayed. They were sent to a camp in the freezing northeast of China for reeducation instead. This was maybe in the Western year of 1967 or 1968. Yuan was sent to an orphanage and never saw his parents again. He later learned that his parents had been beheaded by the Red Guard, executed in a public square as an example to others."

Alex could tell that Peter was choosing his words with great care. She listened to them in the same way.

"It was said that the parents of Yuan were saying prayers to Jesus when the executioners' swords descended upon their necks," he said flatly. "And I have no reason to doubt that story. Lee Yuan, however, made the best of his new life," Peter continued after a moment. "He studied in the orphanage. He became an outstanding officer in the army, then moved to state security and intelligence. As an adult, he didn't practice religion but he always had an interest in it. And why not? Religion had led him to be who he was, by his parents' practice of it. So in that way, it may have been part of him too. Who is to say?"

"Did you ever discuss any of this with him?" she asked. "Christianity? His parents?"

"No. I knew the history. There was nothing further I wanted to hear. Equally, I've learned in life that there are doors you must not open, windows you should not look through. Questions you do not ask. So I knew not to ask more. When the pietà disappeared from the museum, Lee Yuan took a special interest. He was fascinated by the fact that it may have been touched by a saint, buried with a saint, and the inspiration for Michelangelo's great Christian work. And it touched upon his parents' dear St. Francis, as well. You can imagine. Spiritually, it must have made him feel so close to the people he had lost so early in his life. Spiritually, if his parents had connected with this one saint, and then he connected to ... well, you see. Superstition? Faith? I do not know. None of us do. But I know he went to Switzerland to acquire this piece on the black market. For himself."

"And he was double-crossed?"

"Yes. The transaction was to take place in a remote monastery. Yuan liked the idea of that, as he was fascinated with the places where Christianity was kept alive through the Dark Ages. He saw parallels with recent Chinese history. So against his better judgment, he agreed to visit the place and complete the transaction there. He was never seen alive again."

"But you and your associates have come to complete his mission," she said.

Peter's eyes said yes. So did a slight nod of his head.

"Official policy of your government?" she asked. "Or something more personal?"

"Both," he said, "but neither entirely."

"What?"

"Well, you see," Peter said with a smile, "nothing is ever all one thing or all another. Think of it as sunlight shining over a mountain but the mountain is in a valley, and in the valley, Yin and Yang exist, the two opposite parts of the truth, which by themselves are both true and false. Yin is the dark area where the mountain stands and blocks sunlight. Yang is the place of direct sunshine. The sun traverses the sky and Yin and Yang trade places with each other. What was dark becomes light and what was obscured is revealed."

"Are you answering my question of just obfuscating it?"

"I'm answering it," he said. "If a Chinese agent is harmed anywhere in the word, a team of us will come after him to finish his work and to serve notice on those who would harm any of us. In the case of the noble Lee Yuan, he was much loved by many of us. So a professional mission became increasingly personal. The dark became light. Is it more of one than another? I don't know. It changes. The central truth remains — but with gradations."

She blinked. "Okay," she finally said. "Got it."

"If you do, you're better than most Westerners. Westerners see things in finite terms. Asians, not so much."

"Where is it now?"

"The balance of the opposing forces?"

"No," she said. "Where is *The Pietà of Malta?* And I'd like a Western-style answer on that. Don't tell me that its Yin is in Switzerland but its Yang is safely stashed in an outhouse in upper Mongolia. I can't work that way."

He shook his head. "I answered that before. Maybe it's in Switzerland. Maybe it's back in Spain. Maybe shipped to China. My mission is not the black bird and never was. My personal mission is the people who harmed Lee Yuan."

"But it would appear," she said coyly, "that this fellow 'Sun' took care of that?"

"Not completely," he said coldly.

She thought it through, all of it.

"All right," she said. "Your story works. We're still partners."

"That's good," he said. "Because we have company."

"Where?" she asked sharply.

Peter made a gesture with his eyes. Alex had been so engrossed in Peter's backstory that she had missed something. She turned fast and saw Yuri Federov, two bodyguards close behind him, standing near the doorway to the bar. He had just spotted her.

"Trouble?" Peter asked softly. His hand was starting to drift under his jacket.

"No. It's okay," she said. She moved her hand quickly and stopped his before it reached his gun. "It's Federov."

She released. Peter's hand stayed where it was, on his lap, just in case.

Federov approached the table, looked at her, and then looked at Peter.

"Found a new boyfriend already?" he asked in English.

"Don't be crude, Yuri, even though that may be difficult for you."

He snorted. "We can talk?" Federov asked.

His bodyguards were enormous men in black leather jackets. They loomed behind him like a couple of trained grizzly bears, almost as big, almost as wide, and almost as smart. Alex guessed they were the men who had abducted her.

"This is Mr. Chang," she said smoothly. "He's a friend and is assisting me on this case."

Federov, who never cared much for strangers, grunted.

"You can speak in front of him or we can speak privately, Yuri," Alex continued. "But the bottom line is this: anything you tell me I'm probably going to have to tell him. So you can do it whatever way you want, and keep in mind that the Internal Revenue Service will be thrilled by your cooperation."

Federov glanced at Chang. "He speaks English, this Chinaman?"

"Why don't you ask him?"

Federov looked in Chang's direction. "Yes or no? Speak English?"

Chang shrugged. "Some," he said, sounding slightly fresh-off-the-boat. Federov looked back to Alex.

"I have a man in Genoa," he said, "north of Italy. He used to work on one of my ships. My people are holding him."

"I know where Genoa is," she said. "I've been there. Who's this man and where do you have him? In the trunk of a car?"

Federov missed her irony.

"He's at a house I own. He has things to tell you."

"About?"

"Money. And a transfer of smuggled explosives."

She looked quickly to Peter and searched his eyes.

"It will take me a day to get to Genoa," she said.

"Why?"

"Air schedules."

"I have a private plane. It's already at your disposal."

"You're serious?"

"No. I came into the city to tell jokes."

"Are you going with us?" she asked. "To Genoa?"

"It would be a good idea," he said. "I think this man will have more to say if I'm there. I have arranged for an interpreter."

"What does he speak?"

"He speaks Italian and Turkish. Those are the only languages that are dependable."

"I speak Italian," she said.

"He's Sicilian dialect. He sounds like a drunken goat."

She thought for a moment. "Then let me also bring in one of my own people. From Rome, if I can get him."

"I don't mind. Can he be in Genoa by evening?"

"I can call and ask," she said.

Federov reached into his pocket and pulled out his cell phone. He handed it to her, almost rudely.

"I'll use mine," Alex said. "No need to spread private numbers around, is there?"

"None," he said with a grin, taking back the phone.

"Nice try, anyway," she said. Peter smiled. His hand left his lap.

Federov's two thugs still loomed and glowered. Federov looked at Peter. Then, "This Chinaman is coming too?" he asked.

Alex looked to Peter. "Yes, the Chinaman is coming too," Peter said. "The Chinaman wouldn't miss it."

Federov shrugged. "The more the merrier," he said. "Let's get moving."

"Will we have trouble with weapons at the airport?" Peter asked.

"Not if you're with me," Federov answered. "Let's go."

FIFTY-FOUR

MADRID, SEPTEMBER 16 5:49 P.M.

Under the city, Jean-Claude worked with care to remove the final stones and bricks that blocked his access to a chamber under the Calle Serrano. He worked by hand, Mahoud and Samy with him. One by one, the last bricks and rocks gave way. The old plaster and mortar crumbled. They hammered with muffled tools and opened a hole that was wide enough to crawl through. Then Samy, the smallest of them, hoisted himself up, crawled forward, and pulled his way through to the other side.

He was three feet off the ground and did a playful tumble forward. His hands hit the soft dirt. He rolled once and came up on his feet smiling. His side of the wall was in darkness, however. So Mahoud handed him one of the flashlights.

"What do you see?" Jean-Claude asked in Arabic.

"I see a massive explosion that will bring misery to Western imperialists," he said.

All three of them laughed. This was an eerie, dark place. But this wasn't much different from the time they had burrowed under other blocks in this same city to break into the museum several weeks ago. Do anything long enough and you get good at it. The old rule of thumb applied to this also, amateur terrorists tunneling under a city to get what they wanted.

A pack of New Age moles, that's what they were.

Subversives in the old meaning of the word, burrowing underneath the established order. Old Moles, as Marx had once suggested. The small cell of self-motivated, independent jihadists thought of themselves in heroic, romantic terms. They were the substance of the work, the destiny, and the future of persecuted Islamic people in Europe and the saviors of their people, all rolled into one five-piece unit.

Despite betrayal, despite the failure of their culture to adapt to the modern age, these amateur warriors saw themselves making headway. Jean-Claude had read Marx and had pulled some phrases from him.

"We are like a desert stream," he liked to tell his young warriors, "a stream that has been diverted from its course and has plunged into the depths below the sands. And now we reappear, sparkling and gurgling, in an unexpected place."

They knocked away a few more stones and were indeed in a place where no one expected them to be. They were sixteen feet under the basement of the US Embassy. Their plans were right on target and so was their physical position.

FIFTY-FIVE

GENEVA, SEPTEMBER 16, 6:00 P.M.

Alex repacked her bag and checked out of the hotel.

By six in the evening, she was standing in the lobby of her hotel, a few paces back from the door. Peter was already there. They stood apart without speaking.

Federov arrived punctually at 6:00 in a van with a driver and his two bodyguards, one whom he now addressed as Serge, and another whom he addressed as Dmitri.

Peter got into the van first. Alex swiftly followed.

The van took them to a small private airport in the town of Villiette, ten kilometers outside of Geneva. Federov's plane was a Cessna Citation, a small comfortable corporate jet that he had at his disposal. They took off toward 7:00 p.m. as the sun was setting and rose into a sky that was turning gold.

Alex found a seat by a window, sat alone, and looked downward. She enjoyed the tremendous view of the Jura Mountains, which still had some snow on the highest peaks, and the Lake of Geneva. The aircraft took off to the north, banked, and turned southward in the sky. Geneva lay to Alex's right and Lausanne and the other cities of French-speaking Switzerland lay down the lake to her left.

They were out of Switzerland within minutes and flew for an hour over the French Alps and next the Italian Alps. The mountains were luminous with the dying light of day. Then the aircraft reached the Mediterranean, which was growing dark. The plane banked easily to the port side and continued over the sea eastward toward Genoa.

Alex's attention drifted. In her mind several horrible scenarios replayed over and over. The disaster in Kiev. The train to Venezuela that had ended in the blazing shootout at Barranco Lajoya. The gunfight on the streets — and under the streets — of Paris.

"Airplanes took me to all those places too," she thought to herself.

"Not this one airplane in particular, but there were always airplanes getting me to these wretched incidents."

She started to finger the stone pendant at her neck, an old habit kicking in, from the way she used to finger the plain gold cross her father had given her as a little girl.

Her thoughts rambled and in the back of her mind the number *40* rose. As an age, it was not that far away, a half dozen years. By that age, she hoped that she might be married and have a family and be out of this line of work. Not that she hated it, she didn't even dislike it. But she knew the burnout rates and knew the effect that it could have.

Depression. Frustration. Shattered nerves. Sweat glands that didn't work any more or never stopped working.

When would she meet another man? A special man, like Robert had been. Would she ever meet one or would she turn into an old crone? She wanted children. She wanted a marriage. A solid marriage. One in a church like she had always imagined. Maybe she could even have a normal life to go with it if she wished and prayed and worked for it long enough.

Her eyes slid away from the window for a moment as she spotted Federov, moving through the cabin, smoking a small cigar. Marriage. He was probably deadly serious when he kept flirting around the issue. She met the notion with amusement and disgust. She knew she could never love a man like that. And as far as needing a woman to whip his business concerns into shape? He didn't need a wife so much as he needed a secretary of state.

The aircraft's engines hummed smoothly. They hit a little pocket of turbulence, then the air smoothed out. She continued to think. She tried to assess where she was on this case.

What did she know?

It was suddenly the silly season again. Sometimes her mind had a habit of collapsing into nonsense, into gibberish, when she was over tired. Self-defense, she wondered. Did it shut down when she was on overload?

She asked herself again. What did she know? *Que sais-je?* as the French philosopher Montaigne had once asked four centuries ago. Montaigne, whose early works had dealt with spiritual pain and death, concepts very close to her right now. But his later works, after he had had a lifetime to think things over, had been reduced to a few concepts that were very simple, including one that greatly appealed to her: that a person must discover his or her own nature in order to live in peace and dignity.

Had she discovered hers? Had Federov discovered his, which was why he seemed more at peace with himself and the world than when last she saw him?

What about Peter? What about Rizzo? What about her friend Ben back in Washington? She had no idea what Montaigne knew but she knew what she knew.

Que sais je? Montaigne had often asked that question as a way of suggesting that he, or anyone, didn't really know much of anything.

She asked herself again. What did *he* know?

She tried to clear her head and force the analytical parts of her mind into overdrive.

What did she know?

She knew that Jeffrey Dahmer had been the first criminal to rivet her in horror when she was about twelve years old, and she knew that *Ally McBeal* had been her favorite TV show in college. She also knew that someone had swiped a "lamentation" from a museum in Madrid, that at least a half dozen people had been killed over it so far, if not more, that there had been some sort of transaction involved, money to finance something, that the Russian-Ukrainian mob still controlled many ships in the Mediterranean, that Peter was capable of killing people, just like Federov, that this "source" whom they were going to see had better have some good info to make the trip necessary, and that most stolen artwork was never recovered. But she also knew enough to know how much she didn't know; namely, where this case was ultimately headed.

"Water?" came a voice next to her.

Federov had slid into the seat next to her. He handed her a bottle of water. She accepted it. In his other hand, he held something. A book.

"I want to ask you something," he said in English. "You might be the only one I know who can tell me."

"Go ahead," Alex said. "Ask."

He turned the book over on his lap, the battered front cover facing up. It was thin and plain white with black Cyrillic lettering. She looked down at it and read.

Title and author:

Вишнёвый сад
Антóн Пáвлович Чéхов

"Yes?" she answered, after a glance. "I know it."

"What is this?" he asked. "I was told by a friend I should read it."

"In English it's called *The Cherry Orchard*. It's by Anton Chekhov, a great Russian writer."

"He's alive, Chekhov?"

"No, no. He's been dead for many years, Yuri. This is a play. A drama. Theater."

"Oh," he said.

"Who gave this to you?" she asked.

"There's a café I go to in Geneva. There are some young Russian émigrés who go there to drink, smoke, and gossip. This one girl, very pretty, very lovely. She was an actress in Moscow and St. Petersburg. She gave this to me and told me I should read it. She said she once played the part of a girl named Varya. She wants to play the role again and wishes me to finance a production in French."

"I know the character," she said.

"You've read this?"

"Yes. And I once saw the play performed in London."

"What is it about?"

"If I remember correctly," Alex said, "it's about an aristocratic white Russian woman and her family in Yalta about a hundred years ago. They return to the family's estate just before it is auctioned to pay the mortgage. They've lost most of their family fortune. The play ends with the estate being sold and the family leaving to the sound of their beloved cherry orchard being cut down. Varya is an adopted daughter, a mysterious girl who is central to the story."

"Ha!" he laughed. "That's very old-style Russian. They probably sat around trying to figure out what to do and meanwhile their home disappeared."

"That's exactly what happened," Alex said.

"Then I don't need to read it. And the story shows the merits of having money," he said. "If the family still had money, even if they had stolen it from someone else, their estate would not have been sold."

"That's very Russian too."

"What is?"

"Your attitude."

He laughed again. "That is the way of the world," he said. "And that's *new-style* Russian."

"But it's not the morale that Chekhov wanted you to take from the story."

"No? Then what is?"

"Read the play," she said. "Then you tell me what you think the author had in mind."

He nodded slowly, thoughtfully. "This young girl whom I know, the actress," Federov said, "she wants me to finance a small theater production in Geneva so she can play the role again. This time in French."

"And will you? Finance it?"

He smiled. "Maybe."

"If she sleeps with you, you mean."

"Maybe," he said again. "She is very pretty, the way young Russian girls are very pretty at age twenty. If she became my mistress, I would do that for her."

"Does she know that?"

"I've told her."

"And what did she say?"

"She gave me the play and told me to read it."

Alex laughed out loud. "Then you should read the play," she said. "Do yourself two favors at once."

"I had an uncle who was an actor," Federov said. "He was always reading plays and performing. He did Chekhov too, but I never paid much attention."

"Well, now you have the time. So you can read."

"There were a lot of Jews in his theater."

"So what?"

"I'm just saying," he said. "There were a lot of Jews."

"Every time I think you almost might be a normal human being you do something to undermine that notion and offend me."

"What did I do to offend you?" he laughed.

"How much longer is our flight?" she asked.

"Not much longer," he said, taking back the book. "The trip will be worth it," he said. "I know that's something that worries you."

"I just need to get a job done," she said.

"Oh, you will," he said. "I have a matter or two to attend to myself. So this is not bad."

She nodded. He gave her a friendly tap on the nearest knee, stood, and went back to sit with his bodyguards. They were playing cards. She watched him put the book aside. Alex glanced across the aisle. Peter was smiling, having listened in on the entire exchange.

A few moments later, she felt the pilot reduce the thrust of the Cessna's engines. They had started their descent into Genoa.

FIFTY-SIX

ROSANATO, VILLA MALAFORTUNATA, ITALY, SEPTEMBER 16, 7:24 P.M.

They touched down at the landing field in Italy less than an hour later. The field was small and serviced private planes only. It was adjacent to the much larger Genoa airport. The terminal was small, and they walked through customs with barely a nod from the Italians at each of their passports.

Then they were in a parking area. It was past nine in the evening and they walked to a van. Rizzo was already there, having connected earlier with Federov's driver, a young Italian kid with a distinct northern accent. Alex pegged him as a Genovese, but wasn't sure.

They piled into the van, the driver, Rizzo, Federov, and Alex, and one of the bodyguards, Dmitri, who came along. The driver also had some sandwiches in a box, with some more bottles of water.

"It's not far from here," Federov said. "The house where we are going."

"Are you taking some precautions?" Alex asked. "About being followed?"

"Of course," Federov said.

Federov gave the Italian kid a nod and they took off. They were on a motorway within a few minutes. The sandwiches were passed around with the water. They were lifesavers at this point. They hit a village that had a surprising amount of activity for the hour. But it was very late summer, so the Italians were enjoying evenings in their cafes, dining, laughing, and drinking.

Minutes later the van rolled to a halt in front of a public garage, part of a gas station. The garage appeared to be closed, but when the driver of the van honked twice, a large door came up noisily and automatically.

The van rolled in. Federov instructed everyone to get out and move quickly. He led them to a BMW SUV, a big overpowered Black Mariah of a vehicle that had a new driver and its engine running. The group quickly jumped into the SUV, all except for Federov's bodyguard Dmitri, who jumped into a second car by himself, a compact Fiat. Obviously, the bodyguard knew the directions and grudgingly, Alex had to admire the efficiency of Federov's team, even in retirement.

Another door rolled upward in the rear of the garage.

Dmitri hit the gas on the Fiat with a sharp jerk and rolled out first, followed quickly by the SUV. Federov sat up front, his broad shoulders more than filling the seat. The new driver, another Italian kid in a white open-collared shirt and a cigarette over his ear, floored it.

Alex was in the backseat sitting in the middle between Rizzo and Peter. Out they rolled into the darkness.

They went through some side streets with the driver following the first car closely but constantly checking the rearview mirror. But there were no other cars behind them, and they seemed to be traveling cleanly.

No watchers, no shadows. At one point they passed a police vehicle but it gave them no notice. There was no traffic. The driver drove fast but smoothly. Half a moon was shining on northern Italy. They hit one of the older highways that meandered upward along the shore and then along cliffs where the guardrails had been badly dented from years of haphazard driving. At one point on a curve, there was a section that had been knocked out by a car that hadn't quite navigated the turn, either through fog, Alex guessed, or the fog of beverage. But then they were racing down a hill again.

Federov broke out a pack of his inevitable cigarettes, lit one, and offered the pack around the car. Everyone declined except the driver, who lit his smoke from his boss's. Peter made a point of lowering his window by a quarter.

Within fifteen minutes, they were off the motorway and onto a narrow back road. They cut through several residential neighborhoods. New houses, very middle class. No one spoke. The driver had one of those new European sky radio stations that was playing bouncing European pop which fit the occasion as well as anything. Alex liked the music.

Then they went down a final street and Alex could see that the bodyguard in the lead car, Dmitri, had pulled to a stop in front of a house. Dmitri stepped out of his car, and Alex saw he was holding a pistol and waiting.

But there was no reason for alarm. She saw no one else, and she knew he was just doing his job, providing cover. The SUV rolled into the driveway of a house that had its lights on.

The driver hit his horn once and cut his lights into darkness. The downstairs lights in the house went off. Federov raised his meaty left hand to indicate that everyone in the van should remain quiet and still as a precaution. Alex's lateral vision caught sight of Dmitri standing in the driveway, his gun still drawn, his arm at his side, also smoking a cigarette, watching the house.

Then the driver flashed his lights twice.

From within the house, the downstairs lights flashed twice in response.

"Okay," Federov said.

The car doors opened, and they all slid out, Alex exiting on the side of Peter who offered her a hand, which she accepted.

They walked up the front path to the house. The door opened and they went inside. The place was furnished with surprising comfort. They were met by another Russian who must have been six and a half feet tall. He wore a black leather jacket despite the warmth of the evening and went by the name of Grisha. Grisha wore a nine millimeter automatic on his right hip. Alex counted him as another one of Federov's transplanted hoods from Ukraine. When he nodded to Alex and shook her hand, he nearly crushed it. And he was on his best behavior.

"How's Ahmet today?" Federov asked in Russian, which Alex followed easily.

"Better," Grisha answered, whatever that meant. He didn't expand.

"He doesn't have a telephone does he?" Federov asked.

"No, sir."

"Does he take walks?"

"No, sir. Not unattended."

"What does he talk about?"

"Not much, sir."

"Good," Federov said. "Does he have a weapon at all?"

"Just a knife. Makes him feel safe."

They both laughed.

"Should I take it away from him?" the guard asked.

"Don't bother," Federov said. "Any little boy can play with a knife. Maybe he'll cut his wrists later and solve a problem for us."

Dmitri thought this was funny. So did Federov. Rizzo rolled his eyes.

Another man, whom Federov addressed as Ramiz was waiting for them in the living room. He was a small man in his fifties with a sharp intelligent face. Alex took one look and knew he wasn't there for his muscle, so he must have been there for another reason. She soon learned: he was a Federov employee who served as an interpreter in Arabic.

Ramiz sprang to his feet, respectfully and fearfully, when he saw Federov. He joined in the group. They walked to some steps and went upstairs. They headed to what was the master bedroom suite of the new house, Grisha leading the way.

He pushed open a door without knocking, and the whole group walked in.

The room had a claustrophobic and condemned feel. It smelled of sweat, cigarettes, and some spice that she couldn't place, maybe curry. Alex saw a frightened man on a bed, skin of mocha hue, unshaven for several days. This was Ahmet. He was dressed in jeans and a sports shirt. He had a paring knife by his side. Nothing special, just the type of thing that a chef might use to chop celery.

"Get up," Federov ordered.

The man was pale and as jittery as a frightened cat. He couldn't take his eyes off Alex when the visitors arrived and surrounded him.

"Hello, Ahmet," Federov said in English.

Ahmet nodded and continued to stare at Alex. First at her breasts, then at her face.

"We're going to talk about what happened," Federov said. "You're going to sit at that table over there and you're going to tell us everything you know, everything you've done."

Ramiz jumped in, translating into Arabic. As Ramiz spoke, Alex glanced to her right. There was an oblong table, large enough to seat twelve, the type that might be used for conferences. It was so big that it might have overpowered the room, except a wall had been taken down with sledge hammers — a huge gaping gash — and the hole led into the next room.

There was some back and forth in Arabic between the hostage and Ramiz, who blurted out several things quickly. He spoke with great animation and shook his head in Alex's direction. He indicated that he had issues with Alex being there.

"What's his problem?" Federov asked. "Doesn't he know he's not allowed to have problems?"

Ramiz turned back to Federov. Ramiz spoke with a very precise brand of English, almost too perfect, as if he had been educated at British schools, same as Peter.

"Signor Ahmet has informed us," Ramiz said evenly, "that he feels he is being mistreated here. He further adds, and I quote directly here, that he refuses to speak at all in front of this woman."

"Why not?" Federov asked.

The hostage must have understood the question because he offered several utterances in Arabic. Ramiz gave it a moment, as if he were trying to add some delicacy to it. Then he translated.

"Ahmet says he has no desire, sir," Ramiz said, "to be put on display for one of your cheap filthy whores."

Alex blinked. So did Rizzo. Federov nodded pensively. A second passed, during which the prisoner appeared as if he thought he had scored an important point.

In one movement, Federov pulled back his enormous fist and blasted Ahmet in the side of the face. He held him in place with one hand and then delivered a second blow right after the first. Same location.

Never in Alex's life had she seen such a pair of devastating punches thrown by a bare hand. She had gone to prize fights a couple of times with friends in Los Angeles, had sat close to the ring, and had seen the fists land. She had been at hockey games when players had squared off right on the other side of the glass. But she had never seen a one-two punch like this.

The force of the blows crunched into the side of the man's face with hard cracking sounds. Federov let go of Ahmet after the second hit. The man flew over backward onto the bed and bounced. He landed hard against the wall then dropped onto the mattress like a sack of potatoes. Federov's long arms followed him, picking him up, holding him, and walloping him in the gut, and then slamming him backward against the bed and the wall a second time, leaving a pale bloodstain on the wall.

Peter and Rizzo tried to intervene, but not very hard and not very successfully. Alex knew better. Ahmet was cowering now, yelling in terrified Arabic. Federov grabbed him again, by his shirt and by his throat, ripping his clothing as he pulled him upward. Then Federov dragged him across the room. He slammed him down on a hardback chair at the table.

"My guests are personal friends!" he roared in English. "They have come a long way. The lady is a personal friend in particular and works for the government of the United States of America. Not only will you talk to her, but you will answer any question that she asks."

The man sat there stunned for a moment, listening to Ramiz's translation.

"Is all this clear?" Federov bellowed.

The Arab nodded, now in fear for his life. He was bleeding from the corner of his eye and a massive welt had already emerged over his cheekbone.

"Tell him to apologize!" Federov said to his translator. "Now!" Ramiz relayed the request.

"Yuri. It's all right," Alex said.

But the Russian was blind with rage.

Cowering, Ahmet said his only word of English for the evening, looking at Alex. "Sorry," he said. There was blood in his mouth. He sputtered. Part of a tooth came out.

Peter reached in his pocket, found a handkerchief, and tossed it to Ahmet. Ahmet gave him a trembling nod of thanks.

They all settled in at the table. Alex sat between Peter and Rizzo. The hostage had Ramiz to his right and Federov to his left, in case he needed to be encouraged to talk again. There were several empty chairs.

In a surreal touch, Dmitri — all seventy-four inches tall of him — appeared again with a tray. He spread bottles of water around the table, a bowl of fruit, and some chips.

Federov lit one of his cigarettes, waved the match to extinguish it, and threw the match to the floor. He turned back to Ramiz.

"Tell him to speak Italian," Federov said. "I understand it some. Two of my guests," he added, meaning Alex and Rizzo, "are fluent."

Ramiz brought the prisoner up to speed.

Peter leaned to Alex and whispered, "You're my lifeline on this one. I don't understand any Italian."

"I'll fill you in afterward," she said. Rizzo gave a slight nod to the two of them also, underscoring that he was working the same side of the street. Federov stared at Ahmet, barely appeased. The trip had been long and the prisoner finally began to talk.

FIFTY-SEVEN

VILLA MALAFORTUNATA, ITALY, SEPTEMBER 16, 10:18 P.M.

His name was Ahmet Lazzari, he said, switching into Italian. He was a Turk by way of Sicily. His parents had been laborers, his father a bricklayer, his mother a picker in a vineyard. More recently, he and his brother had moved to Genoa, where they had found occasional work on the docks. Eventually, they had worked for one of Federov's shipping companies.

His accent was thick and guttural.

He talks like a goat, Federov had warned back in Geneva. Alex wasn't so sure of that, but Ahmet did have the breath of one.

All of Federov's business had come out of Odessa, Alex knew, but his bases of operation had expanded heavily into the Middle East and the Mediterranean. He thought of himself as a poor man's Aristotle Onassis, with the ships but without the ex-first-lady wife who could give him the big time social and political clout and solve problems for him.

As Ahmet began, Alex quietly brought a notepad and pen out of her purse. Peter sat with his arms folded, elbows on the table. Rizzo sat next to her on the other side, his arms folded across his chest, his facial expression a tight scowl.

Ahmet Lazzari had a stricken look as he launched into his story. He had a prison pallor about him and behaved at times like a stray dog, not knowing whether he was going to be fed or whipped. But he had worked for Federov's companies since 2001, he said, as a warehouseman first, then as a deck hand, and eventually as a member of a crew on the outbound freighters. He'd been clear of trouble for the entire time of his employment, up until about two months ago.

"That's when hell broke loose," he said. "That's when we made some mistakes, my brother, Hassan, and me. Bad mistakes. I regret them."

His eyes darted to Federov and then around the table. Hell breaking loose, he explained next, was when he, his brother, the shipping
company, and a ship known as *El Fuguero*—Liberian registry—all
came together under the same unlucky star.

Ahmet and Hassan had worked together for several years, each
one watching the other's back, working intermittently as merchant
seamen for various companies. They were in Genoa two months earlier when the *Fuguero* was signing on crew. They signed on together.
The bursar and much of the staff were Arabs, many Libyan, a few
Saudis. The brothers had Sicilian names and Italian passports but
were Arabs. So they got special treatment and were hired.

Two nights before sailing, the purser, a man named Abdul, approached them in a café near the docks. He wanted to put an offer to
them, Ahmet recalled, something that would earn them some extra
money. Ahmet had drawn his attention because he was an Arab and
because he had experience working in shipyards and knew how to
weld the inner structure of a ship. So would they be interested in
listening? And would they be able to keep their mouths shut if they
said no.

The brothers looked at each other and didn't think too much about
it. Extra money was important, whatever the job, so they said yes. It
had to do with taking some panels off the wall and sealing some material back in. The brothers looked at each other and laughed.

"Half the boats in the Mediterranean are running drugs," Ahmet
said to the table full of his visitors. "The other half are running guns.
People in suits in offices are getting rich. Men who have yachts and
seven mistresses. So why shouldn't we get some crumbs from the
rich guys' table?"

So they agreed.

Two nights later they were aboard the ship. It had been cleared of
local crew. The brothers were asked to go into the bursar's office with
an array of tools and take out one of the panels on the wall. They did
so. Behind it was a hollow area, about a meter wide and half a meter
deep. It was perfect for storage. They left the new hole in the wall
open and reported back to Abdul.

Abdul came in and inspected their work. He was pleased. The
panel lay on the floor with the bolts that had held it. There wasn't

much of a mess and nothing had been damaged. The brothers had done good work.

"Next, we were told to go below decks until summoned back," Ahmet said. "When we came back down below, the atmosphere on the ship had changed. The crew was gone, almost all of it. In their place, there were some Middle Eastern guys. They had the scarves. Dark glasses. They looked like Egyptians, and they looked like they wanted trouble. They all had Uzi's. They didn't bother us, but they knew we were welders."

"We understood that this was when a delivery was made," Ahmet said. "They didn't want us seeing whoever got on and off."

"We sat in the ship's kitchen, my brother, Hassan, and me," Ahmet said. "We opened a bottle of wine and smoked cigarettes. It must have been less than an hour. One of the gunman came for us. He spoke to us in Arabic and told us we could go back upstairs and finish our work. He asked us if we had more cigarettes, so we gave him a pack. We wanted him to be our friend, you know?"

He searched the table nervously and looked for some interaction from his audience. None was forthcoming.

"We went back upstairs and Abdul was standing there. He was looking into our secret compartment. There was a bag in it. A sack. Rough material, like burlap. The type of thing tools are kept in. He motioned with his head at the hiding place. 'Close it up now!' he said to us. So we did. We put the steel plating back in place and used an automatic drill to put the bolts back. He didn't let us look in the bag. We had no idea."

He drew a breath. Alex interrupted him.

"Ahmet," she said. "What was the exact date that we're talking about?"

He shrugged. "I don't know," he said.

"Try harder than that, if you will."

After some consultation he claimed it was June the twenty-first of this year. Or thereabouts. He wasn't certain.

"Why is the exact date important?" Federov asked.

"Dates are always important," Alex said.

She thanked the Arab and he continued.

"Abdul paid us in cash. So we had some fun with the money in port. Liquor. Women."

"Well, that's not a strict Muslim lifestyle now, is it?" Rizzo chipped in.

Ahmet hung his head a little. He had no idea who Rizzo was and didn't know whether to spit or salute. He did neither. "No," he said. "Would have saved us all a lot of trouble if we'd been strict," he said, "but we weren't."

Federov made a motion with his hand that suggested Ahmet should move the story along. He did. He said they sailed in two days as scheduled, and everything was fine on board. Then after two days at sea, his brother came to him. Hassan had purchased this little electronic tracking device, he said. It had only cost twenty euros. But Hassan had this bold idea. He was going to go into the compartment and slip it into whatever was in the bag. Then they could follow the bag to its ultimate destination.

"For what purpose?" Alex asked. "To steal it back or to blackmail the recipient?"

"I didn't want to go along with this," Ahmet said. "It was my brother's idea. Hassan's. Completely."

"That's nice, but it's not what I asked," she said.

"Blackmail," he said.

"It turned out that he and his brother were stealing from my cargo too," Federov said with bitterness, staring at his prisoner. "They'd break into shipping containers and skim merchandise. They'd smuggle it off the ships and fence it, then the insurance companies would come back to me. Prosecutors in Italy brought charges of fraud against two of my companies two years ago."

"As for these brothers creating problems for me ...," Federov continued, "we're going to discuss it later in the evening."

"My brother's idea," Ahmet said again. "It wasn't me. It was my brother," Ahmet said. "We have an expression in Sicily," he said. "*A cani tintu catina curta.* For a bad dog, a short leash. Hassan should have been on a very short leash."

"But you went along with all of it," said Alex, first in English and then in Italian. "Doesn't that make you equally guilty? And apparently you had been doing this sort of thing for years."

"Exactly," Federov said.

Ahmet looked very ill at ease with the notion, and Federov looked vindicated. Rizzo glanced at his watch. Not that he was going anywhere. But fatigue was starting to take a toll on all of them. "Let's get on with it," he said.

"We waited until we had access to the purser's office," Ahmet said. "We went in one night. We had a shipmate give him too much to drink." He paused, looked at Alex as if he couldn't decide whether to elaborate, then decided to go with it. "There were some women on the ship. Women who worked the freighters in the area. There was a Dutch girl. We made sure she kept him busy one night. We had a whole warning system. She was to signal us if Abdul left his suite."

"Wasn't his office locked at night?" Alex asked. "I would think it would have been."

Ahmet managed a rare laugh. "That was the beauty of it," he said. "The Dutch girl helped us steal the keys too. You know, when he had his pants off. And just overnight so we could get in and out. It worked perfectly."

"Brilliant," said Alex, watching him sweat and noting where his brilliance had landed him.

From there, according to Ahmet's recollection, it was all smooth sailing. Ahmet did the work on the compartment, and Hassam helped with the tools and watched the door. They were both shocked when they got to the burlap bag and opened it.

"We thought it was drugs. Heroin or cocaine. It was a white substance in individual bricks. But both of us had worked light construction and demolition in Sicily. So when we examined it, we knew it was explosives."

"What?" Alex murmured, looking up from her notes.

"Top of the line stuff. The type the Americans use in Iraq. The type they're always using and then getting used against them. Chemicals," he said. He made an expansive gesture with his large dirty hands. "Boom!" he said.

If it was an attempt to add levity to the evening and win new friends, it failed miserably.

Alex put down her pen and leaned back. She took a minute to retrack Ahmet's testimony so far and summarize everything in English for Peter. There had been a whole skein of loose logic that had been hanging together with a few strings. And now the strings were being pulled into place and the logic was emerging.

Ahmet sat on the hot seat and continued to dab at his cheek. He was obviously in considerable pain. Alex guessed that Federov's first punch had fractured the Arab's cheekbone and the second punch had redesigned it.

"I did some further checking on things this afternoon before I left Rome," Rizzo then announced slowly. He spoke English so as to conveniently include everyone except Ahmet. "This man has a long police record in Italy. So did his brother. I ran background computer checks on both of them, then cross-referenced his activities with other investigations involving the national police in Italy. One detail that came immediately to the surface was where Ahmet had worked recently. Aboard *El Fuguero*. This was a ship that was on our list as a possible conduit for some explosives that were stolen from an Iraqi military supply depot after the American invasion. Our intelligence tells us the cache was broken up several times and shipped to the West. Through Cyprus and Sardinia. That's consistent with this ship."

"And consistent with this man's story," Peter said.

"Exactly what *type* of explosives?" Alex asked.

"HMX combined with RDX," Rizzo said. "We think they can be traced directly to a warehouse in Iraq and to a manufacturer in Serbia."

There was an echo somewhere in Alex's memory of the substance. She put it on hold for later when she was back with her laptop. "How much of this HMX are we talking about?" she asked.

"About ten kilos. Or twenty pounds."

She turned back to Ahmet and asked in Italian. "And that's the size of the shipment you saw?" she asked.

"It was about ten kilos," he said. "Ten bricks."

"And so you put a honing device on it," she said.

He nodded.

"Where was it taken ashore from *El Fuguero*?" she asked.

"In Barcelona," he said.

"So we know that the explosives entered Spain?" she said. "We know that for a fact?"

"Yes," Ahmet said. Rizzo was nodding at the same time.

"And what was the date of that?"

"I'm not sure," he said.

"July twentieth or twenty-first," Rizzo said. "The ship was only in port two days. That's when it came ashore."

"Forgive me for a naive question, but exactly how did it get through port security?" Alex asked.

Ahmet snorted. "For a few dollars, anyone can disembark anything," he said.

"Yes, of course," she said.

From there it continued its journey, Ahmet said. Probably by private car, but who knew? His brother tracked it via the homing device, then used a public computer in a café to get the coordinates of the location. One thing led to another. He established the place where the stash was being held. Then he traveled to Madrid.

"Madrid?" she asked.

"Madrid."

"And how did your brother make contact with the people who were holding the explosives?"

"The coordinates were very precise," Ahmet said. "My brother knew all the ways to do those computer things. So he tracked it to a building and — "

"Do you know what building?"

"No. Hassan did all of this."

"Did he tell you anything about the building?"

"No. I was never even in Spain."

"Please, go on," Alex said.

"My brother kept the house under surveillance for a few days. Figured out who was going in and out. He narrowed it down. Ended up leaving a note on the Vespa of a man who was his target. He guessed right. My brother left a phone number and went back to France. We have relatives in Marseilles. He suggested a meeting there."

Ahmet's voice tailed off.

"And?" she asked.

"Apparently, Hassan overstepped," Federov said, almost happily. "When he arrived to pick up his baksheesh, his tender young throat got caught in some piano wire."

Ahmet gave an involuntary shudder.

"Nonetheless," Alex said. "The explosives are still out there. Correct?"

"Correct. And worse," Rizzo said. "I assume the tracker is gone."

"Yes. It's gone," Ahmet said.

"These people are bloody amateurs!" Rizzo snapped with contempt, still in Italian. "The whole lot of them. No wonder they get killed or caught or both."

"That's my *brother* you're talking about!" Ahmet said in Italian.

"Yes, of course it is," Rizzo said. "Hard to tell which of you was dumber. You for being here tonight or him for getting decapitated."

The tension on Ahmet's face was suddenly great. And a sweat broke as he glared at Rizzo. Federov's gaze was frozen on him, but Rizzo was still focused on payback for the needle in his backside.

"He wasn't included very well when the brains were handed out, though, was he, your stupid dead brother? Imagine going to pick up a payoff and not bringing a backup. Typical Arab, really. Plenty of desire, plenty of firepower, but not much between the Muzzy ears. That's why the ears ended up lying on the sidewalk, along with most of the head. Sort of like one of those pig's or goat's heads you see in a butcher's window, revolving on the skewer."

"My brother!" snapped Ahmet.

"You show me a happy Islamic fanatic," growled Rizzo, "and I'll show you a gay corpse."

Ahmet made a sudden openhanded lunge toward Rizzo, who started to laugh.

Alex made a move away from the table, but it was Federov who once again reacted and intercepted. Ahmet's chair retreated and tumbled to the floor and Federov, rising, slammed the Arab down hard onto the floor, breaking the legs of the chair as he threw Ahmet on top of it. Ahmet stayed on the floor and began sobbing. Federov kicked him.

"That's pretty much all of it," Federov said, turning back to his guests. "Does it help?"

Alex flipped her notebook shut. "I think it does," she said. "And I think it will take me back to Madrid first thing tomorrow."

"Then we're finished here," Federov said.

He turned to his guard at the door. "Take care of things, Grisha," he said flatly. Ahmet started sobbing louder.

A few minutes later, the group of visitors was back downstairs, moving toward the door, Dmitri preceding them as they stepped out into the night. There were still stars. The moon had traveled a great distance across the sky.

Dmitri had drawn his pistol again and stood guard at the end of the driveway. Peter, Alex, Rizzo, and Federov moved toward the car under a bright night sky.

When the group was almost to the car, the stillness in the heavy air was broken by the sound of a man shouting within the house. The voice came from the upstairs window, loud enough and frantic enough for Alex to glance upward in that direction.

It was a loud voice and very frightened, intensity rising, speaking in Arabic. Obviously, Ahmet.

Then there was single loud shot within the house. The voice ceased. The group moving to the SUV froze. A second shot followed. Rizzo's eyes found Alex's. Alex felt sick. They looked at Federov who at first said nothing. But he kept moving. As he opened the car door, he finally felt obliged to say something.

"It's my business. I'll run it the way I always have," he growled.

"I'm assuming we weren't supposed to hear that," Alex said. "The execution was probably meant to happen after we left."

"Does it matter?"

"Oh, I don't suppose it does," Rizzo said. "How could it?"

"Ahmet and his brother were stealing from me, stealing from the entire world. They had no honor, no backbone. Why should you care about such men? They were not your friends, they were your enemies."

"And you're still a complete bastard, aren't you?" said Alex. "I'd almost forgotten."

He shrugged. "I've done all of you a favor," he said. "The world is better off without such people. Or do you think otherwise?"

"Murder is murder," Alex said.

Federov shook his head. "And war is war," Federov said. "I did you a service, and you get angry with me. Your government should give me a medal."

Alex didn't answer. She slid back into the van. This time she took a backseat window and retreated into a corner. Peter turned to her.

"Mr. Federov is right, Alex," Peter said.

"What? You agree with what he just did?"

"I agree with what he just did."

"You'd have done the same thing?"

"In one way or another, yes," he said. "Isn't that what we're *all* paid to do? The world has front hallways and back alleys. We work in the back alleys. All of us."

She looked away, then back. "Sometimes I prefer not to," she said.

"Then why are you here tonight?" Peter asked.

"Leave me alone, all right?"

"Don't have an answer to that, do you?"

She glared back at him.

"All right," Peter said. "I'll leave you alone."

Alex was suddenly quite exhausted, quite horrified, and didn't have much to add.

"A Russian can never trust Sicilians," Federov finally muttered to anyone who would listen and when they were finally moving. "Except the dead ones. The dead ones don't bother you."

It was almost a benediction.

"That depends on who finds the body," Rizzo answered, more amused than he should have been.

Federov laughed. "No one's gonna find *that* one."

No one said anything else for most of the time en route back toward Genoa. Alex closed her eyes and slept part of the way. In the moonlight, the van wove its way eastward on the winding motorway back to the city.

The world is better off without such people.

Federov's words echoed in her mind with the same volume and impact as a pair of gunshots, and, for that matter, so did Peter's.

FIFTY-EIGHT

GENOA, ITALY, SEPTEMBER 17, AFTER MIDNIGHT

Alex crashed into bed long after midnight but did not sleep well. The two gunshots that had killed Ahmet Lazzari replayed themselves endlessly in her head. She wondered what Federov's people were doing with the body.

Chopping it up? Dumping it at sea? Burying it in concrete?

She tossed and turned all night. Then, out of sheer nerves and anxiety, and plagued by these dark images, she awakened at eight in the morning, reminded herself that she was still in Genoa and went directly to her laptop.

There were more than two dozen messages. Personal in one account and business messages in the secure account. She scanned the list of senders. Two stood out. The first was from Mr. Collins in New York. He was sending someone as promised, the week of September 18.

Yeah, fine, she answered. She was so slammed that she could barely think about it now. Who knew? Maybe she'd have to duck the guy.

Then there was the second message. It was from "Gutman." Floyd Connelly.

She opened it. She was further surprised to find a full and complete message and then — triple play! — surprised a third time to read the contents.

She stared at the message.

```
Subject:  Pietà of Malta
Date:     Fri, 14 September 2009 7:47:01 - 0400
From:     "Connelly_F"  <Floyd_Connelly@USA
          Customs.org>  Add Mobile Alert
To:       "A_LaDuca" <A_Laduca@usdt.prv.org>
```

```
Alex,
I have a major break in this case. Major infor-
mation. Can you meet me late tonight in Madrid?
Maybe around midnight? My hotel? Bottom of Form
Floyd
```

She stared at it for another moment. Was this utter nonsense or had the political hack bumbled into something? A revisionist thought snuck up on her in her fatigue. Connelly was brilliant: school, church, spy, and government establishment, complete with the Yale sheepskin. The dopey granddad guise was his deep cover, the game was Hide-in-Plain-Sight. What he kept hidden were his brains.

No matter, she reasoned. She would have to follow up. The truth would drift to the surface like a waterlogged corpse. She went back to her notes and contact information that she had acquired on their first meeting. She had his phone and hotel info.

She shook the cobwebs out of her head, ordered coffee and a light breakfast from the hotel dining room, and reached for her telephone. She punched in a number. After three rings a sleepy voice — in more ways than one — came on the line at the other end.

Floyd Connelly.

"Hello, Floyd," she said. "This is Alex LaDuca. I received your email."

A few short beats and Floyd answered. "Oh. Alex. Why, how are you this morning?"

"I'm fine," she said. "I'm also not in Madrid right now."

"Where are you?"

"Geneva," she lied, in case there were listeners.

"Switzerland?" he asked.

"Not Wisconsin. Am I disturbing you?" she asked. "Waking you up?"

He laughed. "I had to get up anyway, might as well be now," he said. "You have a nice phone voice."

"As I said, I received your email. You have something on *The Pietà of Malta*?"

He snorted. "I've got the whole case, that's what I've got," he said happily.

"How could that be?" she asked.

"Ha. A compilation of sources! Some help from Washington, some help locally from the Spanish fellas. I've been around a bit. Went to school with the former president, did you know that?"

"I suspected," she said.

He paused. "I developed an underworld source here or there in Madrid. From hanging around the right places. People say things. They talk if you know how to get them to talk."

"Is this phone secure, Floyd?" she asked.

"Yours? I wouldn't know. Can't tell from this end."

"I meant yours," she said.

"Hardly matters, does it?" he asked. "You know, a lot of people think I'm getting slow in my old age, but it's not the case at all. I've got this case on a platter."

"Uh huh," she said. She didn't know whether to be infuriated that the case might be resolved without her or relieved if it was. Yet she knew things like this happened all the time.

"Look, here's the story," Floyd said. "The pietà is gone. Disappeared in Switzerland. Either got destroyed or sold. Anyway, the point is that the baby Michelangelo got traded for some explosives or something. Might have been a three-way deal. Then — "

"Floyd, are you *sure* this line is clear?"

Floyd said he was sure, and he couldn't stop talking.

"See, there's a further rumor that a load of explosives came through Madrid, then moved on. Got sent up to France, and some of the local towel-heads are planning to blow up some railroad bridges or something in Provence in time for the fall tourist season. Anyway, just to make sure nothing's going to blow up locally in Spain, we've put all the big time targets on alert. Some places are being checked by the bomb-sniffing dogs. I've got emails up the wazoo on all of this. That's what I'm going to show you. I've downloaded them into my laptop. Once everything's clear we all get to go home. What do you think?"

Alex wasn't sure what to think. She felt a frown forming on her brow along with the incredulity that went with it. "That's fine if it's true," Alex said, "but if the investigation is over, I need to hear that from my boss."

"Who's your boss?"

"Mike Gamburian at Treasury in Washington."

"Don't know him. Call him and ask."

"The protocol is that he should call me."

"Well, do it that way if you want," he laughed. "You can probably squeeze a few days of vacation out of this if you do it that way. Me, I can't wait to get home. How many bullfights can you go to in this city? You watch a bullfight and you know who's gonna win, anyway." Connelly ran from sentence to sentence like a reckless driver sailing through a string of stop signs. "I've got some more information on this too. Names, addresses. Laptop. Why don't you come over tonight, and I'll boot it up and run through it. That's if you're not busy."

"Is this a business request or a social one, Floyd?" she asked.

"Little of both," he said after a pause. "I'm at the Hotel de Cataluña. That's over by — Wait a minute. You said you were out of town?"

"Flights are only about ninety minutes," she said. Travel time from Genoa and Geneva were identical. "I can be there by this evening. And I'll meet you in the lobby, not your room," she said. "We can talk there."

"Oh, all right, all right. Be a good girl if that's how you want to be," he said in a deafening bellow. "I'm an old guy, you know. There's not much you have to fear from me."

"What time?" she asked.

"Let's do it late," he said. "I've got a dinner with one of my sources. You know how Spain is. They don't eat lunch till five p.m., then dinner at ten. I should be back to the hotel by eleven thirty or midnight."

"I'll be in the lobby at eleven thirty," she said. "Okay?"

"That's fine," he said.

She rang off, highly skeptical, shaking her head. "What a— —," she mused.

And then for several minutes, she sat in the room alone.

Was Floyd blowing smoke, or did he actually have something? If he had something, how? She was dubious about everything he was saying, yet she had now committed to go visit him that night.

She went back to her laptop, shifting gears now, trying to assimilate the story that Ahmet had told the previous evening.

She went back into the attachments that she had downloaded from Colonel Pendraza. She quickly pegged to points of reference, material she had read before. This, she realized, was why Ahmet's account rang a distant bell.

She reread,

> *Item*: Noted in passing, al-Qaeda leaders have frequently threatened to strike again in Europe in audio and video warnings. Antiterror experts within the *Policia Nacional* said recently that the pace of the warnings has picked up in recent weeks.
>
> *Associated item*: Intercepted al-Qaeda documents have indicated activities of small sleeper cells within Spain, intent on acting independently but with major force.

She did a web search on the missing explosives. Within another few minutes, more pay dirt. From the *Washington Post*, she had another piece of the story:

Iraqi Explosives Missing, UN Is Told

US Disputes Timing of Loss of Munitions Sealed by Inspectors at Weapons Facility

By Colum Lynch and Bradley Graham

Washington Post Staff Writers

Tuesday, October 26, 2004; Page A18

UNITED NATIONS, Oct. 25—The UN's nuclear watchdog agency reported Monday that massive quantities of high explosives at an Iraqi weapons facility have disappeared, including some material under UN seal because of its potential use to detonate a nuclear bomb.

UN and Iraqi officials indicated the explosives were lost while the country was under US occupation. But US officials suggested that the munitions may have disappeared before the US-led forces established full control over the country. They said a search of the facility by US troops shortly after the fall of Baghdad last year turned up no evidence of the explosives.

She fired off an email to Mike Gamburian's office in Washington asking if he could send her any files on the case. No immediate response, so she closed down her laptop.

Half an hour later, she met Peter in the lobby of the hotel, as well as Rizzo and Federov. In an expansive mood, perhaps on a personal high after ordering a murder the previous night, Federov offered another of his private jets to take Peter and Alex back to Madrid. Gian Antonio Rizzo would return to Rome via commercial flight. Federov stayed in Genoa to shore up any damage done by the late Ahmet and his even-later brother.

FIFTY-NINE

MADRID, SEPTEMBER 17

The irony: The HDX and the RDX were powerful enough to bring down an urban block. And yet there was no danger of them going off accidentally. They lacked fuses and detonators. Nonetheless, Jean-Claude worked carefully to get them into their proper position.

It had taken three trips through the tunnels, caverns, and crawl spaces under Madrid to get the whole cargo of ten one-kilo bricks of explosives to where he wanted them. But here, now, in the middle of the night, he finally had them in place.

At one stretch under the city, the narrowest crawl space, Jean-Claude relied on Samy to move the explosives along. Samy's shoulders were narrow. And he was flexible, like an eel. In some of the crawl spaces rocks had crumbled and bits of mortar had created little cave-ins. The passageways were increasingly dangerous. And there was always the chance of a big cave-in. Anyone caught in one would die. There was no mechanism for rescue, only martyrdom, which wasn't a bad thing either.

They had assembled six bricks of explosives in the sub-chamber under the embassy. But getting the explosives in had become increasingly difficult. The narrow walls and tunnels just *felt* like they wanted to collapse sometime soon. Well, Jean-Claude reasoned, soon enough everything would turn to dust. He himself was already making plans to leave Madrid soon after the big blast. As for his confederates, no one would know who they had been or where to find them. They would disappear easily back into the fabric of the city.

In the end, the final four bricks of explosives had been placed on a small panel, and the panel had been tied to a rope. Jean-Claude teed up the parcel from one side and Samy pulled it through the crawl-space. Samy then waited for a few hours, listening to music on an MP3 player under the embassy.

Jean-Claude had heard from the merchant in the Rastro, Madrid's flea market, who had fuses and detonators. His devices were ready. Once they were secured, and once Samy arranged things right, the big surprise could be set off under the embassy. He would use a timer that would time the attack for midmorning. The block would be rubble within seconds, and every living thing—Americans, Spaniards who worked there, casual passers-by—would die in the conflagration, no concessions to humanity whatsoever.

So he was thinking, 10:00 a.m. might be good. A twelve-hour timer would be perfect. The hour was near to visit Farooq.

SIXTY

GENOA TO MADRID, SEPTEMBER 17, MID-AFTERNOON

Not surprisingly, Federov's other jet was a thing of beauty: a Learjet 55 with a crew of four. The plane seated eight in addition to the crew, but she and Peter were the only passengers.

Alex settled into a seat by herself in the rear. The aircraft took off from the same private field outside Genoa where she had arrived. She opened her computer and found a response from Mike Gamburian.

It was a CIA file. She entered her security codes, held her breath as she waited for them to apply properly, then breathed easier as the files opened.

Then she confronted additional pieces of the backstory.

The explosives that Ahmet had undoubtedly spoken of were a powdery plastic called HMX. They were combined with a similar substance named RDX and were manufactured in Serbia. They were some of the most powerful conventional explosives used by the world's militaries.

Serbia, unlike Spain, was the one place in the world where HMX and RDX were manufactured. The path of the particular batch of explosives that would turn up in western Europe was a grim echo of the dark events of the last quarter century.

In the 1980s, the Iran-Iraq war was only one of a series of crises during an era of upheaval in the Middle East. There had been the revolution in Iran that deposed the Shah, the occupation of the American Embassy in Tehran by militant students, and the Soviet Union's occupation of Afghanistan. There had been the invasion of the Great Mosque in Mecca by antiroyalist Islamists, and the bitter clan fighting among different factions of Syrians, Israelis, and Palestinians in Lebanon. All of these events and more had maintained the Middle East as the tinderbox of the modern world, ready to ignite larger conflagrations if any side overplayed its hand.

The Iran-Iraq War followed months of rising tension between the Iranian Islamic republic and secular nationalist Iraq. In mid-September 1980, Iraq under its new, young military dictator, Saddam Hussein, attacked Iran in the mistaken belief that internal Iranian political disarray would guarantee a quick victory. The gambit proved wrong.

The international community responded with UN Security Council resolutions calling for a ceasefire and for all member states to refrain from actions contributing in any way to the conflict's continuation. The Soviet Union, opposing the war, cut off arms exports to Iran and to Iraq, its ally under a 1972 treaty.

The US had already ended previously massive military sales to Iran when the Shah had fallen in 1979. By 1980 the US had broken off diplomatic relations with Iran because of the Tehran embassy hostage crisis. Iraq ended ties with the US during the 1967 Arab-Israeli War.

So the US was officially neutral in the Iran-Iraq War, diplomatically recognized neither side, and maintained that it armed neither. Iran, however, depended on American weapons. Anywhere in the world, if there is a potential buyer of arms, there is always a potential seller. So Iran quickly acquired American arms through merchants from Israel, Europe, Asia, and South America.

Iraq had started the war with a large Soviet-supplied arsenal but needed additional weaponry as the conflict defied a quick resolution and wore on. Initially, Iraq advanced far into Iranian territory, but was driven back within months. By mid 1982, Iraq was on the defensive against Iranian human-wave attacks. The United States, having decided that an Iranian victory would not serve its regional interests, began quietly arming Saddam Hussein's military in Iraq.

Negotiations already underway to upgrade US-Iraq relations were accelerated, high-level officials exchanged visits, and in February 1982, the State Department removed Iraq from its list of states supporting international terrorism. It had been included several years earlier because of ties with several Palestinian nationalist groups.

Iraq also received massive external financial support from the Gulf states and assistance through loan programs from the US. The White House and State Department pressured the Export-Import Bank to provide Iraq with financing, to enhance its credit standing, and to enable it to obtain loans from other international financial institutions. The US Agriculture Department provided taxpayer-guaranteed loans for purchases of American commodities, to the satisfaction of US grain exporters. As the war ground onward, chewing up close to a million casualties on both sides, North American agribusiness profited handsomely.

The United States formally restored relations with Iraq in November 1984, the time of Donald Rumsfeld's more than convivial meeting with Saddam Hussein. But the US had begun, several years earlier, to provide Iraq with clandestine intelligence and military support, in secret and contrary to America's official neutrality, in accordance with policy directives from the White House.

Among the materials received by Saddam Hussein's military was a seven-ton shipment of HDX and RDX, brokered by the Central Intelligence Agency, from a factory in Serbia. The explosives were delivered pursuant to the National Security Study Memorandum of March 1982.

The explosives were stored at a weapons complex at Al Qaqaa, about thirty miles south of Baghdad. Over the course of the next six years, much of the supply was used by Saddam Hussein's soldiers against Iraq's enemies — Iran and internal dissident tribes — and gradually depleted. But not *all* of it was depleted. Another two tons remained over the course of the next fifteen years. And there it sat, much like the rest of Saddam Hussein's massive stockpile of conventional weapons scattered across Iraq, when US forces swept across Iraq in March and April 2003. During the invasion, the Iraqi army abandoned the site. And no one in the American military received an order to secure it.

Unobstructed, thieves entered the Al Qaqaa warehouses and removed the entire two tons. Half of it was trucked to a pro-al-Qaeda terrorist training camp near the city of Mir Ali in Pakistan. The other half, sitting in the back of a single diesel truck, arrived in Damascus, Syria, two weeks after it had been looted from the old storage facility.

In Damascus, a mix of German and Italian converts to Islam, and Arab and Turkish immigrants coalesced in an extremist cell at a radical mosque. They divided the shipment again. Half of it went to an Egyptian imam who directed an Arabic-language school in Cairo. The other half, in bulk now no larger in size than an old fashioned steamer trunk, was trucked to Beirut where, under the cover of night, it was packed into the aft hull of a speedboat.

It went next to Cyprus, where, acting on tips from the CIA, Greek and Turkish police raided several cells of radical Islamists looking for the explosives. The raids came at a time when authorities in southern Europe were increasingly worried about the threat from al-Qaeda in the Magreb, an Algerian-dominated network that had pledged allegiance to Osama bin Laden. A radical Muslim named Ayman al-Zawahiri, considered deputy leader of the broader al-Qaeda movement, had recently issued a videotaped statement repeating his exhortations to the North African group to strike European countries.

But the Greek and German police didn't find the explosives.

They didn't find them because the shipment never came on shore in Cyprus. Rather, according to CIA informants, it went into an industrial packing crate that was marked as a factory refrigeration unit and packed into a different ship. And from there, conveyed by homegrown European radicals now, it went to Brindisi in the south of Italy.

There local gangsters hid it in a picturesque white-walled old monastery within an olive grove, without knowing — or wanting to know — what they were hiding.

By now, according to Italian police, control over the shipment was held by a local radical Muslim named Habib, who ran an Islamic school in Naples. Habib was constantly under surveillance but never made a slip. Rumor had it that he had stashed the explosives in a farmhouse somewhere outside of Naples. But police never were able to locate it.

Several weeks passed. Surveillance on Habib was dropped due to lack of results.

Police who had been attempting to track the shipment went on to other assignments. And there the trail ended for everyone involved with the case.

Until now, thought Alex.

Until now, she reasoned, when the late Ahmet and the even later Hassan, had tracked the next part of the explosives' journey and linked it to a Jean-Claude al-Masri who had formed his own terror cell in Madrid.

But why now? she pondered. She leaned back in her seat and felt the bumpy hot air of a late Spanish summer buffet the aircraft. Suddenly she had it. She gazed out the window, her mind a warren of certainties, theses, and suspicions.

Because of the black bird, she realized. Because, as she had learned, art theft frequently finances crime or terror. Because of *The Pietà of Malta*, the explosives had now made their way to Madrid. Because of the theft of the pietà, because a dead Chinese collector had come up out of the snow, all these events had followed.

The thieves had stolen it from the museum to raise money to buy explosives from anti-Western sources. But then the brokers had burned the purchaser and not delivered, either out of greed, stupidity, or the desire to capitalize even more.

That misstep had brought Peter into the case.

She closed down her computer, closed her eyes for the rest of the flight, and tried not to hear Federov's two gunshots for the hundredth time.

Peter and Alex disembarked in Madrid by three in the afternoon. Alex checked back into the Ritz, a smaller accommodation this time, by 4:00. Peter stayed at El Mirablau.

Settled in by 5:00 in the afternoon, Alex went to email yet again and now heard from her Roman buddy, Rizzo. The DNA samples had come back from the skin that Rizzo had scratched in the nightclub from the face of his assailant.

The DNA had finally triggered a match.

The match named a Frenchman of Algerian heritage named Jean-Claude al-Masri. The latter had a small-time police record in three European countries and an address in Madrid.

The Policia Nacional had already been asked to pick him up.

SIXTY-ONE

MADRID, SEPTEMBER 17, LATE AFTERNOON

On a cluttered back street next to the Rastro, in the rear of a small locked store, Jean-Claude stood in a closed room and obtained the final ingredients for mass homicide.

His detonators were in a small bag on the counter.

The old Arab named Farooq motioned to it when the younger man came in the door. The proprietor also held a pistol in his hand the entire time as Jean-Claude made the pickup, just in case. He hated the sight of such people and sometimes hated himself for having to deal with them.

But Jean-Claude caused no trouble.

He gathered the detonators and pushed them into a backpack. He gave the old man a smile, went out the door, and prepared to head home.

The Metro was giving him the creeps today, and he also had some hotel business to attend to. He had even pulled his Vespa out of storage for the occasion.

SIXTY-TWO

MADRID, SEPTEMBER 17, LATE EVENING

Alex paid her fare at the window of the taxi cab and stepped to the sidewalk on the Carrera de San Jerónimo. Across the street stood the Hotel de Cataluña. She tipped the driver generously and turned as he gave her an appreciative nod. It was only then that she noticed that there was some disorder, that something grievous had happened.

The hotel was a restored nineteenth-century building not far from the museum triangle. A thick, hot night gripped the city. Several meters from where Alex stepped onto the sidewalk, many of the patrons of the Café Giron, where intellectuals had gone to argue for generations, stood looking up into an alley. Several couples stood on the opposite side of the street, discussing what had happened. Their faces were contorted. They spoke in hushed tones. Two women jockeyed for a good view of what had happened, got one, then shielded their eyes and abruptly averted their gaze

Alex looked up, scanning the side of the building. She was staring at the back wall of the hotel where Floyd Connelly had said he was staying. There were human figures at several windows, people looking down, gawking at a spot where a knot of other people had gathered below in an alley. One woman on the third floor was holding her hands to her face in horror. A man poked his head out, looked down, and quickly looked away. Alex worked the side of the building with her gaze. There was a seventh floor window that was wide open with window drapes out and flapping gently. She recalled where Connelly said he was staying — *habitation 734* — and she knew that whatever he had to say to her wasn't going to get said.

For good measure, hoping against hope, she tried Connelly's cell number. His voice came on. Voice mail. She disconnected.

Alex crossed the street. She walked to an alley that led behind the hotel. In front of the alley was an ambulance and in front of the ambulance was a police car. Emergency vehicles, but no one seemed to be in much of a rush. The police weren't setting much of a perimeter yet. They had that "just arrived" look.

She passed between two iron gates that led into an alley. The alley led to a place where garbage was stored and where service vehicles could enter the hotel's service entrance. But the garbage and the vehicles didn't matter right now.

A Vespa with a rider on it emerged from underneath of the hotel and with a whining whirring noise, accelerated as it climbed the driveway. The small knot of men who had gathered there, some in police uniforms, gave way to the bike and rider. Alex stepped back so the vehicle wouldn't run over her toes.

The boundaries of the alley were marked by a high, old wrought-iron fence with spikes on the top. The spikes resembled old-fashioned spears. Part of the spiked railing had been torn from the rest of the fence. It was there that the knot of men were focused.

Alex pushed through the crowd. She could see partially what had brought everyone together. A man in a blue police uniform knelt over a bulky body that was sprawled in impossible directions. The body wore suit pants and a blue shirt with a necktie, but already the color combination had turned from the prosaic into the grotesque. Fragments of the victim's skull, tufts of white hair caked with crimson fluid, were not far from the corpse. Other men stood awkwardly behind the policeman, peering through whatever inches of space were possible between bodies.

Alex worked her way to the edge of the small crowd and managed to slide her way to the front where she could get a good look at the corpse. A wave of nausea overtook her. She suppressed it. She had seen atrocities in her life — human beings torn apart by bullets in Venezuela, by a rocket attack in Ukraine — but this was the worst she had seen.

She looked at the fence, looked upward at the seventh floor window again, turned away, and looked back. It was all clear.

Connelly had come out of the window.

He had plunged from a hundred feet up and crashed into the fence full force when he'd come to earth. The spikes had torn into and through his upper body, ripped his neck apart, had taken off half his skull. Some of the spikes had impaled themselves in his upper chest. But the impact of the big man's fall had taken out a section of the old iron fence and brought it to the concrete with him.

And so there he lay, dead as a crushed bug, his bodily fluids continuing to flow, not a breath of life left in him. He didn't look like Orson Welles anymore, and he didn't look like Gutman. He didn't look like anything human.

For a moment, which turned into several moments, all Alex could do was stare. She stared and wondered what it was that he had wanted to tell her, what it was that he wanted to pass along. It must have been good because people don't voluntarily go out windows when they're waiting to share a secret with a lady. Not usually. It had to have been good unless it had been nothing.

A black vehicle pulled to the curb behind her, not far from the death scene. Alex recognized it. Bodyguards jumped out and opened the door for a man in the backseat. Colonel Pendraza of the National Police emerged. Her heart beat a little faster.

Pendraza's security people stayed with him as he approached the death scene. The uniformed police present recognized him and gave way. Miguel, his lead bodyguard, seemed to be always on duty. He was standing point as the colonel moved toward the fallen body. Alex saw the flicker of recognition in Miguel's eyes when he saw her.

Pendraza moved to the front and looked at the body. Alex gave him a few seconds, then walked toward him. One of the bodyguards intercepted her, raising a powerful arm to block her path.

"I need to see the colonel," she said in Spanish. She spoke past the bodyguard who stopped her, and addressed Miguel.

Miguel turned to ask the colonel, who was a few feet away. The colonel glanced in Alex's direction. He gave a nod. Alex moved past his bodyguards and into the small group that surrounded the corpse.

They too spoke Spanish. "Bad night," she said.

Pendraza had seen his share of corpses in his career. "They've *all* been bad recently, the nights," he said. He paused. "American, right?" the colonel asked.

"Yes."

"I recognize him," the colonel said. "Or what's left of him. The pietà again?"

"That would be my guess," Alex said.

An electric drill went on with a screech. Emergency workers started to cut away the sections of the fence that had impaled the body. It sounded like dental work on steroids. Alex looked away. The workers were disengaging the spiked rails from the corpse, and to do that, they needed to cut away a small section of Connelly's shoulder.

"It's been a completely rotten day," Colonel Pendraza said. "There was a woman murdered in the Metro a day or two ago. One of our track walkers. They only found the body this afternoon."

"Where exactly?" Alex asked.

"It was up by the Calle Maldonado," he said. "Nice neighborhood. What's this city coming to?"

She thought about it. Then it hit her. "That's not too far from the US Embassy," she said. "Isn't it?"

"About a block away," he said. "And there are a lot of embassies in the area. Not just yours. Don't jump to conclusions."

She tried to assimilate the information. "Where was the body found? In a Metro station?"

"No. In one of the underground tunnels."

"What tunnels?"

"There's a whole network of them," he said. "Don't worry. They're old and they're sealed. There's no danger."

"Can I have a look?"

His eyes narrowed. "At what?"

"The area where the body was found. The tunnels."

"Why would you want to?"

"Because it's near the US Embassy."

"If you wish to," he said. "Call my office in the morning. I'll arrange a police permit and keys to some of the locked doors."

"Should I clear it with the Guardia Civil?" she asked.

"If you want to waste your time, certainly," he said.

"Thank you," she said.

Two police technicians were removing the spikes from the corpse, working by hand. Alex fought against a feeling of sickness. She stepped back from the work that was being done. Her eyes wandered, then did a double take.

Peter Chang stood on the opposite side of the street. He was in a suit with a computer bag on his shoulder.

"Excuse me," she said to Colonel Pendraza.

Pendraza nodded. Alex moved through the crowd and crossed the street. She found a different Peter Chang than she had ever seen before. Peter's fine suit was torn in two places. He had a small welt across his cheek and another across his forehead. No blood, just the evidence of combat.

"Peter, what are you doing here?" she asked.

"Same as you, I suppose," he said. "Let's move," he said. "I want to get away from here."

"I'm not leaving just yet," she said.

"Well, I'd like to get off this block before the police seal it up."

She looked at the rips in his clothing and the gash to his temple. "What's going on?" she asked. "You were in a fight of some sort?"

"Yeah, I was."

"Heck of a coincidence, you should be here," she said suspiciously, suddenly wary of him. "Every time I see you after dark, someone winds up dead."

"Yeah. Midnight in Madrid. Not healthy. Someone always gets killed."

"Why *are* you here?" she pressed. "And what happened to you?"

"I was supposed to meet him," he said, motioning to Connelly. "I got a call."

"From Connelly? Why would he call you? How did he even *know* you."

"He didn't. I got a call from my own people."

"Who? Your government? *Guojia Anquan Bu*. Your Ministry of State Security?"

"That's them," Peter said, speaking rapidly. "And Mark McKinnon called them. Do I have to remind you, he works with them when it suits common purposes."

"Peter ...?"

"Come on along," he said. "Talk to me." He took her arm forcefully, and they moved several paces away.

She sharply pulled her arm away. "Don't force me along. I don't like that!"

"I need to be out of here," he said.

"Why? What happened here?" she demanded.

"Connelly came back here with a woman about an hour ago. I asked the hotel staff. He expected to get lucky, and my guess is she let her friends in. That, or the friends were waiting. Lurking maybe. Either in the hall or in his room."

Alex shuddered. She looked carefully at his clothing.

"I arrived at his suite and the door was unlatched," Peter said. "I pushed it open and ran smack into them. They must have just shoved him out the window."

She was having trouble believing him. This was John Sun speaking, suddenly.

"They charged right into me. I tried to grab them and bring them down, but there were three of them. Speaking Arabic, by the way, in case that drops you a hint of any sort. There was a scuffle. They got the first hits in, and the next thing I knew I was on the floor."

Alex knew that Peter could take out three people easily; he could take out *ten* people. And he was armed. This wasn't adding up.

"I didn't know what happened," he said. "I went in, saw the open window, and looked down. Then I got out of there fast," he said. "I didn't have time to look around. I just grabbed his laptop and his notebooks," he said. "That's all I could get."

"You did what?"

He motioned to the cache he had in the computer bag. "You want the Spanish police looking at this stuff?" he asked. "Might as well have the contents published in *El Mundo*."

"You could have stayed for the police," she said. He started to move down the block and she followed, with both reluctance and persistence.

"Oh, sure! After what you told me about the Swiss? And bloody Interpol? I have to get out of this country," he said. "My picture is all over the hotel security cameras, and they'll be going through them tonight. Count on that."

Peter was still moving, looking around, highly nervous, highly agitated.

"Uh oh," he said. "Look at this. The cops are setting a ring around this place. Look. There are cops on each end of the block."

"That's normal," she said.

"Not good for me, Alex," he said. "Let's just get out of here."

She looked at Peter, and something clicked in having to do with his trepidation of the Spanish police. It seemed so obvious that she realized that she had been suppressing it since the first time she saw him in this place tonight.

Peter had killed Connelly. His face was battered and his suit was torn because the chunky failing old Yalie had put up the fight of his life. Peter had beaten her to Connelly because Connelly had something to tell her that reflected unfavorably on Peter. Peter, in short, was a double agent of the most treacherous sort. He couldn't be trusted any more than she could throw him. Peter was the most dangerous liar she had ever met in her life with a spirited competition in progress for second place.

An entire kaleidoscope of deceit opened before her as she gazed at him, new vistas in every direction, forming and reforming in endless patterns of duplicity.

He must have sensed what she felt because he raised his eyes, looked at her, and became colder than ever.

"Look," he said. "Talk to Mark McKinnon if you can ever get him on the phone. It's obvious all those explosives are in Madrid. Connelly heard from an informer that there was going to be an attack on the embassy. Right now it's been shut down, the embassy. There's a US Marine bomb squad going through with dogs and radio detectors."

"Why do you know that and I don't?"

"Because I talked to McKinnon and you haven't," Peter said. "He was going to give us the details. Mark asked *me* to get over here, obviously Connelly wanted to see *you*. It's pretty clear that he was set up. Connelly bought half a bill of goods from someone, but his good information was laced with the bad stuff. But he stumbled across enough solid stuff so that he took a pavement dive from a hundred feet up."

Peter continued to glance around nervously. As he spoke to Alex, his eyes frequently went over her shoulder, back to the death scene.

Again, Peter's hands were moving quickly. He reached inside his jacket and pulled out a leather billfold. From it, he pulled a small laminated card, the size, shape, and texture of an American driver's license.

"Keep this for me," he said. "Keep this until I ask for it back. Please! It's critical."

She looked at it. It was his Swiss consular ID. Well, it wasn't Peter Chang's; it was John Sun's.

She stared at it and looked back up. "This links you to a couple of murders, doesn't it?"

"Maybe," he said.

"I honestly didn't want to believe that about you," she said. "That you were capable of that."

"Aren't we all, under the right circumstances?"

"It's not a situation I ever hope to be in again," she said.

"Nor I," he said. "But as long as you or I carry a weapon and are sworn to protect ourselves, innocent people, and our countries' interests, the possibility will be there."

"Maybe you just seem a little too enthusiastic about it," she said. "Killing people."

"And maybe someday you'll hesitate too long and wish you hadn't," he answered.

There was loud conversation from the group of police across the street. She looked back down to the John Sun ID that she held in her hand.

"Why are you giving this to me?"

"Because I trust you to do the right thing," he said. "And I don't want to have to walk past the police with it. Not here, not tonight. If they stop me and find me with two IDs, I'm going to be answering questions for ten years. All right?"

"All right," she said, taking it.

"Who's the old fascist over there?" he asked. "The one everyone is sucking up to?"

She glanced. "That's Colonel Pendraza. Policia Nacional."

"Yes. Of course. He knows who I am," Peter said softly. "I need to get out of here," he said again.

"Is there really going to be an attack on the US Embassy?" she asked.

"I'm told the information is solid."

"Who's the information from?"

"Chinese and American sources," he said. "And I never told you this, but there's some British thrown in. Some MI6."

"How did that get into the mix?" she asked.

"When the explosives were sold out of Cyprus, the British were within a day of seizing them. They made arrests anyway. Two of the men arrested told the same story: that money had come from Spain, money raised by a museum theft, and now the value was returning to Spain in bombs and bodies."

"If I can ask a dumb question, why are the Brits being so generous with you?"

He spread his hands. "Hong Kong, lady, remember? I'm one of the 'good' yellow people. Isn't that how it works? I'm 'Western,' so I can be trusted."

"Do the Spanish police know there may be an attack on our embassy?"

"I don't think so."

"Then why aren't we telling them?"

"Same reason I'm working this case," he said. "We're trying to take care of things unofficially. Is that so difficult?"

"We could use their help," Alex said. "All I've got to do is cross the street and talk to the colonel."

"Don't bother," he said softly. "In fact, that would be very unwise."

"Why?"

"Alex, do you have a gun?"

"You know I do. We just discussed — "

"Are you allowed to use it?"

"In self-defense. And in defense of anyone I deem fit. Even you."

"I'm honored. But that's where we're different," he said. "And it's another reason I'm still here."

"I just lost you."

"If Mark needs someone taken out, hit, killed, he can't ask you or even one of his CIA lackeys to do it. Not without special permission. And for that he has to go back to Washington, and the request has to go to an intelligence committee, and after a week or a month or a year he *might* get a go-ahead. And he might not."

Two uniformed Madrid police approached them. They seemed to be looking cross-eyed at Peter, but they kept going.

"But if Mark asks *me* to do it, or my team," Peter said, "and it coincides with our interests, well, it gets done, doesn't it? No questions asked, or more to the point, no answers needed to be given."

"Oh, Lord," she said with a shudder.

"Someone has to get the dirty work done," he said.

"Sometimes I'd prefer to be back at a desk in Washington, dealing with financial squabbles."

"But instead you're out here," Peter said. "On the front lines. Where it's more exciting."

"And where I feel more compromised," she said.

He laughed slightly. "Let me ask you," he said, "if you could have stopped the September 11 attacks on America by personally shooting every one of the hijackers, would you have done it? If you could have murdered Hitler and Stalin and avoided World War II, would that have been worth two bullets to end the lives of two thoroughly evil and godless men?"

"I would have looked for some other way to — "

"That wasn't the question," he said. "And I think I know your answer."

She snapped back defensively, the flash of police beacons still illuminating the streets with harsh staccato lights. "What *are* you?" she asked. "A philosopher with an Uzi?"

"Everything is a situation."

"Have a nice night," she said coolly.

Alex turned away in growing distaste.

"And you also," he answered.

She glanced to the opposite side of the street, trying to sort out her thoughts. She noticed that Colonel Pendraza had disappeared. She turned back to talk to Peter again, maybe to voice some uselessly argumentative tract about violence and murder breeding more violence and murder until it bred even more violence and murder. Or maybe she'd just ask him straight up if there had really been three young Arabs or if he had defenestrated blustery old Connelly himself, and if so, on whose orders.

But by then, with her mind teeming with questions and paranoia, Peter was gone too.

She looked in every direction.

No Peter Chang.

Like the Swiss police a few weeks earlier, she had never before encountered a man who could disappear into thin air so quickly and efficiently.

She left the block and retreated to a quiet doorway. She pulled out her cell phone and called Mark McKinnon. She reached him and reported what she had seen, what she knew. An attack on the US Embassy in Madrid was perhaps imminent.

Quietly, McKinnon took the information from her. He promised to alert embassy security immediately. But beyond that, he offered nothing in return and rang off.

From talking to McKinnon, she had the same sense as talking to a wall.

She pondered not returning to the Ritz that night. She felt vulnerable. So she found a late bar, stayed there for a few drinks, and pondered checking into a different hotel. Then she decided not to.

Instead, she returned to the Ritz and entered her room with her pistol drawn. She searched it thoroughly, found no intruder or evidence of an intrusion, and threw all the bolts on the door.

Then, riding the worst wave of paranoia in her life, she eventually dummied up pillows from the closet to resemble her body and put them under the blankets in the bedroom.

She turned around the living room sofa and slept there, facing the door and the locked balcony. She kept the pistol at arm's length.

Sleep, what there would be of it, did not come easily.

SIXTY-THREE

MADRID, SEPTEMBER 18

The next morning, Alex obtained her necessary permits and keys from the Policia Nacional as well as the City Police. She also placed a second call to Mark McKinnon and demanded an urgent meeting with him late that afternoon. He resisted at first, then relented. He asked that she find her way to a bench in a busy downtown area on the Calle de Bailén, across the street from the Palacio Real, the royal palace where the king no longer lived but where state functions were held. The meeting time was set for the window between 4:00 p.m. and 4:15.

Alex traveled there by buses, three of them, a roundabout route. She got off the first bus quickly, reversed her path down a busy street, then caught the second and the third. Each time, she jumped off abruptly just before the vehicle was to pull out of a stop, each time watching to see if anyone followed. The only other American at the meeting involving the pieta's theft had gone out a tenth-floor window, probably not voluntarily. One could never be too careful.

She found the designated bench in the shadow of the Grand Palacio. Across the street was the Cathedral of the Virgin of Almudena, patroness of Madrid. Alex's eyes swept the block for danger. She saw none, but her insides were as jittery as a half-dozen frightened cats. She didn't see McKinnon, either.

The security code with McKinnon: if she felt she had been followed, she would be reading a newspaper. If she was sure she was clean, no newspaper open. She felt secure. She sat down on the bench at a bus stop with a copy of *El Mundo* folded neatly across her lap. She picked up on the activities of passers-by. She noted footwear. She was wary of anyone with concealed hands. She carried her pistol in a holster on her hip.

She asked herself: How fast could she have her gun out and ready?

One second? Two?

She drew a breath, then let it go. It was 4:00 p.m. Then six minutes past four. Where was McKinnon?

A homeless man approached her. He engaged her in a pointless conversation and eventually asked for money. She gave him two euros, and he went about his way, replaced immediately by a twenty-something couple holding hands, smooching, and not saying a thing as they seemed to wait for a bus.

Then the man took out a cell phone, made a call, and the two of them turned to walk away. There needed to be nothing to it, but linked to the homeless man, the events were consecutive, overlapping by seconds, as if the three of them were one of McKinnon's pavement mini-teams, the first man pegging the prey, the couple keeping watch while Mark approached from somewhere. And, thinking back, the homeless man hadn't had a homeless stench.

Or was she imagining things, she asked herself. She glanced at her watch.

Ten after. The heck with the pavement teams, maybe Mark was blowing her off with a no-show. She held her seat on the bench across from the palace. She watched the guards. The palace was magnificent, built to impress, just like Versailles, just like Buckingham Palace, just like Donald Trump's home in Florida.

She tried to settle herself.

She turned her attention to the cathedral. The history gene within her reminded her of the Roman Catholic Church's centuries of influence in Spain, from the pilgrims in the first ten centuries after Christ, through the Inquisition, through the Franco regime, and more subtly, into the present day. Her eyes drifted thoughtfully over the architecture, a gray neoclassic façade that echoed the architecture of the Palacio Real across the street. The pairing of the two buildings, the similarity in their feel and appearance, had been intended to emphasize the Church's relationship with the Crown.

Four fifteen. She glanced at her cell phone. No calls. No alert involving Jean-Claude. Typical in this line of work. One never knew what was going on. Never.

She grew restless. Her back started to cramp. She stood up and strolled the block. A raging paranoia was rolling in on her, a sense that something big had been missed.

She came back to the bench. She felt eyes on her. She kept looking over her shoulder as she walked. The smooching young couple reappeared, hand in hand. The lovebirds stayed a constant half-block away from her.

Yeah, she had made them, all right. Now, with their reappearance, she knew Mark was imminent. So she remained seated. Four twenty. He was late. But sometimes late had no significance other than *late*.

The heat and humidity assaulted her. Rain clouds had formed. A few sprinkles came and went. Then, bingo. She saw a car stop quickly on the palace side of the street. Mark McKinnon jumped out. McKinnon was in a suit, a white shirt, and tie. She slid her gaze to her left and saw that the lovebirds turned tail immediately and departed. She noted the time. Four twenty-six.

She watched Mark and knew the drill with the vehicle. His car would circle the block while they met, and somewhere another car had probably put one or two bodyguards on the street.

She scanned the block nearby, more carefully than ever. There was an ill-dressed man looking through a souvenir stall, but not really looking. A man in a small truck with Madrid plates had pulled to the curb right behind her, stopping in contravention of all traffic rules, and was talking on his cell phone.

She doubted that McKinnon had more than two guns backing him up, but it barely mattered. Mark had already told her so much. This was one high-testosterone operation in progress today if Mark had this sort of entourage.

That, or she had imagined everything. But she didn't think she had. This venue was like a fuse to a cherry bomb.

McKinnon jaywalked lazily toward her, stepping between angry drivers. Then he quickly jogged the rest of the way across the street and came to the bench where she sat.

"Hello, LaDuca," he said. "What's got your panties in a twist today?"

"I need to know a few things," she said.

"We all do," he answered. "What's on your list? Then I'll tell you what's on mine."

He sat. She stood. "Let's walk," she said.

"I'd prefer not to."

"Let's do it anyway."

With a sigh, he acceded. He was up on his feet.

"Did you contact Peter yesterday and ask him to go see Floyd Connelly?" she asked as they moved.

"Distrustful, aren't you? You're checking up on Peter Chang."

"That's right. I am."

"Peter's your partner. What am I to think?"

"I'm being thorough. Could you answer my question?"

"Yes, I asked Peter to go over to see Connelly," he said.

"Why?" she asked.

"Why? Why *not*? That's how I often do things if they're important," McKinnon snapped. "If I ask two people to do something, maybe one of them will get it done. You okay with that? — because I don't care if you are or not."

"You didn't ask him to kill Connelly, did you? I know you didn't ask me to."

"Ha! No. Why? Do you think I did?"

"A lot of things cross my mind," she said. "Our black bird isn't the most normal case."

"What case is?" he asked. "Are you the normal working girl from Treasury? Is Peter the normal Chinaman from Shanghai? Lighten up, LaDuca. There *is* no normal. If something were normal, it would be *abnormal*, which would make it suspicious."

"Even if you didn't order it, I'm wondering if Peter freelanced it," she said. "His interests in this case coincide with ours, but they're not perfectly compatible."

"Oh," McKinnon said dismissively, "I doubt that he did. But if he pushed old Floyd out of the lousy window, so what, really? Floyd was a liability. Senior moments, twenty-four seven. And that hotel he was staying at. It wasn't the Four Seasons; it was more like a One Season. Bad publicity, my buttcrack! They probably won't even bother to get their fence fixed. They're going to parlay the publicity and sell out all summer to the tourists from Kansas. They'll probably open a café in the alley and name a drink after Floyd. They'll call it 'The Dead American' and put a couple of little skewers through it."

"Mark, would you come down to earth?"

But Mark didn't. "I've got this theory, you see," McKinnon continued. "More than a theory, really. An analysis of what's been going down. Floyd was the leak in the room at the embassy, you see. We *know* that. In the room and for many months dating back. He's the one who nearly got you killed by letting go with inside information and not securing either his computer or his phone. He'd get soused and pop off at the hotel bar about why he was in Madrid. Used to trade info for sex. Did you know that? Did you know he mentioned your name a couple of weeks back to some bad people. Did you know that he used to play golf with a cranky old dinosaur of an arms dealer in Switzerland named Tissot, who payrolled a mistress for him, and set up a bank account for him?"

"Is that true?" she asked.

McKinnon laughed. "You Treasury eggheads might dislike all us Agency people, Alex," he said, "but we do know a thing or two. Connelly was a health hazard to all of us. So I'm not bawling my eyes out this morning. It's pretty clear that Floyd was finally set up. Outlived his usefulness to the opposition and in fact had turned into a liability for them as well as us. He bought half a recent bill of goods from someone, but his good information was laced with the bad stuff. And yet he stumbled across enough solid stuff so that he decided to play Clark Kent out of the hotel window. I say, good riddance! He got killed instead of you getting killed. So even if Peter freelanced, so what?"

"Maybe nothing, unless you're Connelly's family back home."

"Floyd had a big government insurance policy. It actually will save the taxpayers some money. Maybe his wife had him pushed. I hear she's not that upset, a bit of a merry widow. It's as if she won the lottery, you know, and she doesn't have to be worried about a wandering husband any more."

"You disgust me sometimes, Mark. That's a human life you're talking about."

"What else is on your mind, LaDuca? You carry yourself well, but you can be a pain in the neck."

They stopped walking. He glanced at the palace and continued before she could say anything.

"Hell of a building, isn't it, the palace? But you know what? They should chainsaw that palace into condos and make some money with the way the economy is crashing. I don't care much for the Spaniards, truth be known. They invented the auto-da-fé here, you know. What's the old jingle? *What a day, what a day, for an auto-da-fé*."

"This 'Jean-Claude al-Masri'," she said. "You know about him?"

"We have some of the same sources, so yes. Of course I do. A potential suspect. Marvelous. Whoop dee do."

"Are the Spanish police going to bring him in?" she asked.

"Hell, no."

"Why not?"

"The Spanish police are involved in the black fricking bird, not in the plot against the embassy."

"What?"

"This is the twenty-first century. We handle these things directly."

"Give me a break."

"No, LaDuca, you give us one and don't exceed your assignment here. These things take care of themselves when we're lucky," he said.

"What are you doing behind my back?" she asked. "I need some help with this, Mark, and you're not coming across with it."

"The world is imperfect, but we just discussed that."

"What about the embassy?" she asked.

"What about it?"

"I'm told it's in stand-down today," she said. "Being searched roof to basement."

"Who told you that?" he asked.

"Colonel Pendraza."

"He's kind of sweet on you, the old guy, isn't he? Feeds you tidbits so he can hang out with a girl a third his age. You know, I think he'd like to get you in bed at least once. It would kind of cap his career, if you want to give it some sympathetic thought."

"At least he acts professionally."

"Okay," he said. "Touché. And he's only two and a half times your age. Listen, Madrid is in Spain, Spain is in Europe, Mercury is in retrograde, I'm in a good mood, and the embassy is in stand-down, yes, as are several dozen other locations around Madrid. We make sure the premises are clean and then we triple the security on anything or anyone coming in."

"What about underneath the embassy?"

"What? The sewers?"

"Has anyone considered that the embassy could be accessed from underneath?"

"Pretty miniscule, the possibilities."

"So was flying a pair of planes into the World Trade Center."

McKinnon was silent. Then, still in Spanish, "But for the dual sake of both argument and personal irritation, I'll give you a minute to convince me," he said.

"This in an old city, one set of walls and ruins on top of another," Alex said. "Same as Rome, London, Paris, Vienna. Ever see *The Third Man*? Ever see *Ocean's Thirteen*? Ever read about Dien Bien Phu where the Viet Cong came up out of underground tunnels to blow the French out of Indochina? You had a tunnel under the Berlin Wall, and you got tunnels under the Tex-Mex borders in Arizona and Texas that you can drive small trucks through. And how about this? Did you read about the way the thieves got into the Museo Arqueológico to steal the bird the first time? There's twelve centuries of stuff under our feet, Mark. They're always finding Moorish walls and cellars in all those places, so it's not outside the realm of possibility that someone could be burrowing."

"Even if you burrowed, you'd need a real wallop of explosives," he said.

"Yes. Like HMX with RDX. That's exactly what's out there somewhere."

"Uh huh. Look, it's *under control, LaDuca*. Stick to your job, which is the stupid figurine. Now, what else do you want from me?"

"You're head of the Agency in Europe. I could use some help examining the area around the embassy. The underground pathways and all."

"What? You want to go looking for souvenirs of the Inquisition?"

"I want to be thorough."

"Thorough!" he laughed. "Have you seen our budget this year?"

"How much does a search cost compared with the cost of if we miss something?"

"You're good. I should send you before Congress and you can ask them that. Someday, they're going to ask me why I do things the way I do, and I'm going to reply by asking them why they use a jet bomber to kill a couple of camels. Dialogue. Socratic method. You like it?"

She seethed. "Can I get some help around the embassy? Please?" she pleaded. They were back at the bench.

"I'll tell you," he said. "You make a point. So maybe. Next week. How's that. In the meantime, go to a hardware store, get a pick, a shovel, some gardening gloves, and a pair of bib overalls, and feel free to look around all you want, okay?"

"Why are you playing dumb, Mark?"

He ignored the question.

She scanned the street around them, the people, the traffic. "With all due respect, you're being a jerk, Mark."

"Yes, yes. What else is new? Request denied. I have to keep a lid on the budgets. And I'm not convinced enough that you know what you're talking about."

"No?"

"No," he said.

"Why? Because I'm female?" she asked, heating up.

"No, because you see things that other people don't see, which would be fine, except the things you see sometimes aren't there. See that lamppost over there?" He waited for an answer.

She glanced. "I see it," she said.

"Nice lamppost. Distinctive Madrid architecture. Quite charming. Except *you* probably look at it and see a potential gibbet."

"Not to put too keen an edge on it, but in the Middle Ages, that's exactly what they used the lampposts for. Hanging people."

"See. That's what I mean. Did anyone ever tell you that you're overeducated?"

"Frequently," she said. "It's how I got hired."

"There you go. But I didn't hire you. I go for more utilitarian types, like Peter."

"Four," she said next.

"Four?"

"Four guns," she said. "That's how many people you have watching your back right now. You've got the guy at the souvenir stand, and the guy in the maintenance truck. Then there's your driver who's been circling the block. I also see," she said, indicating, "the guy standing outside the leather shop. He's supposed to look like a customer, but all he's been doing is watching us, and he's got American shoes. If you want to have a pavement team, do something about the shoes."

"You *are* good," he said. "I wish you also understood when you should just shut up and let our people handle things."

"You've got your own back covered nicely, Mark. Unless the embassy blows from underneath, in which case people are going to ask how it could have happened, and I'm going to tell anyone who asks that it started with a theft of a 'lamentation' from the Museum of Old Stuff here in Madrid, and the CIA guy wouldn't listen to me. So *now* can I please have some backup? Or assign your own people and let me go with them."

He thought further and sighed.

"I got to admire your nerve. You're a bureaucratic extortionist. You don't even work for us. You're Treasury."

"But we're both looking out for American interests, aren't we?"

"All right, all right," he said. "Maybe next week. Maybe by Monday. I can pull some people off some cases in Malaga and bring them up here to burrow through the dirt with you. The people they're working for won't be happy, but let 'em scream. They're not as smart as you, they shut up sooner, and they're not in my face every day. How's that?"

"Not acceptable. I need something sooner," she said.

"Yeah," he said. "Right. So would everyone. That's all, LaDuca. Have a good evening." He turned away from her.

A moment passed, and he drew ahead of her. Then, furious, she followed him and stepped in front of him, blocking his path. He stepped around her and moved to the curb. His car, already shadowing him, moved to a sudden jerky halt in a no-stopping zone and waited for him. Behind it, an irate Madrid cab driver blasted a horn. McKinnon's driver rolled down his window, raised an arm, and responded with a universally understood gesture of ill will.

But she fell into stride right next to him. "Okay, now I'll remind you of something else," he said, moving toward the car. "What's your assignment here, your mission?"

"To find the pietà and discover why it was stolen."

"What's Peter's?"

"I assume it's to take care of business for the late Lee Yuan," she said after a moment.

"Don't lose sight of that," he said. "Connelly's laptop had everything in it we needed. Names and addresses. The whole Madrid network that wants to bomb our embassy. A handful of amateurs and one very dangerous central guy. We even have a photo now. The ones we don't get will be hiding in caves eating beetles with their spiritual leader for another twenty years. So we're going to roll them up."

"Roll them up, how?" she asked.

McKinnon arrived at his car and opened the rear door. "In the only way that it will stay rolled up," he said. *"So stay out of it!"*

McKinnon arrived at his vehicle and attempted to step into it. Alex drew her weapon and held the door with her other hand. She pointed her pistol at the car's rear tire.

McKinnon looked at her in openmouthed bewilderment. His driver started to make a move to get out. McKinnon waved him off.

"Tell your ape to stay behind the steering wheel," she said softly. "And if he hits the gas, I pull the trigger." McKinnon gestured again, and his driver eased back into the car.

"You're crazy!" McKinnon said. "You fire a shot here and — "

"And the Madrid police will be all over us. But I've got permission to carry a weapon here, Mark. Do you? Are you carrying a piece? Does the Spanish government know you have an operation going here? They know *I* do. In fact, I'm here with their permission. Can you say the same for yourself?"

The eyes of McKinnon's driver were burning a reflected gaze at Alex through the rearview mirror. She glanced his way and back quickly.

McKinnon threw a long line of expletives at Alex. She gave him a similar one in return, nice and fast, his own attitude zapping back at him like a verbal yo-yo. She held her pistol steadily on the right-side rear tire.

"Give me something more, Mark," she said to him. "I want to recover that piece of art, and I want to know where else this case is going."

A second elapsed as he considered his many alternatives.

Then, "May I reach into my jacket pocket without you blasting my rear tire?" he asked. "That's a new Pirelli back there. I'd hate for something to happen to it."

"Try it slowly, Mark. You'll find out quickly."

He reached to his left side pocket and pulled out a cell phone. He punched in some numbers. Then he handed the phone to her. The small screen came alive, and on it was a clear image of a man who appeared to be in the custody, temporarily at least, of the Madrid police.

"That's our pigeon," he said. "Jean-Claude al-Masri. French citizen, Moroccan born. Resident here in Madrid. We've got the whole book on him, from smuggling explosives to recruiting his own terror network here in Spain. The dumb local cops had him, then let him go. What do you expect? We're not going to let that happen twice. His file is attached to the photo."

"It is, is it?" she said.

"It is."

She looked at the photo. Then, with a quick one-handed procedure, she worked his phone keyboard with her thumb as he spoke.

"If you don't believe me," McKinnon continued, "then talk to your buddy Colonel Pendraza because two hours ago he gave us a thumbs-up to whacking Jean-Claude just as long as Pendraza doesn't officially know about it. Oh, and your other new best friend Peter is on the case right now."

She was still making thumb entries on his keyboard as he watched her.

"LaDuca, what are you doing?" he suddenly asked.

"I just sent myself the photo and the file," she said. "I want both. Now I have them. Thanks."

She started to politely hand the phone back to McKinnon, but he snatched it away from her. She put away her weapon and stepped back from the car.

"You know enough now. So stay away," he said.

McKinnon slammed the door and barked an order to his driver. The vehicle screeched out into traffic and was gone in an instant, flagrantly running a red light in the process.

SIXTY-FOUR

On a side street café in the Rastro, business was finally slacking off in the early evening. Samy had been nervous that day, waiting for some kind of shoe to drop and wondering why there had been no massive explosion under the United States Embassy. But Samy had also stayed true to Jean-Claude's command to go to work as usual, act as usual, have a normal day as much as possible, and pretend that nothing strange was going on at all. Anything else might attract suspicion.

After all, no one knew who the conspirators were, Jean-Claude had sworn, other than each other? They just needed to wait.

Nonetheless, Samy had been on pins and needles all day, waiting to hear something, waiting for a special report to break into the news on Spanish television, watching everyone with paranoia, particularly anyone who looked like a cop or who looked in any way suspicious.

Gradually the little café called Klafouti had emptied out. Now it was almost midnight. There were two couples there at separate tables and a single man in a suit, an Asian, sitting by himself, reading. One of the couples got up and left. Then the other couple, by virtue of the blackberry wine they had been drinking liberally, started cuddling and smooching. Soon they got up and left too, weaving merrily toward the door.

Ali, the heavy man with the moustache who was Samy's boss, spoke to Samy in Arabic. "I'm going to put the *Cerrado* sign on the door," Ali said, indicating he was ready to close. "And I'm turning the window light off. Let's go home."

Samy thought that was an excellent idea.

Ali went next door to use the bathroom at the grocery store that was run by his cousin. In the rear of his store, Samy started cleaning the counter behind the pastry display case. The single man who had been reading a newspaper, the lone customer remaining, got up, yawned, stretched, and gave Samy a nod.

"Buenas noches," Samy called back.

The man nodded in return, then took some steps toward the door.

Samy turned his back and busied himself with neatening up. Then Samy heard the door close and he heard steps. He figured Ali was back and said something to him. But there was no answer. A second later Samy felt something indefinably amiss and knew something was wrong.

He turned abruptly. The single man, the Asian, was standing on the other side of the pastry case, staring at him. Samy froze. He knew this was trouble.

David Wong looked at Samy carefully.

"¿Qué quiere usted, Señor?" Samy asked. What do you want?

"Do you speak English?" Wong asked in English.

Samy understood but quickly shook his head. The Asian's eyes were fixed on him like lasers.

Wong reached into a pocket and pulled out a picture of Lee Yuan, his mentor, just as Yuan had been Peter's mentor and the mentor of his partner Charles Ming.

"Do you know anything about this man?" the Asian asked softly.

Samy shook his head again. He looked to the door, the escape route. The man in front of him had closed it, locked it apparently, and pulled the shade down.

Samy fumbled in English. "I don't know any Chinaman," he said.

"Now you do," Wong answered.

For a moment Samy was paralyzed. Then there was a knocking on the front door. He heard Ali's voice calling. "Samy? Samy, you in there?"

"Ayúdame! Ayúdame!" Samy screamed in Spanish. Help me! Help me!

Samy suddenly backpedaled. He tried to edge around the display case to where there was a narrow passage on the far side from where he could sprint to the door.

Wong lowered his left hand, and the picture of Lee Yuan was gone. Then the right hand came up, and it held a small gun, one of those Italian jobs that are just perfect for killing in small areas like stores, washrooms, and public transportation.

Samy yelled in terror when he saw the outline of the weapon. At the front door, Ali knocked sharply now, frantically next, then started to pound at the wooden frame. When all that failed, he hit the door with his shoulder.

Samy scrambled but Wong fired. The first bullet caught the waiter in the shoulder but hurled him sideways against the wall. Then the well-dressed Asian was on him like a big cat. Samy began to sputter and plead, half prayers, half curses, a desperate plea for his life.

Wong wasn't listening any more than a cat would consider pleas from a mouse.

Wong pounced on his fallen prey, pushed the nose of the pistol to Samy's head. Samy tried to cover it with his hands, but Wong pushed the gun between the Arab's frenzied trembling palms and fired point blank.

One shot. Two shots.

The bullets blew out Samy's eye socket, half of his brain, and the back part of his skull, all of which splattered and coated the floor beneath him.

Wong quickly stuffed his gun back under his suit jacket and went to the door. He threw the door open. Ali now stood in front of him in shock and surprise.

"*Buenas noches,*" Wong said.

"What's going on?" Ali asked in Spanish.

Wong smiled. "*Nada,*" he said.

As Ali spoke to Wong, his gaze traveled past Wong and settled on Samy's sprawled body on the floor. Wong caught the moment of realization in Ali's eyes and jumped on it.

Wong brought up a knee that impacted like an express train into Ali's groin.

When the café owner doubled over in absolute agony, Wong uppercut a vicious fist into the man's face, crushing his nose with a tremendous crunch, splintering it to pieces within its skin. A downward smash of the elbow to the back of Ali's head, sent him to the floor. There Wong left him, sobbing in a huddled mass at the doorway to his café, but in all ways better off than Samy had been for the encounter.

Wong straightened the lapels of his jacket and departed at a normal pace.

SIXTY-FIVE

MADRID, SEPTEMBER 18, EVENING

The local police granted Alex permission and provided keys to the forgotten underground Madrid. The Policia Nacional offered her a backup, but she declined. She went by herself, stubborn and overconfident, bearing her weapon, a hand lantern, and a GPS compass that she had bought for the occasion.

She unlocked a creaking old door that led to an old service passage that was at the far end of the Metro stop at Nuñez de Balboa. She prayed she wouldn't get lost in the subterranean labyrinth.

Carrying a lantern, she found herself wandering long-forgotten underground chambers that were unknown and unimaginable to the people of modern Madrid. Outside light disappeared quickly, and she relied on her lantern. There was movement around that was nonhuman. First she saw one rat, then she saw ten. First she had ample overhead clearance and then, as she neared the newer construction near the embassy, she had little. Then none.

She walked in a crouch. In her free hand, she carried a piece of chalk, marking passages as she went through them. She encountered stray cats, some alive, some dead. She came across a rat writhing in the agony of a poisonous death. Her nostrils were assaulted by the rancid odors of sewer leaks and the ground was wet and uneven under her feet.

It was cold. Then it was hot. Then it was cold again. An hour passed.

Then a second. She continued to prowl through the winding maze of underground tunnels, crawlspaces, and abandoned passageways that led toward the United States Embassy from the Metro stop at Nuñez de Balboa. As she moved, she constantly consulted her handheld GPS.

She felt as if she had stepped into a moonscape or a surreal bombed-out world of a future that had endured a nuclear catastrophe or a plague or maybe something even worse. She sidestepped old sewers and crossed dried-out viaducts. She passed mute walls that had once been basements, some of which even bore graffiti or artwork. Damaged structural supports sagged overhead, and water trickled in various filthy urban streams. There were old plaster walls, etched with names that appeared to be those of soldiers because many bore ranks before their names, and some had written prayers also. She wondered how many of the prayers had been answered or whether a single one of the names on the wall still belonged to someone living. She doubted it.

Alex recalled that during the bloody final days of the Civil War, troops massed underground and then came up out of manholes into the streets to kill their enemies or be killed by them. On other walls, legions of live insects fed on smaller insects.

She wandered through derelict bunkers where white plastery stalactites hung like daggers, and she crossed an obsolete rail track where no train had probably passed within the last century. At some points, the passages were peaceful, the way a crypt is peaceful, and at other times there was a stinking fetid squalor beyond comprehension, and she had to hold her hand to her mouth for fear of getting sick.

Her compass told her, however, that as she worked her way through the underground maze, she was indeed drawing closer to the area under the embassy, which meant that if she could access the area, anyone could.

More graffiti. Then a handful of murals, some of them pornographic, by artists no doubt long dead. Decrepit rungs that led nowhere marched upward on walls that had been truncated by newer construction. It was utterly silent in most places, and yet from time to time a cool wet breeze slapped her in the face, and she felt as if she were a frightened little girl exploring the basement of a haunted house.

Another mural, one of a man in prison. A mess of terra-cotta tiles. A quote from Cervantes in Spanish and a poem about tuberculosis written in black paint on yellow brick. Old shoes and bottles and newspapers emerged in the ray of her flashlight, and then another mural, a breathtaking rip-off of Dali's *Melting Clock*.

Old steam pipes. Meter after meter of them. Sealed vaults in the walls. Bricked-over exits. A tipped-over rusting gurney. Pools of water, red with rust. Ghostly staircases that led into uneven walls of concrete or granite. Utter blackness, relieved only by her light.

Years ago, she had read T. S. Eliot's *The Waste Land*, and now as she prowled under a modern city, she thought of Eliot's unreal metropolis where dread lurked in the shadows, terrible things emerged by the gleam of light, her shadow near midnight rose to meet her and where she saw fear in a handful of dust.

In another thirty minutes, she found the flashlight most recently discarded by Jean-Claude, outside a low crawlspace that led to a narrow tunnel. According to her GPS, the tunnel would lead the final few meters toward the embassy.

Alex looked at the flashlight. She knelt down and looked into the tunnel. Incredibly, there seemed to be light at the other end of it. The tunnel looked to be secure and wide enough for passage.

She picked up the flashlight. The bulb was dim but she could see.

Decision: go forward or head back? She had always learned to go forward. She decided to do something impetuous and stupid. She took off her jacket and knelt. The tunnel didn't look too bad. She would crawl in.

Time to get dirty.

She got down on her stomach and leaned in, pushing her own flashlight ahead of her. And she entered the tunnel. A few seconds later, she was on a slow horizontal crawl through a wet partially manmade tunnel under the streets of Madrid. It was no one's idea of fun.

She crawled her way through the passage for ten feet, then fifteen. Moving slowly. The walls then started to seize up around her.

Uh oh . . . The flashlight started to flicker. So that's why it had been abandoned. The tunnel narrowed slightly.

Maybe this wasn't such a good idea. Just so that she understood her options, she tried to move backward. Okay, a few paces. She could go either way.

Bad idea! Bad bad bad idea! Claustrophobia started to settle in.

She started to cough.

Oh, Lord, no!

The coughing stirred up dust and mortar, her eyes smarted. She coughed more.

She tried to back up.

She couldn't.

She was stuck.

SIXTY-SIX

MADRID, SEPTEMBER 18, EVENING

No more than three blocks away from Samy's bistro, through the maze of streets in the Rastro, Basheer sat nervously in the living room of the small house he shared with his wife, Leila. He was watching the late sports on television and was particularly interested in a match of his adopted land Morocco against Cameroon.

Leila came out of the bedroom to see what he was watching. She was wearing only a linen robe that she normally wore around the house. When she saw her husband was viewing sports, she gave up on getting his attention.

"I'm going to take a shower," she said softly. "Then let's get into bed."

Basheer grunted his approval. It made sense: first his favorite activity, then his second.

Leila went to the bathroom and started the water for her shower. Playfully, she stood in the doorway and slid out of her robe. Then she tossed her robe into the living room and stood naked before her husband, trying to interest him.

Her husband smiled but didn't budge from the sports. "Later," he said.

A minute passed. Maybe two.

Basheer heard a noise in the entrance hallway behind him, but the account of the game he wanted was seconds away. So he didn't investigate. There were only friends in this building, anyway, so what could go wrong?

A few seconds later, he heard a creak behind him on the old floorboards. The creak finally caused him to turn and glance behind him. He did a double take and jumped from his chair.

A Chinese guy! Stealthy as a giant cat! How the — —?

Charles Ming stood with his arm extended, with a gun pointed forward.

Basheer opened his mouth to scream but never had the chance. Charles Ming squeezed the trigger hard three times. Three bullets slammed into Basheer's chest before he had the chance to duck for cover or even scream. He hit the floor hard and in deep pain. He knew life was ebbing out of him, and all he could think of now was that this must have something to do with the bomb that didn't go off.

Ming stepped over him and sent another bullet directly through his heart.

Ming looked at the linen robe on the floor. He heard the shower water running and knew how easy the end of this job would be. He stepped over the robe and walked to the bathroom door, which was half open.

He pushed it the rest of the way.

Behind a vinyl see-through shower curtain, he could see the body of a woman. She was young and a little plump, with black hair and very pale skin the color of a fish fillet. He studied her for a moment because he had never before seen a woman undressed without having to pay for it. He reasoned that her skin was pale because it never saw the sunshine. Unlike Western or Chinese women, she never wore a bikini or went to the beach.

But Ming made no special note of her. She was an assignment, same as her husband who was dead on the floor behind him. He gazed at her with curiosity for a few seconds. He wondered how long he could stare before she saw him.

He had his answer a few seconds later. She turned.

Her eyes went as wide as saucers. Then she screamed.

The sound of the scream pulled Ming out of his mini-reverie. He raised the pistol sharply and fired three shots into the woman's body from a distance of five feet.

Her knees buckled, her body slammed against the back wall of the shower, and her voice went quiet like a television suddenly turned off. She dropped like a sack of potatoes, made a gurgling sound, and was still.

As a courtesy to the people downstairs, Ming stepped forward and turned off the water before he departed.

SIXTY-SEVEN

MADRID, SEPTEMBER 18, EVENING

Trapped in the claustrophobic hell of the small, rancid underground tunnel, Alex pushed with her arms. She prayed. Oh, she prayed! She almost prayed out loud, and she cursed herself for getting this far along. She stretched out her arms with every inch she could, dug her fingernails into the sandstone that formed the floor of the narrow passage, and she pulled with all the strength she could muster.

Nothing.

She tried again. There were tears forming in her eyes.

Nothing.

She tried a third and final time, pulling in her breath, trying to scrape through.

Nothing.

Then, something.

She groped along. She moved an inch. Then a few more inches. Then, ahead of her, a small trickle of sand and a mini cave-in.

She fought to suppress the panic. Once, years ago, she had read about miners who had been trapped in a cave-in. She felt in her gut the terror of their claustrophobic ordeal as water rose past their knees, their waists, their shoulders, their necks until they had only a few inches of breathing room at which time rescuers found them.

Well, that was them. This was her. She closed her eyes against the dust ahead of her and figured she was dead.

But she wasn't. The dust had loosened the tight walls of the passage. She pushed the sandy dirt away and she started moving again, pushing the lantern forward with her head.

Then suddenly she could move a few inches at a time. Crawling on her stomach like an infantry soldier under live rounds, she was able to push several inches ahead at a time. Then her motion was unabated.

She pushed forward with her knees and traveled several feet. The other end of the tunnel loomed in front of her.

Six feet. Then three. Then two and then her head nudged the lantern forward and it rolled forward and dropped with a clack. But she could still see the light of the lantern. And she could hear a sound of a person working.

Or something.

She reached the end of the tunnel with her hands. She dug in with her fingers and pulled herself free, the greatest feeling she had ever encountered in her life. And then she was on her feet, covered with dirt and crap and coughing and so delirious with joy over just being free and alive that she was almost oblivious to why she was in this damp, dark chamber and what she was looking for.

She coughed again.

Then she saw that there was one more small chamber where there was a light similar to hers. She managed a glance at the GPS. She knew that she was under the embassy. She heard footsteps.

SIXTY-EIGHT

MADRID, SEPTEMBER 18, LATE EVENING

Mahoud had been looking forward all day to a shower after work-ing in the hot kitchen of an Ethiopian restaurant on the Calle de Montevideo. He had been jittery all day but had calmed as night had fallen and as midnight came and went. Perhaps the whole thing was just one tremendous mistake, he thought to himself. He still harbored his deep hatred of the United States and Western culture, but he was half-relieved that the big blast hadn't happened.

Once the bomb went off, nothing would ever be the same again. He would be frightened of every shadow and would jump at every knock on the door. Every day would be like this one, except worse. Planting the thing had been one thing, almost a challenge to see if it could be done. The actual detonation of it was something else, some-thing secretly he hoped would never happen. But he couldn't tell any-one that. He would have seemed like a traitor.

He thought of all of this as he walked the final block to his home in the Arab quarter, past the closed fruit and produce stands that would open again at dawn. It was now past 11:00 p.m. and he *was* looking forward to bathing.

But the end of the bombing mission had him spooked. Everything bothered him today. Well, at least he felt safe in his own neighbor-hood. As safe as one could be.

He cautiously approached his doorway. He saw a problem, but not an unusual one. There was a vagrant asleep on the sidewalk, a slight man in an old coat that was too hot for this weather. But there were *vagabundos* all over this neighborhood. There had been one lying in this doorstep for a couple of weeks and no one did anything. And these bums wore everything they had all the time.

Mahoud cut a wide berth around the downtrodden figure. Under

Mahoud's own coat, he had a kitchen paring knife, just in case of trouble.

He stepped around the man and reached his doorway, noting in passing that this was a different bum tonight and the regular man was gone. Well, *sic transit gloria* in the world of hobos, he thought. Give a bum, take a bum. Maybe, he reasoned further, someone from the neighborhood had done a public service and set the other hobo on fire. Maybe that's what he would do to this one, he thought.

Images of flaming bodies made him think back to the explosives he had helped plant. He really did have mixed feelings about that charge going off. He really wondered if —

Then he heard his name.

"Mahoud?"

A voice in the darkness spoke softly. He jumped.

In his attention on the hobo, Mahoud had not even noticed a man sitting on the steps to the next building. He was a sturdy man but obviously way out of place in this neighborhood.

The man had a foreign face. Asian, of some sort. Japanese. Chinese. Who could tell the difference, anyway?

"Mahoud?" the man said again.

Mahoud's hands went to his knife and held it under the jacket. But the man held up his hands to show that they were empty and that he meant no harm.

"Who are you?" Mahoud asked in Spanish.

'm a friend of Jean-Claude," Peter Chang answered in Spanish. "I bring you news."

Mahoud answered cautiously. "I don't know any Jean-Claude," he said.

Peter Chang laughed. "Of course, you do, my friend," he said. "Don't be so frightened. Your entire group, you all are under *my* command. Don't you think Jean-Claude has a commander? Do you think he was able to do everything by himself?"

A pause as Mahoud considered it.

"What is the news?" he finally asked.

"Come closer," Chang said.

"Tell me from there," Mahoud said, taking one step toward the doorway.

"I'd rather not," said Chang.

"What is the news?" Mahoud repeated with insistence.

"The news is that everyone will die tonight," Peter Chang said.

Mahoud flinched, wondering just how that was meant. Then there was a further explanation of the news. The vagrant had risen to his feet behind Mahoud and had slid out of his coat. The vagrant had slid, in fact, into his own true identity, that of Charles Wong. And Wong, like Chang, was there to conduct business.

Wong slapped one hand across Mahoud's face, holding a filthy rag to his mouth and his nose. Mahoud fought back with his elbow and tried to kick at the instep and shin of the man behind him. But Wong had two hands. The other one, in a glove, held a butcher's knife with a blade that was ten inches long. It was the type that in the primitive regions of China was still used to slaughter chickens or pigs.

With one sweeping gesture, Wong swept the blade of the knife into and across the throat of the third embassy bomber. The pain shot through Mahoud like an electrical current. He would have screamed, but his mouth was firmly covered, and the hacking, slashing sweep of the blade across his throat was so deep that his vocal chords were severed in addition to his cortical artery.

Mahoud's body jumped at first like a great fish on a line, then went slack and buckled. He felt himself drop hard to the sidewalk. Distantly, as he lay in agony dying, he listened to the quiet footsteps of the two men walking away. And he wondered for a final time why the big explosion had never happened.

Several minutes later, Peter Chang moved quickly to a fourth location, accompanied by Wong and Ming. With little effort to conceal their faces, they arrived at the building where Jean-Claude lived in a rambling, cluttered four-room apartment.

Chang and Wong took the front stairs and Ming went to the rear where, at a synchronized moment, he hoisted himself up to a second floor window via a gutter pipe from the roof.

Here was the moment Peter had been waiting for. He wanted to savor it. Jean-Claude had been the instigator of the events that had left Yuan dead, and Chang had special plans for Jean-Claude.

They would ambush Jean-Claude in his home. But killing him swiftly would be too good. They would tie him and sit him down. Chang would show him a picture of Lee Yuan, who had died in a cold, smoky mountain castle in Switzerland.

In Peter's mind, Jean-Claude would shake his head and deny knowledge of any man named Yuan.

Chang, as it played out in his mind, would become animated.

"This man's name was Hun Sung Yuan. We knew him as Lee Yuan," he would explain evenly. "Hun Sung Yuan was my friend. He was my mentor. He trained me when I entered the service of my government."

Jean-Claude would listen in terror.

"Yuan was a boy during the Great Leap Forward," Peter would explain. "He was five years old, and his family was sent to camps in the countryside for reeducation. Yuan's parents were practicing Christians during the Cultural Revolution. Practicing religion was considered social turmoil. So they were held in a Beijing detention center for nearly a year as the Red Guard considered what charges to bring. Then Yuan's parents were sent to a camp in the freezing northeast of China for reeducation instead. Yuan was sent to an orphanage. As an adult, he didn't practice religion, but he had an interest in it. Christian items that may have been touched by a saint. Yuan was a fine man, but he had his superstitions. Which was his right."

Jean-Claude would continue to stare. Maybe he would kick. Maybe he would protest. But he would be gagged with duct tape, so his protests would find no ears.

"As years went by," Chang would explain, "Mr. Yuan became prosperous. And he wished to possess certain items. One was *The Pietà of Malta*. Mr. Yuan felt that he purchased the item very fairly. But through you and your people, it was not delivered to him. Instead, when he came to retrieve it, your associates murdered him. Do you think that was a wise thing to do?"

Jean-Claude, rethinking his position on recent events, would shake his head.

"You're right," Chang said. "It was not a wise thing to do."

And then Chang would take out a long knife from under his suit jacket, a very sharp one normally used for trimming meat. He would let Jean-Claude stare at it with wide eyes while Ming and Wong approvingly watched their new master.

Then Chang would reach slowly — because he wished to draw it out — to Jean-Claude's left ear. And with a quick powerful slashing motion he would thrust the knife into his victim's neck and slash hard from left to right, cutting the man's throat.

Then he would step back quickly and watch Jean-Claude begin to die in agony, even though no one had been gracious enough to be with Yuan in his final minutes. And then Peter would wash the knife off and take it with him. It would take a man about fifteen minutes to bleed to death after such an incident. And Peter needed to wrap things up and get out of the country quickly.

So there was no time to waste.

Except, this was only how Peter had planned it from the start.

In the final execution, it didn't go that way.

When Peter, Ming, and Wong broke into Jean-Claude's home, their victim wasn't there.

That changed everything.

SIXTY-NINE

Jean-Claude was elsewhere, putting the final touches on the charge of explosives.

Working alone in the narrow, cramped chamber under the American Embassy, he braced his flashlight between an old brick and a stone. Working with the low beam from the flashlight, he spread before him the ten different detonators from the pack he had purchased.

He was taking no chances. He would use all of them. He only needed one to trigger the ten kilos of explosives he had spread in separate packets around the chamber. If just one ignited, chances are much of the block would implode.

On the first Number Ten Delay switch, Jean-Claude used a pair of pliers to crush the end of a thin copper tube containing acid. There was no need to crush the end of the tube completely flat. All he needed to do was crush it sufficiently to break the glass vial, thereby releasing the liquid within. Then he removed and discarded the safety pin holding back the striker. Finally, he inserted the other end of the pencil detonator into a brick of explosives. His charges were good for twenty-four hours, meaning they would blow the next night around midnight, give or take.

He repeated the procedure four more times. He then drew back and fought for his breath. The air was disappearing in this cramped hole. And he was sweating profusely. It occurred to him that if there were some sort of freak accident with the acid leaking too quickly into the explosives, he would be blown into oblivion. So, twenty-four-hour timer or not, it was wise to move as quickly as possible.

There! Everything was set!

Then something clattered in the small adjoining chamber. Jean-Claude froze.

"What the — —?"

It wasn't that unusual for rocks or pieces of concrete to crumble and fall, or for a rat to disturb something. But this sounded different. It sounded like a tool, a flashlight or something, dropping.

His eyes went to the portal that led to the next chamber. He saw a flicker of a light waving. Good God, he was not alone!

What the — —!

Then he heard something human. A cough! The cough of a woman!

He left the detonators where they were, set to blast away within twenty-four hours. Angrily, suspiciously, he drew his gun from his belt.

Whoever was in the next chamber sounded as if she was getting to her feet after somehow burrowing in.

Well, he'd killed that busybody woman who had worked for the Metro, and he would kill again.

Jean-Claude checked his pistol and readied it for a quick discharge. It was completely loaded. Whoever was there, he would cut them in half, no questions asked.

He held his pistol aloft and went to the passageway where he could ambush his intruder.

SEVENTY

MADRID, SEPTEMBER 19, MIDNIGHT

Somewhere in the back of her mind, Peter's words floated like a ghost.

A philosopher with a gun ...

Well, at least I'm a philosopher ...

On her feet in these strange chambers under the embassy, she thought her heart was going to burst from her chest. She drew her own weapon.

... if you could have murdered Hitler and Stalin and avoided World War II, would that have—?

The shadows shifted in the portal to the adjoining chamber, and she pointed her weapon in that direction. Out of instinct, she identified herself. "Hello? Hello? Police?!" she said.

But the frame of a man quickly bolted into view in the doorway. The gunman gave her less than a second. She could see arms and legs and a head, a trim body and a half-crouch. One of the arms was extended and swung a gun in her direction, and everything she had ever learned at the target ranges in California and Washington kicked sharply into gear, and it was surely a beneficent God that had trained her to be such a good shot.

As his arm swung into its final position to aim, Alex unloaded four staccato shots from her own pistol. The sound was deafening in the tiny dark chamber, followed quickly by the scream of the man she had hit four times, squarely in the midchest and then upward as he was propelled back until the final shot blew away his nose and the front part of his face.

He managed to get one shot off, possibly two. There was a clatter of ricocheting bullets around the chamber, and something smacked her flashlight and took it from her hand.

Then it was all very still, and the man was lying dead. Her lamp flickered.

She examined the body where it lay in an impossibly twisted heap. She stared into the dead eyes, or what remained of them, since one was loose from its socket. She fought back the urge to throw up over what she had done, and her insides were set to explode. By force of old habit, her free hand found the stone pendant at her neck, and she whispered a few words to herself.

She moved to where the man had been working, and with horror she looked at the mounds of explosives, detonators already set. She said another prayer.

Out of instinct, she tried her cell phone. No reception. All she could do now, she hoped, was to get out and get the bomb people in here as soon as possible. She had no idea how much time she had ... or didn't have.

She took the dead man's torch. Its bulb was dimmer than hers and was wearing down. Suppressing a surge of horror, she returned to the fetid tunnel that had led her there.

She pulled herself into the hole and prepared herself for the final crawl toward open space. As she crawled, edging along in the tight tunnel with mortar and sand coming down on her again, she was almost overtaken anew by the claustrophobic panic that had pursued her like a demon for this whole episode.

But she kept telling herself, she had done this before, she could do it one final time. It was only twenty meters or so. As she proceeded, she took care to drag her feet and push carefully against the clutter and stones.

Then, just as it had previously, more of the sandstone started to trickle down. One inch worth. Then two. *OMG!* This time it was closing up her passage.

She moved forward with a jerk, trying to get some momentum. She got some.

She slid forward another foot or two.

Bad idea, bad idea! Bad idea.

The worse idea you've ever had.

Get out! Get out!

This time, by moving forward too quickly, she had dislodged some heavier pieces. And they fell in her path, pinning her left arm.

You've dug your own grave! No one will ever find you!

You're dead! You're dead! You're dead.

A million and one thoughts pounded her at once.

But one overpowered all the others. *This time you're dead. If the explosion doesn't kill you, suffocation will.*

Robert, where are you? Robert, if I die will you greet me in heaven?

She screamed. She screamed a second time.

No human voice could hear.

Oh, God, oh, God, Oh God in heaven, if you're there, if you're listening …!

Please! Please, spare me. I do not want to die! Not here, not today. Not in this horrible, wretched place!

As she managed to crawl a little bit farther forward, agony and ecstasy, heaven and hell, were all wrapped up in one. Her knees crunched over coarse gravel and sand. What was that? Glass? Something cut her knee. Low on her hip was her weapon but she wished she could have jettisoned it. No way she could reach it.

Oh, my God, oh, my God! How foolish could she have possibly been?

She screamed again. No answer. Just an echo of horror in her ears.

The sweat poured off her.

The moisture — the sewage mixed with underground condensation — was already seeping through her clothing. If Alex could survive the crushing claustrophobia of this time and place, she reasoned, she would never feel it again. That too went on her wish list. That, and seeing daylight again.

And then, once again, for a final time, she felt the aging brick and cement walls narrowing on her. She tried to buoy her spirits. Sure, she could make it. Sure, she could get out of there.

She tried to fight off the notion of death. Death was unimaginable in a place like this.

The passage narrowed again, worse than it had been when she had come through. Her flashlight died. She was in complete darkness. She tried to go forward on her back.

No go. She tried to calm herself.

Okay, okay, okay.

She would have to back up. Going forward made no sense. She put everything into her arms, pushed and pushed hard, and managed to go backward.

There! Progress. She was moving.

Then she heard it. The worst sound in creation. A rustling, crumbling, collapsing sound behind her. She could even feel it. A little cave-in. Sand and mortar drifting down, blocking her retreat.

She pushed mightily, but now it was like a heavy car stuck in snow. She wasn't going to go anywhere. She was stuck, stuck, stuck!

No way to call anyone, no way anyone would know where she was. *Stuck!*

Hello! It's official. She would starve to death or suffocate or be blown into oblivion. *Blown into heaven*, she prayed.

Oh Lord, oh Lord, oh Lord ...

She prayed like she had never prayed before.

Minutes had the weight of hours, small eternities passing in a living hell of a grave. She was beyond panic but not beyond fear.

She had prayed, but no answer yet.

Her heart pounded and pounded. She almost wished it would stop, that death would claim her gently.

Instead, she would have to wait for it, greet it with courage. Where was her faith? She summoned it as best she could. With all her heart, with everything she believed in, she prayed to God, prayed to Jesus.

Fatigue was settling in. She was motionless. Her energy was gone. She tried in desperation to nudge forward with her shoulders. She couldn't squeeze forward. She couldn't squeeze back. It was so tight here that even breathing was now a problem. The stone pendant on her chest felt like an anchor.

Stuck meant death. How many hours, she wondered, when every minute was torture?

Alex broke a sweat. She continued to struggle against the tunnel that now held her so tightly. She hunched her upper body, careful to allow herself a final edge of wriggle room.

His stomach, her nerves, felt as if they were turning to water. Her anger, her desperation, were turning to acceptance of death.

Alex wriggled again and worsened her situation. In her mind she saw her parents waiting for her. Her grandmother, for whom she had lit all those beautiful *luminarias* and set them afloat on a country stream.

There! When she held on to thoughts like that and felt the strength drain out of her, it didn't seem so bad.

Oh God, please take me to heaven . . .

The silence was the same immense size as the darkness. Up ahead, a few yards from Alex's head, there was a slight scratching. Alex, her head at an impossible angle, knew they were rats. Alex spat at them, gave a flick of her head, and screamed!

Couldn't she even die in peace? They'd be back to get her body after she died, wouldn't they?

She fought tears.

Now her neck was cramping. Badly. She had no way to relieve the pain. She dug in with her shoes. She pushed again and felt the stone around her grow tighter and sharper. It tore at her clothes.

She sucked in all her strength, dug in her sneakers, pushed with her arms and pushed with all the strength she had left.

A few inches.

Nothing else.

The air in the tunnel was becoming thin. Then thinner.

She summoned up what was left of her courage. A deeper darkness was starting to swallow her.

Now she knew. She was a goner. A few moments later, locked in place, she started to lose consciousness.

In her father's house, she knew, there were many rooms. And deep down, she also believed, someone had gone ahead to prepare a place before her.

It was easy, really; much like falling asleep.

SEVENTY-ONE

MADRID, SEPTEMBER 19, SHORTLY AFTER MIDNIGHT

Alex's eyes flickered open, and she thought she had her first glimpse of heaven.

She was wrong, but every bit as pleased.

At the end of the tunnel in front of her there was a light, then a stronger light. And all around her now was the sound of tapping.

Tapping, tapping, tapping, growing louder.

Then hammering. More hammering. All around her hammering!

She yelled. "I'm here! I'm here!"

There was the sound of machinery. She could feel vibrations behind her. A rescue team had knocked their way into the same tunnel. The next thing that happened startled her all the more.

Her feet. Something touched her feet. Hands. Human hands. And after that, someone had pushed a hose past her and was pumping air into the narrow passageway. Breathing became easier. An air pump was part of the machinery she heard. Up ahead of her, she could feel a drill.

A voice in English screamed. "Alex! Alex, we got you!"

"I'm here!" she yelled again. She fought back tears, tears that none could see, but which she could feel cascading down her cheeks. Ahead of her, the light became more intense as workers had broken through the basement floor of the embassy to where the explosives had been stashed and then defused by bomb experts.

Then part of the wall behind her broke away. Her legs were free. So was her upper body. Hands in heavy gloves worked their way up to her hips. The hands cleared debris from the wall.

Firemen. Rescue teams from the police. Rarely had she been so happy to feel strange male hands upon her. Stuck for hours, she was being freed within minutes, once they had located her.

A voice in English. Familiar. "Alex?"

It was Peter.

"Yes! Yes!" she gasped in response.

"They're going to pull you backward gently. Are you okay with that?"

"I'm okay!" she yelled.

They pulled. And she slid. It was the greatest ride of her life. Ten feet, a dozen, maybe twenty as her jeans and shirt dragged and ripped. They pulled her out into the light, into the clammy underground cavern where she had entered the tunnel.

She turned over and trembled, trying to sit up. Peter knelt down and wrapped his arms around her, and as he embraced her for a moment, she sobbed almost uncontrollably.

They wrapped her in a blanket. They stood her up. Her legs were unsteady, rubbery, but they supported her. The rescue workers had unlocked some doors in the old tunnels and broken through a wall.

"How did you ever find me?" she finally asked. "How? How?"

"Your wallet," he said.

"What?"

He made a motion to where her wallet rode in her back pocket. She pulled the wallet out and handed it to him. From it, he pulled the Swiss consular ID card that he had forced upon her the day before.

"I doctored it," he said. "Homing device. After you disappeared once in Switzerland, I wasn't going to let it happen again."

She wasn't sure whether to laugh or cry. So instead, she did both.

Distantly, as they evacuated her, the sound of demolition grew louder from underneath the embassy.

SEVENTY-TWO

MADRID, SEPTEMBER 21, AFTERNOON

Two days later, after a single night of hospital recovery, Alex found herself at Madrid International Airport, seeing Peter off on his return flight to China.

They stood together at the departure gate. She saw some emotion in his eyes, but she equally saw him retreat from it, as if it would be a dangerous place for him to go.

"I guess I better get moving," he said.

"Guess so," she said.

For a moment they stood apart. Peter took her hand, and there was something in his eyes that she still couldn't fathom. Again, he didn't smile, not at first, but then he did. The small gesture served to only confuse her more.

In assessing Peter Chang, she had come to know him quite well, yet not know him at all. She didn't know whether the man before her was large and grand or small and mean. Nor could she fathom his moral compass, though she was certain he had one somewhere.

He had murdered savagely and vengefully, something that she couldn't accept. Yet he had twice saved her life. There were aspects of him that reminded her of Yuri Federov and yet there were strains in him that reminded her — unless she was deluding herself — of her late Robert. Or even herself.

After all, weren't they all in the same line of work?

Wasn't everyone imperfect? Wasn't life a daily compromise? Were there absolutes? Were all ethics at least partially situational? Weren't we *all* sinners?

He reached under his jacket and removed his firearm. He bundled it and gave it to her, concealing it. She pulled it into her purse.

"That's a heck of a souvenir," she said with half a smile.

"I'd say put it to good use," he said. "But don't take that the wrong way."

"I won't," she said.

"Are you going to be okay getting out of Spain?" she asked, eying the security controls.

"Oh," he laughed. "Sure. Your pal. McKinnon. Another little souvenir," he said.

Peter pulled out a passport from his inside jacket pocket. American. He flipped it open and showed her. He was now William Kao, a native-born American who was an IT expert from New York.

She shook her head. "Do you ever lose sight of who you really are?" she asked.

"Sometimes," he said. "Same as who I'd really like to be. Sometimes it's confusing."

She allowed that it was.

He continued. "Hey," he said, "if you're going to the safety deposit box, you might want to stash this for me also," he said. "Never know when I might be back. If ever."

"Probably sooner than you think," she said, "but I wasn't planning to go to the safety deposit box."

"Maybe you could. For me. As a final favor."

"All right," she said.

"Oh, and listen," he said. "There's something I'd like you to have."

He reached into his pocket. His strong hand came out with a small jeweler's bag, a light blue one. She had seen it before, held it in her hand before.

"I don't get it," she said.

"Open it."

She did. Into her hand fell the eighteen-karat étoile bangle that had been in the jeweler's box in the safety deposit box.

"Put it on," he said.

She did.

"There," he said with an approving smile. "If that doesn't make your Russian hood jealous next time he sees you, I don't know what will."

"Peter, it's gorgeous," she said, reaching to take it off, "but you bought it for someone else."

His hand stopped hers. "No, I bought it for you," he said, "the first day we met. Then I rewrapped it with paper from Switzerland. I figured ahead of time that I'd want to give you a souvenir of our 'vacation' in Spain. I do things impulsively and ahead of time, as you know."

"But you said there was a woman in China."

"From time to time, I lie —," he said, "to protect everyone. And now I will be deeply insulted if you don't keep it."

"All right." She relented and admired it on her wrist. "It's beautiful," she said.

"It's exactly where it belongs."

He laughed. Then he did something that shocked her.

He leaned forward and pressed his lips to hers, and she allowed him.

He held her for several long seconds. Then she pulled back.

He took her into his arms again, holding her tightly. This time the embrace was longer and lingered. She stepped back and stepped away.

"Travel safe," she said.

"You too."

"I'm anxious to get home," he said. "Ever been to China?"

"No."

"You should come visit someday. There are ways to let me know if you visit. Channels."

"I know."

"I know you know."

A moment, and "I'm very sorry," he said.

"About what?"

"I'm very sorry that I'm obliged to live half a world away from you," he said.

His words had the effect of knocking the legs out from under her.

She fumbled for the words of recovery but had none.

Peter was about to say something further, but then didn't. It was almost as if for the first time, he was ill at ease with something — a feeling, a thought, an emotion, maybe. In any case, he gave it no voice. Instead, he turned and gave her a quick final hug. Then he turned away quickly and went to the first class check-in line for Iberia. His trip was to be a long one. Iberia to New York, then China Air to Hong Kong, and a connecting flight to Beijing. It would be twenty-seven hours before he set foot on his home soil. And who knew when or to what he would next be assigned?

She watched him all the way through the passport check, the ticketing, the checking of two sizeable bags. She had the wistful notion that someone she liked very much was stepping out of her life. She would miss him.

A quick reality check reminded her that he was a hired agent and assassin of a state that wasn't always on the best terms with her own. And then a third instinct clicked in, that Peter Chang was a man who had done what he had to do, done it with honor, and done it in a way that she could respect.

In that way, he had been a soldier. A soldier and a very good one, one in which she had also fought with in the trenches. She respected soldiers.

As for his country, his employer, she didn't care much for their system and their shortcomings, and vastly preferred her own. But his system worked for him, much the way hers worked for her. So who was she, she wondered, to pass judgment? At this stage of her life, he had been exactly what she had needed, in ways large and small.

She had more than the notion of liking him. She *did* like him, and it would take some time to adapt to the new reality of daily life without him.

She stood near the exit gate, not wanting to pull herself away. Her eyes were on him. There were police all over the place. She wondered, *Were the police looking for Peter?*

Suddenly, he turned. He scanned the terminal and found her. He said something to the security people. They nodded. He turned and jogged briskly in her direction.

Now what? Passport trouble? Was he going to make a run for it? He came to her.

"Sorry, I meant to mention something," he said. "I left the box for your bracelet at the bank. In the safety deposit box in the vault. I like to keep things tidy. Can you deal with that for me when you stash the pistol?"

"Of course."

"You can dip into some of the money too, if you want. I did. No one will care. Expenses, you know. Don't be greedy, but I know you won't."

He jogged back to the line, nodded with a smile to the security people and proceeded. Her eyes were still on him when he took his suitcases to be X-rayed, and put them through the giant scanners. The security people nodded and waved him along.

He turned toward the place where Alex stood from a distance of maybe a hundred feet. Somehow he knew she hadn't left, and somehow his eyes found hers immediately, even across the crowded entrance lobby of the bustling airport. Across many travelers, a multitude of cultures, across more languages than anyone in the room could count. This was how they had met and how they would separate.

He gave her that big smile again, raised a hand and waved.

She raised hers in response but without much enthusiasm. Then he turned and was gone through the security gates where they examined his shoes, his belt, and made him stand for an electronic, and then a manual, frisk. An absurd and amusing notion struck her. If these security people only know who they were frisking, she thought to herself. Well, it happened all the time.

She caught one more glimpse of him. Then he was gone.

Completely.

She walked out of the gates to the departures lounge and onto the sidewalk, lost in many thoughts …

She went back to the car and sat for several minutes. The degree to which she was rattled surprised even her. Time spiraled a little. So much had happened in so short a time. It seemed as if it had been only a few seconds ago that she had been emerging from the warm surf in Barcelona and answering the phone. Then she had been in Madrid, then Switzerland being undressed and re-dressed by Federov, then Rome, then back to the Spanish capital where she felt as if she had lost five years of her life pinned in a filthy tunnel under the streets — where she might have lost her life completely if Peter and his hit team hadn't found her.

She shuddered. What kind of bizarre angel had been her guardian this time? If she believed in God at all, in what ways did He work? Would human beings, would *she*, ever understand anything?

She searched the geometry of events. In Kiev, she had lost a man who loved her, and lost a piece of jewelry. Here she had gained a piece of jewelry and found —

She examined the gold bangle on her wrist.

And then a realization hit her. It more than hit her. It jolted her.

She glanced at her watch. It was past 2:00 p.m. She turned the key in her ignition and jerked the car into reverse. She had to hurry. There was still some wrapping up to do, and she just had time today.

SEVENTY-THREE

MADRID, SEPTEMBER 21, AFTERNOON

She drove faster than she should have getting back into Madrid. The traffic was thick but allowed her to move around quickly. Her first stop was the rental car company. Quickly scanning the car to check for any of her own property, she found the black box in the trunk — the stealth box that would beat bank security — that Peter had mentioned.

She placed it in a black tote bag and took it with her. She dropped off the paperwork and the car keys, without going to the desk. So much the better, she mused. She had never been listed as an insured driver, so just as soon skip the desk. Nothing good could happen there.

She was in the old city. She knew the neighborhood well enough to know that the branch of El Banco de Santander where Peter kept his stash was a pleasant ten-minute walk away. She had on a good pair of walking shoes and a comfortable skirt. She pushed her sunglasses in place and hoofed the few blocks to the bank.

Twenty minutes later, she sat in the small private room that she had visited once in her life. A bank security man wearing white gloves delivered the safety deposit box to her. This was her first trip to the box alone, but obviously Peter, as he had casually said a few days earlier, had returned on the afternoon of the Connelly murder.

He had returned and made some adjustments.

"Muchas gracias," she said to the bank guard.

"Da nada, Señorita," he said with a slight bow. Spanish bank employees tended to elevate courtesy to an art form.

When the clerk was gone, Alex opened the safety deposit box. Everything was exactly as she had last seen it, with the exception of the cash, which Peter had drawn on. Well, those Madrid evenings, she noted with a wry smile, didn't come cheap.

She lifted the gift box out, the one with the wrapping paper from the Swiss jeweler, and set it aside. It was slightly heavier, and she could see that Peter had opened it and rewrapped it. Typical male fingers, good at larger, more complicated tasks, not so good with the small stuff.

She smiled to herself at the thought.

She looked at the two stacks of money, the dollars and the euros. About twenty-five thousand dollars in US currency, depending on how much the people in the foreign exchange section upstairs were finagling with the daily rate.

She fingered the money and shook her head. She didn't need any and didn't want it. Her employer paid her for an honest day's work and got it from her. She didn't need to drink from a pool of poisoned water.

Twenty-five grand. In her grandfather's day you could have bought a small house for dough like that. In her parents' day, you could have made the down payment. These days, you were lucky to get lunch.

She pulled the black box, the one with Peter's gun in it, out of her tote bag. She positioned it into the deposit box. It fit easily with the gift wrapped box gone.

She smiled again and gently slid the gift box into her tote. She completed her business in the bank within a few minutes, politely thanked the guard and was gone.

It was only three o'clock. She was doing fine.

She took lunch at one of the local cafés, relaxed slightly, added a bold glass of chilled Spanish white Rioja to her meal, then a second glass. She felt her nerves finally settle. She was surprised that she felt that way because the meeting at the museum was still in front of her and she was guarded about what direction it would take. She took out her cell phone and made some calls.

She emerged from the café less than an hour later and walked directly to the Museo Arqueológico. Rivera, the curator, was there in the lobby to meet her.

"Thank you for phoning ahead," he said. He spoke English out of courtesy and out of gratitude. "I might have been out. But I cancelled the rest of my afternoon."

"Thank you," she said. "It will be worth it."

They met in a special conference room. Colonel Pendraza of the National Police arrived next and Colonel Sánchez, the real Colonel Sánchez, of the Guardia Civil entered at almost the same time. There were no police there from foreign agencies, though Alex had notified them all. The meeting had been called too quickly for any to attend, and in any event, Alex had notified them by email or phone that the issue of the stolen pietà had been resolved to the likings of two governments. Floyd Connelly, of course, remained booked out of town.

Rivera convened the meeting and turned it over to Alex.

"I suspect several of you have been briefed so far," Alex said. "To backtrack, we know that a small *objet d'art* disappeared from this museum several weeks ago. Within the past fortnight some of us in this room came together to see what the implications of the theft were and whether, in the best of all possible worlds, there was any room for recovery of the item."

The men assembled in the room waited.

"I'm happy to announce that this is one of those rare cases where justice, perhaps in a crude way, has been dealt to those who engineered the theft. They were also on the path of a greater evil, which has quietly been averted. And as an added bonus, *The Pietà of Malta* is back here for the people of Spain."

She set the gift wrapped box on the table.

Pendraza looked at the box. "How do we know it's not going to explode?" Pendraza asked, making a joke of it.

"It hasn't yet," she said. She paused. "Don't worry. It won't," she said.

The package sat benignly in front of all of them.

"You're the curator," Alex said, turning to Rivera. "You're used to dealing delicately with fine objects. Please open the package."

Rivera's fingers did the walking. In the quiet room, the ribbon came off. The curator smiled and worked with the joy of a little girl opening a present on Christmas morning. Then away came the firm tactile wrapping paper and within was a wooden box. The box was nondescript, unmarked, sturdy but light, the type of thing that might normally house Japanese chocolates.

The curator held the box carefully in his hand, raised his eyes to

Alex again. "Are you sure you wouldn't like the honor, yourself?" he asked her.

"No, thank you," she said

He opened it and, although he knew what to expect, astonishment crossed his face. He stared at it for several seconds and no one else in the room could see.

From his pocket, he took out a small velvet pad, the type upon which jewelers place diamonds on for inspection. He laid the pad on the table. And then, from the box that Alex had presented, he removed the contents and placed it on the mat to the further astonishment of those gathered.

And there before them was the primitive miniature carving that had served as the inspiration for Michelangelo's masterpiece. There in the center of the room sat *The Pietà of Malta*, the earliest lamentation known to the art world, a tiny replica of Mary comforting and caressing the body of the slain Christ.

Across eighteen centuries, perhaps in and out of tombs, there it was.

There were gasps around the room.

"Think of this as a gift from the people of the United States to the people of Spain. The return of your black bird."

"How on earth — ?" Rivera began, shaking his head.

"A contact in the underworld and some invaluable assistance from another intelligence service. I'm equally grateful and indebted to both for their assistance and good will."

"Extraordinary," said Pendraza. "Excellent work."

"I can tell you this much," Alex said. "Your thieves were home-grown and highly amateur, based right here in Madrid. But they were also unpredictable and tightly knit, which made them both dangerous and a challenge. Your security system was compromised, and they walked through it. They made contact with forces within the Middle East and set in motion a terrorist plot against the United States of America. But like most amateurs, they committed mistakes that caused their undoing. Their first mistake was greed. They attempted to sell the pietà to a collector in Asia. They never delivered because they were greedy. They wanted to try to sell it twice to raise twice as much money. It turned out to be a bad way to do business."

"Please tell us enough to make proper arrests," Pendraza said.

"A friendly intelligence service already put them out of business," said Alex. "I don't even know where the bodies are. I'll review the details with you privately if you wish. I will also need to teleconference later with the French police, the Swiss, and Interpol to cover some ancillary details. My recommendation, however, would be to terminate this inquiry and everything related to it. No good will come from any further investigation. Any subsequent time and expense will be wasted."

Pendraza held her steadily in his gaze, as did Sanchez of the Guardia Civil.

She addressed them in return.

"Related to this is the death of the unfortunate worker in the Metro system," she said, "the track walker Maria Elena Gómez. I suspect she stumbled across something she shouldn't have. In any case, those responsible, and those who would have been responsible for an even more horrific incident at one of the embassies on the Calle Serrano, have been summarily brought to justice. This was not of my doing specifically. Again, another intelligence service acted, but they acted with lethal efficiency."

Colonel Pendraza's eyes went to the lamentation at the center of the table. "And where did you find this?" he asked.

"The actual retrieval of the pietà took place, I would surmise, in Switzerland. It would appear that an agent of another service called upon a businessman in Geneva, a man of questionable commercial affairs. My guess is that the agent came across the 'lamentation' in the man's possession. The agent surely would have been looking for it. In any event, he passed it along to me for return to its rightful owners."

Pendraza nodded thoughtfully. "I'm just curious," Pendraza said. "Certainly you knew that this team from a 'friendly' intelligence service was in Spain."

"Yes, I did," she said.

"Did you know that their ultimate task was to use lethal force on the conspirators?" he asked.

"No, I didn't," she said. "I didn't even know that had happened until I was released from the hospital a day later."

"Who told you?"

"A friend of mine and, I would submit, a friend of the Spanish and American people, considering how many lives were saved. And putting two and two together, I now realize that the gentleman who approved this exercise on behalf of US intelligence was trying to distract me during the final hours of the exercise. I met with the gentleman across from La Almudena late three afternoons ago. I couldn't understand why he was allowing the Spanish police to act so slowly. He just wanted to get to these dangerous amateurs first."

"Understandably," said Pendraza.

"So while it was not my decision to launch an execution team," Alex said, "once that team was launched there was no holding them back. And honestly, I have reservations about what happened, the fate of those who were executed. They were a small band of amateurs playing at being world-changing revolutionaries. The leader, a misguided young man named Jean-Claude, organized his own murderous little cell."

"Hundreds of innocent people might have died at their hands." She smiled wryly. "What can I say? I tend to be a person of faith who tries to live her faith. God sometimes works in strange ways." She paused. "Then again, to paraphrase a personal friend, a streetwise philosopher of sorts, 'The world is better off without such people.' "

"So the terminations took place on Spanish soil?" Pendraza said.

"That is correct," she said.

"Was it done in conjunction with the American intelligence service?" Pendraza asked. "Or with their approval?"

"To answer that, Colonel," Alex said, "let me just say that if I decline to answer your question, then, if asked, you won't know the answer."

He smiled faintly and nodded.

"I would have to agree with your philosopher friend," Pendraza said. "Certainly Madrid is better off without a few extra individuals prone to terrorist attacks. I could argue that the world is better off too."

"I have some homicide reports this morning from the city police," Sanchez of the Civil Guard said quietly. "Four murders, maybe five. Including a fire. Related. No further victims of the fire fortunately."

"The further details are known only to the participants and to God," Alex said. "I suspect that might be the best way to leave things."

Pendraza glanced around the room. "I suspect it might be," he said.

"Is there anything else?" Alex asked.

"Maybe, if we inquire, the rival service that solved this problem for us would be able to give us a few more details," Sanchez suggested.

Alex shook her head. "Don't even bother asking," she said. "They won't. And I'm not planning to divulge what country's intelligence service helped us. I'm disinclined to discuss it. Even when I'm back in Washington, I suspect my memory will grow hazy."

She glanced around.

"Now," she said, "unless anyone has something else, I'd like to excuse myself. I believe this investigation is finished. *Muchas gracias, Señores.*"

Alex rose. The small group in the room rose with her. One by one, the men around the table offered congratulatory handshakes, which she accepted as she moved toward the door. Sanchez gave her an embrace. The last man to stand before her was Colonel Pendraza of the National Police.

His eyes were gray and almost sad. He gave her a slight nod. "I have many questions, but I'm going to pose none of them," he said. "But I wish to thank you. You and whatever other service you worked with. You spared us enormous problems."

"De nada," she said.

"No, no. It was more than *nada*," he said. "It was everything."

Then he too gave Alex a hug, replaced his cap, seemed to stand an inch taller on the spot, and was on his way.

She walked back to the hotel.

It was evening now and a warm evening gripped Madrid.

In a way, she felt suddenly very alone, that strange kind of loneliness that one can only feel in a large city when one is surrounded by millions of people, but all of them are strangers, and everyone else seems to be in the company of someone else.

Back at the hotel a short time later, she wandered into the bar on the first floor. She ordered herself a cognac and sat at a quiet table in the corner. From her table, she could watch the street and the nearby gardens.

She settled back and relaxed.

She pondered. Peter's flight would have departed by now. So he was well on his way back to Shanghai. Federov was back in Zurich, Rizzo in Rome. What a weird world it was. Violent, beautiful, and unpredictable, a world in which an ancient carving of a slain man of peace and charity could set off a bloody chain of events.

She had already decided what she would do. She would check out the next day and go somewhere. Maybe Paris. Maybe London. Not Washington just yet. Maybe back to Barcelona.

That was it, she decided after another sip of cognac. Back to Barcelona. No one would know her there; this time no one would find her. She fingered the pendant at her neck, then released it.

She could use the relaxation and a week at the beach. If she worked it right, it would seem as if she had never left. She looked forward to finishing her vacation.

Then her eyes glanced to the left, from the gardens and skylight of a great city to the entrance to the bar. Her eyes focused on a man who had just entered, and the shock of recognition was immediately upon her.

He was ruddy faced and wore glasses. He wore a light blue suite, white shirt, and tie. He had one of those straw hats that she always associated with men in their sixties or musicians of the Buena Vista Social Club.

"Oh, Lord," she muttered to herself.

The man, Sam Deal, spotted her at the same time and smiled. Then she realized. It was the week of September 18, and as promised, Mr. Collins had sent an emissary.

And of all people, he had sent Sam. His South American hatchet man.

Sam grinned broadly, walked to her, and sat down.

"Hello, Alex," he said.

"Hello, Sam."

"Funny coincidence. Fancy meeting you here, Alex LaDuca," he said.

"It's not fancy, and it's not a coincidence, either," she said. "But as long as you're here, you might as well order a drink."

Sam signaled to a waiter who was already on the way over. Sam ordered something cold and powerful.

Then he turned back to Alex.

"Venezuela?" she asked.

"Order yourself another drink," Sam said, "and I'll explain."

ACKNOWLEDGMENTS

In addition to having visited Spain, the author is grateful to many sources for background and research on Madrid and the Spanish Civil War. Among them, the *New York Times*, the *Washington Post*, the United States Department of Justice, Wikipedia, *The Columbia Encyclopedia*, and *The Encyclopedia Britannica*. Also, *The Spanish Civil War* by Hugh Thomas, originally published in 1961 and revised in 2001, remains a definitive account of that tragic stretch of history. The wonderful book for children *Farolitos for Abuelo* by Rudolfo Anaya was also an excellent introduction to the traditional use of luminarias in North America. And as usual, I'm grateful to my good friend Thomas Ochiltree for his endless insights on international politics and diplomacy. At Zondervan, at various times, Andy Meisenheimer, Bob Hudson, and Alison Roth saved me from the thicket of my own verbal excesses. Thanks, guys. Equally, I'm ever grateful to my wife, Patricia, for her help, advice, and support in more ways than I can ever calculate.

The author welcomes comments and correspondence from readers either through the Zondervan website or at NH1212f@yahoo.com.

Conspiracy in Kiev

Noel Hynd

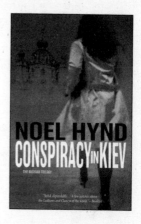

A shrewd investigator and an expert marksman, Special Agent Alexandra LaDuca can handle any case the FBI gives her. Or can she?

While on loan from the US Department of the Treasury, Alex is tapped to accompany a Secret Service team during an American presidential visit to Ukraine. Her assignment: to keep personal watch over Yuri Federov, the most charming and most notorious gangster in the region.

Against her better judgment — and fighting a feeling that she's being manipulated — she leaves for Ukraine. But there are more parts to this dangerous mission than anyone suspects, and connecting the dots takes Alex across three continents and through some life-altering discoveries about herself, her work, her faith, and her future.

Conspiracy in Kiev — from the first double-cross to the stunning final pages — is the kind of solid, fast-paced espionage thriller only Noel Hynd can write. For those who have never read Noel Hynd, this first book in the Russian Trilogy is the perfect place to start.

Softcover: 978-0-310-27871-9

Pick up a copy today at your favorite bookstore!

Share Your Thoughts

With the Author: Your comments will be forwarded to the author when you send them to *zauthor@zondervan.com*.

With Zondervan: Submit your review of this book by writing to *zreview@zondervan.com*.

Free Online Resources at
www.zondervan.com/hello

 Zondervan AuthorTracker: Be notified whenever your favorite authors publish new books, go on tour, or post an update about what's happening in their lives.

 Daily Bible Verses and Devotions: Enrich your life with daily Bible verses or devotions that help you start every morning focused on God.

 Free Email Publications: Sign up for newsletters on fiction, Christian living, church ministry, parenting, and more.

 Zondervan Bible Search: Find and compare Bible passages in a variety of translations at www.zondervanbiblesearch.com.

 Other Benefits: Register yourself to receive online benefits like coupons and special offers, or to participate in research.